What the critics are saying:

Le Mystère

"Le Mystèere" by Winston tells the tale of Jesse Dubois, a lost soul who was killed 25 years ago. When Luke finds this beautiful woman in the swamp, he is overwhelmed... What is the mystery that brings Luke and Jesse together? Will Maman Rubie, a voudon empress, bring Jesse to peace? ~ *Robin Taylor for Romantic Times*

Embrace the Moon

"...*Embrace the Moon* is a wow-inspiring story. Author Patrice Michelle gives us a story filled with action and very steamy sex. Her hero is a man you just have to love and want. While he is sinfully sexy he is also a man who is made up of very many intriguing layers...Embrace The Moon is one great story that should not be missed." - *Lisa Lambrecht for In the Library Reviews*

Malédiction

"Ms. Windsor provides you with action and adventure within a plot that has more twists than a back road...This story alone is worth the price of the book." - *Faith Jacobs, Just Erotic Romance Reviews*

Discover for yourself why readers can't get enough of the multiple award-winning publisher Ellora's Cave. Whether you prefer e-books or paperbacks, be sure to visit EC on the web at www.ellorascave.com for an erotic reading experience that will leave you breathless.

www.ellorascave.com

Cajun Nights
An Ellora's Cave Publication, September 2004

Ellora's Cave Publishing, Inc.
PO Box 787
Hudson, OH 44236-0787

ISBN #1-4199-5024-X

ISBN MS Reader (LIT) ISBN # 1-84360-665-8

Other available formats (no ISBNs are assigned):
Adobe (PDF), Rocketbook (RB), Mobipocket (PRC) & HTML

LE MYSTÈRE edited by *ALLIE McKNIGHT*
EMBRACE THE MOON edited by *MARTHA PUNCHES*
MALÉDICTION edited by *ANN RICHARDSON*
Cover Art by *DARRELL KING*

CAJUN NIGHTS

LE MYSTÈRE
SAMANTHA WINSTON

EMBRACE THE MOON
PATRICE MICHELLE

Malédiction
Annie Windsor

Prologue

Sunset prowled Louisiana's Atchafalaya Basin, thieving glimmers from the swamp's unrelenting black surface. Tributaries became dark wells. Slow-moving rivers grew bleaker than the Styx and twice as deadly. Like veils between worlds, Spanish moss hung from cypress branches, concealing more than most dared to imagine or understand.

Snakes sliced across inky surfaces as owls preened and readied for the night's hunt. Here and there, crickets and toads rehearsed for a deafening performance, and a bull gator's heart-chilling bellow cleaved the humid air. Birds struggled to find roost before they fell victim to the swamp's insatiable appetite—and as for bipeds, human or otherwise, they hurried to the nearest refuge. Only fools and murderers remained in the Atchafalaya after nightfall, along with a few brave souls and yet a few more lacking sanity's wisdom.

Rubie Breaux counted herself among the former, and sometimes the latter. Sometimes, Rubie thought she'd been born with the Atchafalaya, and when she died, the old Basin might just wither with her bones—or at least Daemon Swath, the isolated patch of mud, rock, and swamp grass where she lived and farmed and saw to ceremonies in her *oum'phor*, her Voudon temple.

"Foolishness," she muttered. Talking to herself had become second nature long before *Maman* Rubie forgot how old she was getting. Now, she could scarcely remember the spelling of her name, who loved her enough to call her *Maman*, who knew her enough to address her as *Tata*, and who simply pointed and whispered about "dat old *mam'bo* on dat damn cursed island." She could no longer fully remember even the gentle lines of her Haitian mother's sweet face. She recalled what was important, though. What had to be done. She didn't dare think about what would happen to the world she knew when she died. Those thoughts were simply too horrible to bear.

As darkness stole across her herb beds and chicken yard, covering her vegetable garden and her clothesline draped with newly laundered ceremonial flags, Rubie moved quickly despite her white-clad bulk. Adjusting her cotton dress and apron, she leaned forward and touched up the paint on the trunks of her *reposoirs*, the trees where the *loas*, the gods, lived. She took care to use the exact shade of each *loa*'s favorite color. She knew exactly what the gods liked to drink, what they chose to eat and how to cook it—and this was fortunate, for Rubie and her foremothers tended the most unforgiving of *mystères*. *Maman* Rubie and her people kept the Pethro Rites. They served—and to some extent, contained—the darkest of *loas* and the darker sides of benevolent gods.

She finished painting the base of the last live oak at moonrise, then glanced toward her two-room shack. It would feel like paradise to slip inside and take a short nap, but many hours of work awaited her in the *oum'phor*. The wooden building's four rooms needed to be swept, and the packed-earth *peristyle*, or courtyard, too. The *peristyle*'s central post and the nearby *pé*, or altar, needed dusting, as did the two Pethro drums. Rubie's *asson*, the calabash rattle filled with stones and snake vertebrae, sacred symbol of her power—well, that was looking dusty, too.

Rubie sighed. Sometimes, she wished to be a young initiate again, free of the burden of leadership. Or maybe just a *hoodoo* adept like most in New Orleans, casting love charms and simple spells, barely noticed or known by the *loas*. Such was not her lot, though. Rubie Breaux was a *mam'bo*, an empress of Voudon, and she knew her responsibilities all too well.

Mustering her waning strength, she started for the *oum'phor*—then froze and shivered.

A strange spirit energy had crossed onto Daemon Swath.

"Something that don' come often." *Maman* Rubie sniffed the thick night air, hoping for a scent, a perfume, some clue to tell her which *loa* had chosen to make a visit without being summoned by the drums, chanting, dance, and offerings of a proper ceremony. Such things were unusual, but not impossible, especially in times of trouble.

Rubie sniffed again. "Smells like...hmmph. Fancy European toilet water. What you be doin' here, Mademoiselle Charlotte?"

Of course, the capricious *loa* refused to answer.

Heaving a sigh, Rubie changed course and hauled her old bones back to her cabin. It took her a good hour to collect and prepare what she needed: a cup of syrup-sweetened water, a glass of clairin, and a plate of just-cooked tender meat of a very young chicken. Rubie arranged all of this on a tray lined with pink, Mademoiselle Charlotte's favorite color, and she carried it through the darkness, out to the edge of the yard, and placed it at the base of her only pink dogwood.

Minutes ticked by.

Mosquitoes worried Rubie's arms and face. She swatted at them, but didn't even consider going inside. Charlotte was the trickiest of tricky. Temperamental. Headstrong. She'd take her time, *mais, oui*. Just to be a dickens.

After another few seconds, the contents of the cup, glass, and plate vanished.

Before *Maman* Rubie could move or speak, Mademoiselle Charlotte's presence seized her like a storm. Pictures flooded her tired mind.

A dark man, with wicked purpose.

A woman sought by a man outcast, even from his own heart.

A cursed man, bearing blood-burdens and grief.

And more. Infinitely more. Perhaps the breaking of all she had protected, the finish of all she held dear. Maybe even her own doom.

By the time Mademoiselle Charlotte departed and left Rubie to fall to her aged, aching knees, the *mam'bo* of Daemon Swath realized great good and great evil would come home to the Atchafalaya. The fate of many souls turned on the actions of the three people she had visioned. May the gods help them—and all the lives they would touch.

Two of them would be her visitors, no matter that they weren't initiates, and no matter her personal feelings. One man was her long-lost foster son, heading to the swamp in great peril. Charlotte had instructed Rubie to answer the questions they would pose. For what purpose, Rubie could but guess.

Mademoiselle Charlotte, a mystery among *mystères*, rarely shared her intentions, be they fair or foul. Rubie knew one thing for certain, though. With Charlotte involved, nothing would be simple...and everything would have a price.

LE MYSTÈRE

Samantha Winston

Prologue

Bayou Lafourche, Atchafalaya Basin, 1977

In the black, velvet night, someone hunted her.

He'd been following her since she left the *bastringue*. At first she hadn't been worried; lots of folk took the short cut across the swamp after the dance. Simon had accompanied her as far as the fork, and then had asked if she'd be all right. She'd just laughed. The bayou was her home and she knew it well. The path was wide and the pale sand glowed faintly in the moonlight.

The air stood still. The heat in Bayou Lafourche was oppressive, sending stinging, salty sweat into her eyes. Mosquitoes whined, some landing on her arms and legs. Their bites stung, but she didn't dare move. She didn't dare breathe.

Then the clouds had covered the moon. Quiet footsteps had come closer, but when she asked who was there, no one answered. Now she crouched in a small bush, painfully aware of how poorly it hid her.

A bullfrog croaked, making her jump.

Close by, there came the sound of a low laugh. Gooseflesh prickled on her neck. Her heart hammered madly. She couldn't see anything in the pitch darkness. But she sensed a presence. Someone came near, closing in on her...chuckling as he approached.

Her nerves stretched to the breaking point. A splash sounded on her left and she bolted, rocketing out of the thicket. Her feet hit the familiar path leading to her shanty, but the laughter came closer. A hand grabbed her and she lost her balance. She fell, grunting as she skinned her hands and knees. Before she could recover, hands were around her neck.

She wanted to scream, but she couldn't. The hands were tightening, and a harsh voice whispered in her ear.

"Sorry ma belle, but I need you dead...and buried where no one will find you."

She tried to breathe, tried to escape, but the hands were too strong. The last thing she knew a flash of light blinded her and then…nothing.

* * * * *

Twenty-five years later…

The *mam'bo* stared at the man. He was evil, she sensed it. Badness surrounded him in an aura that pulsed with each breath he took. "What do you want?" she asked, her voice low.

Outside the crickets stilled. In the quiet, the man spoke. "I seen her." The skin around his mouth and nose whitened.

The *mam'bo's* eyes narrowed. "Seen who?"

"Non, *mam'bo*, I ain't sayin' her name. Be enough to say she's dead, been dead twenty-five years, yet for two weeks now in my dreams I seen her standing in a patch of moonlight, lookin' jes like she did twenty-five years ago. The same dream comes back every night, and in it, she looks straight at me and says it's my turn now." The man shook his head. "She's dead. *Defan* bitch!"

"Twenty-five years?" The *mam'bo's* skin was prickling now. She looked out the window. "You said it is the same dream?" She shook her head. "Bad signs. Dreams about the dead are bad signs. Twenty-five years is a quarter century, with the moon—"

"I don't care about that. Tell me what I got to do to make her go away and never come back."

The *mam'bo's* lips tightened, but she nodded to a bench and he sat down. She went to the corner where a black hen and a white rooster were penned. She reached into the cage and selected the hen.

She did her business in this room. Callers came at night usually. She ushered them into the peristyle, where most rituals were performed. Partly enclosed, it was adjacent to the holiest room in the *oum'phor*. Baskets, rattles, and trays hung from the ceiling. A burning fire cast red light on the man's face.

On the hard, earthen floor, an intricate *vèvè* glimmered malevolently. She'd drawn it with chalk and, in the dark, it took on a greenish glow. The *mam'bo* took pungent, stinging leaves out and

14

crumpled them, inhaling their bitter scent, then sprinkling them on the lines of the *vèvè*.

She grabbed the black hen and tore its head off. The bird's wings flapped, but she held it over a jar until no more blood trickled from the neck. She set the bird down and picked up the jar. Holding it towards the fire, she peered at the quantity and color. Too dark for her liking, too thick, clinging to the side of the glass. Not a good sign. She hesitated and then took a sip. The hot blood burned. She held the blood in her mouth then swallowed.

Her hands shook as she set the jar down. She walked in slow circles around the bloodied *vèvè* — seven times — praying to the *loa* she was summoning for help. Her eyes closed. Would Charlotte help her now? Where was that *loa*? Time passed. Sweat rolled in huge droplets down her face. A whiff of perfume tickled her nostrils, but it wasn't Charlotte's French scent. It was lighter...like lily of the valley and cool dew. And then images appeared.

Darkness, a white path. In the middle of the path a huge bullfrog crouched; it swelled and then vanished. People appeared, but they were transparent and dressed in outdated clothes from the seventies. A pair of scales. A clock. Dancing shoes. A woman, shadows, and mist. The woman was blurred but something glittered on her hand. The *mam'bo* strained, but the image wouldn't come clear. The *loa* left her and the vision vanished. Time for something else.

"Give me the rooster."

He did.

She twisted the rooster's neck and threw the bird in the air. "*Dis moi tout!* Tell me all!" The dead bird hit the floor, nerves making its legs pedal. Wings flapping, it skittered from one side of the *vèvè* to the other, coming to rest near the left hand side. "In the bottom quarter," muttered the *mam'bo*. She had rarely seen such bad signs. This man was evil, but whatever he was up against was strong. The images were starting to make sense. He wasn't lying. Whoever this man had seen *was* dead and had come back for revenge.

"What do I have to do to protect myself?" the man asked, impatience clipping his words.

The *mam'bo* pursed her lips. "You must take this person's bones and burn them. When they are ashes, you'll be safe."

The man nodded thoughtfully. "Any particular day or night?"

"It has to be done before the moon wanes. Afterwards, she'll be here to stay, or you'll be gone with her."

The man nodded. "Last question. Do you know why she's back?"

Such evil intentions seeped from this one. For a second she considered not answering, but she had to. *Mam'bos* didn't question evil or good, fate would take care of him. "She's back to set something right. What it is, I don't know, but I see something glitter in her hand. Is it a wedding ring? A bracelet? I don't know. But she's looking. Yes, she's looking for something. There is a *lien*— a link, between the *bijoux*, the woman and you. But what it is, I don't know."

"Forget you saw me, *mam'bo*." He took her hand and pressed a wad of bills into it. She winced as his fingers dug into her wrist. If she hadn't sensed the evil within him, she would have cursed him to his face. "Forget I ever came here. *Maintenant, adieu.*"

"Yes sir," she muttered angrily, glaring at his back and rubbing her bruised arm as he walked away. "*Adieu.* You ain't ever coming back here again. I saw that too."

Chapter One

Luke kept his eyes on the old oak. He'd caught a glimpse of white as he'd rounded the bend. The oak was dead; the long strands of moss hanging from its branches made it look like a weeping willow. He'd cut the boat's motor, and now he glided silently downstream in the darkness. Was it a deer? He picked up his binoculars and peered through them, but even the night-enhancing lenses didn't show anything. Could have been a deer, maybe an albino, or a possum coming down one of the branches. It probably wasn't a poacher, but his job was watching for poachers, so he wasn't going to leave until he'd settled the question one way or another.

Making sure his gun was in its rack, he dipped his paddles into the black water, moving the boat towards the low, sandy bank. It grated softly as he pushed it on shore, then, moving lightly, he grabbed his gun and leapt out of the boat, crouching in its lee. Poachers often took offense at being caught. His last partner, Dan, had been shot a month ago, and so far no one had been sent to replace him. Dan was out of the hospital but still on sick leave. Well, the Louisiana Department of Fish and Wildlife probably had better things to do than find replacements for rangers in this neck of the swamp.

Luke stared at the sand. The moonlight showed nothing. Not a trace of hoof or foot. If anything had been here, it would have left tracks. He ran his hand thoughtfully over his jaw. He had seen something though. Maybe it hadn't been close to the water. He stood up and tilted his head, listening hard. After a moment he flicked his flashlight on and ducked under the curtain of Spanish moss. His beam of light fell on a white figure and he raised his gun automatically. At first, his brain thought that his eyes were playing tricks on him. His feet stumbled to a halt. His whole body froze. He found himself staring down the sights of his gun at a young woman.

She knelt at the base of the oak. She'd been digging — he could see that. For what?

She stared at him gravely, no sign of fear in her eyes. He lowered the gun.

"What are you doing here?" His heart still pounded in his chest; the last time he'd come across someone hereabouts there'd been a shoot out.

The woman frowned. "I'm not sure." Her voice was lilting and had an accent he couldn't quite place.

"*Patois, eh?*" She looked Cajun, with dark hair and eyes, and pale skin.

"*Mais, oui.* But I prefer English, if you don't mind." The young woman got to her feet and brushed her hands off on her white dress. Her dark hair floated about her shoulders in a soft cloud. She straightened, pushed her hair back, and looked around. A puzzled frown twisted her face. "I'm not certain," she murmured.

As she stood, Luke's breath caught in his throat. His heart, instead of calming down, thudded painfully against his chest. There was something enthralling about the woman, something bewitching. He couldn't find his words, and he knew his cheeks must be burning under her level gaze. Finally he managed to blurt, "What do you mean, you're not certain?"

"I'm not sure what I'm looking for." Her grave voice echoed strangely in the night, and her eyes were bottomless wells of pure sorrow. The moon moved behind a cloud. In the darkness, a shiver of unease ran over his body.

"Can you help me?" she asked plaintively.

"Help you do what?" Luke kept his voice very gentle. He could not tear his eyes from the slender woman. She was so beautiful, with her white, white skin, black hair, and black eyes that seemed to hold the entire night within their depths.

"I don't know." She shook her head and her long, dark hair swirled around her shoulders. "I have to find something, but I don't know what. I just know that I must find it."

"Something buried around here?" Luke looked at her hands. They were covered with dirt and her nails were broken. Disquiet prickled his skin.

"I'm confused. Here, or nearby. Or maybe on the other side of the river. It's all mixed up in my head." She put her hands on her temples and pushed. "I can't seem to remember anything. I don't even know my own name."

Luke was startled. "You don't?" That was odd. Perhaps she was injured. He shined his flashlight on her face. Bruises covered her neck and scratches marred the side of her face. Why hadn't he noticed that before? "I have to get you to a hospital, mam'selle." How had he missed that? She needed help and all he could do was stare at her! What was wrong with him?

"No!" She stepped towards him, her expression beseeching. "Please, you have to help me."

"I will. Don't worry, I will." Close up, she became even more ethereally beautiful. A pang stabbed at his heart. She was so lovely. She reached her hand out, and he took it.

Ice stabbed at his arm. He cried out. At the same time, a flash of greenish light so bright it hurt his eyes seemed to flare off her body. The icy pain in his arm swept over him like a jolt of electricity. Everything happened in a second—the cold, the light, the shock. And then he was holding a warm, very solid hand. The pain passed. *Mon Dieu!* Had he'd simply imagined it or did he just have a minor heart attack? He gasped and let go of her to press his hand to his chest. His heart beat, strong and steady, but sweat chilled his back and chest.

What the hell?

The woman looked at him and her face bloomed into the most beautiful smile he'd ever seen. "You agreed to help me." To his consternation, she burst into tears.

"Hey! Hey there, don't cry." Luke patted her shoulder awkwardly. His rifle was hooked over the same arm holding the flashlight, and he was still shaky after the chest pain. He couldn't quite gather his thoughts. One thing he knew, he couldn't leave her here alone. Luke put the gun and the flashlight down and pulled her into his arms. "It's all right. You've had a nasty shock. When I get you to the hospital, they'll take care of you, don't worry." He spoke into her hair. Tendrils tickled his nose, and he caught a whiff of a flowery scent—it reminded him of lily of the valley. His granny always picked huge bunches of the fragile white flowers in the spring.

In his arms, the woman stopped trembling. She snuggled close to him. Her body might be slender, but her breasts were well-rounded and pushed softly against his chest through the light cotton shirt he wore. As he tightened his arms around her body, he grew conscious of her curves, of the width of her shoulders and slope of her back. When her thighs pressed against his, his loins tightened. In a minute he was going to have a raging hard-on.

What would she think when his cock stiffened against her? Would she be upset? Frightened? Or would she respond to his sexual invitation? For a minute he wanted to lay his naked body onto hers, to let her know how she affected him. But then he remembered she was injured. What had he been thinking? Had he gotten moonstruck? His granny had warned him that might happen if he stayed out in the moonlight too long. He'd mocked her, but now he started to have doubts. How else could he explain his overwhelming response to this woman?

"Um, I'm going to take you to my place now, all right? Then I can get you to a doctor. You need some help." Luke stepped back, regretfully letting his hands slide from her body. Afterwards, his hands itched to touch her again. Was she ever beautiful! But that didn't explain the urgent aching in his belly. He'd never been able to get aroused without the cold grip of reality grabbing him and waking him up. After what happened to him, he'd never approached a woman. He couldn't. That hadn't bothered him before. So, why did he react so strongly to her? His whole body tingled at her touch and his cock swelled uncomfortably. *Merde*, his jeans had never been this tight.

The woman stood still, her eyes closed. Another tear wandered down her cheek.

"What is it?" Hot anger boiled in his chest. Just the sight of that lone tear and the bruises on her fragile neck made him crazy. Whoever the hell had done that to her, he wanted to bash his face in. How dare they hit a woman? He unclenched his fingers, trying to get a hold of his temper. What on Earth was going on here?

She looked up at him, and his breath caught in his throat. He'd never seen such an intense gaze. "I'm starting to remember things," she said in a low whisper.

"Can you remember your name?" Luke took her hand again. The urge to touch her was too strong to resist.

"Jess...Jessica. No, Jesse." She spoke haltingly. "Jesse...that's my name. I can't recall anything else. Except music. There was music." She pressed a hand against her forehead and grimaced. "Everything is jumbled. I can't remember anything else. Just my name—Jesse. And music." Her hand fell to her side and she staggered. Luke caught her just before she fell.

She weighed no more than a bird. Her bones seemed fragile, like spun glass. *Spun glass?* The strangeness of the night had made him fanciful. He didn't usually think in such terms. This woman was a mystery he needed to solve. Plus he'd never met anyone like her, especially out here in the middle of nowhere. And that was another riddle to be solved — he knew all the locals, and he knew he'd never set eyes on her before. He'd have remembered her.

"How did you get here? Did you come in a boat or by foot? At least try to remember that." Luke carried her to his boat and set her down on the bank.

"I can only recall pitch darkness and some music." She shook her head and her face crumpled. "I'm sorry, maybe I fell and hit my head. It feels really strange."

"Here, let me help you get into my boat, Jesse." He settled her in, and then he put his gun away and pushed off. Once in deeper water, he pulled the engine cord and the motor started with a sputtering roar. Turning the boat back upstream, he took the left branch leading back to Bayou Lafourche. On the way, out of habit, he glanced up at the towering structure on the hill. Overlooking an unnamed corner of the Atchafalaya Basin in solitary splendor was an old mansion. Luke knew it well, and with cause.

"What are you looking at?"

Luke blinked and pointed through the trees. "That old house."

"The Braquesmar mansion?"

"No one calls it that anymore." He frowned. Braquesmar was his last name, but he didn't want to say that. "How did you know its name?"

"I...I don't know." Jesse shook her head, an expression of frustration marring her smooth features. "I just know it, that's all. Why isn't it called Braquesmar anymore?"

Luke shrugged. "It's now the Lesnoire estate. No one lives there. It's been abandoned since it changed hands. The present owner bought it as a favor to my granny." His voice took on a bitter tone.

"It used to be your granny's?"

"My great-grandfather built it. My family lived there until the tragedy." Luke tore his eyes from the mansion and looked at Jesse.

"Tragedy?"

That was an understatement. "Everyone knows about it. My father was accused of murder, and that lost him his reputation, his job, his home and ultimately, his life."

Jesse rubbed her forehead. "That sounds awful, but familiar somehow. Tell me more. How did your father die?"

Luke didn't particularly want to talk about it, but it had all happened so long ago he'd stopped feeling anything but frustration that the police had never managed to prove anything. "He hanged himself, after protesting his innocence."

"I'm so sorry. That must have been hard for your mother."

More wounds to open. It must be the night for grief from the past. Maybe this woman was a spirit. In her white gown, with her pale skin and dark eyes, she could pass for one of *Tata's* invocations. A wry smile quirked his lips. He had definitely stayed too long in the moonlight. "My mother died giving birth to me, so my granny was left alone to raise me. Mr. Lesnoire made my granny an offer she couldn't refuse. She sold our house."

"Why is it abandoned now? It's almost a ruin." She turned her head to catch a last glimpse of it, then looked at Luke expectantly.

Was she doing it on purpose, digging up his past like so many bleached bones? "Jacques Lesnoire tried to make the house into a luxury hotel, but it's surrounded by National Park land—nothing around it can be developed. He tried everything, from bribing the governor to threatening to turn it into a casino. Then he tried to buy our land, adjacent to the house. But my granny won't sell the land, and the only thing that he got was the house and a couple acres leading to the river. Nothing he could exploit." Luke gave a hollow laugh. "Out of spite, Jacques Lesnoire decided to close up the manor and leave it to ruin. In a few more years, it will be overgrown with weeds and look like a ghost mansion." As he spoke, the hair on the back of his neck prickled.

"How sad," Jesse whispered. "But at least you still have the land."

"That's nothing." Luke shrugged again. "The land isn't worth much, it's all swamp and bayou." For a minute he wondered how it would have been to grow up in the mansion, and then he sighed. No use fretting over things that couldn't be changed. As his granny would say, *ne te tracasse pas, fiston.* Don't worry, son.

"It's so pretty here. I think it's worth something. It's worth the peace and quiet, and the wildlife that lives here is priceless." Jesse spoke in an impassioned voice, startling Luke into looking around him differently. The light of the full moon made everything appear as if cast in silver, and some of the peace Jesse spoke of crept into his soul.

The riverbanks were still as the boat glided by. Sometimes they caught sight of raccoons fishing in the shallows, and once they startled a deer as it lowered its head to drink. Fireflies floated through the dense underbrush and flickered in starry patterns above the marsh grasses. Luke found the silence restful. He was used to it—used to the bayou and the dry, whispery sound of the grass as the night breeze moved it, but he hadn't appreciated it in a long while.

The woman sitting in the boat was wrapped in silence too. She sat, her knees raised, her arms curled around her legs. Her dress was light, but the night was hot. She shivered.

"Are you cold?"

She looked up at him, knocking the breath right out of his lungs. *Mon Dieu!* Such a beauty!

"No, I'm fine. Just a little tired, that's all." She went back to staring at the riverbank.

"Who hit you?" Luke asked, after a while. He couldn't believe someone had lifted a hand against her. Whoever had done it was a bastard. His blood boiled, and then he took a deep breath. *Calm yourself, Luke. Ne te tracasse pas.* He couldn't help her remember anything if he frightened her.

She turned her face to him. In the moonlight, it was very pale and the bruises stood out like dark stains on her neck, stirring sharp pity in him. "I don't know." She put her hand to her neck and winced. "It's as if I woke up under that tree, and everything before that moment is a blur. All I can recollect is the music." She shook her head. "I'm sorry."

Music? "What kind of music? Rock, classical, jazz?"

She gave a small laugh. "It's an old folk song. *A la Claire Fontaine.*" She hummed a few bars. "Someone was playing this on an accordion and singing."

That made no sense. "Were you at a party? A dance? You were definitely attacked. It looks as if someone tried to strangle you." Whoever had attacked her might have killed her. She looked fragile still, not quite right. As soon as he got her home, he'd call a doctor. He'd feel better then.

She looked uneasy. "I know someone attacked me, but I can't remember who, or why. When I think about it, it's all dark, and I'm afraid."

"What are you afraid of? That he'll come back and try again?" He was upsetting her, so he tried a different tack. "Where do you live?"

She hugged her knees tighter. "Around here, I think. I'm not certain, really. It's so odd. I have no recollection at all of living anywhere. I know it sounds strange…" Her voice trailed off and she looked at him. "Something is wrong. I know that. It's more than my bruises or being attacked. There's something I have to find, and if I don't find it, something terrible will happen to me."

Another prickle of disquiet shivered Luke's skin. She spoke so strangely sometimes, he could hardly understand her. *Something terrible?* Worse than being attacked and nearly strangled? "You have amnesia. The doctors will be able to help you, Jesse. *Ne te tracasse pas.* Don't fret."

She nodded. "I'm not." But she didn't sound convinced. Her voice was faint and she looked tired all of a sudden. Luke wanted to hold her again, to press his body against hers and keep her safe in his arms.

His whole body yearned for this woman. This strange, beautiful woman. It excited him and frightened him at the same time. But for now she had to get well. When she recovered, he'd… What? In his mind he saw himself standing at her doorstep—wherever that was—holding a bouquet of yellow honeysuckle. She would smile at him, her face lighting up, and then she'd kiss him. Her mouth would taste sweet, like a honeysuckle flower, and her lips would be like satin. Their mouths and bodies would…

He shook his head sharply. He was mad. He'd gone mad. She'd cast a spell on him. But what a spell! His mouth twitched in a rueful smile. He wanted to see her again soon. Hopefully she lived nearby.

"Here we are." Luke cut the motor and the boat glided to the pier. He caught sight of her pale face. "Hey, are you all right? Stay there, I'll tie her up and help you out." She looked as if she were about to pass out. He'd never seen anyone turn so ashen.

He caught the post and swung out of the boat. The planks creaked under his weight. Working quickly, he tied the boat up and secured it to the dock. Out of habit, he glanced at his house. The screened in porch which jutted out over the water was dark, and he couldn't see if his granny waited up for him or not. She sometimes sat there at night, when the heat wouldn't let her sleep. Perhaps she was there, sitting, watching. What would she think of Jesse? He'd never brought a woman to his house.

Then he turned back to the boat. Jesse was gone. She'd vanished without a sound. Where was she? Had she fallen overboard? He rushed to the water and looked in, but nothing had fallen into the river. The water stayed smooth, only the faint current rippled the dark surface. Besides, the water only reached his waist here. If she had fallen in, she could just stand up.

He scanned the dock. Beyond, tall trees shadowed the path leading to the house. Where had she gone? "Jesse?" There was no answer. Uneasy, he picked up his rifle and trotted down the wooden pier. He looked in the shade beneath the live oak, but there was nothing. No one was sitting on the old, wrought-iron bench overlooking the landing. He bounded up the steps to the house three at a time and pushed in the screen-door. His granny was on her rocking chair, looking at him with a worried expression. In the dark, the whites of her eyes glinted.

"What is it, Luke? Why are you back so early?"

"Where is she?" Luke set his rifle in its rack and turned to his granny. "The girl in the boat with me. Where did she go?" Foreboding prickled his skin.

His granny shook her head. "Luke, what are you talking about? You were alone in your boat. There was no one with you."

* * * * *

It seemed as if a cloud covered the moon. In an instant, darkness enveloped her and she found herself alone on the dock. Dry leaves blew across her feet, skittering across the dock with loud rustles.

Where had Luke gone? Where was the boat? She stood, shivering, with only the wind rustling in the trees as company. Wait a minute. The wind blew through bare branches. Hadn't it been summer a minute ago? Where were the fireflies and the croaking frogs? What was happening?

A voice rose above the wind. "Jesse! Jesse?" It sounded like Luke!

"I'm here!" She shivered and walked to the end of the pier. "Where are you?"

"Laws chile, ain't you finished yellin'? You's gonna wake up the dead!"

Jesse whirled around and found an old man sitting at the end of the dock, fishing. Brown skinned and white of hair, the man wore patched and baggy trousers held up with suspenders. His jacket lay on the dock next to him, along with an antique, wicker fishing basket. He hadn't been there a second before.

"Who are you? How did you get here?" Jesse's voice quavered.

"Oh honey, I been here for ages. Done fell off this here dock one day, had a heart attack I s'spect, an' now I come back here and fish whenever I long to. Ain't hard to explain." He patted the wood next to him. "Have a seat. I can tell you's confused. Ain't nothing wrong with that. You jes don't know you're dead yet. Happens sometimes."

Dead? Jesse started to argue, but instead, she sat down heavily next to the old man. Her legs dangled into the water, but she didn't feel the current or the wet. She tried to dredge up some tears and couldn't. "Why can't I cry?" It was a silly question, but the words popped out of her mouth before she could think. *She was dead?*

"Just a minute, I think I caught something." The man reeled up his line, but the hook was empty. "What were you sayin', chile? Oh yes. Tears. Ain't no tear left in you, honey. No substance to you at all. What I'd like to know is, why you come back all a sudden like this. Normally, we hang around where we died, sometimes we leave, and sometimes we come back. Time don't mean much to us. But you don't belong here, and I ain't never seen you before."

"I don't understand what is happening to me." Jesse touched the wood. Her hand distinguished hard and soft, but nothing else, as if she wore heavy mitts. Her feet, dangling in the water, might as well be dangling in thin air. Even her emotions seemed lacking. She could dredge up no fear or horror, only a dull sort of anger she couldn't comprehend. *Dead!*

"But shouldn't I remember how I died?" She realized that she'd accepted what he'd told her. Somehow she believed him. This was no dream, but she also knew, obscurely, that something was wrong.

"You know, I believe I have an answer to your dilemma." The man stood up, packed away his fishing gear, and then slung his coat over his arm. "Come with me, chile. We're going to see Charlotte."

"Charlotte?" Jesse followed the man to the end of the pier.

The man stepped off it and seemed to hover over the water. He turned and shot an amused look at Jesse. "Come on, you won't sink. Hold my hand, I'll take the shortcut."

Confused, she stopped at the end of the dock. "But I don't want to leave Luke!" Luke...she couldn't leave him. She had to find him! An emotion stirred through her, bringing a sudden tingle of sensitivity to her hands.

"Who is Luke?"

"He's the man who found me and brought me here. He lives in that house." She looked up at the darkened building. A shutter flapped in the wind, and it seemed to her that the house looked suddenly derelict, as if no one lived there. However, a force held her pinned to the dock. Luke had something to do with it. Her bones, when she thought of him, ached. When she turned to the old man again, he smiled at her gently.

"Then he must still be alive. You won't find him here, honey chile. You're not in the same time frame now. Can't rightly explain it, but if you want to see him again, you best hope Charlotte can help you."

She wanted to see Luke again. With a sigh, she stepped out over the water and touched his hand. The air grew warmer and a bit lighter, and she found herself standing in front of a white door. She tried to dredge up some sort of emotion as she stood there. She'd just floated through space. Why wasn't her heart pounding with amazement? But all her feelings seemed locked away inside her, beyond her reach.

"Knock," said the old man. "I got my hands full holdin' you an' the basket."

Jesse did as she was told. The door shivered and vanished. "Come in," said a light, girlish voice. Jesse stepped into a vast room. She recognized the place as being a *mam'bo's oum'phor*.

Now, how had she known that? She must have come to a *mam'bo* once before. Before she had died. A shiver ran over her.

"Well, don't just stand there. Come sit down!" The speaker turned out to be a haughty looking young woman. She wore beautiful, old-fashioned clothes and her hair curled in a golden chignon. She smoothed her hand over the brocaded hoop skirt and gave a little tug to the lace sleeves of her opulent chemise. "I'm Charlotte," she said. "Where is your other shoe?"

My shoe? Jesse looked down. Why hadn't she noticed before? She only had one shoe. "I don't know." *How odd.*

"And your dress is all torn. *Mon Dieu*, you look a fright!"

The old man stepped forward and spoke a little impatiently. "Miss Charlotte, this here gal needs help. I done brung her here for *Tata* Rubie, so you be nice and go get her now."

Charlotte tossed her head and sniffed. "I certainly don't have to take orders from a slave, Pishou."

"Why Charlotte, I had hoped a few hundred years would teach you a little humility. I guess you'll never learn, will you?" The new voice was cultivated and slightly mocking. As Jesse watched, a tall man in riding clothes materialized.

Charlotte smoothed her hands over her hair and tugged on her dress, descending her already low neckline. Her nipples almost peeked out from the froth of lace on her bodice. "Oh, Sir Quentin," she cooed. "How lovely it is to see you tonight. Will you be staying for a while?" Was it her imagination, or did Charlotte flush when Sir Quentin appeared? She seemed to grow more, intense, somehow. Jesse watched closely as Charlotte draped herself on the new ghost's arm.

"Charlotte." His voice held a stern note. "How many times must I tell you nice women don't undress in front of men, nor do they press their charms too closely?" He patted her hand and stepped away from her, adroitly disentangling himself from her arms.

He brushed an imaginary speck of dust off his impeccable waistcoat and bowed over Jesse's hand. "So pleased to meet you, my dear. I am Sir Quentin. May I have the pleasure of knowing your name? Don't mind Charlotte, she never learned any manners in that cat house she grew up in."

Charlotte whirled around and glared. "I was just teasing Pishou. I'll go tell *Tata*." Then, gaze softening, she asked, "You're not mad at me, are you, Sir Quentin?"

"Why should I be mad at you, Charlotte? You didn't insult me. Pishou, on the other hand, deserves some respect. If you want me to pay my respects to you one day, you have to prove you are worthy of respect. Spreading your legs, showing your breasts and insulting your friends are the signs of a spoiled slut."

Charlotte paled, and then whirled around, her face twisted in what looked like despair. "I am sorry, Pishou."

Jesse blinked. Emotion! Charlotte could feel things. Could it be linked to her passion for Sir Quentin? Perhaps love had something to do with her vibrant looks and nature.

Or perhaps there was something else special about her. She seemed very...powerful, despite her capricious ways. Whatever the reason, next to Charlotte, Jesse had the impression of herself as a wisp of smoke.

"Luke," she whispered. A powerful vibration surged through her. A fragile pulse beat in her chest. What sort of chain bound her to Luke? She had to find out.

The old man scratched his head and spoke, interrupting her thoughts. "I don't much like being reminded I was a slave, just as you don't like it when we call you a whore."

"I said I was sorry." Charlotte gave a little huff and disappeared.

Pishou chuckled loudly. "My an' don't Miss Charlotte mind her manners when you's here, Sir Quentin. Sure is nice when you show up."

"Please excuse her, my dear," said Sir Quentin, appearing at Jesse's side. "We do tend to take advantage of her. You see, she is the strongest of us and can appear at will to *Tata* Rubie, and we have to use up a lot of energy. So, tell us your name and how you came to be here?"

"My name is Jesse, but I can't remember anything else."

"Ah. A murder victim," Quentin said airily.

"Or it could have been an accident." Pishou shrugged. "Sometimes it happens so quick a body don't know he's dead. Ain't that so, Quentin? Seems we had a time convincing you that *you* was dead."

"I just couldn't imagine ever falling off my horse." Quentin heaved a great sigh. "I'd agree with you, Pish old friend, but look at her neck. Not exactly accidental bruises are they? Think Jesse, can you recall being strangled?"

Jesse winced. Her emotions might be dulled, but the word strangled made her throat hurt. Why? Love and hate were two sides of the same coin. Could those passions have animated her? Was that why she'd come back? She put her hand to her neck. "I just don't recall."

Pish patted her shoulder, but she didn't really feel his hand, more like she felt the idea of his hand patting her shoulder. "Don't fret, Jesse.

Tata Rubie will help you. If that flighty Charlotte tells her you're here she'll summon you soon. So why don't you sit over here and relax."

She did, settling near the fire. As with the river though, she didn't really sense the heat from the flames. She stretched her hand towards them, but the firelight seemed to flicker through her skin, as if it were transparent.

A small log rolled off the fire and began to smoke, so Jesse reached for the poker to prod it back into the fire. Her hand slid over it and she couldn't touch it. It was like trying to grab something in a mirror.

"Don't bother, *cherie*," Sir Quentin said, waving towards the fire. "*Tata* Rubie will do it later. You can't touch anything anyway."

She examined her hands. How odd. Luke had touched her though. How had he done that? There had been a flash of light and an electrical jolt when they'd touched.

She frowned. Something had happened when she'd met Luke— not only to her, but to him too. Something had flowed from her spirit into his, and now she knew that there existed an invisible but strong bond linking them. Luke. Even just saying his name seemed to pierce through her strange apathy. When would she see him again?

Please, let it be soon.

Chapter Two

The paper was yellowed with age and so brittle that Luke was afraid to touch it. Carefully, he smoothed it on the table. His granny poured tea into their mugs, and they sat, side by side, and studied the old document. It was a local newspaper clipping. The photo showed a young woman staring at the camera with a serious expression. It was a high school photo, but Luke recognized Jesse. How could it be possible? Dead! The woman of his dreams had been killed twenty-five years ago. His throat tightened as he read on.

The Mystery — Five Years Later

Jessica Dubois. Disappeared in nineteen-seventy-seven, presumed dead. Last seen at the Saturday night dance with Simon Braquesmar, who was also spotted accompanying Jesse from the bastringue. Several witnesses saw them leave the dance together. Traces of a violent struggle were found on the path leading to her shanty. A shoe was discovered in the underbrush, as well as her underwear, torn in two. There was some blood, but no body was ever found.

Although it is nearly impossible to prosecute without a body, Simon Braquesmar, a widower, and only son and heir of Léon Braquesmar, was accused of murdering her. The police arrested him on a count of manslaughter. In the weeks that followed, the police tried to put together a case, while the Braquesmar fortune was spent on defense lawyers and private investigators, all of whom turned up nothing. Debts the Braquesmars owed were called in, and the bank declared Simon Braquesmar bankrupt. He hanged himself in his attic three months after Jesse disappeared. His son Luke and his mother, Mrs. Léon Braquesmar, survived him. The mystery of Jesse's murder was never cleared, but in Simon's last letter, written to his mother, he tells of his innocence.

If anyone has any information about Jesse, contact the editor at The Daily Gazette.

Luke's granny cleared her throat. "You sure that's the girl you saw?" Her hands trembled on her teacup, rattling it.

"Oui, j'en suis sûr." Of course he was sure! How could he forget that beautiful face? Entirely sure, certain. *"Sûr et certain."*

There was a deep silence between them. The night birds called to each other across the bayou. Finally his granny stirred. "You best go see *Tata.*"

"Now?" Luke glanced at the clock. It was three a.m.

"Best go now." His granny folded the paper and tucked it back in her photo album. "Tell *Tata* I say *bonjour*, and don't forget to flatter Charlotte."

Luke rubbed his chest. The pain had gone, but the anxiety remained. And now he was heading to another daunting place. *Tata* was his granny's friend, but he'd always been terrified of the tall, black woman whose eyes seemed to look right through him.

When he was younger, he'd been sure she knew about every single time he jacked off or did something bad. And Luke had been bad.

When he was a kid, the worst trouble he'd even been into was at *Tata's* place when he set loose her snakes. She'd caught him, nearly flayed him alive. Then he'd spent seven days in the bayou at night catching each and every one of the poisonous copperheads he'd released into the wild. It was a wonder he was still alive. He'd been bitten twice. Each time *Tata* had fixed him up. The second time his arm had swelled up like a watermelon.

As a teenager, he'd been the worst of the bayou's hoodlums — stealing cars, breaking windows, selling dope or whatever he could get his hands on, and generally getting into trouble. He'd gotten caught, and the judge had sentenced him to social services. He'd somehow managed to keep out of prison because he was a minor. Except for once. Just once. That one time nearly killed him. Afterwards, he'd spent three weeks lying in *Tata's* house between life and death while she nursed him and somehow convinced him to go on living.

His granny had just about despaired of him, and then, for some reason, he'd grown up. "Some reason? Hell," he muttered. "Got your ass raped in jail and decided that wasn't the life for you." His voice sounded loud in the dark and he clamped his lips shut, steering the pirogue up the narrow creek leading to *Tata's* house. He'd gotten a job with the Fish and Wildlife Department and since then had kept his nose clean. So why did he always feel like he was seven years old when he went to see *Tata*?

Because she knew all his secrets, that's why.

* * * * *

He docked his boat on Daemon Swath and rubbed his face nervously. It was three-thirty by his watch. There was a light in the *oum'phor* though. As Luke stepped onto the rickety dock, a cool breeze caressed the back of his neck, sending gooseflesh down his arms.

"*Merde*," he said under his breath. He hefted the burlap bag in his hands and from it an angry hissing sound came. On the way he'd spotted a water moccasin and he'd caught it. *Tata* liked presents. "Don't worry, you're going to like it here." The snake just hissed.

"Hurry up boy. You plannin' to stay there all night?" *Tata* called to him, her hands on her hips, her eyes flashing in the dark.

Luke winced. She sounded pissed, almost like she'd been expecting him. How would she—no, best not wonder how she knew things. Well, he was here now. He held the bag out in front of him. "*Bonjour Tata*. Here's a gift for you. I know how much you like snakes."

"If I didn't like snakes, I wouldn't like you." She snatched the bag from him. But her voice was teasing and she reached up to ruffle his dark hair. "Luke Braquesmar. My favorite hood. So, what brings you out here tonight?"

"A ghost. Hey! Careful with that, you don't want to stick your hand in that bag."

She ignored him, reaching in and drawing out the snake. She held it just behind the head. It twisted its long body around her arm. "What kind of ghost?" she crooned to the snake.

Luke stepped back, his eyes on the serpent. "Jesse Dubois." He slapped at a mosquito sting on his forearm.

"Jesse Dubois? The woman your daddy was accused of murderin'?" *Tata's* eyes sharpened with interest. "So that's what

33

Charlotte tried to tell me. She showed up all in a fuss complainin' that Pishou was givin' her orders again and that Sir Quentin had insulted her because of a woman with a missing shoe…

"She didn't make any sense at all, and when I questioned her she looked strange all of a sudden. Almost like she wanted to cry. 'She'll come if you call,' she said, and then she vanished.

"Well, come inside boy, the mosquitoes gonna eat you up alive." She led him into her house, not the *oum'phor*, and she put the snake in a wicker basket, verifying the lid was on tight. Then she put some water in a kettle and set it on the stove. "Sit down Luke. I'm making some tea."

"Oh, granny says *bonjour*." Luke sat on a wooden chair at the kitchen table. His eyes picked out the nicks and scratches he'd made as a child. How many hours had he sat here while his granny talked with *Tata*? He used to feel at home here as in his own house, as long as *Tata* wasn't looking at him. He sighed, fidgeting in his seat. If only he hadn't been such a crazy, stupid teenager.

"Luke, the past is the past," said *Tata*, as if reading his mind. She put some herbs in the hot water and then poured it into three mugs. "Here, this will help you relax. I swear, watchin' you is like watchin' a June bug in a henhouse." She sat down with her mug in front of her, and put the third mug between them in front of an empty chair.

"Which *loa* will come?" His skin was prickling again. "Is it Charlotte? Sir Quentin?" *Tata's* eyes were closing and she was breathing deeply. The light flickered and went out. "Wonderful," Luke muttered.

"Jesse Dubois, I summon you," said *Tata*. "Come now, or leave my *fiston* Luke alone."

"Tata, I…" Luke's heart was hammering in his chest. Oh great, he thought, I'm going to die of a heart attack. Tata can cure snakebite, but I bet she's never had to revive someone from a heart attack —

A white figure appeared in the third chair. "What the fuck!" In his hurry to get up, he tipped his chair over. The figure shivered, wavered, and then solidified into a person. Luke jumped backwards, his feet caught in the chair and he hit the floor with a crash.

The lights went back on, but the white figure didn't disappear. She leaned over and looked at Luke. "Hello again."

Luke's mouth was so dry he couldn't speak. His legs were trembling so hard his heels drummed the floor. *Merde! Triple merde!*

"Luke's a bit shy," said *Tata*, patting the girl's hand. "Here is some tea, *chère*. Drink up, it will give you strength. Luke, get up and sit down properly. You'd think you never saw a ghost before."

"Charlotte never shows herself to me, and besides, I didn't know *she* would show up." He didn't want to look at her, but at the same time, he longed to grab her and hold her tightly. His heart pounded frantically and waves of heat washed over him. A ghost! Seeing her face in an old, faded newspaper hadn't brought that fact home. Seeing her appear from thin air sure did.

It figured. He finally met a woman he wanted to get to know, and she was dead. His whole life was a fuck-up, why not his love-life too? Well, he wouldn't have long to feel sorry for himself. His heart would give out any minute now.

"Luke, *fiston*, we have to talk now." *Tata's* voice was gentle and she took his hand in hers. She took Jesse's hand too, and then Jesse took Luke's hand, joining them in a triangle. A soft light flowed from Jesse and surrounded them. It didn't feel like the same violent shock as when Luke had first touched her. This was a quiet, slow seepage of energy.

"That's right," *Tata's* voice was soothing. "Ghosts ain't nothin' but troubled energy. Too much disturbance, and everything all knotted up. Got to sort all that out. Got to settle it down." She closed her eyes. "You're back for a reason, child. Got to find somethin', that right?"

"Yes." Jesse sighed deeply. "Something is lost, and I must find it. But what?"

Tata nodded, her whole body moving like one of her snakes. "Bones. You have to find your bones."

"Why?" Luke couldn't help blurting out. Damn, *Tata* didn't like it when he interrupted.

Tata frowned but kept her eyes closed. She seemed to listen to a tiny voice in her head. She nodded slowly. "You have to find your body, Jesse child. When you find your bones, you'll have solved the mystery."

But, no one knew what happened to her body. Was that the mystery? Or would that solve the murder? "And then what?" Luke asked.

"That's not clear." *Tata* opened her eyes and peered at Jesse. "You have to hurry. Someone else be searchin' for your bones."

"Someone else? How do you know?"

Tata turned her gaze to Luke. "He came to see me an' asked about her, that's how I know."

"Who was it?" Luke's voice was hard.

"Jacques Lesnoire." *Tata* let go of their hands and leaned back in her chair.

"But…" Luke sputtered. "Jacques Lesnoire? What the hell he be wanting with Jesse's bones?" Lord, he must be tired. He was starting to sound Cajun.

Tata's eyes narrowed. "I be wondering the same thing, *fiston*. If you want to know, I think maybe he has somethin' to do with this whole story. Maybe this is the time to set things right."

Luke frowned. "If Jacques had something to do with this, can't we just call the cops?"

"And say what? You don't know where her body is, so the police can't do anything. You have to help Jesse, Luke. She came back for you."

He looked at the woman—no, ghost. His fists tightened as fear churned his stomach. "I have a job to do, I can't do this. I can't help a ghost. I'm…" His thoughts flew like leaves in the wind, fluttering madly.

"Your job takes you into the bayou, into the swamp. Chances are her body is nearby where you found her. You'll have to go back and seek out her bones." *Tata's* voice was stern. "You have to help her Luke. You were chosen. It's time you cleared your father's name."

"How?" Clear his father's name? Was it possible?

"First, you have to make Miss Jesse stay." *Tata* looked up at the clock ticking on the wall. "The sun will be up in an hour. You'll have to hurry, boy. In an hour, she'll fade and she won't be able to come back. It may be too late. She needs to be here in flesh and blood, and only you can do that. Give her your seed, she'll be fixed here. Your seed or your blood. It's up to you."

Luke stared at *Tata*. His body trembled. "You don't know what you're asking of me," he whispered. He would not panic, he would not. But did she mean what he thought?

"Please?" Jesse had been silent until then, but now her voice broke past his defenses. Her eyes were pleading. "I need you, Luke."

Images of another night flashed in his mind. He winced. Why did Jesse have to look at him so hopefully? How could he ever tell her?

"I'm going to the *oum'phor*. I won't be back before full daylight." *Tata* chortled then patted Jesse's shoulder. "My *fiston* will help you. I give my word."

"*Tata!*" A feverish heat coursed through his body and his cock stiffened almost painfully. A sweet yet spicy taste clung to his lips. "What was in that tea?"

"Somethin' to make your task easier for you, *fiston*." For once *Tata's* voice was soft when she spoke to him. "Don't think I don't remember what happened to you. I remember everything, boy. If I could have somehow stopped what happened to you that night, I would have. But the past is the past. It's time to put that behind you. I healed your body. She will heal your mind. Go with Jesse. She needs you."

"What if she doesn't want me?" hissed Luke. Lights were dancing in front of his eyes. He blinked, trying to clear his vision, but *Tata* was gone. The door swung closed, and he was alone with Jesse. He tried to fight the waves of arousal washing over him but it was impossible. His cock, aching with need, strained against the fabric of his jeans. His heart pounded in his chest and his breath came in quick gasps.

No, it's all right. They won't get me. It's over, finished. But somehow, since that night in prison, his body equated arousal with rape. He'd never dated because of that. He had to tell Jesse. He'd tell her now. He gripped the table with his hands and looked up, expecting to meet her sad stare. Instead, her chair was empty.

He blinked and looked around. She'd vanished. "Jesse? Where are you?"

"Don't fight it," said a voice at his ear. Fight it? Of course he would. The last time someone touched him, he nearly died.

Calm down, Luke. This is not the same. But where had Jesse gone? Who had spoken? "Charlotte, is that you?" Damn, as if one ghost weren't enough.

Something touched him on the jaw. A hand. An invisible hand. He leapt out of his chair and spun around, but nobody was there. "Who are you?"

"It's me, Jesse. I'm right here. Can't you see me?" She sounded surprised.

Luke strained his eyes. Nothing. "No." His senses were heightened. Each touch, each sound seemed amplified a hundredfold. His shirt scratched roughly against his skin and sweat popped out on his forehead and upper lip when another wave of heat submerged him. He groaned as invisible fingers undid the buttons on his pants, setting free his erection.

"Don't—" he started to say, but an invisible hand covered his mouth.

"Do you choose to help me?" Her voice seemed to come from far away.

Did he? What would that mean? Giving up a part of him, but could he do it? Yes, he wanted to clear his father's name. He'd been living with the shadow of a murderer hanging over his head for too long.

No, he didn't want to get involved with a ghost. Just the thought made him shiver with fear.

Or was it something else? His cock swelled, grew heavy, and suddenly he longed for release. Release from his memories and release from fear. The fear he could control, but the memories…they hurt him. So far, he'd been good about suppressing them. But Jesse needed him. He pictured her standing before him, her dark, soulful eyes full of hope.

"Yes," he breathed. "I will help you." There, he'd said it. A quiver ran over him, and another wave of desire, brought on by *Tata's* damn potion no doubt, made his buttocks clench. He gritted his teeth. "I have to tell you something though."

"Hush. Whatever it is, it will keep."

"But I want to—"

"Later."

Maybe she was right. Later he would think. Right now, he had the impression he stood alone in the kitchen and talked to a wall. He reached over and turned off the light. A candle still glowed from the counter, casting a flickering, orange light over the sturdy wooden table and chairs.

"That's better," Jesse said. She ran her finger over his cock, and he could hear her practically purring.

Trembling, he stood still while sensations assailed him. Lips as light as a butterfly's wings touched his mouth and a slender body pressed close to him. No warmth emanated from her, but he touched cool, smooth skin and his hands brushed against soft, full breasts. His hips thrust of their own accord, and he uttered a strangled moan of frustration. In a second he was going to come. It was building just behind his balls, a tidal wave of passion waiting to unfurl.

Damn potion. Damn *Tata*! *Merde!* He tried to hold on, and slowly gained control of his body.

Curiosity warred with his fear, and the curiosity won. He ran his hands over the invisible body. His palms slid up her slim waist, over her delicate shoulders, touched soft hair he could not see. He tangled his hands in it and leaned into her embrace, eyes closed, seeing her with his body. Jesse. Her name stirred his heart, or was it her touch? His own heartbeats nearly deafened him. His erection pressed into her belly, and she shifted, catching it between her thighs.

No. He stepped back, his heart pounding. Other memories kept intruding, violent, hurtful memories.

Let me. Please? Jesse's words were like a light touch on his mind.

Eyes still shut against the terrors of his recollections, he reached up. Blindly he traced the delicate contours of her face. Her sweeping eyebrows, narrow nose, full lips. She caught his fingertip in her teeth and bit gently. There came the sound of the chair moving and he sensed her rise and sit on the table. Clasping his hips, she pulled him to her. He slid between her open thighs then slick heat covered his cock. Tight, slick and faintly pulsing, it clasped him closely. Panic welled then subsided just as quickly. Her mouth was on his now, lips open, tongue seeking his. Hands guided his hard cock into her close-fitting, slippery cunt that grew warmer as he thrust.

"It's all right. Doesn't that feel good?" Her soft voice tickled in his ear, no more than a whisper.

The hurt and the panic that had seized him before faded. In its place grew a throbbing urgency. His cock had no problem forgetting what had happened to him. Instead, blinding waves of passion washed over him, leaving his body quivering with lust.

"Wait!" he cried, shuddering with the need to explode. He didn't want it to end. He wanted to—

The body he couldn't see bucked against him. Breasts rubbed his chest; a leg wrapped around his waist. The table moved as he thrust forward. Now he opened his eyes and looked down. He wasn't sure what he'd expected to see.

His cock stuck straight out in front of him. Even though he felt it surrounded by throbbing, hot flesh he saw his cock as he sheathed himself in her, saw the way it twitched in her invisible body. She moved her hips back and forth, and his cock bent to follow her movements. Hard yet supple, it slid into her flesh and bobbed up and down as she rose and fell. Her leg hooked around him to give her leverage, her slim calf pressing against his. She slid deeper.

He grabbed her by her invisible hips, pushing his body into hers. There came the sensation of heat as he entered her flesh, and cool as he pulled out. Slowly—now what would it feel like really slow? He felt little spasms shaking his balls, like he was just about to come, but he gritted his teeth and struggled to hang on. Slow and easy now.

"Harder," she cried. She mewed and writhed against him, her fingers digging into his shoulders. Faster now. He dragged the air into his lungs and plunged into her body, as hard and fast as he could. Friction heated his cock like a blow torch. He thrust harder, his cockhead hitting her womb at every long, hard stroke.

Good, no, good didn't describe it. Heaven, he'd died and gone to heaven. A laugh escaped him. Who had died? Not him. His blood sang in his ears, his cock twitched and throbbed. The need to fill Jesse with his cock, with his seed, grew stronger with each passing second.

Little moans and kitten cries sounded in his ears. Her lips brushed against his mouth, and then he shattered.

He reached down and grabbed her ass, holding her close, a harsh cry torn out of his throat as he emptied himself into her. His milky seed left his cock and it grew into a cloud, spreading through her body and giving it form. It swelled up and down like a mist, until her body once more became visible.

Luke shook uncontrollably. He still held Jesse in his arms—he couldn't let go if his life depended on it. He'd brought her back; he'd done it. His whole body wrapped around her and held on.

Jesse uttered a muffled sob and buried her face in the crook of his neck. His scent, musky and male, soothed and excited her at the same time. Hot tears ran down her cheeks and this time she could feel them. She could cry. Emotions battered her, but she welcomed them. She felt so alive. She was alive! And Luke had made this happen.

"Why are you crying?"

"I'm finally here." Her lips brushed against his ear as she spoke and she stopped to run her mouth over his ear, reveling in the shell-like curves.

He stroked her back, quieting her. His warm hands rubbed the tension out of her back and neck, but at the same time, made prickles of delight run down her spine. Then, to her regret, he stepped away, holding her at arm's length. "What is happening?"

She wished she knew. For a minute, she tried to sort out her thoughts. Questions jumbled in her head. Had that been the first time she'd made love? Did it always feel so good, and leave her so sticky, satisfied afterwards? Did he feel the same? "I'm not a ghost anymore," she finally managed to say. It sounded so silly.

He didn't seem to think so. His eyes softened and he smiled at her. Relief flooded her as she saw that all traces of fear had left his gaze. "Can you recall what happened now?"

She tried, but she had no memories of before, just a frightening blankness that her mind shied away from. "I think *Tata* Rubie is right. I came back to set things right and you are supposed to help me. From what I understand, your father was accused of murdering me." She paused. That sounded so odd. She was dead, or was she alive? She poked herself in the arm. The strange cold numbness that surrounded her as a ghost had disappeared.

"That's right, my father supposedly murdered you." Luke's voice sounded cool and she shivered.

Please, don't let him hate me, I can't survive without him. I need him in order to stay alive. No, that's not the only reason. Tata said I would need him and I do, but not how she meant, at least, I don't think so. It has to do with him and me, not just me. Luke is the one I need, it couldn't have been just any man.

He stopped to help me, and he grew upset when he saw my wounds. He cares. I can sense the good in him. Is that why I need him?

"What are you thinking about?" He put his finger under her chin and turned her face to his. His eyes were questioning. "Why do you look so sad?"

"I...I don't know. Perhaps it's the shock of knowing I caused your family so much pain."

"No, not you." His eyes were cold splinters of ice now. "Jacques Lesnoire is responsible, not you. Never say that again." He pulled her into his arms and kissed her.

Her heart raced. Could he tell how much she needed him?

Warmth enveloped her now. A knife of sheer passion stabbed her in the belly. More, her body ordered.

I obey, she told it, as her blood seemed to reach the boiling point and her nipples stiffened into painful peaks.

She ran her lips down the side of his jaw, her mouth coming to rest on his. Her lips were soft, sensual and warm. As her kiss deepened, she used her tongue to tickle his upper lip, begging him silently to open his mouth.

A groan left his throat as he met her tongue with his, teeth clicking together. He tightened his arms around her, grinding his hips to hers. Her leg, still wrapped firmly around his waist, flexed and drew him even closer. His cock hardened so fast his head spun. He staggered and would have fallen, but Jesse held him upright. Her arms were strong now. Her face, turned up to his, was glowing.

A vibrant, living woman stood before him. Now warmth emanated from her smooth skin. Warmth…and the scent of aroused pussy. His head spun as he caught a whiff of her. Desire surged into his groin, and his balls pulled tight.

Exhaustion made rational thought impossible. He wanted to stop, to analyze his feelings. But Jesse's face shone like a new penny. With his heightened senses he could almost hear her heart beating and feel the new blood rush through her veins. Her hands massaged his shoulders, sending waves of pleasure right to his toes. His cock grew even harder, if possible. Could it explode?

Okay, so we think about this later. He grabbed hold of her hips and nudged his cockhead against her inner thighs. She opened them wide, and he groaned again, louder, as she speared herself slowly onto his cock. The angle didn't allow for much penetration. Luke bent his knees a bit, trying for some thrust.

His head swam and he had to stop for a minute.

"Let's go into the bedroom." Her voice sounded loud in the quiet kitchen. She pulled away from him, his cock slipping from her wet cunt with a sucking sound. The cool, night air struck him as she left him.

She slid off the table and strode to the doorway. He stepped after Jesse, nearly falling because of his pants wrapped around his ankles. Cursing in impatience, he kicked his pants off. His body still burned with unspent desire, so he hastened to follow the sexy spirit into the bedroom.

How had Jesse slipped past his defenses so easily? Could it be because she was dead and he pitied her? No, don't think that. She wasn't dead, not now. His steps faltered. How long would she be able to stay with him? Would she have to go back? God, no! Pain tightened his throat into a knot. *Jesse! What have you done to me?*

He shook his head to clear it. He would think of that later. *Or not at all*, said a tiny whisper in his mind.

Candles flickered in the darkened room, casting mysterious shadows on the wall. Jesse lay on the white sheets, her raven-colored hair spread on the pillow, a smile playing about her full lips. As Luke watched, mesmerized, she stroked her breasts, pinching her taut nipples. Electric shocks burst in his nipples as he saw this, and his hands fumbled at his buttons. He tore his shirt off and threw it across the room. The air seemed too thick to breathe. Panting, he threw himself on the bed and rolled onto Jesse's willowy body. Holding her in his arms would chase away the last demons hiding in the corners of his mind. Fucking her made him whole, made her whole, and somehow made them one. A shiver of excitement made his cock stiffen and twitch. The passion that grabbed him was nearly supernatural.

Her legs parted and she lifted her hips higher, her hand coming down to seek his cock and guide it into her wet cunt. Without faltering, he plunged into her, gasping as his cock slid its whole length into her snug sheath.

"*Mon Dieu!*" Luke cried raggedly, trying desperately to regain control of his body. But his body wasn't his to control. Fire coursed through his veins instead of blood, and it pooled and concentrated in his loins. His cock throbbed with each rapid heartbeat and he thrust his hips faster, trying to outpace the pressure building in his groin.

She twisted beneath him and the sting of her nails as she raked her fingers across his back urged him on. Her stiff nipples pressed into his chest like pebbles, and her strong legs wrapped around his waist, her heels drumming against his ass. He imagined himself a wild colt, being driven by its rider. Her heels spurred him on. His balls slapped against her wet flesh in time to the beat of her heels on his ass.

Black spots danced before his eyes as another orgasm grabbed him by the belly and shook him from head to toe. He cried out, his body convulsing as he shot his seed deep within Jesse's tight cunt. His body drained itself into hers. Gasping, he poured everything he had into her throbbing flesh. *Oh Lord, there's no more of me, I've given her everything.* He collapsed onto her stomach. A deep satisfaction stole over him.

"More!" she begged, rubbing her naked body against his.

"I can't," he gasped. Part of him wanted to laugh, but he could hardly open his eyes. "You're insatiable." He grinned down at her.

She pushed him off her and he rolled onto his back. "Is that bad?" she asked, straddling him. Legs wide, she leaned backwards, offering herself to his view. Luke swallowed hard and his cock stirred, even though his eyelids seemed to weigh three tons. Her cunt was inflamed, swollen with desire, and as he watched, she reached down and touched her clit. Her finger rubbed it, circled it, and teased it.

"I don't know." Could he get drunk on sex? In another minute, his head would fly right off his shoulders.

"Give me your hand."

Luke did, and she rubbed her glistening cunt against it. She gave a harsh groan and pushed hard against his hand. Hot liquid gushed onto his palm, and his fingers slid right through her labia, past her outer lips, and into her tight vagina. His cock, hard again, pressed against her soft thigh. With a ragged moan, he thrust his fingers deep into her cunt, loving the slippery, tight wetness. He could get used to doing this three or four times a night. His stomach contracted as a stab of pure lust hit him. "Jesse," he moaned.

"You like it?"

You're incredible. He wanted to say it. He wanted to say more, but she bent her head down and kissed him, her mouth covering his. He kissed her back, tasting her lips, her tongue, the sweetness of her mouth awaking a fierce hunger. More, he wanted more. More of her slow, sweet kisses, her slick pussy. More of Jesse. His mind shied away from the eventuality of losing her. Instead, he would lose himself in her body.

She seemed to read his thoughts. Her kiss became soft, tender, her lips barely brushing his. "I don't want to leave you. I don't want this night to end." She spoke softly, her mouth still touching his.

"Me neither." There, he'd admitted it. He needed her. A knot pulled tight in his throat and he pressed his hand harder against her cunt, his fingers reaching deeper into her tight passage, trying to chase away the thought that she could not stay.

"Then let's make it last forever." A tear slid down her cheek. He kissed it away, licking the salty tear from her lips.

Now his cock was so stiff it hurt. Little spurts of liquid shot from its head. Luke withdrew his hand and grabbed Jesse's hips. Roughly, he pulled her onto his cock and thrust.

Knees spread wide, Jesse impaled herself on his cock. Luke watched as it disappeared into her cunt. Fully sheathed now, her black, curly pubic hair hid his shaft from view. He could just make out his thick root as she slid back and forth. The silky friction drove him crazy, so he grabbed the bedcovers with both hands, holding tight while she rode him. Her hips slammed back and forth, and her fingers dug into his shoulders as she held on to his body, urging him on, calling his name with a voice that made his hair stand on end.

Then Jesse threw her head back and uttered a raucous cry. Her cunt gripped Luke's cock, massaging it with pulsing contractions. All at once, something deep inside his body unraveled; his whole being shuddered and emptied his seed into Jesse's body. Long, hard spurts shot out of his cock, and he dug his heels into the bed and drove his hips upwards.

His body jackknifed, and he rolled over Jesse, pouring the last of his sperm, the last of his soul, it felt like, into her. Over and over his body convulsed, the hot spurts finally dying away, the flood becoming a trickle. His hoarse panting quieted, breathing evened out, and his eyes closed.

Make the night last forever, he thought, desperately trying to stay awake. But blackness swirled around him. As sleep claimed him, he lay splayed on the bed like the victim of a shipwreck.

Chapter Three

Jesse propped her elbows on the window and watched as the sun rose. Behind her, sleeping deeply, was the man who'd saved her. She held her hand up to the pale pink light and marvelled as her skin glowed. She didn't become transparent and vanish; instead she seemed to become more solid as each minute passed.

Turning, she gazed at the man on the bed. "Luke," she murmured. Just the sight of him made her whole body burn with a fierce heat. She wanted to wake him up and stroke his cock hard again. She needed it buried deep inside her. A stab of desire made her pussy clench and she slid her hand between her legs. Her fingers found her clit and she rubbed it, trying to still the twinges inside her cunt. But the ache was too deep; she needed a cock, a long, thick cock to stretch her out and pump her full of life. And yet, she didn't just want any cock. She only wanted Luke. Nobody else, just Luke.

Was it just the effects of *Tata* Rubie's potion making her so desperate? Whatever it was, it made her like a cat in heat. She needed cock and she needed it bad. Had it been the same when she was alive? She didn't know; she didn't remember anything but vague shadows, hushed whispers and Zydeco music. Her memories started with Luke. The first time she'd looked up into his angular face with its blade-like nose, sensual mouth and black, burning eyes she'd been lost. He'd stepped out of his boat, his expression wary, suspicious, yet ready to be of assistance if he could. When he'd set eyes on her all his reticence had vanished and he'd focused on helping her.

The good within him seemed to shine out of him like a beacon. She couldn't believe others didn't see it as well. A man lay asleep behind her, someone she could depend on, someone who would protect her with his life, if need be. It was the sexiest feeling in the world to know that. And speaking of sexy...his body was long and muscular. His cock matched the rest of him—bowed slightly towards his flat stomach and made to fit her body perfectly. Just thinking about it made her achy; slick moisture spilled over her fingers.

She thrummed her fingers against her clit, pressing hard to bring herself to climax, but it didn't help. She couldn't reach orgasm. Only frustration grew as her fingers slid into her slippery flesh. Her cunt swelled as desire grabbed her by the throat. Prickles of electricity tingled in her belly. With a muffled groan she crawled onto the bed next to Luke. He stirred, but didn't waken. Under the light covers, he was naked. She reached down, her hand sliding over his smooth skin, until she reached his cock.

"Wake up." She prayed he'd forgive her for waking him from his sound sleep.

He groaned, throwing his arm over his eyes. "What time is it?"

"Time to make love to me." She pumped his cock with her hand. It hardened, sending another thrill of desire streaking through her. She lay on top of him, and his cock, fully-erect now, was like an iron brand on her thighs. She opened her legs and pressed her cunt to him. When the tip of his cock parted her sensitive flesh, she groaned in satisfaction.

Taking a deep breath, she sat up, balancing on her knees. Now his cock was upright, the tip nestled in the folds of her labia, poised at the entrance of her cunt. She sat down fast, a guttural cry welling up from what seemed like the depths of her soul as his hard shaft penetrated her, stretched and rubbed against textured flesh. Sharp tingles of delight filled her belly, and she rocked her hips forward, glorying in the pleasurable sensations.

She threw her head back and thrust down harder. His hands came up and grabbed her hips, holding her even closer to him. Eyes still closed, she reached for his hands, clasping them to her waist. Without sight, her sense of touch was heightened. She felt the whole length of his cock as it slid into her body. Tensing her thighs, she rose above him. The glorious fullness lessened, withdrew, and there was just the slippery, hard tip to tease her with the promise of satisfaction and bliss. The flared head paused as it caught in her tight entrance. She lowered herself again, this time slowly, eyes squeezed shut. Inch by incredible inch, his cock filled her, searing her cunt with its throbbing heat.

"Look at me," ordered Luke. His voice came out harsher than she'd ever heard it. "I want to see your eyes when you come, look at your beautiful face. I want you to see me, and know that it's me, my cock, giving you this pleasure."

Jesse's eyes fluttered open.

Her cunt was throbbing and burning. It was like being on the top of a volcano about to erupt. In a minute, she would be swept over the edge. Desire was the current pulling her along. Luke's coal-black eyes were fixed on her face. He pumped his hips faster, and then froze. His body shook, and Jesse felt his cock spasm inside her. Spurts hit the back of her womb, exploding from his body in a burning stream. He uttered a harsh cry, his fingers digging into her flesh.

She gasped as she was swept over the edge, falling into the molten lava. Her body seemed consumed by searing rushes of heat, carrying her in a mad, headlong rush into blinding ecstasy.

* * * * *

"We have to find your bones." Luke gently touched her face. He sat on the side of the bed, fully-dressed.

Jesse blinked. "Was I sleeping?"

"You looked so peaceful, I didn't want to wake you. But we have to go now. *Tata's* day-time clients will start coming, and I don't want them to see us."

Jesse sat up, groggy. For a minute, she didn't remember where she was, or what had happened. Then memories of the night rushed in. Heat rose into her cheeks and she ducked her head. What must Luke think of her? A bitch in heat couldn't have been worse! Then another thought struck her. Was she still solid, flesh and blood? Hesitantly, she touched her face, running her hands over her cheeks and hair.

"Yes, you're still here." Luke's voice held a note of tenderness in it. "Hey, I really enjoyed last night." He tipped her chin back with his hand, forcing her to meet his eyes. "Don't hide from me. We know each other too well now."

"Are you glad I...I stayed?" She had to know.

His eyebrows rose. "Of course I am." He hesitated. "We have to go soon. Are you still tired?"

"No, I'm fine. Just let me get washed up. Where's the bathroom?"

Luke pointed. "Over there."

Everything seemed strange and new; the sting of the water in the shower, the towel against her skin, slipping the cotton dress over her head. She moved clumsily and it was as if she were doing everything for the first time again. In a way, it was true. Her hands were hypersensitive and she smelled and tasted everything as if experiencing it for the first time.

However, her memories remained stubbornly hidden. Even her face in the mirror didn't stir anything but a whisper of disquiet. Who was she? *What* was she? Was she really alive? Fear crouched stubbornly in the back of her mind. What if she turned back into a ghost?

No, don't even think about that!

Her stomach growled loudly. She jumped at the unexpected sound. At least her appetite had returned.

When she stepped out of the bedroom, dressed and ready, Luke had stripped the bed and piled the sheets and towels in the hamper.

"Are we just going to leave?"

"Don't worry, *Tata* won't mind if we leave without saying good-bye." He took her hand and pulled her out the bedroom door, through the dark, silent kitchen and outside. A rooster crowed not far away. The sun shone over the treetops, but there was still dew on the ground, and gray mist rose off the river. Their footsteps sounded loud on the wooden dock.

Luke helped Jesse into the boat and cast off. Silently, he poled into the middle of the river, and then he let the current pull them along.

The sun had fully risen now, and it soon burned away the mist. Jesse sat in the boat and looked at the quiet beauty of the scene.

"Do you recognize anything?"

She shook her head, frustration bubbling in her chest. "Nothing. I can't remember anything."

"Let's have breakfast, and we'll look at a map. Might as well do this the right way." Luke gave another push to the pole, then set it inside the boat and started the motor. Water curled in froth at the bow as he steered the boat up the river branch leading to his house. As before, the mansion on the hill caught his eyes and he looked upwards.

Jesse followed his gaze and her skin prickled. She shook her head. Jacques Lesnoire? The name meant nothing to her, but somehow he was mixed up in her story and Luke's past. But she didn't know how. Only shadows were in her mind, only shadows. A sigh left her and she rubbed her forehead tiredly. All her hopes were pinned on Luke. She looked at him again. Strong, yet somehow fragile. He looked able to wrestle an alligator, but when she touched him, he trembled.

Something had happened, something bad. She was positive. "What happened to you? What was *Tata* talking about when she said she wanted to stop what had happened that night?"

A muscle jumped in his jaw. "I got into some trouble a few years ago. Hung out with the wrong crowd, listened to the wrong people, and did stupid things. I got caught." He stopped speaking. The outboard engine purred, then he cut it, drifting to a stop at the dock.

"Go on." Jesse took his hand before he could get out of the boat and held it tightly.

"You don't want to hear it."

"I do."

His face was bleak. "They threw me in jail. There were a few guys in there who thought I needed a lesson."

Jesse nodded. "Did they hurt you?"

He wouldn't meet her eyes. He looked away, across the river, and his mouth twisted. "You could say that. Yeah, they hurt me bad."

"What happened?"

"Three held me down while the others took their pleasure with me. Then they beat me senseless. *Tata* bailed me out. She and my granny came to get me. *Tata* took care of me afterwards. I don't remember too much. It's probably better this way."

"I'm sorry." Jesse's heart contracted with a sharp pain. He wouldn't accept her pity, she knew this. But what about her love? Could he tell she was falling in love with him? She shivered as the futility of her situation struck her. In a day, a week maybe, she would be gone.

He looked so angry. How could she wipe those bitter lines from his face? A thought struck her. She would help him, as he helped her. Together they could do anything.

He shrugged and pulled his hand away. "No big deal. I was just another statistic, that's all."

"Like me. We're both statistics."

He looked at her then, and his dark eyes filled with a strange sorrow. "I'm still alive, and I'm fine now. You were killed. It's not the same thing at all."

Jesse's mouth trembled. His words hurt. She knew she was dead, damn it, but she loved him anyway and had since the first second she'd seen him!

Well, her torture wouldn't last much longer. "I'm sorry anyway."

"Don't be. It's over now. *Tata* nursed me back to health." He got out of the boat and held it steady while she stepped onto the dock.

"So I was your first woman." She stepped closer to him.

He looked away, a flush staining his cheeks. "Yes."

She didn't know whether to laugh or cry. Were all men so proud? Her memories stayed securely locked away, so she had no idea if she'd ever made love before. "Well, if it makes you feel better, you're the first lover I've been able to remember." Her own flippancy surprised her, and she was glad when he turned to her, a grin on his face.

"You can stop feeling sorry for me," he said, tying the boat to the pier. "I got over it last night, thanks to you. Now it's my turn to help you, and I hope I can do more than just make you scream with pleasure." He looked at her with a hooded gaze, giving her goosebumps. "For whatever time you're here, you're my woman, Jesse."

He'd said she was his woman! Joy swelled her heart. When she passed near him the heat of his body touched her, she caught a whiff of his spicy scent. She swayed towards him. He took her in his arms, and she marvelled again at how strong they were. He grabbed her and gave her a hard kiss on the mouth.

She kissed him back, hungrily, their bodies pressed together. Through the light cotton of her dress, she felt his cock stiffen against her thigh. A stab of pure desire rushed through her. She imagined him pushing her against the oak tree, lifting her dress, and taking her right there by the river. She could almost feel the rough bark pressing into her skin and his cock driving into her hot cunt.

Instead, he drew back, a clouded look in his eyes.

"What's the matter?"

He shook his head. "Let's go have some breakfast. My granny must be waiting for me."

His Granny lived here—so that's why he pulled away. He must be worried about shocking her, and he must think she might terrify the old woman. She darted a glance up at the porch, jutting out over the river. "Is she up there?"

"Of course."

Jesse held back. "I don't think I should go up there. What if she sees me? Won't I scare her?"

"Frighten my granny? I don't think so. You don't look anything like a ghost." He gave her a reassuring smile, and her heart grew lighter.

He led her across the dock and past the old oak tree leaning over the dock as if it were sheltering it. Jesse walked up the old stone stairs after him, her body curiously tense. Just the sight of him made her blood boil. It was hard not to touch him when she was near. Was it because he was part of her? His seed had gone into her making. A shiver ran down her spine. All she wanted was to run her hands over his flat chest, down his taut belly, and over his—

"Careful, this step is loose." Luke held the screen door open for her and pointed downwards at the same time. "I haven't got around to fixing it," he added apologetically.

Jesse stepped inside the house and looked around. It was a comfortable house, with crocheted rag rugs and wooden furniture that gleamed from years of use and polish. The porch had a daybed and two rocking chairs. A bookcase stood in the far corner of the porch, next to a bench covered with plants. In the living room, a cast-iron pot-bellied stove faced the threadbare sofa and two armchairs. The kitchen was large and surprisingly modern. Jesse blinked as she stepped into it.

"My granny likes to cook." Luke turned on the coffee machine.

Jesse looked at the black and white tiled floor, the glass fronted cabinets and the state of the art oven and fridge. "It's very nice." She ran her hands over the smooth granite-topped counters. The chrome sink caught her eye, and she tilted her head. "Where are the hot and cold faucets?"

"You lift this lever and push it right or left." Luke grinned. "In twenty-five years, some things have changed. I bet you didn't have a computer."

"A computer? Why would I need one of those?" Jesse lifted the sink lever and washed her hands. She had to think of something besides fucking Luke. Even though that's all she wanted. Had she been wanton when she was alive? No. She knew, somehow, that wasn't right. She shook her head, trying to clear it. *Think of other things.* "Can I set the table?" She wondered what else had changed in a quarter of a century. The appliances didn't look that different, except for the sink.

"Of course, dishes are in that cupboard, silverware in this drawer. Granny will be in soon."

Jesse laid the table then sat down, her hands in her lap. Luke fried eggs, put bread in the toaster, and made fresh orange juice. His movements were spare and precise. She loved the way he frowned as he concentrated on a task. She tried to tear her eyes from his face but couldn't. His tousled black hair framed his angular face, accentuating his eyes which never lost their eagle-fierce intensity. What had he looked like as a child? Thin, with scraped knees and eyes too big for his face, she bet.

A woman's voice startled her out of her reverie. "Hello Luke, I didn't hear you come in. And...*Mon Dieu!*" The woman in the doorway turned deathly pale.

Luke was at her side in an instant. "Granny, let me explain."

"I'm sorry, I was startled, that's all. You can't be Jesse Dubois. You gave me such a scare. But it's uncanny how much you resemble her." The woman took Luke's arm and patted it. "It's all right, I'm just being fanciful. Of course it's not..."

"Grandmère," said Luke, his voice grave. "I went to see *Tata* last night. She said I might have the chance to clear papa's name." He stopped and glanced at Jesse. "This is Jesse Dubois, grandmère. She came back to help us, and *Tata*, well, *Tata* found a way to make her real for a while."

For a while! The words stung, though Jesse tried not to show it. "I'm sorry about all this." Why was she apologizing? She hadn't gotten killed on purpose.

The old woman blinked, then shook her head. "*Tata*. I should have known." She fixed Jesse with a bright gaze. "No, no, don't be absurd. None of this is your problem. It was brought upon us by *le mal*, and we will overcome it. Here, I'll sit with you, and you can tell me what happened."

"You're not afraid of me?" Worry gnawed at Jesse's heart.

"No, heavens child! I lived in the bayou all my life. You aren't the first ghost I've seen. Some days I catch sight of an old black man sitting at the end of my pier. When I go down to say 'hey', he vanishes. And I see Charlotte too. She likes to try to startle me, but *Tata* always scolds her." She gave a chuckle.

Jesse sighed, relief washing over her. Luke's granny wasn't horrified, and she didn't blame her for what happened. "I wish I could tell you what happened, but the last thing I remember is music. Then I woke up beneath a tree. I had to dig, for some reason, but I must have been in the wrong place. I was about to go somewhere else when Luke came by. He found me, and saw I'd been hurt. I rode in his boat, but when I wanted to get out, I couldn't. It was like going to sleep—I was so tired and everything grew dark.

"The next thing I knew, I was standing all alone on the dock. I met someone called Pishou and he took me to see Charlotte. It's all sort of jumbled in my head now. The next clear thing I recall is sitting at the table with Luke and a big, black woman with fierce eyes."

"That would be *Tata*." Luke's granny settled her crocheted shawl around her shoulders, the white wool almost matching the short curls on her head.

"Luke…helped me stay here." Jesse frowned. She was afraid to look at Luke. Just thinking about him made her dizzy with need. She clenched her thighs together beneath the table. Now was not the time to get distracted. But she wanted nothing more than to touch him, to kiss him, to run her hands over his strong shoulders and—

"Here's some coffee," said Luke loudly, setting a mug in front of her.

She sipped it gratefully and turned back to Luke's granny. "Mrs. …"

"You call me Granny, child, like everyone around here." She hesitated, and then patted Jesse's hand. "You're nothing like that flighty Charlotte, are you?" She smiled.

A knot of tension dissolved in her chest. For some reason, the woman's kindness made her want to cry. She sipped her coffee. Her emotions were new and raw, she decided. She was…what had *Tata* called her? A jumble of energy, that's it. And yet, she was human and she felt alive, especially when Luke held her in his arms. She looked at him and their eyes met. His were black as night and smoldered like a barely banked fire. A frisson ran down her back.

He blinked and looked away. "Let's eat and then study the map. Granny, can you go get that old map we had of the bayou? It may help us find Jesse's bones."

"Of course, poor child."

Jesse was ravenous. When Luke put her plate in front of her, she had a hard time not scooping up all the eggs and toast at once. "So good!" she exclaimed around a mouthful of eggs. "Everything is delicious."

"It's like you haven't eaten in years." Luke cleared his throat and looked embarrassed. "Sorry."

Jesse put her fork down and sighed. "You're right. I haven't. Everything feels, tastes, so strong to me. It's as if I've been scraped raw and all my nerves exposed."

Luke's granny nodded. "It's to be expected, I suppose. Maybe it's like waking up after a long sleep."

"Maybe." Jesse watched as Luke's granny rummaged in a drawer. Abruptly, the fear of disappearing again tied knots in her stomach. If Jacques found her bones first, Luke would not be able to clear his father's name, and she... She couldn't eat another bite. She had no idea what would happen if Jacques found her bones first, but the thought frightened her.

"Here, I've found the map. Shall we clear the table and look at it?"

They peered at the map. Jesse recognized some things, but most of her memories stayed locked inside of her. Frustration welled in her throat. "This isn't working."

"The name Jacques Lesnoire doesn't mean anything to you?" Luke asked.

"No, not at all!"

"Jacques? What does that scoundrel have to do with Jesse?" Luke's granny frowned.

"*Tata* said he came to her asking about Jesse. She thinks he had something to do with her, maybe he even killed her. We don't know."

Granny shook her head. "That bastard. He always wanted the Braquesmar mansion and our land. I'll never sell to him, and he knows it. But to stoop as low as murder—"

"We don't know. He could be searching for her bones for another reason altogether, but I have no idea why." Luke sounded as frustrated as she did.

"If he can prove your father killed her, he might think I'll sell him the land." Granny shook her head doubtfully. "More likely he needs her bones for something else. *Tata* didn't know?"

"No, and this talk isn't helping us. Let's try something different. This is where your shoe was found." Luke grimaced as he pointed to a spot on the map. "Here is the path leading to the *guinguette* where there used to be the *bastringue*, dances and..." his voice trailed off. "You were at the *bastringue*. That must be the music you keep hearing in your mind."

Jesse nodded and hummed a few bars of a song. "I keep hearing that music over and over."

"Is it loud?" Luke's granny leaned over the table and took her hand. "Close your eyes and listen carefully. How close is it?"

She tilted her head, eyes closed. An accordion played a slow tune. "It's faint, but I can hear it still."

"Hear any voices? Maybe one you can identify?" Luke asked hopefully.

"No, it's too far to hear voices. But the music carries over the water..." Jesse's voice cracked and she shivered as fear stabbed her. "Why did I say that?"

Luke's granny tapped on the map. "He carried you over water and buried you. Over here is out of sight of the crowd at the *guinguette*, but still within hearing of the loud music. There were speakers at the time, set up on the roof. Most folk danced outside under the live oaks. I remember going there on Saturday nights. From May till October, there were dances."

"We should look around here then." Luke pointed to a bend in the river. "Look here. It's across the river from the dance. You could still hear the music, I bet. But there aren't any houses around."

"It's on state property," mused Luke's granny. "That's a pretty smart move on the murderer's part. No one would dig up a body by accident there. Yet I seem to recall they searched damn carefully thereabouts, with dogs too."

"I can guess why it never got found. If the murderer knew the area and knew of a deep hole, it could remain hidden. A strong scent could throw off the search dogs," Luke added.

"A strong scent?" What did he mean?

"Muskrats. If the murderer shoved the body up into a muskrat hollow beneath the water level, it would have been impossible to find." Luke heaved a sigh. "I better bring my wetsuit and diving gear. We'll head out as soon as you're ready, Jesse."

"Where to?"

"It must be somewhere around here." His finger pointed to the curve in the river. But instead of a solid line, the map looked like it had been cut up in a lacy pattern, reaching far inland.

"What is that?"

"Swamp. There's only one way into this place, a single path through the forest. Otherwise, you can get there by boat. We'll take my boat. Afterwards, I'll swim along the river while you go by the path. That way we'll be sure to find the muskrat den. I'm convinced that's where he hid your...body." He grimaced. "Sorry."

"I'm ready." Her heart beat painfully. The map had stirred something, or maybe it was all the talk about her body. Horror prickled along her backbone.

"What is it child? You're as pale as a—"

"A ghost. I know Granny. I think I finally realized what happened to me, that's all." Jesse gave a faint smile. "I'm frightened."

"Everything will be fine," said Luke. "I have confidence in *Tata*. She wouldn't have brought you back if there wasn't a chance we'd succeed. Come on Jesse. Someone else is looking for those bones too, you know. Seems you're mighty popular, Miss Dubois."

Jesse gave a start. "I think I would have rather not been so popular," she murmured. "There are things I'm starting to recall. Music, and men, lots of men, asking me to dance. If only I could see their faces!"

Luke's granny looked at her with narrowed eyes. "Hang onto your memories, girl. They might save us yet."

"I'll try my best." Jesse shivered. Everything depended on her memories. *Please don't let me fail.*

* * * * *

Luke hustled to get his gear. Hurry! urged the voice in his head. If he finds her bones first, Jesse will be lost to you forever.

"She already is lost," he muttered as he tapped the valve on the back of his tank. Sorrow as sharp as a knife cut into his heart. The pain nearly made him double over. "Jesse," he moaned.

Why did she have to be a ghost? Last night had been the most incredible experience of his life. Just thinking about it made his cock hard as a rock. He rubbed it, trying to ease the sudden tightness of his jeans. He unzipped his bag, wishing he could unzip his jeans and get himself off while dreaming about last night, about Jesse's sweet lips kissing his, her hot cunt wrapped tight around his —

His cock gave a strong twinge, but he shook his head sharply. No, he had to hurry.

Swearing under his breath, he checked the bag, making sure his goggles and flippers were there. Then he unhooked his wetsuit from the wall. He wanted to remember each second of the night before, never forget a single one. But all he could think of, staring at the wetsuit clutched in his hand, was how much it was going to hurt when she was gone. "*Et merde*," he groaned, tossing the wetsuit into his bag and pulling savagely at the zipper.

Wouldn't you know? He'd fallen in love with a ghost.

Chapter Four

Jesse admired the way Luke steered his boat through the narrow channel. He cut the motor, and now he poled the boat between the cypress trees, gliding it around exposed roots and sandbars. Jesse sat in the front, sitting with her back to the sun, her face in shadow.

"Are you all right?"

"Shhh." She raised her hand and pointed towards the shore. Through the trees, Luke could see a deer. The animal raised its head, ears pricked towards them. Then, with a graceful bound, it sprang into the underbrush and disappeared.

"You've got keen sight." He gave another push to the long pole and angled the boat towards a low bank. "We'll go ashore here. The park's land starts just up the river."

Jesse nodded, and when the boat ran ashore, she leapt out lightly and grasped the bow, holding the boat steady as Luke took his gear and lifted it ashore. To her dismay, she found she could hardly hold the boat. It kept slipping from her grasp, although she tightened her fingers.

Horror iced her spine as she realized that her body had started to revert to a ghost-like state. She uttered a little cry of distress. Not now! She had to help Luke. He needed her! What could she do?

A glance at Luke gave her the answer. As soon as she set eyes on him, her cunt gave a twinge of desire. Well, why not? No noise came from the forest. Nobody could see them. She shivered with delight and a welcome flood of desire dampened her underwear. She gave a last look at Luke, then darted behind a tree and slipped off her dress. As soon as her skin was bared, the breeze tickled her nipples, hardening them.

"Luke!"

Luke wasted no time shucking down to his shorts, but before he could step into his wet suit, Jesse called him.

He raised his head, but couldn't see her. Where had she gone? He ducked under a branch and stood, transfixed. Jesse had taken her dress off and stood, naked, on a sandy patch of ground in front of a tall tree. "What are you doing?" His mouth went dry at the sight of her. *Mon Dieu!*

Her eyes held his as she slowly turned her back to him and bent over, her hands pressing against the tree-trunk. Her buttocks turned towards him, she glanced back at him. "I think I'm about to vanish," she whispered. "Come help me." Standing like that, her body brazenly displayed, she looked like a sexy wood nymph. He caught a glimpse of her shiny, pink labia within her dark pubic hair. That sight and her words ignited the fire smoldering in his blood. A flame of desire leapt to his groin and his cock hardened painfully. In two strides he was beside her, his hands running up and down her smooth flanks.

"Come on baby, give it to me." She turned around, her breasts now brushing against his chest.

He had to get inside her. Now. But first he put one hand on her chin, turning her to face him. "I want you to know I'm not just doing this to keep you from vanishing."

Surprise and a smile lit her face, as tears filled her eyes. "Thank you." Her voice was rough with emotion. She blinked and a tear slid down her cheek.

Without thinking, he bent down and licked it away. Salty sweet, it tingled on his tongue. Jesse, his Jesse. God, why couldn't it be forever?

He slid one hand between her thighs and she rubbed against him wantonly. Her slick juices gathered on his fingers. He couldn't suppress an excited hiss when she reached for his hand and pressed it harder against her hot pussy. His finger slid into her tight flesh and she writhed on him, holding tightly to his wrist. Rapid contractions massaged his finger and Jesse groaned. His cock flexed against her firm thighs. His legs shook. He took a deep breath and dipped another finger into her hot folds. That felt so good. His engorged cock gave another jerk. *Easy, not so fast.*

He wanted this to last forever, and he wanted to hurry, to find her bones. *But if I find her bones, she'll vanish.*

So I stay here and make love to her. I'll keep her as long as possible.

No, hurry! It'll be too late!

Why couldn't he find a compromise? Both ideas jumbled in his head—keeping Jesse and losing her. It hurt too much to think of losing her.

Velvety, smooth skin hugged his fingers, scattering his thoughts. He imagined his cock sunk deep inside that slick heat. At that, his cock gave another twitch and he had to lean his head against her shoulder so as not to fall down. He still wore his shorts, but he opened the fly and freed his stiff cock. It throbbed in time to his heartbeat, getting harder every second.

Her chest jutted just in front of his eyes, and he lowered his head, his lips following the curving lines of her body, over the gentle swell of her breast. Then he found her nipple and he pulled it into his mouth, sucking greedily. She tasted so good, her skin so sweet it made his head spin. Her breast throbbed in his mouth and he swirled his tongue around her now stiff nipple.

He was hard as a rock, his cock pushing into her leg, his hand pressed to her cunt. His fingers snaked into her tight passage and twitched. "Yes," she cried, panting in sharp gasps.

His cock nudged against her cunt and she opened her thighs. When his cockhead lodged in between her labia, her silken heat seared him, urging him on. With a deep groan, he pushed slowly into her. He would keep her a little while longer.

"More!" Her whole body was throbbing with lust. His arms around her and his cock buried in her body made her feel so vibrant and alive. His body pressed against hers intoxicated her senses. Rough tree bark rubbed against her back and beneath her feet the sand was cool and soft.

"What do you want?" His voice sounded thick. He pulled out of her body, teasing her with his cock, pushing it against her cunt then withdrawing it when she tried to press closer.

"I'm turning around." Her breath came in sharp gasps. Now, she needed him inside her now! She braced her hand on the tree and spread her legs.

He took her from behind, slid his cock into her slick sheath. He eased into her, slowly taking possession of her body. "Please," she moaned.

Grabbing her waist with both hands, he obliged and thrust into her. The tip of his cock reached her womb.

"Faster Luke, faster!" Was that her voice? She didn't recognise the raw need she heard coming from her throat, sounding almost like a sob.

His balls hit her clit with each stroke, taking her even higher. She was so wet her juices slid down her thigh. His cock filled her and stretched her, eliciting little whimpers from her throat each time he pounded home. With each strong, long stroke her head just about left her shoulders. A quiver started in her belly and spread towards her cunt. The burning sensation inside her grew immense as she found herself tottering on the edge of orgasm. Her heart raced, and her cunt clenched with need for release. Any second now—

A branch broke nearby. Then, a man's voice said, "Why, if it isn't a free girlie show."

Luke jerked out of her cunt, and to her horror, his hot seed spurted onto her leg. "No!" she gasped. Shame and fear turned her knees to water. Without Luke's seed, she would surely vanish for good.

"Well, well, well." The voice, coming from behind them froze Jesse's blood. It was a sly voice, with a note of evil triumph in it.

"What the hell?" Luke flung his arms around her protectively and pressed himself to her. His body sheltered hers from the view of the man stepping out of the undergrowth. His cock, soft now, rested in the crack of her ass. She glanced down. He still had his shorts on. Maybe she could help him—after all, this was all her fault. With her hand, she tucked his cock back into his fly, her hand lingering on his strong thigh, seeking reassurance. She trembled like a leaf in a high wind.

"Well." There was a pause and then the man came into the clearing. Jesse couldn't see him, but she heard his heavy footsteps. "I don't need to ask what you're doing, Luke Braquesmar. So those stories I heared about you weren't true. I thought that you couldn't get it up with no girl, that since your little trip to jail, you prefer men. Seems they was wrong. Just goes to show you can't listen to rumors, eh? So, step aside boy and show me who you got cornered."

"What are you doing here?" Luke's voice was flat.

"Me? Looking for something I lost. I guess I don't have to ask what you're doing." He gave a raucous laugh.

Jesse gave a shuddering moan. That voice! In an instant, her world shook violently right off its foundations. Flickering pictures came back into her head. *A white path. Running. A strong shove between her shoulder blades and landing on her knees.* She looked down. Blood ran from fresh scrapes on her legs, as if she'd just fallen down.

"Come on boy, don't I deserve a little fun?"

"Get the hell out of here." Around her, Luke's body tensed with fury. She couldn't say anything. Her neck hurt. Hands were around her neck, squeezing, and that horrible voice was whispering in her ear. Air, she needed air!

"Fine. You asked for it boy." The man called Lesnoire gave a mean laugh. Then Jesse heard a metallic click. "Now, I'm asking you nicely to step aside."

Jesse couldn't breathe anymore. Rushes of scenes flashed in front of her eyes. In her visions, she saw the *guinguette* now—the little dance hall on the waterfront. It was too far away from her though. She could see it, but it was on the other side of the river now and the music drowned out her frantic cries. *Oh Lord, help me! It hurts so much!*

Luke grabbed her tightly, bringing her back to the present. "Put that gun down and get out of here." His voice was tight.

"Hell no, I'm too curious. Let's see who you got there."

Jesse uttered a strangled gasp. "That voice! It's the man with his hands around my neck. It's him! He killed me!" She pushed Luke aside and came face to face with her nightmare. "Jacques Lesnoire." The name fell from numb lips. How could she have forgotten?

He stared at her, all color fading from his face. "Impossible." His gun wavered, but he held it trained on Luke. That sight made Jesse stop a second and reconsider. Maybe she could get him talking and Luke could escape. *Please Luke, run away!*

"Why did you do it?" Jesse had to know. She recognized the voice and the man now, but she still didn't know why he'd killed her. "We hardly knew each other!"

Jacques still looked shaken, but he answered easily enough. "No, I didn't know you. But you danced with Simon all night long, and I, well, I needed a way to get something I'd been wanting for a while. Something Simon wouldn't give me."

"The mansion," Luke breathed. He stood next to Jesse and his arm quivered where it touched her side. "You bastard!"

Jacques stiffened, then his face relaxed and he sneered. "Well, if fate don't play tricks on us all. Here I am, trying for years to get my hands on your land, and tonight I walk right to the answer to my prayers. Just think. I burn Jesse's bones so she can't come back and haunt me, and I shoot *fiston* Braquesmar here and stuff him in Jesse's grave. Why, I believe I'm on a lucky streak tonight." He chuckled meanly.

Luke gave an enraged bellow and lunged past her towards the man, and then there was a loud popping sound. Luke's body dropped to the ground.

"Luke!" She whirled around. Lesnoire pointed his gun at her and pulled the trigger.

Jesse noticed several things at once. Luke was wounded, but not dead. He groaned as he lay on the ground and tried to hitch himself onto his forearms. When Jacques shot at her, the bullets went through her body and hit the tree behind her with loud thwacks, but she didn't feel anything. She looked downwards, but there were no wounds. Her body was rapidly fading away.

Jacques uttered a loud, raucous laugh. "It's too late, *ma belle*. I'm going to find your bones and I'm going to burn them. Then you won't ever come back to haunt my dreams, like you been doing these past weeks. That's why I went to see the *mam'bo*, and seems she gave me some good advice. Goodbye, and good riddance. I'm off to dig me up a muskrat den."

He turned and walked out of the clearing, his laugh echoing in her ears.

To Luke, it seemed a tree had fallen on him; he couldn't move. Were his legs broken? Nothing made sense, his head was whirling and thoughts churned as his hands scrambled for purchase on the sandy ground.

Why was there blood? A thin stream of it wet the ground and he groaned again as a sharp pain darted through his shoulder. A black veil lowered slowly over his vision. As the light grew dim, he saw Jesse standing in front of him. She was nearly transparent, but as he watched, she began to gain substance even as the light all around him faded. She stared at him urgently and her lips moved. What was she trying to say? Lassitude filled his body. He wanted to sleep, just to lie down and sleep. But Jesse stood over him, her eyes blazing, and she wouldn't let him slide into that peaceful oblivion.

He tried to make out what she was saying. *Your father,* she mouthed. Why couldn't he hear her?

Father? His heart gave a lurch. He was supposed to be saving Jesse and finding out who had framed his father. Now he knew. Jacques Lesnoire!

The veil over his eyes lifted as he remembered the shot ringing out and the shock of the bullet striking his shoulder. Would he be able to find Jesse's bones before Jacques did? That bastard must be out there searching right now. And he had been right here. That meant he wasn't far. He was getting dizzy again, but Jesse, nearly transparent now, was waving to him frantically.

Get up, get up! she seemed to be saying.

He drew himself to his knees, and then got slowly to his feet. The ground swayed, but he caught himself before he fell.

Jesse was pointing at the wet suit, still in his boat. *Muskrat.*

That helped. He knew where to find the old muskrat den. The water level had risen these past years, flooding had changed some of the landmarks, and maybe he would find her body before Jacques. The path through the forest was overgrown and wound back and forth. The river would lead straight to it, if he could get there. At the thought of the man who'd killed Jesse and framed his father for murder, his blood boiled. He would do anything to get revenge now.

Putting on the wet suit proved to be hellish. Pain lanced through his body when he tried to move his left arm. Blood still seeped from a hole in his shoulder and trickled down his arm. Finally he managed to slide his arm into the sleeve, though his knees buckled from a fresh onslaught of pain. It took all his concentration not to pass out. All the time Jesse grew dimmer, so that when he finished putting on his suit, she was hardly visible.

"All right, I'm ready." He tried to keep her in sight. She'd faded into mist. "Can you guide me?"

She nodded, her face worried.

Her body had nearly vanished. Luke knew he had little time left. He adjusted his mask one-handed and awkwardly swung the air-tanks onto his back. He winced as the weight pulled on his shoulder, but at least the pain kept his head clear. He slipped into the water.

The current kept the river fairly clear, and visibility was good. He had dived here before. Part of his job was checking for illegal trapping and keeping the park waterways clear. He knew the river, and he also knew the path. With luck Jacques did not, and would take a long time to get through the forest. Optimism spurred him on.

A branch loomed out of the dark water. He pushed it away, and regretted it when his shoulder cramped. He paused to catch his breath. The water was deeper here and the riverbank rose steeply. Muskrat had hollowed out part of the bank. Their burrows ran deep. If Jacques had stuffed her body into a muskrat den that night, he must have dug into one from the shore, and after finding the cavern, pushed her in and covered her up. Now it would be a toss up as to whether her bones lay underwater or in the dry burrow.

Please, let me find the bones before Jacques. Are you there, Jesse? He reached out with his mind, trying to contact her. Faint warmth filled his heart. She was still there, but her presence was so frail.

Luke swam with the current, his hands gliding along the silt at the bottom of the river, his eyes searching for clues. Cypress trees hampered his progress; their roots formed a labyrinth. But he swam through the underwater forest without losing sight of the riverbank.

A dark hole caught his eye. He checked his air, but he had another thirty minutes left. His heart beating with anticipation, he swam to the hole and looked in. It seemed to widen beneath an overhanging ledge. It was just the place he'd been searching for, the ledge he'd been trying to find.

Since the river had risen and covered the ledge, maybe Jacques couldn't find it! Using his right hand, Luke started the painstaking job of digging into the bank. Luckily, the waterlogged earth crumbled easily.

After a few minutes he grew exhausted and had to rest. But Jesse's disembodied voice sounded in his ears. *Hurry, Luke, Hurry!*

Yes, hurry. Don't let Jacques find Jesse first.

He redoubled his efforts and a huge portion of the ledge sank into the water. For a moment, swirling mud and silt blinded him. Then the current pulled it away and he found himself looking into a vast cavern.

Muskrats had dug it, but someone had enlarged it. There was light gaping from the top—the ceiling of the den had caved in. No, someone had excavated it. A vast, empty hole gaped now.

Urgency prodded him into action. This must be where her bones had been hidden, and Jacques had certainly taken them away. He had to be quiet, not make any noise. He drew long, deep breaths, calming his racing heart. *Now, slowly, pull up by the roots. There, that's right.* His hand slipped and he gasped, pain stabbing his shoulder, but his feet had gained purchase in the soft riverbank, and he stayed upright. Where was that bastard? The trees grew densely here, and he was not in the perfect position to look around. Carefully, as silently as possible, he crawled up to the top of the bank and stood, his knees shaking under his weight. Something hot ran down his arm. Blood. Don't think about that. Look. *Look!*

A flicker of light caught his eyes. Jacques crouched near a canister, a cigarette lighter in his hands. He flicked at it again, but the flame refused to work.

Oh my God. Luke's eyes fell on a pile of gleaming bones at Jacques' feet. The acrid scent of kerosene assailed his nostrils. Damn him!

Luke launched himself through the underbrush. No time to think about not making noise. As he broke through the branches, Jacques whirled around, his face a mask of surprise. He hadn't counted on anyone coming from the river. The grim satisfaction Luke felt faded as Jacques sprang to his feet and faced him.

"Don't give up, do you?" he snarled.

"You bastard!" Luke bellowed. "You killed her and framed my father."

"Prove it." Jacques suddenly lunged at him and punched him hard in the side. Searing pain nearly made him lose consciousness, but white-hot rage kept Luke on his feet.

Luke jumped at Jacques again, but Jacques had picked up a branch now and waved it threateningly. Luke tried to grab it, but the branch came down on his arm. He heard a sharp crack, and a blinding pain seared from his wrist to his shoulder. His arm dangled at his side. He feinted left, then kicked at Jacques' legs, knocking him backwards.

Jacques dropped the branch and rolled out of Luke's way, knocking over the canister of kerosene and scattering the bones. He got to his feet and reached into his jacket, grabbing for his gun.

Luke froze. He wondered when his life would start to flash before his eyes. Did it go slowly, or like lightning, he wondered. Would he meet Jesse on the other side? That would be all right. He closed his eyes.

"No boy. Watch." Jacques, with his other hand, grabbed his lighter. He kicked the bones into a pile with his foot, then, still holding the gun trained on Luke, he bent to light the fire.

"Bastard," Luke hissed. "Just get it over with." He steeled himself, waiting for the burst of flame and the gunshot that would kill him.

Jacques flicked the lighter, and fire leapt from it. As he bent to hold it to the bones, Luke caught sight of a nearly transparent figure.

Jesse! She wavered then took shadowy form.

"Come to save yourself?" Jacques laughed meanly. "You're nothing but mist."

She appeared next to Jacques and pushed her hand at the lighter. Nothing happened.

"Ha, told you so." He held the lighter towards her now and jeered. "Let's see if ghosts burn, shall we?"

A look of terror twisted her face.

Jesse, I'm sorry, Luke mouthed. Pain blinded him as he thought of her vanishing from his life forever. *Good-bye, my love.*

She nodded and the terror faded some from her face. *I'll see you again, Luke.* Then she shoved again. Suddenly the flame blew backwards and licked Jacques' sleeve. With a loud *'whoom'* his jacket burst into flame. In the inferno, Jesse's diaphanous figure disappeared from Luke's sight.

Jacques screamed, reeling backwards, his arms windmilling frantically.

"Get down you fool! Roll in the sand!" Luke cried.

Jacques must have heard him. He threw himself to the ground. But he landed in a puddle of kerosene. Horrified, Luke watched as a fireball enveloped Jacques. Jacques uttered an inhuman scream. His skin crackled, intense heat radiated off him as he turned black, and a dreadful smell arose with the smoke. His body thrashed and the screams continued non-stop. There was no time to save him; it happened too fast.

Luke staggered backwards, shock turning his blood to ice. And then he saw a stream of flame start towards the pile of bones.

"No!" He dashed forward and kicked at the flame, putting it out the best he could. Then he began dousing the bones with dirt. He tried to dig, but only one arm worked. Heedless of the agonizing pain, he dug until he found himself on his knees instead of standing.

How did I get here? A spell of dizziness made coherent thought impossible. As he leaned over the bones, something caught his eye.

He frowned, then blinked, trying to see better. What was that bright spot?

The spot grew brighter, turned into a gold medallion, and suddenly he heard sirens wailing. Someone must have seen the fire and called the police. About time. He slumped over, his head coming to rest near the bones. About bloody time the police got here. *Thank God.*

Chapter Five

The hospital bed hurt his back, his cast itched, if he saw one more serving of Jell-O he would throw up, and he couldn't get to sleep without the familiar sound of the bayou night. The sound of cars, trucks, sirens and footsteps kept him awake. He needed the hum of mosquitoes, the quiet slap of water, and frog song.

"When can I go home?" He didn't mean to sound so peevish. The nurse was only doing her job. But his limit had been reached. He couldn't take any more coddling. And after five days of no sleep he was about to go mad.

"Relax. Try to get some sleep. You're a hero now." The nurse gave him a smile. She closed the door behind her, after turning off his reading light. Luke turned it back on again.

Okay, so he was a hero now. Luke had cleared his father's name, recovered Braquesmar mansion, and solved the mystery of Jesse's death. His picture stared from the front page of no less than six local newspapers and even two or three national papers picked up the story. Reporters came to interview him, and his granny cried tears of sheer joy for three days straight. So fucking what? He felt like shit. He felt like…like a kicked puppy, that's what. No matter the nurses vied for his attention, no matter he now had money in the bank, his father's honor restored, and his granny's gratitude. It wasn't enough. All he wanted was Jesse. *Jesse.* Even her name hurt him.

He looked despondently at the newspaper on the bedside table. Bizarre Twist in Murder Case! Yeah, bizarre all right. Luke knew the story by heart. Murderer burned near his victim's bones. A gold medallion found with the bones identified Jacques Lesnoire as Jessica Dubois' killer. While making a routine check of the shoreline, ranger Luke Braquesmar stumbled upon Jacques Lesnoire about to burn a pile of old bones. In the resulting scuffle, Mr. Braquesmar received a bullet wound, and Mr. Lesnoire met his death in a bizarre accident.

Well, the bullet wound happened before the scuffle, but saying he'd been shot while trysting with a ghost hadn't seemed the right answer to "when did you get shot?" The tricky thing to explain had been the lack of a bullet hole in the diving suit, but he said he'd been shrugging out of it when the gun went off.

Moonlight streamed into the window. Outside came the sounds of traffic on the thruway, some voices arguing in the parking lot, a siren wailing. How could anyone sleep in the city?

Luke took a deep breath. Well, only one way out of here.

Climbing out the window with a cast would be a new experience for him, and one he would not be looking forward to repeating. What he really hated was pulling his I.V. out. Now that hurt. And the damn tape pulled all his arm hair off. Nothing wrong with his legs though.

He headed for the thruway and stuck his thumb out. Surely someone would give a wounded hero a lift back home?

* * * * *

"I had a feeling you'd be comin' here, Luke *chère*." *Tata* leaned back in her chair and fanned herself with a folded up magazine. Moths blundered into the candles' flames, their wings sizzling.

"Then you know why I'm here." Luke sipped the tea *Tata* had given him as he'd stumbled into her house. Maybe being a hero wasn't so bad after all. But now his arm throbbed, his head ached, and he had a nagging suspicion he was starting a fever. Great.

"I can't call her back." *Tata* leaned over the table.

Luke's heart cracked in his chest like broken marble. Tears blurred his vision, and he turned away, a bitter taste in his mouth.

"Luke." Her hand covered his but he didn't want comfort. He pulled away. She held on tight though. "Luke! I can't call her back. Only you can do that."

He shook his head. "I've tried. Every minute, every second, I call her back. I've begged. I got down on my knees and begged, but she didn't come back. I don't know how." He wiped his eyes with the back of his hand. Damn, he definitely had a fever. His cheeks were burning.

"You know how." *Tata's* voice held a note of teasing in it. He flashed her an irritated look.

"I do?"

"*Oui.* How did you get her to stay the last time?" *Tata* leaned back in her chair and peered at him, a flicker of amusement in her eyes. "Dawn is coming soon. I'm off to check my traps. Go lie down in my room. You need some rest." She heaved her body out of her chair and tossed the magazine onto the table. "Blow out the candles." She walked into the night, humming softly.

Luke snuffed the candles and lay in the bed. Mosquitoes whined, frogs croaked, the river gurgled softly, and the night owls hooted. A raccoon chittered, the breeze rustled the Spanish moss, and peace stole over his body.

"Jesse," he whispered. "I'm home."

He kept his eyes closed and imagined her. Stepping out of the bayou. Walking lightly on the sandy path winding through the cypress grove. Hair dark as night swirling around her bare shoulders. A slip of a white dress moving in the breeze.

"Come closer," he whispered.

Eyes as deep as wells, starlight sparkling in their depths. Her chin down, her mouth curved in a shy smile. *Jesse!* Her arms outstretched.

Come get me. Please. Her voice! Shaking, he reached for her.

I love you. He hoped she heard him. Hoped she believed him. "With all my heart, I love you," he said fervently. "Why didn't I tell you before?"

Warmth flowing over him in a golden cloud. A smile, and tears like stars in dark eyes. Soft hands clasping his own. Pulling her close, as if pulling her through thick water. Then her face next to his. *Kiss me.* Her voice just a sigh in his ear.

Lips soft against his mouth. Arms wrapped around his shoulders. Her lithe body settling by his side... His cock twitched restlessly.

Yes, that's it. Running his hands down her sides, down her long thighs. Inside her thighs. Such soft skin, like satin. She moaned softly, but Luke kept his eyes closed. He could almost feel the weight of her, lying next to him on the bed. The breeze stirred the curtains and he heard them rustle. Or could it be soft breathing? He didn't dare hope. *Focus.*

Parting her legs, stroking the soft hair between them. Beneath his touch she sighed and moved her hips suggestively, opening her legs wider. His fingers slipped along her cleft, teasing it open. Moisture made her flesh slippery and he leaned over, careful of his arm, and pressed his mouth to her sex. Eyes tightly shut, he kissed her sex, teased it with his tongue, seeking the hard nub of her clit. Sweet and musky, salty and tart, her taste intoxicated him. His tongue slid along the inside of her labia, nuzzled her clit, lapped at it until it swelled and quivered.

"Oh yes." Had she said that, or he?

Waves of desire made his cock as stiff and heavy as if it were carved from granite. His hips moved of their own accord, humping against the bed, bunching the covers next to his thigh.

"Take me," said her soft voice. Or was it the wind? He dared not open his eyes. He buried his face in her cunt. This had to be real. He could never have imagined anything so good. He moaned, thrusting his tongue deep into her cunt. She grew wetter, and his cheeks and chin grew wet too. It might just be tears. He eased his hand upwards, skimming along her hip then to her stomach. Her body quivered beneath his touch, when he slid his hand up to her ribs and breasts. God, could it be Jesse?

He pinched her nipple gently, rolling it between thumb and forefinger. It hardened, and another rush of liquid filled his mouth. He lapped greedily. He wanted to tease her breast some more, but he was propped on his bad arm and it hurt too much. He let go with regret, and then ran his tongue along the sensitive flesh inside her labia.

His cock was about to explode, but he wanted to taste her, experience her contractions with his tongue and his mouth. He prodded her clit hard with his tongue and was rewarded with a quick pulsing. It nearly set him off though. He groaned aloud, and then something grasped his cock.

His eyes nearly flew open. He kept them closed just in time. He would never be able to take the disappointment of losing her again. "Jesse?"

No answer, but something pushed him over onto his back. He caught the scent of her aroused pussy, and then her lips surrounded his cock. She went down slowly on his cock, licking and sucking, swirling her tongue back and forth over the hypersensitive head.

"Open your eyes."

He did, but darkness, like blackest velvet, surrounded him. He couldn't see anything but the faint outline of the doorway and the window. Swallowing hard, he stared into the obscurity at his erect cock. It throbbed as invisible hands stroked it, and then a hot mouth took possession of it again. He saw a tiny spurt of milky sperm shoot into the air and disappear.

His heart was racing madly, and he clutched at the covers with his good hand. He was about to come. Oh, Lord, he was about to come. His arms and legs didn't exist, only his cock. His cock existed alone, and it was about to explode. His stomach tingled and his hips jerked.

"Jesse!" Her name tore from his throat. His cock grew suddenly cool as the night air hit it then incredible heat enveloped it tightly. Slowly, a tight, hot sheath sank onto his hard-on. It slid all the way down then it started to rock. Friction sent the temperature soaring. His cock was buried in fire. He gasped, pressed his heels into the bed, and uttered a wild cry. No way could he control himself another second. His seed shot out of his cock. As before, it seemed to coalesce in thin air, swirling into a shadowy form.

"Yes!" Luke thrust upwards, watching in amazement as his cock jerked and shuddered then disappeared. Black curls nestled against his pubic hair, two long thighs spread like wings on each side of his hips. Then a slim waist, high, round breasts, long graceful arms, and at last, a pale face surrounded by tangled black hair appeared.

"Jesse!" She slumped onto his chest, her hair spilling over his shoulders and face. Sweat made her body gleam in the darkness. Her body convulsed against his, and he held her tightly. Her breath was hot on his neck, her tears scorched his cheek.

"You called me back."

"I had to." He cupped her chin in his hands and kissed her hard. "Stay now. Promise you'll stay."

"I'm real now." She looked deeply into his eyes. "You called me and ordered me to stay. I'm yours now, yours until we both die."

"And then, we'll still be together, won't we?"

"Yes." Laughter bubbled from her mouth. "You're going to have some trouble explaining me to the authorities."

"We'll think of something." Luke sighed and stretched. *Mon Dieu*, he felt good. "*Tata* will have an idea. She always does."

"What happened to my bones?"

"Buried in the cemetery next to my father's grave."

She wrinkled her nose. "They're not mine anymore, are they? They belong to another woman, one who lived a quarter of a century ago."

"Do you recall anything about her?" Luke stroked her cheek and her eyes clouded.

"I still don't remember much." She shrugged. She didn't look too worried, and neither was he. She'd remember eventually. Until then, they would live day to day, here, in the bayou where they belonged.

Luke kissed her. "It's over. Now we start planning our wedding, all right?" His heart was so light he thought maybe helium filled his chest. His fever was gone. Except for his arm, he felt perfect.

Rose-colored streaks tinted the sky. A breeze moved the curtains, and Jesse snuggled next to him, her arms wrapped firmly around him. They'd fix up the Braquesmar mansion and they'd live in the bayou. They would raise a flock of black-haired, bright-eyed kids with their mother's sweet smile.

"I love you, Luke," she murmured as she drifted off to sleep.

Luke didn't dare close his eyes until the sun rose fully and cast its golden light over his lover's sleeping face. Then, reassured that she was with him for good, he finally drifted off, the sounds of the bayou in his ears.

About the author:

Samantha Winston is the pen name for Jennifer Macaire, an American freelance writer/illustrator. She was born in Kingston, NY and lived in Samoa, California and the Virgin Islands before moving to France. She attended Parsons school of design for fine art, and Palm Beach Junior College for art and English literature. She worked for five years as a model for Elite. Married to a professional polo player, she has three children.

After settling in France, she started writing full time and published short stories in such magazines as Polo Magazine, PKA's Advocate, The Bear Deluxe, Nuketown, The Eclipse, Anotherealm, Linnaean Street, Inkspin, Literary Potpourri, Mind Caviar and the Vestal Review. One of her short stories was nominated for the Pushcart Prize. In June 2002 she won the 3am/Harper Collins flash fiction contest for her story 'There are Geckos'.

As Jennifer Macaire, she has written a series of seven fiction novels based on the life of Alexander the Great – the first, Time for Alexander published by Jacobyte Books in April 2002. Book two, Heroes in the Dust, will appear in March 2003, also with Jacobyte. Her science fiction novel Virtual Murder will be published by Novel Books, Inc. in March 2003, and Angels On Crusade, a fiction novel about the ill-fated eighth crusade, will appear in October 2003.

Samantha Winston welcomes mail from readers. You can write to her c/o Ellora's Cave Publishing at 1337 Commerce Drive, Suite 13, Stow OH 44224.

Also by Samantha Winston:

A Grand Passion

Darla's Valentine

Gladys Hawke

Once Upon A Prince

The Argentine Lover

The Frog Prince From Marecage

The Phallus From Dallus

EMBRACE THE MOON

Patrice Michelle

Acknowledgments

I would like to thank my family for their unerring support of my writing and the crazy hours I keep. I love you all!

Special thanks goes to Trish and Gail for the valuable resource roles they played for this book. I hope you enjoy Rafael, ladies. :o)

Prologue

Hanging moss slapped at his face as he dashed through the dark, murky swampland, adrenaline pumping through his veins in an all-time high. The squishy sound of the damp earth beneath his feet only echoed the vibration of his pursuer's surefooted steps as he chased him deeper into the bayou.

Rafael Delacroix glanced back, his heart racing. He caught sight of the hunter's silky dark hair as he gracefully jumped a fallen tree. Gritting his teeth, Rafael increased his speed, refusing to let the old childhood fear take over. But try as he might, he couldn't completely extinguish that frightened feeling that came from deep within and now lurked just beneath the surface...a feeling he'd buried underneath a calm, cool exterior more than forty years ago.

Fuck the bastard who dared to wreck his private solitude. Clenching his fists, Rafael slowed his pace, letting the hunter draw near. Screw him and those like him who killed his family and by the nature of that act, his very security and identity right along with them.

Ripping his shirt open, Rafael tugged the damp silk from his body. The sultry night air, combined with his exertions, didn't make undressing an easy task, especially while running. When he tossed his shirt away, a contemptuous smile tilted the corners of his lips as he stopped running, kicked off his pants and waited for the hunter to attack. He closed his eyes and inhaled, noting a change in the air surrounding him—an indication the hunter had leapt into the air.

Rafael turned and shifted to his wolf's form right as the attacker connected with his body. Both wolves hit the ground hard, rolling until they tumbled over an embankment. As they slid down the incline, they inflicted damage, teeth ripping at fur covered flesh. They snarled and snapped, each trying to find the other's weakness. Wet, slippery leaves, smelling of musky earth, clung to their bodies, making it difficult for Rafael to catch an identifying scent.

When they reached the bottom of the embankment, the adversaries slammed into the water. Rafael recovered first and managed to paw his way out of the sucking mud in the bottom of the swamp. But he barely had time to recover before the black wolf was on him, pinning him down with his thick paws as he clamped his massive jaw around Rafael's neck—a jaw that could so easily snap it if he moved even an inch.

Fear me not, the wolf spoke in his mind. *I'm your alpha. I mean you no harm.*

Panting, Rafael responded mentally, his tone calm but commanding, *I answer to no one.*

The wolf growled and tightened his hold. Rafael fought the innate urge to submit to the obvious alpha above him. But he'd spent his entire life depending only on himself for too long to do anything less than rebel. Kicking his back hindquarters, he managed to rack the wolf good in his testicles. To his credit, the alpha wolf only flinched, never releasing his hold.

His attacker's canines imbedded into his flesh and Rafael inhaled, accepting his fate. But the deep inhalation brought the alpha wolf's scent deep within, unlocking a familiar smell that gave him strength in the early years after his family's death and his prolonged isolation.

Before he had a chance to respond, he saw a gator out of the corner of his eye, ready to attack the alpha above him. At the bull gator's bellow, Rafael instinctually growled deep in his throat and then touched the large reptile's mind, telling him to shove off.

The alpha wolf had released his neck and stared at the gator. His body stiffened, ready to do battle, but the gator took heed to Rafael's warning and slipped quietly back into the dark, murky water.

The wolf turned his crystal green gaze back to him, tilting his head in curiosity.

Now I know for sure. I'm glad you made it, Rand. The wolf panted, his jaw widening into a huge smile. *Baine and I had hoped…*

Rafael heaved a deep, pained sigh as his body naturally shifted back to human form. Holding the form for as long as he did outside of the full moon's tide weakened his strength.

Lying underneath the alpha wolf, the confining position made him feel threatened—more than a little too much like the experience he'd had as a teenager. He pushed against the wolf's chest, shoving the animal off of him.

Rolling away, the black wolf easily shifted back to human form, a wry laugh echoing in the woods. "You never could hold your wolf form for very long."

Rafael slowly stood, heedless of his naked state as he brushed leaves and forest debris off his body. "And you always were a cocky bastard, Ethan. It's Rafael now. With my new life, I created a new identity."

Ethan gave an easy laugh and stood as well. He glanced at the gator swimming just below the surface. "I'm glad to see you've tapped into your vampire powers, my friend. The ability to touch animals' minds is quite a gift to possess."

"It's both a blessing and a curse," Rafael responded wanting desperately to shake the man's hand who had saved his life years ago. Yet, at the same time he fought down the desire to punch him square in the jaw for not giving him a choice to stay and protect his family. Even though Ethan and his brother knocked him unconscious, he did owe them a debt of gratitude. Without them, he would have died four decades ago. During the lonely years that passed, there were many nights he wished he had died, but some inner demon never let him give up, driving him to survive, despite himself.

The emotions warring within him, churning his stomach and burning his chest, couldn't stop the inner joy he experienced upon seeing another wolf after so many decades — one of the few he could call a friend.

Instead, he reserved his excitement at seeing Ethan as he awaited the man's reason for seeking him out. He met Ethan's emerald gaze and his lips twitched in amusement at the realization that Ethan had matured into a man a good three inches taller than his own six feet two inch height — such towering height keenly appropriate for a Chief Wolfen.

The memory of that very title caused fury to sweep through him. He clenched his fists and said in a low voice, "You've called yourself alpha. Tell me that means you've displaced Haden and sent his treacherous soul straight to hell."

Ethan ran a hand through his shoulder length pitch-black hair and sighed. "No. Over the years, the older I got, the more Haden resented my ability to shift to wolf's form at will and not be bound by the moon's cycle."

Rafael curled his lip in disdain. "Welcome to my world."

Ethan turned a sad gaze his way as he placed a hand on his shoulder. "As half-werewolf, half-vampire, even at fifteen years old you represented a far greater threat to Haden than Baine and I ever did. If nothing else, with your vampire blood, you would have outlived the bastard. I'm sorry we didn't get there in time to save your whole family."

Rafael's heart ached at the mention of his parents and sister. Their deaths hung heavy in his heart. If he'd been a little older and more in control of his powers, he could have stopped the killing frenzy Haden and the wolves in his pack—his very own fucking pack—had embarked on that early morning so many years before. When he tried to stay and fight, regardless of the odds, Ethan knocked him out cold.

He furrowed his brow. "Did Haden punish you for helping me?"

Ethan clenched his fists and snarled. "No. He was too busy going berserk to notice us carrying you out."

Never one to mince words, Rafael got right to the point. "Why are you here, Ethan?"

Ethan walked over to the swamp and squatted, washing the mud off his hands while he spoke. "I left the pack. I'm too alpha to be under Haden's rule. He knew it and I knew it. It was only a matter of time before he went on another 'house cleaning' spree."

"Why didn't you challenge him?" Rafael asked, incredulous. "Surely, the entire pack would benefit from his death."

Ethan scooped water in his palm and let it trickle through his fingers. "The pack is Baine's, Rafael. I couldn't stay. I'm just as alpha as my brother. When Baine takes over, you know as well as I do two alpha males in a pack spell trouble."

Rafael folded his muscular arms across his chest. "You still haven't answered my question as to why you're here."

Ethan glanced over his shoulder and smiled, his teeth flashing white in the darkness of the dimly lit bayou. "I'm starting a new pack and I had hoped to convince you to come with me."

He whistled softly three times and Rafael looked up at the sound of someone exiting the thick woods. When a white wolf emerged, it's sleek stature smaller and more delicate, Rafael couldn't help the slow smile that spread across his face.

"Hello, Tayen."

Good to see you healthy and well, Rand. Or did I hear it's Rafael now? she responded mentally in an upbeat tone. Brilliant blue aquamarine eyes, just as startling as he remembered, stared back at him.

She bounded around, turning in circles, still the same energetic white wolf she'd been as a young pup. He admired the positive aura she'd always projected, especially considering her plight. Everything about Tayen was polar to the rest of the pack. Her coloring was stark white while the others were shades of gray, brown, and black. But the most unusual aspect of Tayen was that she remained in wolf form all month, only shifting to human form during the full moon's cycle while all the other wolves roamed on four legs.

The only reason Haden didn't kill her was because she posed no threat, not to mention the fact that in human form Tayen had been the most striking young woman he'd ever seen. Rafael could only imagine what she looked like now that she'd fully matured.

"Tayen joined me when I left," Ethan spoke, jerking him out of his reverie. "I had hoped to find you and offer you the same, Rafael—a home and a pack to join where you'd be appreciated for your differences, not persecuted."

"We make quite the group of misfits, don't we?" Rafael gave a self-depreciative laugh.

"No," Ethan said forcefully, unfolding his tall frame to face him as a scowl drew his dark brows together. The hard lines on his face softened and he gentled his tone continuing, "Not ever with me, Rafael. You'd be appreciated for the unique powers you would bring the pack, not ridiculed."

He sensed the power in Ethan, the pure alpha dominance he exuded with every word, every slight movement of his body. Rafael's mind rebelled against such dominance while the ingrained wolf instincts within him urged him to accept the closeness of the new pack life Ethan offered him.

He gritted his teeth and fought the urge. Shaking his head he replied, "I have made a life for myself here, Ethan. Thank you for the offer, but I must decline."

Ethan met his gaze, staring deeply into his eyes. "Have you mated then?"

Rafael shook his head. "No, I don't need a mate."

Ethan smirked. "The instincts to mate are strong, Rafael. Living out here in the bayou, you've been able to ignore them. You need to get out more, mingle, mix with others."

Rafael's body tensed in a defensive stance. He frowned at Ethan. "Like you know so much. I see no mate traveling with you, old friend."

Ethan gave him a feral smile. "That's because I won't settle down until I find her."

"Won't Haden hunt you down considering you're trying to establish your own pack?"

Ethan nodded solemnly. "All the more reason to find my alpha lupina sooner than later. If you change your mind, just follow your instincts. Now that my scent is fresh in your mind, you shouldn't have trouble finding me."

Ethan started to walk away, Tayen following in his wake. He turned back saying, "When you find her, your lupina's scent will drive you insane until you've well and truly mated. A home with a pack is what you'll need then. We'll be waiting."

"Don't hold your breath," Rafael mumbled.

Ethan chuckled and walked away saying, "You always were a stubborn Loup."

As Ethan and Tayen made their way back through the woods, Rafael heart went with them.

He gritted his teeth and shook off the need for company. He'd lived his entire adult life alone, well, save Cordelia, but she knew when to leave him be.

Ethan's words echoed in his head, 'You always were a stubborn Loup.' Loup. Ethan had always seen him as an equal wolf, even considering his half-vamp status. The warm evening breeze blew softly against his bare chest, drying the dampness that clung to his skin as he exited the swamp lands and made his way back to his house on the outskirts of the Atchafalaya Basin.

Chapter One

He ran through the swamp lands, his pulse racing as his bare feet dug into the lush forest floor. But it wasn't a survival instinct that had his senses on high alert. This emotion felt different – primal, exciting, urgent. He inhaled deeply, taking in the scent of gardenia all around him.

The flowery aroma suddenly changed, slamming his senses with another scent – honeysuckle and peaches. His smile turned devilish as he picked up his pace.

Up ahead she gave a teasing laugh. The sun sliced through the thick foliage overhead, reflecting off her fair skin as she dashed around a cypress tree, her petite frame lithe, almost pixie-like. She could never hide from him. No matter where she went, he'd scent her.

His cock hardened and anticipation coursed through him, increasing his body heat at the thought of sinking into her warm flesh. He knew he could easily use his vampire power to compel her to him, but the hunt, ah the hunt only heightened his arousal.

When it came to mating, his wolf instincts took over…well, all save one. His heart pounded at the thought of clamping his teeth onto her neck while he slid inside her warm walls. He wanted to taste her spicy, exotic blood, savor it with the knowledge she was his and no other's.

He heard her heartbeat's rapid increase, smelled her desire wafting through the air like a beacon guiding him home. A deep, long howl ripped from his chest and he closed the distance between them. It was time to mate…

Rafael sat straight up in his bed, his heart pounding, his cock rock hard. He yanked the white Egyptian cotton sheet off his sweat-drenched body and kicked his feet over the side of the bed. Bright early morning sunbeams streamed through the room, streaking across his chest. He squinted at the light, sensitivity to bright sunlight his only holdover from his vampire heritage. Shoving his hands through his short-cropped, rumpled hair, he placed his elbows on his knees and drew in long, deep breaths.

It had been two moon cycles since Ethan's visit and Rafael had had the same dream with recurring frequency since then. The dreams became more intense, more vivid as each full moon neared, increasing his need to hunt with more frequency during the full moon to stave off the feeling of pent-up urgency that pumped through his veins.

Rubbing his face, Rafael looked up and caught his naked image in the mirror above his wood dresser. Running his hands through his dark brown hair once more, he noted the tired lines around his eyes as he scrubbed his fingers across his goatee. Should he shave it? He'd had the beard for several years. It had become almost a part of him. But maybe…maybe he needed a change.

It was the dreams—the freakin' dreams were driving him nuts. How long had it been since he'd gotten laid? A month? Two months? He rarely went to town, only when he needed supplies. But when he did make that occasional trip, there always seemed to be a willing woman to help assuage his sexual needs. He couldn't remember the last time he'd gone into Baton Rouge.

"Up and at 'em, lazy bones," Cordelia announced as she barged into his room. "Your paintings might have made you enough money to live your days out in peace, but I won't let you sleep your life away." Ignoring his naked state, she began collecting the sheets from his bed.

"Get your rear in gear," she paused waiting for him to stand. Rafael stood, turning away from her so she wouldn't see his amorous state, but obviously he hadn't moved soon enough, "Sunshine," she finished with a wink. "Wet sheets again?" she asked. Her short silvery-white hair bobbed around her face as she pulled the bottom sheet off the bed. "You know, you really need to find a woman and settle down."

Rafael set his jaw and wondered for the thousandth time why he kept her around.

"Because you need me, hon." Her steel blue eyes met his as she balled the sheets in her arms. "Else you'd go crazy out here alone in the bayou."

Rafael ignored her remark and walked into the bathroom. How'd she do that? The woman always seemed to know what he was thinking.

"Because that way you don't have to say any more than you need to, oh man of few words," she called out in a cheerful voice from the bedroom.

Right she was, he thought with a chuckle. Rafael never said more than was necessary. Before Cordelia came along he would only speak when he went into town.

He turned on the shower and stepped under the water, his shaft throbbing painfully. The full moon was only two days away.

Tomorrow, he'd go into town, work out his sexual needs, and be done with it. He didn't need the distraction. The pent-up frustration he'd been feeling had affected his concentration. Try as he might, he just stood there in front of the canvas, brush in hand, staring into space.

Rafael bowed under the steaming hot water and laid his forehead against the cool tile. Why couldn't he picture her—the woman from his dreams? She had a petite body, but no features, no hair color for which to place her. She teased and tormented him only with her infectious laughter and her intoxicating scent. He'd never forget the scent from his dreams. It was forever imbedded in his memory. To his knowledge he'd never run across that arousing aroma before.

He closed his eyes and inhaled, bringing her scent to the forefront of his thoughts. While he stroked himself, he imagined driving into her warm, welcoming body, imagined her cries of passion while her body began to quake around him. As his own body tightened for its impending release, Rafael struggled with the conflicting emotions battling within him. She was like a drug, this unknown woman— addicting yet dangerous to his desire for solitude.

When Rafael finally came, his groan sounded more like a growl. God, he hated this need, this insidious hunger for a mate...no, *one* mate, his lupina mate, that had wormed its way not only into a physical response but into his psyche, disturbing his sleep, keeping him on a tense edge, destroying his peace.

Damn Ethan! Anger rose within him and he slammed his fist into the wall, punching a hole clean through the dark blue tile and sheetrock behind it.

Well, shit. Rafael sighed and turned off the shower. Water trickled down his body as he assessed his handiwork, shaking his head. *Where'd that steely control I'd spent my entire lifetime building go?* he wondered wryly.

After he dried off, he pulled on a black T-shirt and faded jeans and walked downstairs. Cordelia didn't even look up from cutting fresh, raw meat into bite-sized chunks. "Think we should just keep 'ole Jack on a retainer?"

Irritated, Rafael glanced down at the meat she prepared, his kill from the night before.

As she dropped several chunks in Scout's silver bowl, she continued in a dry tone, "I'm just wondering how many holes he can patch before the entire wall caves in."

His hunting buddy, a full-blooded gray wolf, scarfed down the meat in two quick bites and looked up at Cordelia, panting expectantly.

"Very funny," Rafael replied as he opened a drawer in the kitchen desk, pulled out a pen and pad, and jotted down a list of painting supplies he needed to pick up.

"You goin' into town?" Cordelia asked as she washed her hands.

At his nod, she dried her hands on her gingham apron. "Want something to eat before you head out?"

"Nah, I'll grab something in town."

Handing him some paperwork from the desk, she replied, "Here, take your latest check to the bank then. It'll save me a trip."

He slipped on his sunglasses and walked out the door, Cordelia calling out behind him, "One last thing: either get laid or go see *Maman* Rubie before you come back here tonight."

Rafael chuckled at her gruff tone as he climbed into his Mercedes SUV. To suggest he go see the *mam'bo*, the empress of Voudon called *Maman* Rubie, Cordelia had to be worried about him. She'd been with him for twenty years. Only once had Cordelia complained that it wasn't fair how much slower he'd aged. Yes, she knew exactly who and what he was.

Before he set the paperwork on the passenger seat, he looked at the check she'd asked him to deposit. He smirked at the exorbitant amount someone paid for his Haunted Woods painting. The irony never ceased to amaze him that people paid him for working out his own inner demons in his paintings.

As he drove down the road he wondered why was he having a mental block with his painting. He'd always been able to pour out his emotions in his work before. Why was now any different?

Rafael gripped the wheel and set his jaw, determined to rid himself of this emotional roller coaster he'd been living on for the past couple of months. A long afternoon of heart pounding, sweaty sex was exactly what he needed and he damned well planned to find a willing woman to accommodate him at the earliest opportunity.

By the time he reached town the sky had darkened. Gray clouds rolled in, announcing an impending storm. Rafael took off his sunglasses and hooked them on the collar of his shirt. It wasn't often that he was able to go without his shades in the early morning.

He'd heard of half-humans, half-vampires who were able to abide the sunlight, but for him having wolf night vision mixed with vampire heightened senses meant his eyes were ultra sensitive to bright sunlight. The artist in him took advantage of every opportunity to see the true colors of the world without the dark lenses filtering out the brilliant hues nature intended.

✳ ✳ ✳ ✳ ✳

"Hey, Liv," Roxanne Waters called out as her friend strode past her with a mission in her eyes and a big smile on her face.

Liv glanced back at her and then quickly looked at the entrance to the bank.

"Got any bank business you need to take care of, hon?" Liv asked in a hopeful tone as she tucked a strand of her straight shoulder length auburn hair behind her ear.

"Er, no. I just dropped off the weekly deposit for Bender's," Roxanne replied, wondering where Liv was going in such an all fire hurry.

"Well, you're no help." Liv rolled her eyes and threw her hands up in the air in an exasperated gesture. Her multicolored bead bracelets clanked together on her arm as she rifled through her purse saying, "Man, and I left my own deposit on my desk at Escapes."

Roxanne really liked Liv. After moving from Virginia to Baton Rouge two months ago for her new job as a junior accountant for Bender's Motors, Roxanne had been so busy learning her job, she'd met very few people. But when she walked past Liv's relaxation therapy spa one day, she just couldn't pass up the opportunity to buy some of her favorite aromatic oils and bath beads. Even though her eccentric friend sometimes lived in her own world, Roxanne had taken to Liv right away. "Why do you need to go to the bank?"

"I don't really *need* to go to the bank, but I want to get a closer look at Rafael Delacroix."

"Who's Rafael Delacroix?"

Liv rolled her eyes and licked her lips. "Only the sexiest famous painter I've ever seen. The man just makes me melt. He's such a recluse too, rarely coming to town from his plantation home in the Atchafalaya Basin." She grinned. "I noticed he wasn't wearing his sunglasses when he walked into the bank."

Roxanne smirked. "Well, duh, it's cloudy and getting ready to rain."

"No, no, no," Liv tsked. "He always wears his dark sunglasses. My guess is he doesn't want to be noticed when he comes to town." She chuckled. "As if one wouldn't notice a six-foot-two-inch sexy man with a body to die for...and that goatee, and those high cheekbones, ooh and his eyes...mmmm yum, eyes the deepest blue I've ever seen..." she trailed off as a dreamy expression crossed her face.

"What about Henry?" Roxanne teased her friend about her longtime boyfriend.

Liv snapped out of her reverie and met her gaze with an amused look. "Henry's my rock. But I'm not dead, Rox. I can still look."

Roxanne laughed. "Well, for pity's sake. This Rafael person is just a man, Liv. Just walk into the bank even if you don't have business in there and ogle him."

"No, you don't understand. He seems to sense when you're staring at him. He has a way of looking at you with those intense blue eyes that will send shivers down your spine. It's...it's almost as if he can see right through you, hear your heart pounding a mile a minute."

Roxanne shook her head at Liv's fanciful notions about Rafael Delacroix. "Really, Liv. No man is that good."

"Ooh, but he is, *mon ami*!" She leaned in closer and whispered, "Rafael doesn't come to town very often, but rumor has it that when he does, he's got one thing on his mind." Liv waggled her eyebrows as she finished.

"Okay, let me get this straight. This really hot guy..." Roxanne ticked off the attributes on her fingers, "is an artist, is filthy rich, and lives alone in the bayou." She stopped talking and arched her eyebrow. "What the hell's wrong with him?"

"Nothing, other than being known as a man of few words whose very stare will send you up in cinders, whose touch is enough to make you melt."

Roxanne snorted. "So why hasn't anyone snagged this paragon of masculinity?"

Liv grinned. "That's one of his most appealing qualities, Rox. He's unattainable."

Thunder rumbled above her, causing Roxanne to look up to the sky with a frown. Glancing back down at her white silk blouse, navy linen skirt, and matching pumps she said, "Well, I'd better get back. It was such a nice morning, so I parked at Cup of Joe's, ordered a coffee to go, and walked the two blocks to the bank." She waved to her friend and started down the sidewalk.

Thunder boomed again, quickly followed by bright flashes of lightning in the darkened sky. Roxanne smiled at the smell of rain in the air. *She loved a good thunderstorm, but not being caught in one*, she thought as she picked up her pace.

When she was within thirty feet of her car, the sky opened up. The wind blew and sheets of rain pounded on her, soaking her through before she dashed under the closest awning of a street-side store. Great, just great. Now she'd be a late, wet, drowned rat!

* * * * *

Rafael tucked his recently purchased art supplies under his arm as he entered the bank. As soon as the door closed behind him, a feminine smell permeated his senses. The scent from his dream...that unique aroma seared in his memory for all time was very, very real. Where was she? He looked around the small branch, first left, then right and inhaled deeply. Nothing. The scent he'd caught was latent as if she'd been there and gone not too long before he'd arrived. His heart raced at the idea of finding this woman, seducing her, and working out all his sexual tension. He'd make sure she enjoyed herself. He wasn't a selfish lover, but he needed to get on with his life.

What if she were dating someone, or married? He shook his head. He didn't scent another smell along with hers. If she were intimate with someone, he'd damn well know it. The thought of another man's odor mixed with this mystery woman's made him clench his fist, crumbling the check he needed to deposit.

The sound of the crinkling paper reminded him of his errand. Though he wanted to immediately leave the bank and track her down, he held back his natural primal instincts. He needed to prove to himself he could control his emotions when it came to the effect this woman's scent had on him.

After standing in line for ten minutes, Rafael tapped his pen impatiently as he waited for the teller to complete his transaction. His entire body felt like a tightly coiled spring held together by a thin thread. He'd never felt so wired in his life. Running a hand through his hair, he barely noticed the cheerful smile and dreamy eyes the teller turned his way when she completed the transaction.

"There you go, Mr. Delacroix. Have a great day."

When Rafael walked toward the exit, he noticed a red-headed woman staring at him as she stood near the counter, her pen poised over a deposit slip. That scent, a mixture of exotic honeysuckle and peaches, clung to her as if she'd stood very close to the woman he sought.

"Morning, *chère*." A devilish smile tugged at his lips when he heard her heart rate increase ten-fold.

She blushed and mumbled, "Good morning."

Rafael walked outside and immediately turned right, his senses taking him in the direction he needed to go. Scanning the crowd in front of him, he had no idea what to look for since he didn't have a clue as to her physical attributes. But her smell. Man, her smell blew him away. His cock hardened at the thought of holding her, burying his nose against her neck, and inhaling in long, deep breaths.

Raindrops started to fall, causing him to take longer, more determined strides. His pace increased as the moisture in the air began to mask the scent he tracked, scattering the beckoning aroma in several directions, confusing his senses. When the rain picked up, he remembered the art supplies he'd tucked under his arm. Following a group of people caught in the downpour, he crowded under a hunter green awning in front of Jean Claude's restaurant to wait out the rain.

The pouring rain usually had a calming effect on him, but today the sound barely touched his psyche. He appreciated a good storm, the elements giving their best, but today the rain's timing shot his euphoric mood to hell. Crowded behind several wet bodies, Rafael closed his eyes and concentrated on reining in his heightened senses and stormy emotions.

His highly developed hearing took in every single drop that hit the awning above him. The rush of the torrential rain seemed to echo his raging hormones. He took a deep breath to calm himself and in doing so caught her scent again, faint though it was.

Rafael kept his eyes closed and turned his head, inhaling once more. The floral scent lingered. The rain slowed somewhat and with the lull her scent wafted to him like a red flag, strong and close, very close.

His pulse raced as he opened his eyes and looked around at the fifteen or so people that crowded around him. Which one? A few men close to his height stood in the crowd so he couldn't see all the women. Ah, but he could smell her. *Move*, he gave the compelling command to the people around him in order to give him space to maneuver. As he inched his way closer to the scent, Rafael noticed a pair of sexy, toned calves. Damnit, the people weren't moving fast enough. He shouldered his way closer and noticed how the dark, wet material of her skirt clung to her perfect ass.

His stomach clenched as he stepped within a foot of her petite form, his primal instincts telling him to grab her and take her off to the nearest hotel. She stood with her back to him at the front of the crowd, a manila folder opened above her head. Due to her wet state and a clip in her hair, he couldn't tell the exact color of her hair or even how long it was.

Impatience mounted as he took the final step in order to speak to her. But just as he stepped beside her, the woman dashed into the street and headed straight for a silver coupe. Rafael started after her but as he walked out from under the awning the sun suddenly peeked out from the clouds, blocking his vision with its intense light. Annoyed at his temporary blindness, Rafael quickly retrieved his sunglasses, but by the time he put them on her car was a half a block away.

Chapter Two

Rafael walked into his house, slamming the door behind him, his mood dark, brooding, almost explosive.

"You're back earlier than I expected," Cordelia called after him from her chair in the living room. "I take it you didn't follow my advice." He heard the amusement in her voice as he stomped through the house.

"Remind me never to follow your advice, *vieille femme,* old woman," he grumbled in a low voice as he exited a side door and made his way to the art studio.

"I heard that, *vieux homme,* " she shot back with a snort.

Old man? With his hormones raging, that was hardly how he felt. Rafael set his art supplies on the table and pulled a sketch pad out of the bag, his emotions whirling.

After he'd lost sight of the woman from his dreams, he spent the morning with the art gallery curator, discussing his latest sale. Alfred tried once more to get him to do a full-fledged show, but he refused. He didn't care to mingle with people and schmooze with the wealthy buyers. If they liked his work, fine, buy it. Otherwise, don't.

He'd spent lunch in Remy's Bar N' Grill. While he drank his beer, he noted the looks passed his way by several of the women patrons. He could smell their desire and knew a few of them would have been more than receptive to an 'afternoon delight', but once he discovered the woman from his dream, that her scent was real and not just a figment of his imagination, he couldn't muster the desire he needed to pursue another. He wanted her. No one else would assuage the sexual need coursing through his body.

Then, in the afternoon, to add insult to injury, he did take Cordelia's advice. He went to see the *mam'bo, Maman* Rubie, to try and get an answer as to why he was so unsettled lately. Did he need to join Ethan's pack? Is that what all this unease he'd been feeling lately was all about — that he'd somehow subconsciously conjured up a fictitious woman in his mind based on Ethan's parting words? If he ever saw Ethan again, he'd deck him.

Rafael picked up his charcoal and sketch pad and sat down in his favorite leather chair near the window. His hand flew over the paper, giving vent to his pent-up emotions. He drew without conscious thought, his mind on his visit with *Maman* Rubie. Though he held the *loas*, gods, in high respect, Charlotte was in a particularly mischievous mood tonight. He knew he owed her for her counsel, but Charlotte refused the chickens he'd brought as payment—a traditional gift for a *loa*. Instead, tossing her golden curls, she demanded payment with a riddling answer in her cultured English accent: "Someone will soon need your help. Get involved, Rafael."

He squinted, noting the overcast afternoon light showed more harshness to his drawing than he intended. Rubbing the paper, he softened the sharp lines, his thoughts once again returning to Charlotte's demand. Not only did the frustrating *loa* not answer his question, but she then proceeded to lock him into helping someone. Get involved. He snorted. He preferred solitude, not mixing with humans who didn't understand his race or anything about him.

Raphael held up the drawing and stared, amazed at the mood he'd captured on paper. He'd drawn a petite woman standing in the swamp, water swirling around her firm calves. She had her head turned away to where he could only see her jaw line. Her hair was wet and hung over one shoulder, barely covering the curve of a breast. Small, firm breasts with pert, upturned nipples and a waist he knew his fingers would easily span, drew his attention.

His body hardened instantly as he touched her body with his fingers, wishing she were with him. His gaze traveled the trees and moss surroundings he had created until his eyes settled on something peeking above the water a few feet away from her—a bull gator lurked under the surface, waiting to strike.

His heart froze.

What did it mean? Why had he drawn such a picture? Rafael closed the sketchpad and sat back in his chair, thinking of the woman from today and how he planned to approach her once he found her. He *would* find her. Guaranteed.

* * * * *

How did her day manage to go to hell in a hand basket so quickly? Roxanne wondered for the hundredth time as she dashed through the swamp lands, losing one of her slip-on tennis shoes in the process.

She stopped to take off her other shoe and tossed it to the side mumbling, "Well, damn, I liked those shoes." But she quickly took off running again at the sound of footfalls crashing through the woods and men's voices behind her—Scott Bender's goons.

Moss clung to her hair like spider webs, *eeking* her out but she didn't have time to work up a major scream. She might have practically lived in the forest as a kid, but she'd never learned to like spiders. Instead she slapped at the tendrils that seemed to surround her while all the animals and insects in the bayou made noises near her as if announcing her location. Right now the only animals that brought her the most concern were the two-legged kind chasing her through the bayou.

"Come on, *chère*," one of the men called out. "We just want to talk. Nothin' else. Honest."

Yeah right, she thought as she slipped behind a huge oak tree. She moved further into the bayou, her heart racing as anger and fear fought for dominance in her psyche.

The forest grew darker the deeper she ran, making her stomach clench and her palms sweat, but an inner voice drove her to push onward. And that's when she heard it...the sound of rushing water. Roxanne broke through the clinging vines to a clearing where a murky river, its brown water moving ever so slowly downstream, greeted her. Straight ahead she noticed an old tree that seemed wedged in the water as if it had fallen across the river a decade ago and remained right where it fell, becoming a part of the river itself.

That old fear gripped her, making her chest contract while she stared at the moving water. Her heart raced as she immediately turned in the direction of the tree and gauged her luck of being able to walk across the length of the old log without falling in. If she made it across, would she be able to jump the rest of the way to the other side? How deep was it out that far? Did the muddy sludge supporting the log just drop off at that point and the river was deeper than it looked? She couldn't swim and the idea of falling in terrified her.

As she debated her odds, the men drew near, making her decision for her. Roxanne placed a bare foot on the thick log and raised her arms to balance herself as she stepped up with the other foot. Curling her toes, she clung to the log as cool water rushed around her feet, making her hold tenuous on the slimy, moss-covered bark.

Roxanne gathered a deep breath and started walking, sweat trickling down her temples. Why had she worn a skirt to the office today? It was Sunday for pity's sake. Her heart skipped a beat or two as she almost lost her balance.

Where the slime stopped, the unforgiving bark bit into her soles as she slipped and regained her footing a couple of times before she made it to the end of the log. While she walked, Roxanne kept her gaze focused on her feet, making sure to take careful, precise steps. But when the two men chasing her emerged from the forest, she looked up, her heart pounding as her blood pressure rose.

What should she do?

"*Chère?*" A man's voice said from in front of her, causing her to jump and almost lose her balance once again.

A strong hand grabbed her outstretched one as she teetered, ready to fall. "I believe you need a ride, no?"

Roxanne turned her gaze to the man in surprise. He stood there in a boat, a pole jammed into the water to keep the craft still in the rushing current. The wiry man, his thick salt and pepper shoulder-length hair tied back with a leather strap, gave her a wide grin. When she met his dark, hawk-like eyes Roxanne couldn't explain why but she immediately felt safe. She nodded and let him lower her into his boat, a pirogue, she'd heard them called.

"My name is Aiden," he said in a calm voice.

Roxanne quickly sat down as the pirogue rocked with her weight. Keeping her eye on the two men making their way across the log, she said, her tone tense, "Um, Aiden, think we could get this boat moving along?"

"To be sure, *chère*," he drawled as he used a long pole to push the boat away from the log in unhurried movements.

"Tell us where you put the ledger, Roxanne..." the stocky man called after her.

"Tell Scott he can go screw himself...oh wait, he already did that, didn't he," she taunted with a smug smile.

The short, stocky man reminded her of a human bulldog as he shook his fist in the air, his face turning red. "Running will do you no good. We'll find you."

"Gotta catch me first," she shot back, comfortable in the knowledge Aiden had already put enough distance between them.

"We'll be waiting," the taller one called out in a bland, deadly voice, his lips curled in an evil smile. Now, *he* scared her. Shorty, she could handle. With his volatile temper, she could easily egg him into doing something stupid. But tall and slim...a shiver passed through her.

And that's how she ended up in this predicament, damn it. Roxanne blew a piece of her wavy blonde hair out of her eyes and put her chin in her hand, contemplating the events that led to her current dilemma.

After she'd gotten caught in that rainstorm on Friday, she was so drenched she had to run home and change clothes. By time she returned to work, she'd been gone for a couple of hours and lost a good part of her workday. Feeling guilty, she decided to make up the time on Sunday when the office was quiet.

Plus, she'd intended to speak to Jake Bender. She really loved that man. Tall, with a barrel chest and a booming voice, laid-back Jake reminded her of how a dad should be. Not that she knew much about dads since her own father had run out on her mom when Roxanne was just an infant. And during her formative years, her mom, a good woman at heart, spent more days half-lit off vodka than sober. Yep, if Roxanne could've picked traits for a dad, Jake fit the bill.

If nothing else, his offering her a job despite her criminal record made him an 'A' player in her book. So many prospective employers had turned her down once they found out about her past.

"Roxanne," Jake had said to her as he looked over her resume and job application. "You were young and you made mistakes. We all deserve a second chance in life. I've seen what you've accomplished despite your family circumstances. "

At her surprised and embarrassed expression he continued, "While I trusted my son's judgment to bring you here for an interview, I'm still a business man and yes, I had you investigated. It might have taken you a few years to get your head on straight, but you worked your way through college, you've earned your degree. Now let's see you make something of it, shall we?"

She could've kissed the man! She really could've. Instead, she tamped down her excitement and calmly shook his hand, thanking him for the opportunity.

And then there was Scott Bender. What a crook Jake's son turned out to be. She'd never seen a more controlling, power-hungry person. How he came from Jake's genes she'd never know. Scott had his fingers in everything around town. Known as a huge supporter of Sam Duprey, the puppet-on-a-string in the mayor's office, Scott spent so much time with his nose up other politician's asses, she was surprised it wasn't permanently brown.

And that was the thing…she never could figure out why he recommended her for the junior accountant position under him. He never let her 'be' a junior accountant. He tallied the receipts and just gave her the journal entries to post. Scott didn't seem to mind giving her grunt work, like running the deposits to the bank, but when it came to actual analytical work, he did it all and never delegated to her. Which irked Roxanne to no end. How was she supposed to learn if all he gave her to do was glorified clerical work?

A couple of gators slipped into the water along the edge of the river as Aiden pushed them onward. Roxanne sighed and tucked an errant curl behind her ear as the noonday heat beat down on her. Man, even in the springtime, the bayou felt warm.

"Care to share what all that was about?" Aiden finally spoke, shaking her out of her reverie.

Roxanne looked up at him and smirked. "You want the long version or the short one?"

Aiden grinned. "We've got a ways to go. It's your call."

Roxanne shrugged. Why not? Scott's goons might finally catch up with her and at least one person would actually have a clue as to what could have happened to her enough to tell the authorities.

"If Scott had just given me some real work to do, I might not be sitting in your boat, running for my life."

"Nothin' wrong with being an overachiever," he replied as he maneuvered the boat around a marshy area.

"You see, I wasn't at all pleased that I'd been hired on as a junior accountant but I wasn't given any real accounting work to do. Scott Bender — of Bender's Motors dealership — did all the tabulations of the weekly receipts and prepared the accounting. Then he'd just hand me the journal entry to make in the system. One day, out of sheer boredom,

I decided to add up the receipts in order to tie out to my journal entry, which they did. But I was in a particularly anal mood that day and I skimmed over every receipt. That's when I noticed three receipts with deep discounts to the buyers—discounts worth several thousand dollars, I might add."

Aiden's only response was a raised eyebrow.

"I voiced my concerns to Scott, better known as Snot in my mind, and after he'd dressed me down for recalculating the receipts, he told me he'd talk to Jim—Jim was the sales guy who had given the discounts to the buyers. Scott also said he'd make sure Jim had received his dad's approval for such deep price cutting."

Roxanne noted Aiden's gaze on her bare feet. She wiggled her toes and said with a light hearted laugh, "Not only is my life in danger and I've lost my job, but I managed to lose a great pair of shoes in the swamp too, darn it!"

Rubbing her feet together, she continued, "Two more weeks passed and the same problem occurred—several discounts. This time I kept the info to myself. Scott had to be skimming. I felt even stronger about this after I looked up Jim and a couple of other sales guys' commission checks. The checks reflected the higher sales figures *before* the discounts and Scott had been the one who'd written their checks. What I couldn't figure out was why Scott didn't ask his dad for the money he needed instead of stealing it."

Aiden gave her a blank stare and she trudged on, "I finally decided to talk to Jake, the owner of Bender's Motors and Scott's dad. I knew he might very well fire me for bringing the issue to his attention but I just couldn't stand by and not tell him what his son was doing."

Anger made her cheeks grow hot and she slammed her fist on her thigh saying, "Damnit! I took the same freakin' CPA exam Scott did and even though he apparently doesn't care a whit, I do believe in ethical behavior in business practices."

"I'm sure you do," Aiden replied in an even tone.

"I'd finally worked up the nerve to talk to Jake on Friday when that entire day was shot to hell due to me getting caught in a springtime rainstorm. You know…wet clothes, the look of a drowned rat, having to go home and change into dry clothes, yada, yada, yada."

Aiden nodded his understanding.

She continued, encouraged by his rapt attention, "Going to work on Sunday had a dual purpose. To catch up but also to speak with Jake since I had heard that he often worked on Sundays."

She lifted her hands in the air in an innocent motion. "How was I supposed to know Jake had gone out of town?"

"How indeed?" Aiden responded with a twinkle in his eye.

"So, I get to work and was walking past Snot's...um, I mean Scott's office when I noticed the ledger on his desk. I started to walk into his office and I heard Scott talking out on the patio. He had his cell phone mashed against his ear as he told someone, '"You're not paid to think. Take care of it."' When Scott looked up and nodded to someone, that's when I noticed the two men standing out on the patio as well. Scott looked at the taller one, nodded and said, '"We took care of Jeanie, we can certainly handle someone refusing to sell. Just do your job, Sam, and sway the vote on the zoning request."'

She raised her eyebrows. "Yep, this just gets better. Scott's very political, so I knew he had to be talking to Sam Duprey, the yahoo Council Chief of Staff under the Mayor. I moved closer to hear what Scott was saying and noticed another ledger underneath the one Scott normally worked on. After quickly flipping though the pages of the second ledger, I realized it was a notebook keeping track of all the money he had skimmed." She rolled her eyes and finished, "What an idiot! I picked up the ledger and had just tucked the notebook under my arm when Scott walked back into his office and man, was he pissed," she said with a grin. "I told him I planned to tell his dad what he'd been up to."

"I assume since you're here he didn't take too kindly to your announcement?"

She shook her head. "He said, ''Who'd believe you? *You* made the journal entries. *You* deposited the cash.'" Roxanne didn't tell Aiden Scott's full reply. What he'd also said was, "Who'd believe a woman with a questionable past over a well respected business man's son?"

"I tapped the notebook I held and replied, ''Hey, I got all the proof I need right here, ya dope.''"

At Aiden's bark of laughter she gave him a sheepish smile. "Okay, so maybe calling him a dope probably wasn't the smartest thing I've ever done, 'cause that's when he stopped pretending to be civilized and sicced tall n' slim, and short n' squat on me, but no way, no freakin' way was I going to let him pin this on me. So I did what any smart girl would have done in my situation. I ran."

What she'd really done was dash out of his office and take a side door that led into a hall. Running as fast as she could, she took a different path to her office—a path the two eejits following her wouldn't know—through a couple of offices and the kitchen before she circled back toward her office.

After ditching the ledger under a loose floor board in her office— hey, she needed an insurance policy if they caught up with her—she crawled out underneath the desks on her hands and knees until she reached the entrance to the parking lot. When she peeked through the window, she saw Scott standing by her car as if waiting for her to run out.

She'd doubled back through the maze of offices, managing to miss Slim Jim and Tiny Tim by a hair's breadth before she made it to a side door. Thank God for living on the streets because if she hadn't she never would've been able to hot-wire one of the showroom cars in five seconds flat. Of course, she did this while the two goons hammered on the locked car doors and windows, trying to get to her. Man, talk about pressure under fire!

Unfortunately, her pursuers managed to catch up with her as she made it to the outskirts of town. They chased her down dirt roads for miles until she reached her current location when the damn show car ran out of gas!

Chapter Three

The pirogue bumped and jostled as the flat vessel slid up onto muddy land, jerking Roxanne out of her musings.

"You're here, *chère*," Aiden said. Roxanne looked at the small island with its cabin and another building, some kind of temple, surrounded by a few sparse brightly painted trees around the ritual area. Several goats and chickens milled about in the small yard. "Er, Aiden? Where exactly is here?"

He turned his dark gaze her way as he held his hand down to help her out of the boat. "Daemon Swath. Go meet *Maman* Rubie, the *ma'mbo*. She's been waiting for you."

How odd that some strange woman on some remote plot of land would be waiting for her. Roxanne thought about saying, 'No thanks' but what would be her alternative? Going back the way she came where Rufus and Dufus awaited her return? Nah! Best to take her chances with a kooky recluse. She let Aiden help her out of the boat and watched as he used his pole to push away from the island, leaving her...stranded!

Argh, was she nuts? She started to call out to him when a woman said from behind her, "You come, *chère*. Come inside while Rubie makes an offering for the *loa*. Mademoiselle Charlotte, she don' be sayin' a word without her *poulet*, her chicken, *oui*. Soft and young, that's how she like it."

Roxanne turned to the woman, but she'd already walked away, her big-boned, bent-over figure moving to the eerie rhythm she hummed. She stopped for a brief moment and, with a sweep of her hand, beckoned for Roxanne to come. Shrugging off her unease, Roxanne followed the older woman into her small home.

Rubie bustled around the dim cabin, mumbling to herself, her white cotton skirt swirling around her bare feet as she put cooked chicken on a tray. Strange! But she could deal. Though Rubie might be a bit off by going too long without human interaction, she seemed harmless enough.

Roxanne followed Rubie as she walked out of her house and over to the temple-like structure in measured, even steps as if she'd done this many, many times. Careful to step around the symbols she had drawn in white paint on the dirt floor, Rubie picked up some type of drum and began to chant in a loud voice while she pounded on the instrument.

Roxanne jumped, literally, at the abrupt start of the chant. But Rubie's words and the rapt expression on her wrinkled face drew Roxanne closer. The old woman seemed totally involved in her song, almost as if she were in a trance, as she walked around the tall pole, stepping in and out of the symbols on the floor, but never once touching them.

As Rubie's voice grew louder, Roxanne picked up another instrument off the altar against the back wall, thinking maybe she was supposed to join in. The instrument looked a lot like a maraca and sounded like one too, Roxanne thought as she shook it experimentally. When she hit the maraca-like instrument against her open palm, Rubie suddenly stopped chanting and frowned as she stomped over and snatched the instrument from her hand.

"*Peeshswank,*" Rubie said with vehemence.

Roxanne furrowed her brow at the woman's change in behavior and accusing tone. She wanted her to pay skunk? Running her hands down the front of her skirt, Roxanne quipped, "Sorry, I'm fresh out of skunk today, but," she quickly pulled the maraca from Rubie's hand saying, "How much you want for this nifty little trinket? I could use a neat conversation piece in my apartment, one with the flavor of the bayou." She shook it close to her ear and smiled at the *cha, cha, cha* sound coming from inside. "Whatcha got in here anyway, peas?"

"Give me the *asson!*" Rubie hissed and narrowed her dark eyes as she jerked it from her hand. "Fools who touch the sacred *asson* don' belong here."

Well, that was rather rude. "Hey, if you don't want sell it all you had to say was 'no'..."

"Hush," Rubie interrupted her. "Mademoiselle Charlotte comes."

Taking great pains to set the *asson* back where Roxanne had found it, Rubie then rushed out of the temple. Her bare feet seemed to glide across the ground as she made her way back to her house.

Maybe Charlotte would be a bit nicer than crabby, Roxanne thought as she followed Rubie outside the temple and waited while the old woman walked inside her house and picked up the tray of food. She took a tray of barely-cooked chicken and carried it over to a tree painted pink and set it down.

When she backed away with a look of awe on her face, Roxanne cut her gaze over to the food as the wind picked up.

Limbs swayed and leaves blew on the trees in the yard while dirt stirred on the ground around them. Roxanne squinted as flecks of dirt spattered her face, but she couldn't stop from blinking furiously when the food on the plate magically disappeared right before her eyes.

Whoa mama!

She turned to Rubie and started to ask, "Did you see what I just saw?"

"Ask what you come to ask, *fille fofolle,*" Rubie whispered in a clipped tone.

Somehow Roxanne knew Rubie had just insulted her. What did that mean? Wait...Girl...Silly. Silly girl! Man, for someone who'd been waiting on her, she didn't like her much. Did the old woman know something she didn't? Rubie appeared to be impatiently waiting, ready to strangle her.

Roxanne sighed heavily, "Fine. I'll play. How about: Will my current situation resolve itself or will I always be running?"

"Don' mock a *loa.* You be sorrier than sorry, you do, *mais oui...*" Rubie began then stopped talking as if listening to someone. Her lips thinned and she nodded saying, "Charlotte say somebody will help you so you can stop runnin'. And she say when that somebody asks you for somethin' back, you got to give it. When you do, you got no more debt to Mademoiselle Charlotte. Hmph." Rubie folded her arms. "She be lettin' you off easy, yeah."

Somehow that didn't seem like a fair trade to Roxanne. Looking around at the animals in the yard she turned to Rubie and said in a hopeful voice, "Can't I just offer her raw chicken or something?"

* * * * *

Roxanne stood perfectly still, the murky water swirling around her ankles. Her heart raced at the complete silence. A warm breeze kicked up, teasing the water droplets on her naked body. She shivered. The cypress trees that lined the water's edge, moss hanging from their limbs, made the swamp seem secluded and mysterious. She smiled at the feeling of complete freedom that washed over her. The strong, earthy smell of the swamp and something else…something more primal overpowered the faint scent of gardenia that hung in the air.

Roxanne sucked in her breath when a wall of warm muscle pressed against her back. Now that primal smell – strong, erotic, all male – invaded her senses. A thrill zinged through her body all the way down to her toes, made even more exciting by the fact she had yet to see the unknown man.

When he brushed her wet hair aside and touched his lips to a sensitive spot behind her ear, Roxanne started to turn around. But he growled low in his throat and grasped her waist with his large hands, pulling her flush against his heated skin once more, pinning her still. His aggressive action caused her heart to race, her nipples to tighten, and blood to rush to her sex in throbbing, aching anticipation.

"Who are you?" she managed to breathe out in a gasp as his lips trailed a burning path down her neck.

Splaying his fingers around her hips, he slid his foot in between hers under the water, silently telling her to widen her stance.

The water sloshed as Roxanne took a step without conscious thought. Conscious thought? All conscious thoughts fled the moment he touched her.

When he moved away from her, she almost cried out in disappointment, already missing his heat. Instead she inhaled sharply when he skimmed his fingers down her crack and clasped the flesh of her ass in a familiar, intimate manner as if he had every right.

Spread your legs more, chère. The deep timber of his voice, sexy and confident, entered her head, causing her stomach to clench in tortured suspense. As she moved to do as he asked, he cupped her sex from behind, his hold firm, possessive. When she settled her foot, he slid a finger against her clit once, twice, then a third time, eliciting a keening cry from her before he thrust his finger deep inside her.

Roxanne moaned and arched her back, giving him better access to her body.

"You're so wet," he said with a low groan as he added another finger and moved them slowly in and out of her sheath. "Ready for me already."

She clenched her teeth to keep from coming right then and there. No way would she let him get her off that easy. But God, it felt so good. Roxanne rocked her hips to the movement of his hand, her body clenching around him.

"I want more," he ground out as he withdrew his hand and tugged her down into the shallow water.

Roxanne dropped to her hands and knees, panting, her heart thudding against her ribcage.

Large, strong fingers grasped her inner thighs, pushing her legs further apart, opening her to his every whim.

Her heart raced. She didn't give a whit for the muck she'd just plunged her hands and knees into. She wanted his mouth...

Before she could complete the thought, he swiped his tongue against her throbbing clit, then delved it inside her core, causing her to let out a sobbing cry as she bucked toward him.

He quickly moved to lean over her, his warm breath fanning her neck as he said, "You're ready to mate, bébé. The smell of your arousal has driven me insane but the taste is more than I can take." Nipping at her shoulder he moved his hand around her front and massaged the soft skin on her upper thigh while his fingers moved closer and closer to her entrance.

"Yes," she screamed out, her body so tightly wound she was sure the moment he touched her she'd fly apart or pass out in excruciating agony if he stopped.

"You have to be ready, chère," he said in a strained tone as he moved to cup her breast, then roll her nipple between his fingers.

Intense pleasure rippled through her body, starting from her breast and shooting straight to her sheath as he circled her sex with his fingers, preparing her. When she felt his cock nudging her wet entrance, stretching the sensitive skin, Roxanne bit her lip and rocked against him, wantonly inviting him in.

He laid his head briefly on her shoulder, inhaling deeply.

"Mine," he whispered hoarsely as he grasped her hips and thrust inside in one hard stroke.

* * * * *

Roxanne screamed and threw her arms outward, trying to ground herself as she awoke from her erotic dream to a sense of complete disorientation, imbalance, and sexual frustration. As the floor underneath her rocked uncontrollably, her stomach ached as if it was tied in knots and her sex throbbed, miserably so. She tried to sit up and heard Aiden's amused tone, "Easy, chère."

The pirogue still swayed beneath her from her frantic movements.

Aiden spread his legs on either side of the boat, using his weight to steady the craft as he drawled with a grin, "Based on the sounds you were making, that was some dream."

Roxanne slowly sat up and her head swam. "God, I feel like I've been run over," she moaned. She avoided responding to his teasing. "I just had the strangest dream. I dreamed you took me to see a woman named Rubie and she talked to an invisible god."

Aiden chuckled. "I understand Charlotte was a bit miffed at your suggestion that you'd give her chickens as a gift."

Roxanne jerked her gaze to his. "What? You mean that was real?"

He nodded. "I believe Charlotte knocked you back in her anger, hence your unconscious state up until now."

Come to think of it, her backside felt a little sore, too. She ran her fingers through her hair and gave a short laugh. "That'll teach me to open my big mouth."

Aiden laughed outright and began to pole the boat toward the river's edge. When he stopped near a very familiar looking log, anxiety rose up within her. Glancing at her watch she noted only two hours had passed since she'd left her pursuers behind. Would the two men still be waiting for her or did they follow the direction that Aiden had taken?

"Uh, Aiden, think you might be able to drop me off just a little farther down the river?"

He shook his head. "I'm sorry, *chère*, but your destiny lies where you left off. I must return you to where I found you."

Well, if that didn't just beat all. "You're going to let me off at the embankment at least, right?" Did her voice just crack?

"Where you left off, remember," he gently reminded her.

"But I don't swim."

He just gave her a blank stare.

"Oh, you meant that literally?" she said in a flat tone. Her heart began to race and her palms started to sweat as he bumped against the log. While he helped her onto the old tree, she forced a light tone, "Thanks for the lift, Aiden, and if my destiny is to drown before I make it to the end of this log, it'll be on your head, buster."

"Somehow I think you're too stubborn to drown," he said with a wide grin as he pushed the boat away. "Even though you don't know how to swim, you'd somehow manage to fight your way to dry land. I wish you luck."

* * * * *

Rafael took off his sunglasses as soon as he entered the swamp that ran along the perimeter of his property. He'd tried to paint but instead he ended up sitting and drawing again. He'd drawn yet another picture of the woman from his dreams. This time she lay naked on his couch in his studio, her breasts jutting toward him. But like before her face was turned away. After having spent another restless night dreaming, he'd gone to his studio to try and release some of his tension. In every dream, the woman always remained just out of his reach. Never once had he seen her face. Only her form and her alluring smell remained when he awoke.

Hooking his sunglasses on the open collar of his blue silk shirt, Rafael looked down at his slacks and dress shoes. He chuckled that he'd been so distracted in his need to escape the house, he'd forgotten to change into something more appropriate for walking in the bayou. Shrugging, he looked around, thankful for the darkness the lush thick foliage provided overhead. The dim forest was the one place he could go without his shades on a bright, sunny day, and he relished the freedom. It was one of the reasons he spent so much time in the bayou.

Rafael walked the outer edge of the swamp, projecting a constant warning growl to the bull gators in the area. They'd developed a certain grudging respect for him over the years, but he didn't think for one minute they wouldn't attack if he ever let his guard down. They were, after all, predators. He gave a feral smile as the impending full moon's magnetic pull called to him. He was a predator, too, so he certainly felt right at home in the gators' company.

As he passed by a large oak tree, his senses suddenly honed in on a particular scent—honeysuckle and peaches! Rafael's heart rate increased and his cock hardened instantly. He inhaled deeply and peered into the forest around him. Where was she? Closing his eyes, he took another deep breath and concentrated on the scents around him. His mind immediately identified and catalogued each new scent: the woman's and two others...men. Fierce protectiveness laced with a healthy dose of possessiveness immediately invaded his consciousness. Why was she here with these men?

Rafael ran in the direction her scent took him. Jumping over tree roots and pushing past hanging moss, he moved deeper into the forest. Raging need drove him. Nothing would stop him from finding her.

He scented the men before they caught sight of him. Rafael held back, observing them. A tall, thin man stood cleaning his fingernails with a knife and a short, stocky one sat with his back against the base of a tree.

"I think we should've followed the pirogue," the short man complained.

"Trust me, Joe, she'll be back this way," the tall one said without looking up from his task.

Slapping his neck to ward off a bug, Joe said in a disgruntled tone, "Yeah, right."

When the other man slowly lifted his gaze and pinned it on the man on the ground, the short man replied, "Fine, Rick. I'll wait another half hour and then we're leaving. We can wait outside her apartment. For all we know she's already hitch-hiked her way back to town by now."

What did they want with the woman? he wondered. But Rafael didn't have much time to ponder. Off in the distance he heard a woman's voice. "But I don't swim... Thanks for the lift, Aiden, and if my destiny is to drown before I make it to the end of this log, it'll be on your head, buster."

Several minutes passed. He heard her rapidly beating heart, smelled her scent as well as her anxiety. What was causing her so much tension? She hadn't seen the men yet. He started to skirt around the men to meet her before she crossed their paths but everything happened too fast.

She came running into the clearing where the men sat, spotted the men, and bolted right on past them, calling behind in a sarcastic tone, "Run, run as fast as you can. You can't catch me, 'cause I'm gonna steal your van."

As the two men started after her, she grabbed a low hanging tree limb and pulled it with her, letting it swing back and hit them in the face, effectively slowing the men down. Rafael grinned at her spunk, though he sensed her fear and this time he knew it was caused by the two men crashing through the woods behind her.

* * * * *

Why oh why did she have to test people? Roxanne berated herself as she dashed through the woods, Rufus and Dufus gaining on her. They'd recovered way too quickly from the tree limb smacking against them for her comfort. Her heart raced and her chest heaved with her exertions. *If I make it through this, I'll spend three days a week running my ass off until I drop*, she promised herself. As the men's footfalls drew closer, she noticed with mounting frustration that up ahead a huge tree stump lay directly in her path.

Roxanne gave a quick mental pep talk to her aching thighs, *Okay guys. No more indulgence in mint chocolate chip ice-cream. Just help me clear this stump, please.*

Taking a deep breath, she leapt off the ground to jump over the obstacle. But she immediately sucked in her breath when she was lifted bodily, and before she knew what had happened, she was standing in a tree. A man's chest brushed against her back as her rescuer took her hands and wrapped them around the tree trunk. He leaned over and pressed his lips close to her ear saying, "Not a word, *chère.*"

Chapter Four

Roxanne shivered at the deep timber of the man's voice, the muscular strength of the body behind her, and nodded her agreement.

Okaaaay, now that was the weirdest thing she'd ever experienced, like something out of a Tarzan movie. But she didn't see any hanging vines strong enough to hold her weight. She looked down past the two strong branches supporting her feet and noted she was a good fifteen feet above the ground. Mutt and Jeff, yeah they reminded her of cartoon characters alright, ran past the tree, then doubled back and stood right beneath them.

Squatty said, smacking at a mosquito on his neck, "Where'd she go? Did you see where she went?"

"No, I was too busy jumping over tree roots," String bean replied.

I hope those mosquitoes eat you alive, she thought with a grin, thankful she had the type of skin that didn't attract mosquitoes. While the men talked below them, the stranger clasped her waist and leaned close, burying his nose in her hair at the nape of her neck. When he inhaled deeply and nuzzled her neck, the soft, tickling sensation, caused a sensual heat to spread all over her body. Roxanne marveled at the goose bumps that popped out on her arms. Goose bumps in 100 degree heat? Good Lord but the man affected her. A man she had yet to see, for crying out loud! All she knew was his tall frame made her five-feet-six-inch height feel small in comparison.

She should be outraged, really she should. Better say something. "Hey…" she said in a whisper but stopped short when the man touched his lips to a sensitive spot behind her ear. There went that tickling sensation again. *Ohmigod!* Roxanne's heart skipped a beat and her nipples hardened. She bit back a moan when he pressed his erection against her backside, forcing her hips against the tree. Even through her bra and blouse, her body reacted to his heat and the friction of the rough bark gouging her aching nipples.

When he ran his hands up her sides and rubbed his thumbs over the plump flesh of her breasts, Roxanne pressed her check against the tree and rocked her hips back against his erection.

He gave a low groan and dropped his hands to her hips, pulling her against his erection as he ground the hard flesh against her ass.

"Your intoxicating scent haunts me, *chère*," he said in a low, sexy voice next to her ear.

As he kissed her temple, suddenly, the two men below stopped debating her whereabouts and the shorter one said, "Let's go. I don't know why, but I have this feeling she's gotten a ride back to town."

"Yeah, and it better not be our van," the tall one replied.

As Laurel and Hardy walked away, Roxanne didn't realize she was holding her breath until the man behind her swiftly turned her around and scooped her into his arms. Her breath escaped in a small cry as she groped for something to hold on to. Finally, clasping her arms around his neck, she clung to him and squeezed her eyes shut.

Her stomach dropped as she felt the air stir around her as if she were falling. When he started to set her down, Roxanne held tight, refusing to open her eyes.

His chuckle, a rumbling purr, slid over her body like a seductive, velvet tongue. "It's okay. You're safe now."

Roxanne opened her eyes and realized they were now on the ground. How the hell did he do that without jarring her? For that matter, how the hell did he jump fifteen feet without breaking his legs?

She squirmed to get down and he slowly set her on the ground, but he didn't relinquish his hold on her waist. It was as if he couldn't release her. Roxanne's gaze fixated on his rich Italian leather shoes and expensive dress slacks first. She didn't want to look up. Good Lord, if he looked anything like he made her feel, sex incarnate, she'd be flat on her back without even leaving the swamp. Bad, bad, Roxanne, she berated herself. She didn't even know the man.

Before she could push away from him, he made her decision for her when he hooked a finger under her chin and raised her face up to his. Her gaze slowly traveled up his tall, gorgeous body.

Deep, cobalt blue eyes, fringed with thick, dark eyelashes searched her face. She took in the contours of his handsome, chiseled features; the straight nose, the defined cheekbones, and the strong jaw, partially covered with the sexiest goatee she'd ever seen on a man. *That* was the tickling sensation she'd felt. She took in the fall of dark hair over his forehead, the natural wave that kept it looking not quite tamed but finger combed instead. She itched to run her fingers through the short length to find out if it felt as silky as it looked.

When her gaze met his, a shiver passed through her. The smoldering, intense look he gave her made her feel as if he'd read her very thoughts.

A slow smile spread across his face and he rubbed his thumb over her lower lip. "I'm Rafael and you are?"

"Roxanne Waters," she responded. Did her voice just quiver? Grrr. Chill out, Roxanne. He's just a man. Just a man? Her own words to Liv about that man Rafael Delacroix echoed in her mind. Wait a minute…sexy as sin, lives in the Atchafalaya Basin, dark hair, goatee, and the darkest blue eyes she'd ever seen… *Ohmigod*, she'd just been groped by the reclusive artist, Rafael Delacroix!

"Care to tell me what all that was about, Roxanne?" he interrupted her train of thought.

The sound of her name rolling off his lips with that sexy Cajun accent sent her heart rate into full throttle. Roxanne pulled his hand away from her face as she took a step back. He was so distracting she could hardly think with him touching her. Clearing her throat, she countered, "Care to tell me how you managed to pull me fifteen feet up into a tree, or better yet how you jumped to the ground without breaking both your legs?"

Noting his impassive expression, she shrugged. So what…maybe he did have legs of steel. Man, what would it feel like to run her hands along those rock hard thighs? *Oooh, Roxanne, stop it!*

"It's just a misunderstanding. That's all." Taking another step back, she rambled on, "Listen, thanks for your help, but I need to be going now." Was she *nuts*? She planned to walk away from this hunk-of-burnin'-love who so obviously wanted to show her just how much lovin' he could give.

Yes…yes she did, damn it! Scott Bender was a terrific liar. No one would believe her word over his until she got that ledger back. For some reason she couldn't explain she didn't want this man to believe Scott's lies, too.

She turned to walk away but he moved quickly, clasping her hand in his large, warm one. Threading his fingers through hers, he locked their hands together. "Stay, *chère*. Talk to me," he said in his silky, seductive voice, a voice of pure temptation.

Roxanne looked away from his mesmerizing gaze. Focusing on his chest, she noted how well the material of his expensive blue silk shirt accented his muscular physique. Butterflies jumped around in her stomach at his oh-so-awesome form. Try as she might, she couldn't look away for long. Unbidden, her gaze sought his once more and the confident expression on his face made her want to confide in him, to tell him the whole sordid story.

But somehow she had a feeling he'd want to get involved and she'd always cleaned up her own messes. Untangling her hand from his, she backed away, resisting the magnetic pull he seemed to have over her. "I can't. I really do appreciate your help though."

She took off running when he called for her to wait. She had no idea where she was going to go, but at the moment putting much needed distance between them seemed like a good idea. Her heart raced as he followed her around the swamp. Just as Roxanne exited the woods, dashing into the bright afternoon sunlight, she heard Rafael make a pained sound behind her.

God, she would feel so bad if he had gotten hurt because of her. Turning around she ran back to the edge of the woods. Rafael stood there rubbing his eyes with the heels of his hands. With his eyes still shut he patted his chest and gave a low curse when he didn't seem to find what he was looking for.

"Can I help?" she asked.

He tried to open his eyes to see her, but immediately squeezed them shut again.

"I must've lost my sunglasses while running through the woods," he replied.

She walked back into the dark seclusion of the woods saying jokingly as she grabbed his arm and turned him away from the sunlight, "Man, your eyes are that sensitive to the sun? You don't look much like an albino."

* * * * *

"I'm not, I'm a vampire," he stated in a matter-of-fact tone. He didn't know why those men were chasing her nor did he care at the moment. Later he would get to the bottom of that mystery. Rafael wanted her to know exactly who and what he was before he made love to her. Never before had he told a potential lover about his heritage, but his desire for this woman was too strong. He wouldn't be able to make love to her without tasting her blood, and he wanted her to acknowledge and relish his teeth sinking into her flesh.

"Kewl," she replied and took a step closer, looking intensely at his mouth. "Lemme see your fangs, Count Draaaacula," she finished with an *bwahahaha* evil laugh. Jumping back, she withdrew a long chain from underneath her blouse. "Ooooh, I can't forget this." She dangled a gold cross in front of him and said in a stern voice, "Stay back."

Astonishment flooded through him. No, she didn't? Yes, she *did* just finish that last statement with a hiss. The woman actually bared her teeth and hissed at him. With his steely countenance and reclusive reputation, no one, absolutely no one had ever dared to laugh at him. Yet, here this petite dynamo had just mocked him not once but twice. If he wasn't so turned-on by her vivid green eyes, rosy cheeks, and heart-shaped face, he would have laughed out loud. Instead, he wanted to run his fingers through her shoulder-length blonde hair, pull her against him, and show her just how beneficial making love to a vampire could be.

Folding his arms over his chest he replied in a dry tone, "I take it you don't believe me."

She raised her eyebrows. "Ya think?"

Before he could respond, she took off toward a nearby oak tree, calling behind her, "Better yet…"

Hiking her black skirt up her thighs, she climbed the tree as if she'd been born in one. Rafael's cock twitched at the show of milky thighs and firm calves her actions put on display. His gaze traveled upward as she climbed a good ten feet in the air. When she reached her destination, she stood with her feet braced on the thick tree limbs and leaned her back against the tree trunk. Panting from her exertions, she looked down and taunted him, "Show me what you got, Bela Lugosi."

His cock throbbed at the obvious, 'Come and get me' she'd just thrown his way. His own heart rate roared in his ears at the smell of her arousal. Before she could blink, he was there.

* * * * *

Roxanne's blood pressure skyrocketed when in a matter of a second Rafael cleared the distance between them, gracefully landing on the tree limbs directly in front of her.

"Holy shit! You're for real?" she squeaked.

His only answer was to give her a devilish grin—that displayed two very real distended fangs!

He leaned close to her neck and inhaled deeply saying as he brushed his lips against her throat, "I'm going to sink into your body in every way, *chère*."

Her heart rammed in her chest as he removed her hands from the tree trunk behind her and then positioned them on two limbs above her head, cupping her fingers around the branches.

She had to get control of the situation quickly. My God, this man, this sexy, I-wanna-have-wild-n'-crazy-circus-sex-with-him-so-bad-I-can't-see-straight man was a flippin' vampire.

"I-I don't remember agreeing to have sex with you, Rafael."

He slid his hands down her arms as he stepped close to her body. Nipping at her neck he said in a casual tone, "Really? I hear your heart pounding. Your body heat is at furnace level and," he paused to skim a hand further down her body. Splaying his fingers across the top of her thigh, he continued, "I *smell* your arousal."

Roxanne's body hummed to life at his words. Her arms above her head, her feet spread to balance herself on the tree limbs, she felt exposed to his every whim and damn, the very thought excited her.

"I..." she started to say, but Rafael nuzzled her neck as his fingers slid upward to rub across her damp panties, distracting her.

Roxanne couldn't help herself, she rocked her hips toward his hand when he found her clit and drew circles over the throbbing bud with his fingers. Biting her lip, she held back the moan that threatened to escape as he slipped his hand inside her underwear and teased her folds before he massaged a finger along her slit in slow, purposeful motions.

When he finally thrust two fingers inside her, she sobbed, canting her hips to give him access to her body.

"That's it, *bébé*," he encouraged in a husky voice. "You're so wet. Too damn bad this position isn't conducive to tasting your sweet body, Roxanne, 'cause God knows I want to...badly."

She started to respond to his comment, but his mouth covered hers. All thoughts flew out of her mind as his tongue explored her mouth and danced with hers in a seductive rhythm.

A burning need gathered in her belly as Rafael continued to masterfully stroke her body. When he hit her g-spot while he drove his fingers deep within her, she bucked and whimpered her need for release.

"Please, Rafael," she heard herself begging him between kisses, but she didn't care. His woodsy scent, combined with the hard, muscular frame towering over her bombarded her senses, taking what little resolve she thought she had and tossing it out the proverbial window.

He traced kisses from her mouth to her jaw and then moved his lips down her throat. Inhaling near her throat once more, he caressed the soft skin with one long stroke of his tongue before clamping his mouth on her neck.

Holding her still, he said, *Wrap your legs around me.*

Roxanne stopped moving her hips when she realized she'd heard his words clearly but the words were spoken in her mind.

His low growl made her adrenaline spike. *You have no reason to fear me, Roxanne. I only want to give you pleasure,* he said to her mentally.

When he finished speaking, Roxanne felt a small prickling sensation on her throat as he pressed his chest and hips against her and plunged his teeth into her neck, groaning in pleasure. She gasped and reacted instinctively by pressing against the tree as she wrapped her legs around his waist. With each swallow he took, her desire spiraled tighter and tighter. The very idea that he was taking her blood made her head swim while her heart rate increased at a rapid pace. When Rafael rocked his hips against her, she panted, her chest heaving. Her sensitive nipples rubbed against his chest in tantalizing agony and her sex throbbed, contracting around his thrusting fingers.

Scream for me, chère.

There was something incredibly sexy and wanton about making love high up in a tree, with only her own grip on the tree limbs keeping them both from falling to the ground. She let out a keening, pleasure-filled cry as she came, but Rafael didn't stop his relentless onslaught on her body until the clawing, building sensations engulfed her body twice more.

Three orgasms? In one sitting…er, make that standing? She couldn't believe it. When her body stopped quaking, Roxanne sagged against his hard body, completely zapped.

As her heart rate slowed, Roxanne contemplated what had just happened. She'd just had several mind-blowing orgasms with a total stranger, not to mention the fact that said stranger happened to be a vampire who had also just taken her blood. The whole scenario was just bizarre.

Rafael withdrew his hand from her body and clamped both hands on her hips to steady her while she lowered her legs.

She met his burning gaze and quipped, "I'm O negative, you know. The Red Cross is *not* going to like you at all, mister."

He stared at her intensely for a moment and then his lips twitched in amusement as he ran a finger down her throat. Raising a dark eyebrow, he gave her a heart-melting smile. "I think I'm a very *worthy* cause, don't you?"

Roxanne's cheeks grew warm at his reminder he'd brought her to climax three times — with his hand no less!

Before she could respond, he lifted her in his arms and stepped off the limbs, dropping swiftly to the ground.

The quick change in elevation brought reality crashing back, throwing Roxanne off kilter even more. When he set her on the ground, she nervously smoothed her skirt back down her body and then ran her hands through her tangled hair. *What a wanton mess she must look*, she thought with an inward grimace.

"Well, I guess I'd better be going now."

"Aren't you forgetting something?" he said in a calm voice.

She swallowed hard, her heart rate kicking up once more. "Um, I don't normally let strangers —"

"What? Get you off upon your first meeting?" he stated bluntly.

She winced at his to-the-point statement. "Er, yeah, that." She really did owe him one, no three, she mentally corrected. Sheesh, she still couldn't believe it.

He crossed his arms over his chest. "I was referring to the fact you can't go home, Roxanne."

"I can't?" she echoed.

"Have you forgotten the two men who were after you?"

She gave him a doubtful look. "Of course not."

"Then you know they'll be waiting for you outside your home."

He had a point there. She gnawed on her bottom lip until a solution came to her. "I'll just stay with my friend Liv."

He stared pointedly at her. "I think you should stay with me."

Stay with him! She *so* wanted to make love with this amazing man whose sexy Cajun accent and seductive vampire ways did amazing things to her libido, but she knew Liv would put her up for a few days. At Liv's place, she'd be in town and closer to the office. She had yet to figure out how she would get past the security since she was sure Scott had informed them she'd been fired, but a solution would come to her.

"You *want* to come home with me, *chère*," Rafael said in an even tone, the look in his deep blue eyes willing her to say yes.

"Okay," she heard herself say when she specifically told her brain to say 'no'. *What the heck was going on?*

At his satisfied smile she said, "Hey, I meant 'no' I don't."

Rafael clasped her hand and kissed the inside of her palm. "But I need you, Roxanne."

"I'm sure you do," she replied with a smirk.

He shook his head, his expression serious. "No. Since I can't find my sunglasses, I need you to be my eyes and walk me home."

Weeeeell, she couldn't very well leave him stranded. That really would be leaving him high and dry. She could handle walking him home. Then maybe he'd be nice enough to drive her back to town.

Clasping his hand firmly she said in a upbeat tone, "Tell me the way, kind sir."

He squeezed her hand. "That's my girl."

Now why did those three little words make her feel unusually giddy? she wondered as she followed Rafael's directions to his home.

Chapter Five

The dirt stirred under her feet as she walked down the oak tree lined driveway, tugging Rafael beside her. She admired the thick canopy of trees above her, noting how the dense foliage had grown so wide that the leaves and limbs met in the middle over the double-wide driveway, letting in very little sunlight and creating a beautiful, secluded, and much cooler pathway to his home ahead. Roxanne looked up to see Rafael watching her intently as if he wanted to see her reaction to his home.

She didn't know what type of home she expected Rafael to live in, but a huge, rambling mansion with two huge columns and white-washed wood siding with deep hunter green shutters—an estate that looked like Tara from *Gone With the Wind*—wasn't it. When they approached the house, Roxanne appreciated the cozy look of the oversized rocking chairs that graced the wraparound front porch and the huge potted gardenias flanking either side of the front door. As she opened the front door, she inhaled deeply, enjoying the flowers' delightful aroma.

As soon as she entered the house and closed the front door behind them, an older woman, wearing a white apron, poked her head out of another room. Wiping her hands on a towel, she stepped into the foyer and said in a cheerful voice, "Well, it's about time you brought a guest home, Rafael." She fluffed her short gray hair. "Though it would've been nice to have some warning so I could've been more prepared."

Noting Rafael's slow grin, Roxanne felt compelled to set the lady straight. "No, I'm not staying. I just helped Rafael get home since he lost his sunglasses in the swamp."

The old woman's gaze drifted from Rafael to Roxanne's bare feet, an amused expression on her face. "Shall I make up a guest room?"

His intense gaze met Roxanne's and without looking at the older woman, he said, "Yes, Cordelia, put her in the Garden room."

"Oh? I thought I'd put her in the lady's suite…"

He looked at Cordelia. "No. It's best for her to stay in the Garden room," he replied, his tone adamant.

Cordelia mumbled to herself and walked around the curved staircase to the back side of the house.

When his housekeeper was out of hearing range, Roxanne reminded him, "Hey, I said I wasn't staying. I'll stay till the sun goes down, but I would really appreciate it if you could drive me back to town."

He touched her chin, caressing her jaw with his fingers. When his persuasive gaze met hers, he said in a confident voice, "You will stay for at least tonight, Roxanne."

"Of course I will." She heard herself say. *Where the hell is this stuff that's popping outta my mouth coming from? I know I intended to tell him otherwise.*

It seemed like she stared into his eyes for several minutes, getting more and more lost in his sapphire gaze when she heard Cordelia's voice.

"Room's ready," the older woman called out, breaking the mesmerizing spell he seemed to hold over her. As she walked toward them, the thick oriental carpet in the hall muffled the sound of her clog house shoes. "I still think the lady's suite would be better..." Cordelia started to say, but trailed off for a second before she resumed talking. "But then I guess it's for the best," she finished with a shrug.

A confused expression crossed her face before she made a frustrated sound and turned toward the kitchen. As she started to walk into the kitchen, she stopped short and straightened her shoulders. Without turning, she called out in a stern voice, "Rafael Felipe Delacroix, you compel my thoughts one more time and you and I are gonna go toe-to-toe, *vieux homme.*"

Rafael chuckled and clasped Roxanne's elbow. "I'll show you to your room now."

Compelled? What was Cordelia talking about? Roxanne wondered as Rafael escorted her to her room. When they entered the beautiful room, Roxanne gasped and her chest contracted at the lovely sight.

A dark cherry, four-poster bed, complete with a high headboard and covered in all white linens, sat in an alcove surrounded by floor-to-ceiling windows. Silky hunter green corded rope tied back very fine mosquito netting to each post on the bed. Sleeping in this bed would be the closest she could get to sleeping outside...well, minus a few thousand mosquitoes. Perfect!

On the far side of the room she saw a beautiful, secluded garden through the French doors. Oaks lined the patio and gardenias grew in abundance. Roxanne walked over and opened the French doors, immediately inhaling the gardenia's rich fragrance. She could imagine sleeping in this bed with the doors open or at least the windows so she could smell the flowers.

"So you like it, *chère*?" Rafael inquired softly from behind her.

Sleeping in this bed? Roxanne shook her head to clear it. Wait a minute? Why did I agree to stay here again? She turned and narrowed her gaze on Rafael. Damnit, he'd compelled her. Anger welled and she reacted on instinct, punching him square in the gut. The jolt of hitting his hard-as-a-rock stomach reverberated all the way up her arm, but Roxanne refused to wince. As he bent slightly from the impact and gave a surprised *whoosh*, she said, "Yeah, I love it and don't you ever compel me again. Got it?"

Rafael straightened and rubbed his stomach with a half-surprised, half-amused glint in his eyes, "I'll keep that in mind, *Rocky*." He clasped her hand and kissed her wrist. "Are you still going to stay?"

The hungry look in his eyes washed away her anger and made her melt all over. She knew the emotions she felt had nothing to do with being compelled. God, she wanted to know what he felt like moving inside her, his hard, muscular chest and belly pressing against hers as she wrapped her legs around him. Her stomach clenched and her sex throbbed at her sensual thoughts.

He cupped the back of her neck and leaned close to her ear, his beard brushing her cheek as he whispered, his voice dark, seductive, "Me too, Rocky. Me too."

Rafael spoke as if he knew her secret desires. Her cheeks flooded with heat.

Leaning back, his gaze met hers once more while he rubbed a strand of her hair between his fingers as if the wavy texture totally captivated him. "Your body language tells me everything I need to know, *chère*."

Holy Toledo! This man knew exactly what to say to set her heat-meter on full blast. Her heart pounded and she clenched her hands to keep from pulling him against her. He'd compelled her damnit! She should be pissed at him. Instead, all she could think about was what it would feel like when he touched his tongue and mouth to her clitoris and sucked and nibbled, teasing her body, priming her for his entrance.

Roxanne couldn't explain it. She'd never felt a pull toward another man the way she did toward this one. It was the vampire part of him, she told herself. *That's it. I'm just a freak!* As her gaze skimmed his powerful, sexy body and the throb in her sex turned to a torturous ache, she amended her thoughts with a mental sigh, *Yeah, but at least I know how to pick my creatures of the night.*

She started to say something when a large gray wolf came trotting in from the garden, brushing past them to jump up on her bed and flop down, panting.

"Scout," Rafael said in a warning voice.

Roxanne jumped when the wolf immediately bounded off the bed and came straight toward her, sniffing her legs. She touched the top of his head, noting the tips of his eras had perfect black markings. When he nudged his nose against her crotch, Roxanne laughed and tried to shove him away, but it wasn't until Rafael made a low growling sound that the animal finally sat back on his haunches.

"You'll have to forgive Scout. We don't have company here often, so he's very curious about any newcomer. Oh, and there's another wolf that roams the house and property. He usually keeps to himself, but I just wanted to warn you not to be afraid if you see him about."

He lifted his hand in a commanding gesture and Scout responded by immediately moving to sit beside him.

"I'll leave you to settle in. Knowing Cordelia, we'll be eating dinner soon. I'll meet you in the foyer in twenty minutes."

When Rafael left with Scout following close behind him, Roxanne immediately felt the loss of his presence, his warmth. Despite the heat outside, she rubbed the goose bumps on her arms before she closed the French doors and walked into the bathroom to freshen up.

Ohmigod! she thought as she stood in front of the mirror. Her white silk blouse was missing the top button, exposing a good bit of cleavage. Spots of dirt streaked her shirt in several places. Talk about looking like 'what the cat dragged in'. When she shifted her gaze to her face, she could only chuckle at her bedraggled appearance. Dirt streaked her left check and while the sun from her river ride had heightened her coloring, her shoulder-length, wavy blonde hair looked like she'd just gotten out of bed.

"Well, at least Rafael knows what you look like at your very worst," she said with a sigh as she ran her fingers through her hair, trying to put it in some semblance of order. What she really wanted to do was take a shower but she'd need longer than twenty minutes to do it justice. After she washed her face, Roxanne carefully washed her feet, avoiding the cuts and scrapes as best she could. Tucking her shirt back into her skirt, she felt much better. Well, at least more presentable.

With five minutes to kill before dinner, Roxanne decided to enjoy the garden. She walked over to the French doors, opened them, and strolled out onto the flag stone patio. While gardenias lined the patio, another vine-like plant, filled with beautiful orange blooms, snaked throughout the white arched trellis that crossed over the patio. With the plant's thick foliage overhead, the exit right outside her room remained fragrant and comfortably shaded.

Roxanne walked over and ran her hand along one of the oak tree's trunk. The feel of the rough bark under her hand automatically conjured thoughts of Rafael. Why didn't he give himself release when they were up in the oak tree? Even though she was on the pill, she was a safety girl and usually demanded additional protection. Man, he had her so primed, she couldn't have refused him if she had wanted to. More than likely he didn't have a condom in his pocket, so maybe that's why he held back.

Her heart raced as she wondered what Rafael had planned for them after dinner. As intimate as he had been with *her* body, she felt cheated that she didn't know what he looked like, or felt like. *Was his cock long or wide or*...she bit her lower lip in anticipation, *God help me...both!*

Roxanne jumped when a pair of strong arms encircled her from behind. "Easy, *chère*," Rafael murmured in her hair as he pulled her back against his chest. "I know I said I'd meet you in the foyer, but I decided to escort you to dinner myself."

He smelled like sandalwood soap, clean and all male. Roxanne turned in his arms and took a step back, frowning slightly. Dressed in faded jeans and a white T-shirt, his dark hair still damp and curling on the ends from his shower, he was so damn sexy, he made her feel rumpled and sweaty in comparison.

"You took a shower. Now I feel really grungy and grimy," she said with a sigh.

His eyebrow raised and he looked down at her bare feet. Noting his own bare feet she met his gaze with a questioning look.

"I just wanted you to feel on equal footing," he said with a sexy smile.

Roxanne couldn't help but smile back. Underneath that intense, brooding exterior the man had a sense of humor.

Rafael clasped her waist and pulled her against his chest once more. Rubbing his nose close to her neck, he inhaled slowly, saying in a low, rough voice, "I like the way you smell, Rocky. Your scent is like an aphrodisiac."

He kissed her jaw and then her cheek as he continued, "Sweaty is a state I hope we'll *both* be in soon enough, *chère*."

As if his gorgeous body pressed against hers wasn't enough to cause her body temperature to rise, his words made Roxanne tremble all over. Rafael's lips brushed against hers, softly at first as if testing her willingness to continue. When she touched her tongue to his lower lip, he groaned, slid his hands up her sides, and tugged her closer as he deepened the kiss.

God, he was a fabulous kisser. She wouldn't say overly aggressive, but certainly dominant. With each thrust and retreat, the sensual slide of his tongue traced every sensitive spot in her mouth…almost…almost as if he intended to send every nerve ending in her body into overload. And it was working!

Her heart pounded and her breasts tingled at the intimate sharing of their mouths and tongues. The barest brush of his chest against hers had her nipples hardening to aching, sensitized buds. Roxanne slid her fingers into his hair, enjoying the thick, silky texture. As she pulled him closer, she thrilled at the friction of his hard chest pressed against her breasts and wished there were no clothes between them to separate their heated skin.

When Roxanne's breathing turned shallow, Rafael clasped her waist and set her away from him. Her heart sank and disappointment rushed through her at his abrupt withdrawal. Before she could voice her frustration, he said, "Dinner awaits."

"But I'm not hungry," she insisted. She really didn't want to stop what was happening between them.

His intense deep blue gaze held hers for a long heart stopping moment and all Roxanne could do was stare back. Good Lord, the man truly mesmerized her.

"You'll need to fuel your energy, *chère*." He gave her a devilish smile and finished, "Trust me."

*****

Rafael clasped her small hand in his and directed Roxanne along beside him. He knew his strides across the hall were brisk, but his body was so wound with pent-up desire for this woman, he needed a way to lessen the tension.

He'd never wanted to mount a woman as much as he did this one. There was something about her honeysuckle smell that absolutely captivated him. And when she became aroused, her musky, feminine aroma emanated from her like some kind of wolf-mating pheromone, yet the woman was human!

As they walked into the dining room, her scent wafted to him, reminding him how good her soft body felt pressed against his harder one, how wet she'd been while he stroked her to orgasm, and her taste...Damn, but the woman tasted so good it was all he could do not to sink his teeth into her neck again while standing in her bedroom.

When he'd kissed her the change in her was obvious. Even if he wasn't blessed with heightened senses, he knew Roxanne didn't want to stop what they had started. Neither did he, but he wanted her to know what he was.

He'd only told her half the story.

Tonight, he would tell her the rest. With other women he could control his dominant wolf side, but with this woman...he wasn't so sure he would be able to. The wolf side of him was too strong to hide from this woman, especially when he made love to her.

Rafael gave himself a mental shake to gain control over the powerful emotions gripping his body — the thoughts and desires that knotted his stomach muscles and had left him with a perpetual hard-on since the first dream began.

He pulled Roxanne's chair out for her and as he moved to walk away she leaned forward to scoot her chair up to the table. His step slowed as his gaze immediately locked on her exposed cleavage. The curve of her small, firm breasts peeking out of a lacy white bra begged to be kissed. Dragging his gaze away, Rafael shook his head to clear his thoughts and settled in his own chair.

When his gaze met hers and she gave him a mischievous smile, he realized she knew. Rafael gritted his teeth and bit back a groan as his cock twitched in sexual frustration. Oh yeah, a good, long fuck was exactly what they both needed.

Cordelia bustled into the room and set their plates down in front of them. "Eat up, boys and girls." As she turned and walked out of the room, she called over her shoulder with a chuckle, "Lord knows you'll need it."

Roxanne looked at his plate, full of meat, and then her own well-balanced meal and asked, "Aren't you going to eat any vegetables?"

He met her questioning gaze. "No, other than blood, meat is my only means of nutrition."

As he cut into his meat and the juices ran a deep pink, she replied, "You, uh, might want to ask Cordelia to cook that a little longer."

"I like my meat on the rare side." He held back his grin at his understatement as he put a forkful into his mouth. He'd asked Cordelia to cook his meat tonight for Roxanne's benefit. No need to frighten her.

"Okaaay." She shrugged her shoulders and began to eat. As she chewed, she tucked a blonde strand of hair behind her ear and groaned her approval. "Mmmm, good. I'll have to compliment Cordelia on her wonderful meal."

Rafael's chest swelled in masculine satisfaction as he watched Roxanne enjoy his kill from the night before. He never thought watching a woman eat would be so sexually arousing, but this woman, with her 'yums' of approval, made it an almost orgasmic experience.

Before she ate the last bite, she said, "I don't believe I've ever had this meat before. It's very good. What is it?"

"Venison."

"As in Bambi?" her voice rose and she coughed, almost choking on the piece of meat.

"No, Bambi's uncle," he replied in a dry tone. "I don't kill innocent babes, Roxanne."

"You shot this deer?"

"I took it down, yes," he gave her a neutral answer. She didn't necessarily need to know the details...yet.

Roxanne pushed her empty plate away and cocked her head to the side, her expression surprised and intrigued. "Somehow I didn't picture you as the hunter type."

"You've no idea, *chère*," he replied. The closer it got to the full moon, the longer he was able to hold his wolf form — then the hunt became something to relish, enjoy, and take as much time as he wanted to bring down a prey.

"Of course, I would never have guessed you were a vampire either," she said with a laugh as she looked down at her food.

Look at me, he whispered in her mind. When her emerald gaze met his, he asked, "Does knowing what I am bother you?"

"No." She shrugged. "You saved my life today."

He noted the tinge of color on her cheeks, heard her heart rate kick up. The fact he was a vampire excited her. And she just gave him an opening he couldn't pass up. Maybe now she would tell him what was really going on. "Are you going to tell me why those men were chasing you?"

"I..." she started to say something, then ran a hand through her hair with a resigned sigh before she finished, "It's not important."

It was important to him. Rafael needed to gain her trust, but how? As soon as he asked himself the question, an idea began to form in his head. He stood up and held out his hand. "Come with me, *chère*. I want to show you something."

Chapter Six

Roxanne's hand shook as she put it in his larger one. He pulled her to stand beside him and his towering height, broad shoulders, and seductive presence had her heart thudding in her chest. God, she'd never been more aware of her attraction to another man in all her twenty-seven years of life.

"Where are we going?" she asked while he escorted her out of the room.

"I'm going to teach you something you should have learned a long time ago, Rocky," he answered with a sidelong look.

Oh, she hoped so. This man could certainly give new meaning to the expression 'teacher's pet'. She'd gladly be his student any day! Her breathing increased and her excitement grew with each step they took down a long hall. At the end of the hall, he opened a door and they stepped into a huge master bedroom.

Everything about the bedroom screamed 'all male'. From the dark cherry sleigh bed to the navy comforter and blood-red pillows to the functional dresser and night stand. The only other piece of furniture in the room was a comfortable navy and red plaid reading chair next to one of the windows. Once he shut the bedroom door, Rafael released her hand and stepped back to pull off his T-shirt.

Ohmigod! Roxanne's stomach fluttered and her mouth went completely dry at the sight of his gorgeous chest and washboard stomach. She wanted to run her fingers through the light spattering of dark hair all the way down the V that narrowed to his navel. Her palms tingled with the need to touch every inch of his superb body. When he dropped his hands to the button on his jeans, the flex and play of his defined biceps drew her attention. Well…until he chuckled.

Roxanne met his gaze and noted the devilish gleam in his eyes.

"Look outside, *chère*."

Confused, Roxanne walked over to the French doors and peered outside. Dusk was almost upon them and the late daylight reflecting off the water in the stone swimming pool made the still surface look like a sheet of glass.

Potted plants were scattered on the patio around the pool and several lights reflected from the deep bottom, making the pool appear inviting and warm. Too bad she and deep water just didn't mix. But making out with Rafael in shallow water had its merits.

She stood on her tip-toes to see if the pool had a shallow end. Disappointment coursed through her when she realized the shallowest end appeared to be four feet deep. Not quite shallow enough for her non-swimming butt, darn it!

"Ready to go for a dip, Rocky?" Rafael asked in a husky voice as his chest brushed against her back.

"Um, sorry to disappoint you, but..." Roxanne started to say when Rafael's hands came around from behind her and began to unbutton her blouse.

I know you can't swim, chère, he spoke in her mind as he planted a kiss on her neck.

Another button slipped past the material and her nipples hardened.

"How do you know?" she asked, sounding breathless even to herself.

He kissed her collarbone and another button gave way. "I heard you in the bayou."

When his knuckles gently brushed over her rib cage as he undid the last button, Roxanne gasped at the electric contact.

Once Rafael slipped her blouse off her body, he laid his hand on her bare belly, pulled her back against his naked chest, and whispered in her ear, "I'm going to teach you how."

Mmmm, his warm chest felt so good against her body. Roxanne hooked an arm around his neck and pulled his mouth down close to hers, saying in her sexiest voice, "I'm sure we could find something more entertaining and constructive to do."

Rafael kissed her mouth hard before he quickly turned her in his arms to face him. Placing his hands on her hips, he said in a stern tone, "This *is* constructive, Roxanne. For your own safety, you should know how to swim." Before she could respond, he'd slipped her skirt down her hips until it pooled at her feet on the floor.

Roxanne looked down at his black silk boxers, noted his obvious hard-on, and glanced back up at him with a siren's smile. As beautiful as his swimming pool was, she really, really didn't want to go in that water. Maybe she could distract him away from this 'swimming lesson' he seemed to have his mind set on.

Reaching around behind her, she unsnapped her bra saying, "Well, I don't know from personal experience, but I've heard nothing is more fun than skinny-dipping."

Rafael's gaze dropped to her breasts. Desire sparked in the deep blue depths as he met her gaze once more while a muscle ticked in his jaw.

Moving faster than she could've ever anticipated, he reached around and re-hooked her bra saying in a gruff tone, "I think it best if we both leave some of our clothes on, Rocky."

She stuck out her bottom lip. "Well, you're no fun."

He stared at her for a long, intense moment, enough to tell her without words just how wrong she was.

"Nice try, but you're going in, *chère*." With that he clasped her hand, opened the door, and pulled her outside.

Roxanne inched closer to Rafael as he nudged her to the pool's edge. He must've sensed her nervousness, and before she could change her mind and pull away, he scooped her up in his arms and walked down the steps into the water.

Roxanne's heart raced and fear gripped her as the water touched her bottom and began to surround them. She clung to Rafael's neck whispering, "Don't let me go. Please, don't let me go."

He kissed her temple gently. "This is all about trust, Rocky. You have to trust me."

Roxanne nodded and forced her body to relax, though her heart still raced in fear.

"Understanding how to float is one of the most important lessons in learning to swim." He placed his hand at the small of her back and said in an encouraging tone, "Once you teach yourself to float, some of your fear will dissipate. Lay back, Rocky. Spread your arms wide, arch your back, and lean back into the water."

She gave him an imploring look and Rafael kissed her. When he ended their kiss, Roxanne bit her lower lip and released her grip on his neck, letting her arms slip into the water.

Rafael kept his hand at the small of her back. "Spread your arms wide and arch your back. You have to lay your head back in the water, Rocky, or you won't float."

Aack! Get water in her ears? Around her face, close to her mouth and nose? Was he flippin' nuts? She stiffened in his arms and shook her head adamantly.

"Trust me, *mon amour*."

He'd saved her life when he knew nothing about her, why she was running, or if she actually deserved being chased by Scott's men. Trust him, she told herself. Roxanne closed her eyes and laid her head back into the water.

The water rushing in her ears made her immediately tense. With her ears clogged, she couldn't hear a thing and she felt suddenly alone until Rafael's voice whispered in her mind, *Relax*, chère. *I'm right here. That's it. You've got it.* Then he released her.

And she did it! She was floating! The buoyant feeling of drifting in the water was unlike anything she'd ever experienced. She felt so...free. Roxanne smiled and tried to talk. That was a mistake. The slight shift made water immediately rush over her face. Sputtering, Roxanne jerked upright as her body began to sink. In a split second, she was lifted out of the water.

Even though he set her down in four feet of water and still had a firm hold on her, Roxanne couldn't stop the fear that gripped her.

Rafael cupped her face with his hands. "Are you okay?" he asked, concern in his voice.

She held onto his arms and forced herself to stop shaking. Her mouth curved into a tentative smile. "Yeah, I think so."

Rubbing his thumbs along her jaw line, Rafael's gaze dropped to her chest and his expression changed from concerned to thoroughly aroused.

Roxanne looked down and realized her dark nipples showed right through the wet material of her white bra.

Before she could meet his gaze once more, Rafael immediately turned her around, saying in a rough voice, "Let's work on your stroke."

Her stroke? Was he kidding? She'd gladly show him how well she knew how to stroke, Roxanne thought with a mischievous grin.

Rafael's chest brushed against her back as he covered her arms with his and showed her how to stroke her arms through the water to swim. Roxanne mimicked his movements for a few moments, but when his hand slid down her stomach to support her while she practiced, her body ignited at the intimate touch and her concentration scattered.

Rafael leaned closer, the heat of his body covering hers as he whispered encouraging words, "That's it. Just like that."

Roxanne closed her eyes and inhaled, taking in his exotic smell. That's when the memory hit her. His scent, his heat, his touch...Rafael was the unknown man from her dream. She gasped at the realization and stumbled in the water, accidentally brushing against his rock-hard erection.

When she tried to apologize and pull away, Rafael groaned and clasped her hips, pulling her back against him as he rocked his hips against her.

Turning her in the water, he ordered in a tight voice, "Put your hands on the side of the pool."

Roxanne's heart raced as she gripped the stone side.

He slowly slid his hands down her back to the curve of her waist as if enjoying the feel of her skin underneath his hands.

"Your skin is so soft, so different from mine," he said, his tone husky, reverent.

She closed her eyes once more and savored the sensation of his hands sliding to her hips and clasping them tight.

Lifting her slightly, he pressed the tip of his cock against her entrance and ground out, "You're pure temptation, Roxanne. I want to bury myself so deep in you, I can't think straight."

Roxanne's heart soared at his words. Her sex throbbed at the hard shaft nudging her entrance through their clothes. She arched her back and said, "I'm all yours, Rafael. Take me."

He growled then, a low rumbling that made a shiver shimmy all the way down her spine as he pumped his hips once, twice against her, driving his cock deeper inside her despite the barrier of material between them.

Roxanne panted as her body reacted to his seductive movements. Her stomach clenched and her breasts tingled. God, she wanted him inside her, filling her completely. Now!

He laid his chest across her back and rasped near her ear, "Oh, I will, *chère*. I'll take you again and again, until you beg me to stop, I promise."

Until she begged him to stop? Yes. Yes!

"But not yet," he finished.

Huh? Her stomach pitched.

Rafael released her and Roxanne turned in the water to face him, her expression confused, her body tense.

He backed away, his own expression hooded, inscrutable.

"You only know part of what I am, Roxanne and I won't have sex with you until you know the rest."

"Then tell me," she responded, frustration evident in her voice.

Without a word, he climbed out of the pool and then held his hand down to help her out.

Roxanne let him help her out and as soon as she was on level ground she asked, "Well, are you gonna tell me?"

"In time, *chère*." Rafael led her back into his bedroom and turned on a lamp on his night stand. She watched with growing disappointment as he picked up his T-shirt and laid it across his shoulder before he wrapped a dark blue towel around his waist. He then reached behind his bathroom door, pulled down a white robe, and held it out for her.

Why did he tease her like that and then leave her hanging? She didn't like it, not one bit. Before she took the robe from his hand, Roxanne met his gaze with a seductive one as she reached around, unsnapped her bra, and dropped it to the floor.

A thrill zinged through her when she saw hard lines form around Rafael's mouth and the intense look in his deep blue eyes as his gaze drifted to her breasts. His reaction gave her the confidence she needed to continue. Hooking her thumbs in her underwear, she quickly stepped out of them.

Rafael's gaze swept over her naked body and he balled his hands into fists, crushing the terry robe in his hand. His expression steely, he held out the robe once more, ordering, "Put this on, Roxanne."

His tone and his rigid stance told her she'd gotten to him. Roxanne tossed her underwear to him and reached for the robe. When her underwear landed on his head, she stifled a laugh and averted her amused gaze as she put on the robe and tied the belt around her waist.

Before she could utter a word, Rafael threw her wet underwear to the floor, grabbed the belt where she'd tied a knot, and pulled her out of his room. She had to literally run to keep up with his long, purposeful strides. He didn't stop walking until he set her in front of her bedroom door.

Rafael placed his hands on the doorjamb, effectively blocking her in. Leaning close, he said in a fierce tone, "You will pay for that, I assure you."

"Do you promise?" Roxanne replied playfully as she ran her palms over his chest and down his hard abdomen. God, he felt so good. Sliding her hands around his waist she leaned forward and kissed his hardened nipple.

Rafael sucked in his breath and his entire body went still. She could feel the tension literally radiating off of him. His calm countenance sobered her playful mood. Roxanne looked up and met his intense, burning gaze.

Go to bed, Roxanne.

He handed her his T-shirt. "Here's something to sleep in."

When his fingers brushed hers as she took the shirt, he said gruffly, "I promise, Rocky."

Clasping his T-shirt in her hand, Roxanne watched him walk away. That's when she noticed the tattoo on his right shoulder blade. The design consisted of a blue and black ring that narrowed and twisted into a loop at the top. Two black entwined animals wove in and around the ring in a Celtic-type knot until their heads came face to face above the loop. Unfortunately, Rafael moved so fast she couldn't make out the animal faces. But her curiosity was certainly peaked.

As was her libido! How could he just leave and deny the passion raging between them? Confused and frustrated, she tossed the T-shirt over her shoulder and turned to open the door.

When she started to walk into the room, the T-shirt slid off her shoulder. With a sigh Roxanne noticed the shirt had snagged on the doorjamb. As she reached up to release the material, that's when she saw a deep impression in the wood door frame the exact size of a thumb print. Her heart racing, Roxanne leaned out to look at the other side of the frame. Four deep gouges from his fingers had mangled the wood. Another look and a matching set graced the other side of the doorjamb.

Good Lord! The thought of all that massive strength held in check, made her shiver in anticipation. He wanted her. And heaven help her, she wanted him to let go of that steely control and show her just how untamed he could be.

Chapter Seven

After she took a leisurely shower, scrubbing her body clean, Roxanne dried off and carefully patted the soles of her feet dry. It wasn't until she had some down time and adrenaline had stopped rushing through her veins every five seconds that she realized just how much the sticks, the tree bark, and the general forest floor I-don't-wanna-knows had really done a number on the soles of her feet.

Hobbling over to her bed, Roxanne pulled on Rafael's white T-shirt. While the cotton slid over her head, she inhaled the clean masculine scent that clung to the material. Her stomach tensed and her sex throbbed at the memory of his hands on her body, inside her, bringing her to climax.

She smoothed the shirt over her body and sighed in sexual frustration. What more could he possibly have to tell her? she wondered. Careful of her wounds, she stepped gingerly over to the French doors and opened them. As Roxanne inhaled the gardenia scent, Scout brushed past her and jumped up on her bed once more.

She turned and faced the wolf as he flopped down on the bed, his dark brown eyes staring back at her. She was no match for a wolf, but she'd be damned if she was going to sleep on the floor. Hobbling toward him, she placed her hands on her hips and adopted a stern expression. "Listen Scout, this is *my...*"

A low growling sound from behind her immediately cut her off.

Fear shot through her at the sound. Roxanne slowly turned and stared at the huge wolf standing directly behind her. With brown and black markings and dark blue and brown eyes, he was the most unusual wolf she'd ever seen.

"Hello there. Nice wolfie."

The wolf trotted past her and she finished in exasperation, "Er, why don't you come in, too." The wolf walked right up to her bed and growled once more. Scout quickly jumped down and ran out of the room.

The wolf turned to face her. He stared at her for a long moment before he walked out of the room, his powerful shoulders rising and falling with each step he took. Her entire body trembled as she quickly shut the doors behind the wolves. With a sigh, she decided to open one of the windows near her bed instead.

* * * * *

Roxanne tossed and turned, the bed sheets tangling in her legs, as she tried to fall asleep. Try as she might, she couldn't get Rafael out of her mind or her body for that matter. Every brush of the covers against her sensitive nipples was pure torture, even with the T-shirt as a buffer in between. The shirt carried his scent and only managed to exacerbate her need. The dull ache that throbbed between her thighs made sleep impossible.

The wind had kicked up from a storm brewing outside and the mosquito netting around the bed billowed with the strong gusts coming through the open window.

Roxanne closed her eyes and inhaled, enjoying the faint scent of gardenia wafting through her window. The strong wind had diluted the flowery aroma somewhat as the smell of impending rain hung in the air.

The wind blew harder and a sudden knocking sound at the window had Roxanne sitting straight up in bed, her hand covering her heart. As she turned to the sound, her heart rammed in her chest. She let out a sigh of relief when a small tree limb, rocking in the wind, hit the window once more.

She smiled and climbed out of bed. Walking over to the doors, she opened them wide. Most dogs didn't venture out during storms. *She should be safe from the wolves for now,* she thought as she walked out into the garden.

Spreading her arms wide, she let the wind buffet her body, thrilling at the power of nature at its best. The gusts blew against her in waves, only giving her a second to recover before circling around her and starting the process all over again.

Through half closed eyes, Roxanne noticed a light filtering through the thick forest of trees surrounding her patio. She looked all around her and seeing no sign of the wolves, she stepped into the grove of oaks, seeking the source of the light.

The sound of falling rain penetrated her consciousness long before the first drop of rain ever hit her body. In the seclusion of the forest, the thick foliage protected her from the heavy downpour banging on the leaves above her.

When Roxanne reached the edge of the woods, she realized the source of light came from a small house along the backside of Rafael's property.

As she stared, someone passed by the window. Rafael! No, Rafe. A more intimate name was needed for what she planned to do with him. Her pulse sped up and her nipples hardened instantly. Roxanne walked across the lawn, heedless of the rain pouring over her. This time she'd be damned if she'd let him just walk away.

* * * * *

Rafael leaned back against the windowsill and listened to the rain as he sketched a drawing of Roxanne. God, the woman's smell had been burned into his very consciousness. Everywhere he turned, he smelled her. He wanted her so much his hand shook as the pencil flew across the paper. He'd planned to go to her tonight but he needed to gain control over his emotions first.

When she'd stripped in front of him, it was all he could do to keep from pulling her to the floor and mounting her right there on the carpet. He'd never wanted to fuck another so bad and not just a get-her-outta-my-system fuck either. No, he felt the primal urges and instinctively knew the physical reaction he had to Roxanne wasn't his normal need for a woman.

The fact was he really liked everything about her—her gorgeous body, her spunky personality, her acceptance of their mutual attraction, and her passionate response to him. He knew. He wanted to mate with her. Every fiber in his being told him what a bad idea that was.

After his failure to protect his own family in the past, he'd vowed never to be responsible for another's safety. He didn't want or need a repeat performance. A lupina mate would certainly qualify as someone he would want to protect. The fact the full moon hadn't occurred yet was his only saving grace. Tonight, he would do his best to get this woman out of his system and not have to worry about impregnating her. But first he had to rein in his raging desire in order to stand before her as a man in total control.

Earlier, the sight of her wearing his T-shirt, the light behind her outlining every curve against the white cotton material, made him want her even more. The fact that Scout had ignored his earlier command that he stay out of her room only managed to exacerbate his pent-up desire. He'd warned the wolf off for the last time. What infuriated him more was the insane jealousy he'd experienced over a mere wolf. It's not like Scout was a werewolf vying for Roxanne's affections. Rafael couldn't explain the irrational reaction, he just knew he needed time to get a grip and his art had always soothed the demons fighting inside his soul.

Just as his mind settled and the charcoal moved smoothly across the paper, Rafael smelled her before he saw her. Her arousal reached out and yanked at his senses, overwhelming them. He clenched the pencil tight in his hand and looked up from his drawing when the door opened noiselessly.

Roxanne was soaked and his white T-shirt did nothing to hide her body. If anything, the wet material clinging to her breasts and thighs only accentuated all she had to offer. Small perky breasts and dark nipples jutted toward him, a waist no bigger than the width of his hand begged to be clasped, and the shadow of dark hair between her legs beckoned to him to nuzzle, inhale and taste her scent. His cock rose as his gaze traveled down the rest of her body while she walked over to the couch and laid down.

Skimming her fingers over her breasts and down her abdomen, she asked, "What are you drawing, Rafe?"

Rafe? Damn, he liked the sound of that. The drawing forgotten, his gaze followed her hand as she pulled the wet shirt up and exposed her belly. The pace of his breathing sped up as she trailed her fingers down her wet thigh and then straightened her leg, offering her body to his hungry stare.

* * * * *

Roxanne drank in every inch of Rafe's well-cut body as he propped against the windowsill. He'd pulled on a pair of old jeans but remained shirtless. And what a view his gorgeous pecs and six-pack abs were! His dark blue gaze strayed from hers to follow the movements of her hands. His heated gaze made her stomach flutter as she squirmed on the extra-wide couch. *Mmmm, like a twin-sized bed*, she thought with an inward grin.

She felt totally brazen as she exposed herself to him, but she didn't care. She wanted him and if he didn't respond to her own seduction of her body, then the man was a eunuch.

"Tell me what you're drawing," she repeated as she slid her hand up her thigh and feathered her fingers through the nest of curls covering her sex.

"You," he replied, his tone clipped, almost angry.

Wind gusted outside, thunder rumbled, and lightning lit up the room. The lights in the room dimmed and revived.

Her heart skipped a beat at the idea of making love in the dark, during a raging storm. "See." She gave a sexy laugh. "You needed a live model and here I am to," she hesitated before sliding a finger across her clitoris, "inspire you." She finished in a breathless voice as her body reacted to her own stimuli.

He didn't say a word, just stared at her intensely. But Roxanne could see the barely held control, the tension in his shoulders. He wasn't immune.

The pencil snapped in his hand.

She smiled and met his gaze with a bold one as she slid her own finger inside her slit. Amazed at how decadent she felt with him watching her, she moaned as she rocked her hips against her hand. A loud clap of thunder sounded and lightning flashed again right before the power failed, dousing the room into darkness.

When two strong hands suddenly clasped her thighs, Roxanne let out a cry and grabbed the edge of the couch as Rafael quickly turned her so her legs hung over his shoulders. Before she could recover, he grabbed her buttocks, yanked her to the edge of the cushion, lowered his head to her sex and feasted.

Blood rushed to her core, sending juices flowing, and her heart raced as she moved her hands to his head, pulling him closer as he nuzzled her folds, sucking her clit, nibbling the swollen nub with his teeth. He made sure he didn't miss a single spot and when his tongue finally slid along her slit, she keened at the pure pleasure he elicited.

She was in heaven.

Rafe sat back panting, his expression hungry, almost feral. Sliding her legs off his shoulders, he stood and ripped at the buttons on his jeans. Her sex throbbed in response to his jerky movements as if he couldn't wait another moment and he had to have her right then. Thank God, 'cause she didn't think she could wait any longer.

When he pulled his jeans off, the sight of his large, thick cock on display made her go weak all over, but Roxanne's heart sank when he kicked his jeans to the side without retrieving a condom. Well, crap, he didn't have any protection?

She put her hand up to tell him to stop, but he grabbed her hand and flipped her over on the couch without saying a word.

"Rafe!" she panted as he lifted her hips until she was on her knees. Roxanne grabbed the back of the couch for support and tried to turn around.

Rafe ripped her T-shirt right down the middle and quickly pulled it off her arms. It made a wet plop as it hit the wood floor. "I'm not stopping, Roxanne," he bit out as he nudged her legs apart with his thigh. "I'm too far gone, *chère.*"

Anxiety and sheer excitement over the risk they were taking fought for control in her head. "Hey, you need a condom," she reminded him between gulps of air.

His cock nudged against her entrance and she instinctively arched toward him, wanting him inside her as much as he wanted to be there.

"I'm clean, Rocky, and your body's not prepared to conceive yet, so we're covered," he ground out as he clasped her hips in a firmer hold and pressed his body against hers.

"Mmmm," she moaned and dug her nails into the fabric of the couch as his cock entered her. He was bigger than any man she'd ever been with and her body contracted instantly against the stretching of her sensitive skin.

"God, you're tight," he rasped. Pausing, he slid his hands up her back and around her front until he cupped her breasts. Rolling her nipples between his fingers he tweaked them until she moaned in sheer delight. Accompanying the pleasure he elicited, a gush of warm moisture shot straight to her sex. Damn, he was good.

"Spread your legs more for me, *chère*. That's it," he whispered in her ear as he rocked his hips against her, sliding deeper inside her body.

Roxanne reveled in her body adjusting to accommodate his size. She bit her lip, amazed that his cock seemed to touch every part of her insides. Once he was fully seated within her, Rafe held still, taking long, steadying breaths.

Just as Roxanne inhaled deeply to remain calm, he withdrew and drove back inside hard and fast, once, then twice more.

"Ohmigod!" she screamed as her body reacted instantly to his aggressive thrusts, contracting quickly around his cock.

Rafe groaned at the muscle spasms around him. "You feel so good, Rocky." He clasped her ass and massaged her buttocks as he began to rock his hips against her, plunging deeper and deeper inside her each time his hips met her ass.

Roxanne arched her back and met each of his thrusts with her own counter ones, thrilling in the tightening of her stomach as her body prepared to come while Rafe's hands never stopped stroking her body.

He found her clit and rubbed the nub between two fingers. She panted and rocked her hips, making mewling sounds as her walls began to quiver in small spasms. Rafael growled low in his throat and withdrew from her body.

Before she could work up a good frustration, his slid his fingers inside her body once more. She arched and pressed closer, missing his thick cock within her.

As he obliged and thrust his cock inside her once more, Rafe slid his finger up her crack and massaged her anus. Roxanne gasped at his unexpected touch. She tensed, pausing her movements, secretly thrilled and surprised by the taboo sexual act from a man who appeared so tame and civilized.

"I want all of you, Rocky. Let go and experience, " he insisted, his voice dark and demanding as he rocked her body against the couch with his powerful thrusts. When she pushed back against him, he groaned at the same time he slid his finger inside her anus.

The dual stretching sensation on both her front and her backside sent Roxanne flying over the edge. Her orgasm slammed through her body in rippling, rushing waves. She screamed and rocked her hips, doing anything she could to prolong the most intense, sexually satisfying orgasm she'd ever experienced.

Rafe grunted at her actions and he began to control the pace as each new stroke he took was harder and deeper than the last. In every way, he possessed her. Roxanne used the leverage of the couch to push back against him, clenching her inner muscles, taking back some of the control, until he shouted out with his own climax.

When he came, Roxanne marveled at the feeling of his hot semen coating her core. It felt warm and wet, sexy and wanton, and strangely, right. She'd never experienced sex without a condom between herself and a lover before. God, did his flesh sliding within her feel good. The fact that he pushed the sexual envelope, knowing exactly what to do to make her body sing to the highest note possible, only made her want him more.

Rafe laid his head on her back until his breathing evened out. He kissed her shoulder, then withdrew from her and walked into the bathroom.

A few seconds later, he emerged, washcloth in hand. "Lie down, Rocky."

When she followed his request, Rafe sat down beside her and gingerly wiped her entrance. The washcloth was warm and his attentive behavior melted her heart, but what shook her the most was the look of disappointment that crossed his face while he cleaned his semen away.

Worried he might have regretted making love to her, she clasped his arm. "I'm on the pill. You were right about me not ovulating. But how did you know that?"

He raised a dark eyebrow as if to say, "C'mon, babe, I'm a vampire, remember?"

He gave her a seductive smile, all remnants of his regretful expression gone. "Being what I am does have its fringe benefits."

Before she could respond, Rafael glanced outside and pulled her to her feet. "The storm seems to have subsided a bit. Let's get out of here."

Roxanne started to walk toward the door, but Rafe scooped her up in his arms. "No, *chère*. Not with your feet hurting the way they do. I'll carry you."

"How did you know…?" she started to ask, but instead, she sighed. He seemed to have a sixth sense when it came to her. Wrapping her arms around his neck, she accepted his help.

Walking quickly in the rain, Rafe carried her through the French doors into his room and laid her down on his bed. After he dried her body with a towel and turned to put the towel away, Roxanne finally got to see the rest of his tattoo. The two animals on his tattoo consisted of a raven's head and a wolf's head. *Interesting combination, but still sexy as sin*, she thought as he crawled into bed and pulled her body against his. Pressing his chest against her back, he kissed her neck and said, "Tell me why those two men were chasing you, Rocky."

Rafe's warm body and comforting voice made Roxanne feel safe and secure. She couldn't explain why but she did trust him. He would believe her. She told him the whole story.

When she finished, Rafe said, his voice deadly calm, "Tomorrow morning we'll go get that ledger."

"But tomorrow is Monday. The office will be open and busy."

Rafe turned her over to face him and wrapped his arms around her. Running his fingers through her damp hair, he replied, his voice confident, "I'm going to help you, Rocky."

His words reminded her of the *loa* god Charlotte's prediction. Here was the person who planned to help her. It felt right to accept his help. Her decision made, Roxanne fell asleep to the sound of the pouring rain and Rafe's steady heartbeat underneath her cheek.

Chapter Eight

Roxanne awoke to the sensation of a warm cloth being rubbed against the bottom of her foot. Sitting up slightly, she noticed the covers had been pulled to the bottom of the bed, and the huge black and brown wolf she'd seen earlier stood on the end of the bed, licking the sole of her foot. Scared to even take a breath, she reached for Rafe. When her hand met empty space, she willed herself not to panic.

With each brush of the wolf's tongue, her foot tingled, the sensation overshadowing the pain from the cuts. Now that the storm had passed, the moon's light shone through the windows, giving her plenty of light to see the wolf as he bent down over her foot.

Her heart raced at his large size and the knowledge of the damage he could inflict if he chose. Biting her lip, she debated what to do. She'd heard an old wives tale that a dog's saliva had healing properties in it. Wolves were like dogs, right?

Propping herself up on her elbows, Roxanne let the wolf clean her wounds. What else could she do? As if sensing her watching him, the massive animal stopped licking and raised his head. His steady gaze locked with hers before he bent his head and began to lick her other foot.

Roxanne lay back, strangely soothed by the gentle cadence of his movements. He shifted and his tongue began to bathe her calf. What could he possibly like about her calf? She had no wounds there. When the wolf's tongue laved the side of her leg, she slightly bent her knee, not sure what to do. When his tongue brushed the back of her knee, she opened her eyes and tensed at the achy feeling that gathered in her sex. No man had ever bothered to lick the back of her knee. And damnit, leave it to a wolf to discover such an erogenous zone.

The wolf took a step and lapped at her inner thigh in long, leisurely strokes. Okay, that was too close for comfort. Roxanne started to back away, but the wolf suddenly gave a low warning growl, deep in his throat. 'Don't move an inch,' he seemed to be telling her.

She met his gaze and froze as he took the few steps to the top of the bed, caging her in.

Fear pumped through her, causing her heart to race as the wolf bent and rubbed his nose against her neck gently. Roxanne closed her eyes in shame that she found his physical touch so arousing. But the sensible part of her kicked in and she held herself perfectly still while she gave a silent prayer that he didn't suddenly decide to have her for a late night snack. When the wolf's body begin to shake above her, Roxanne opened her eyes to see Rafe poised over her, his hair damp, and his naked body covered in a sheen of sweat.

Holy Cow, talk about Wolfman Jack! The man could shift to a wolf's form? Shock rocked through her. What more surprises did he have in store for her? For that matter, did she really need to get involved with a man who had more secrets than she did? Nope! She started to move away.

"No!" he bit out as he quickly clasped her hands and held them over her head, pinning her to the bed.

His erection pressed against her thigh and while her mind rebelled, her body reacted instantly. Her nipples grew taut, aching for his touch, and her heart raced in anticipation.

Roxanne's expression must've reflected some of her mixed emotions, for Rafe's face turned grim. "You trusted me to tell me your secrets. I want you to know everything that I am, man and beast alike, Roxanne, because when it comes to you, I have very little control over the wolf side in me."

Still reeling from his revelation and not at all quite sure how she felt about it, she quipped, "Well, now I know why you like the doggie style position so much."

His grip tightened and he nudged her thighs apart with his leg. "You liked it too, Rocky. You can't deny it."

Her chest rose and fell with her rapid breathing and her sex throbbed at the truth of his words. She couldn't deny it.

As he dipped his head and captured a nipple between his teeth, Roxanne gasped and pressed her chest closer while trying to free her hands.

"So your tattoo..." she panted, "...on your back... Mmmm...are you able to shift to a raven as well?" she finally managed to get out her question between exquisite sensations rocking her body.

"Mmmm, hmmm," he mumbled against her breast. *The raven and wolf represent my split heritage*, he answered her mentally.

Rafe shifted and held both her wrists in one hand while he rolled the rosy tip along his teeth, alternately nipping and sucking with just enough pleasure-pain to make her hips intuitively rock at the intense sensations he caused.

Rafe traced his fingers up her thigh and Roxanne wantonly spread her legs, asking him to touch her. When his hand cupped her sex, she moaned and bucked against him. He moved to her other breast and sucked hard on her nipple while he trailed his fingers around the folds of her sex. Using her own moisture to tease her clit, he made his way around her sex in a path of seductive frustration.

As his fingers teased, Roxanne found herself shifting her hips, trying to encourage him to delve into her core. But still he avoided the one place she wanted him to touch.

When she heard a low chuckle, Roxanne realized what he was doing. He was keeping his promise to make her pay.

"Rafe," she whispered, her voice desperate.

His expression sobered and his gaze locked with hers as he rubbed two fingers over her clit right before he slowly slid them inside her.

Roxanne swallowed a sob as he drew tantalizing circles around her cervix. When he used his fingers and thumb to press on all her hot buttons inside and along her clit, she strained against his hold and pressed closer, rocking with the exquisite pleasure.

While he touched her, she wanted to savor his warm flesh and flexing muscles underneath her hands. "Let go of my hands."

Rafael positioned himself between her thighs, pressing her body against the bed with his weight. "Uh-uh, *chère*."

He looked down at their bodies as his cock pressed against her entrance and then met her gaze once more. "You wanted to be taken and so you shall."

Her breasts tingled and her sex throbbed at his statement. The uncontrollable need of wanting him moving within her knotted her stomach. Before she could respond, Rafe laid his hard, muscular body over hers and slammed inside her in one swift thrust.

"Yeeoooooow…mmmm…" Roxanne's howl of shocked discomfort turned to a purr of sheer pleasure when Rafe stayed buried deep inside her. While she met his hungry gaze, he rocked against her clitoris until orgasmic contractions spiraled and splintered throughout her entire body.

"What was that, *mon amour*?" he drawled, amusement lacing his tone as her body shuddered around his erection.

As much as she wanted him to come inside her again, Roxanne wanted to drive him over the edge more.

"Roll over," she demanded.

Rafe raised a dark eyebrow, but he released her hands and complied with a chuckle.

When she started to move off of him, he clasped her arms. "Where are you going?"

Roxanne laughed at his scowl. "I'm going to return the favor."

Releasing her, he grinned. "Well, if you insist."

"Oh, I do," she murmured as she bent down over his cock.

* * * * *

Rafael looked at Roxanne leaning over him, her peachy skin so much more fair than his. He'd never enjoyed making love with a woman as much as he did with Roxanne. Her willingness earlier to try something she'd never done before—her trust that he only wanted to heighten her pleasure—sent his libido into overdrive. While he watched her uninhibited response, felt her slick body clenching around him, his own desire consumed him until he couldn't hold on any longer. He came hard and fast, enjoying every sensual slide against her luscious body, every breathy gasp she took until his body was completely spent.

Roxanne's tongue circling his cock brought his thoughts swiftly back to the present. He groaned and ran his fingers through her tousled blonde hair. Sliding his hand down the nape of her neck and then across the silky skin along the curve of her back, his heart raced. She was a gorgeous creature.

Roxanne's small hand grasped his cock while she took him as deep in her throat as she could. He rocked his hips to the rhythmic movement of her mouth up and down his erection. His heart thundered in his ears as his climax built and when she cupped his balls, he groaned in response, enjoying her warm hand surrounding him.

His heart tripped and anticipation built when she trailed her fingers along the skin between his balls and his anus, then slid her finger lower and applied pressure. Rafael clasped her head and jerked at the erotic sensations slamming through him, calling out her name in a hoarse voice. His orgasm shook him to the very core, taking him to a level of sensuality he'd never experienced in all his forty years.

Roxanne licked the last drop of cum off his cock and gave him a devilish smile. Rafael felt so thoroughly satisfied, he pulled her on top of him and kissed her. Hard. The only thing that would ever top such satisfying sex was a full wolf mating. Some of his euphoria dwindled a little when he reminded himself a mating could never happen between them.

Oblivious to his inner turmoil, Roxanne smiled and tucked her head on his shoulder once more. Running her fingers through the hair on his chest she said with a chuckle, "Who says you need a full moon to howl?"

Yeah, he thought, his heart sinking, *all I need is you.*

* * * * *

Rafael awoke the next morning to the smell of honeysuckle and peaches all around him. He looked down and stared at Roxanne lying across his chest. His heart swelled at the feeling of rightness he experienced while waking with her in his arms. Closing his eyes, he inhaled her sweet aroma. As her scent permeated his consciousness, his stomach clenched and his cock hardened instantly when he caught a whiff of another distinct, beckoning scent—a scent that made his heart jerk in tortured agony.

Rafael fought his body's natural response to the knowledge that Roxanne was in the early ovulation stage—that same instinct that pulled at him to roll her over and mount her instantly. And this reaction was based on her scent alone. What would he do when she awoke and turned those luminescent green eyes his way or gave him her sexy siren's smile?

If he kept his distance, he could resist her sexual lure but only during the day. Tonight, with the full moon's pull upon him, the need to mate, to reproduce and increase the strength of the pack, would be flowing like wildfire through his veins.

In the past, he'd been able to ignore the signs with each full moon, focusing on the hunt for food to alleviate his pent-up sexual tension. But tonight, with Roxanne in her current fertile state, he would be unable to resist making love with her and making her his lupina mate for life.

All the more reason to get her back to town as soon as possible. He clenched his jaw and slowly pulled out from underneath her.

* * * * *

"Rise and shine, hon," Cordelia called out cheerfully as she stood at the end of the bed holding a breakfast tray.

Roxanne awoke quickly at the woman's booming voice. When she remembered she was in Rafe's bed, stark naked, she clasped the covers around her and sat up. Disappointment sliced through her that Rafael had left her alone in his bed, but her down mood was soon replaced with embarrassment as she realized Cordelia had caught her in such a compromising position.

"Do you know where Rafael is?" she asked, trying to keep the disappointment from her voice.

"He's been in the studio this morning," Cordelia replied as she set the tray across her lap. She frowned slightly continuing, "He plans to take you back to town in an hour."

Roxanne sighed. She'd hoped... Ah hell, she didn't know what she hoped. "Yes. He's helping me straighten out a mess I've created."

Cordelia tilted her head to the side and looked at her curiously. "Did he tell you who and what he is?"

Roxanne took a sip of her orange juice and nodded. She set down her glass and met Cordelia's expectant gaze. "Why does Rafael live out here alone? I know he's part wolf and though I don't know much about them, I do know wolves are pack animals, not loners."

Cordelia gave her a wide, knowing smile. "I'm so glad you asked." Sinking onto the end of the bed, Cordelia told her the story about Rafael's past. "I've been hounding him to get out and mingle. Enough is enough," she finished with a frustrated sigh.

Roxanne's heart went out to the young Rand who had lost so much and been betrayed so ruthlessly at such a tender age. How did he manage to keep his sanity and not become a bitter, tortured soul? she wondered.

Munching on a piece of toast, she asked, "So are you saying he's living in exile as some sort of self-imposed punishment?"

Cordelia sighed. "That's about the gist of it. I think he blames himself for his family's demise. Up until a couple of months ago, Rafael just existed, splitting his time between roaming the bayou and painting."

She paused, her brow furrowing. "But something happened to shake him up and he hasn't been the same since. He sleeps very little and he walks around in a state of heightened tension. He won't talk to me about it, but I know something is bothering him. My guess is his body has begun to acknowledge the need for a wolf pack, even if his mind rebels at the idea of losing what he perceives as his peaceful solitude.

"Why can't he have both?" Roxanne asked, genuinely confused.

Cordelia gave a warm hearted laugh. "He can, hon. He just needs to forgive himself first. The rest...well, I think the rest will fall into place."

Cordelia stood up and smiled, nodding to the clothes on the chair near the window. "I washed your clothes and fixed the button on your blouse." She pointed to a pair of black flats on the floor by the bed. "Oh, and I guessed at your size and got a pair of my niece's shoes for you to wear."

Roxanne blinked away the tears. No one had ever been so kind to her. "Thanks so much, Cordelia."

The older lady nodded. "I just wish you were staying with us for a while."

She did, too. Roxanne really cared about Rafe. "I've got to get back and set things straight."

After Cordelia left, Roxanne stepped into Rafe's bathroom. While she waited for the water to turn warm in the shower, she noticed some of the tiles and grout on the side wall looked newer than the surrounding ones. It was rather odd how the newer ones seemed to be in a random pattern.

She stepped into the shower and the warm water beat down on her, lulling her, washing away the aches from her long night with Rafe. When she ran the soap over her body, Roxanne mentally relived every place he touched her. Rafe had been insatiable, making love to her throughout the night, just like he promised he would. Her sensual memories made Roxanne wish Rafe were there with her, stroking her body, sliding against her, surrounding her with his tall, muscular frame all over again. She sighed and turned off the shower, her fantasy disappearing with the steam that cleared as she got dressed.

Rafe stood waiting for her in the foyer. Wearing black dress slacks, a light blue dress shirt and black dress shoes, he looked every bit the steely, confident, cultured Rafael Delacroix his reputation had been built upon.

"Come on, I'll take you to town, *chère*," he said when she reached his side.

Roxanne knew immediately something wasn't right. Was he the type of man who, once he'd seduced and won the woman, he was done with her? She could tell by the stiff way he held his shoulders to the impassive expression on his face, something was bothering him.

She put her hand on his arm and asked, "Are you okay?"

Rafe looked down at her hand on his arm, then met her gaze. A muscle ticked in his jaw before he clasped her elbow and steered her toward the front door saying, "Nothing is wrong, Roxanne. I just want to help you with your problem. The sooner, the better."

Uh-oh, he was back to calling her Roxanne. Yep, something was definitely wrong. Why did she have to fall for the moody type? And that's when it hit her. She'd fallen for Rafael Delacroix. Hard. And in the light of day, he could barely look at her. Damn it, didn't that just round out her last few days on a great note! The man who intended to help her solve one problem was the very center of an entirely different kind of dilemma.

Putting on his sunglasses, Rafael escorted her to his SUV and closed the passenger door behind her. Not a word was said as he pulled out of his driveway and turned onto the road. Noting his tight knuckled grip on the steering wheel and his refusal to look her way, Roxanne closed her eyes and inhaled. At least with her eyes closed she could enjoy his clean, masculine scent and pretend he still wanted her.

She dug her fingers into her palms as she remembered last night and the way he made her feel, his cock driving into her, stretching her, making her scream. Her heart raced and her sex began to throb painfully. She shifted in the seat and crossed her legs, trying to dampen her desire.

"Stop it, Rocky," Rafe bit out.

She jerked her gaze to him, but Rafael refused to look at her.

"What?"

"I can hear your heart racing, smell your desire." He looked at her, his gaze pure steel. "It's driving me fucking nuts."

"And that's a bad thing?" she asked, incredulous.

He looked back at the road. "Yes."

This was insane. He wanted her. She wanted him.

"Why?"

The wheels squealed as Rafael slammed on the brakes and pulled the car to the side of the road under a shady tree.

His hand still on the gearshift, he yanked off his glasses and faced her as he ground out, "Because you're ovulating."

Her eyes widened and she felt the blood drain from her face. "But...but, I'm on the pill."

"Well, apparently it's not working."

His words made her realize she didn't take her pill last night. It was entirely possible she was ovulating. But his tone was so accusing.

"You're blaming me?" she shot back.

"What the hell are you talking about?" he all but yelled.

A clattering sound interrupted him and they both looked down to see pieces of round black plastic hit the console between them before the bits rolled to the carpeted floor. That's when Roxanne noticed the ball from the end of the gearshift had disappeared.

His expression unruffled, Rafe met her gaze. "Tonight is a full moon."

She didn't get what he was yammering on about. Exasperated, she threw up her hands. "Yeah, and it affects the tides and lots of weirdos and freaks do crazy things on a night like tonight and—"

"And werewolves mate, Rocky," he interrupted her, his tone hard.

Roxanne's gaze flew to his intense one. Panic and excitement warred within her. She wanted him. But did she want to be with him forever? The idea of mating with Rafe, the very thought of living every day with this complex man, making love to him, made her heart pound and her nipples harden. Her mind finally caught up with what her body and heart already knew. She wanted to mate with him.

Before she could respond, he turned back to the wheel, put on his glasses and pulled the car back on the road saying in a dull tone, "I'm not ever going to mate."

"But—"

"I'm not the right man for you, Roxanne," he said, his tone distant, almost cold.

Hurt by his blunt words, Roxanne turned to stare out the window as she blinked back tears.

She jumped when Rafe's hand slid underneath her hair. He cupped the back of her neck, his thumb rubbing along the soft spot behind her ear.

"It's not you, *chère*. It's me." He spoke quietly as if a heavy weight laid upon his shoulders.

Roxanne remembered Cordelia's words. 'If only he could forgive himself.' Did his not being able to forgive himself have anything to do with his decision not to mate?

She turned to look at him but Rafe dropped his hand and stared straight ahead. Maybe it was best for them both to change the subject.

Folding her hands in her lap, Roxanne asked, "So what's your plan for getting me in a busy office unnoticed?"

He cast her a cocky smile. The first smile she'd seen from him that day. "We're going to walk right in, *chère*."

Chapter Nine

"Are you *suuuure* no one can see us?" Roxanne looked over her shoulder at Rafe before she opened the entry door to Bender's Motors.

Behind his sunglasses, his brows together, frowning down at her. For that matter, he'd alternately scowled and frowned ever since he'd stepped close to her to show her how they were going to escape detection.

As they entered the building, he kept his hand firmly planted on her shoulder while he removed his sunglasses and put them in his pocket. Reminding her mentally, he said, *Remember, you must touch some part of me at all times to remain unseen.*

"Wouldn't it be easier if you just held my hand," she insisted in a low voice.

Oh and don't forget, no talking.

Grrr. Rafe had thwarted all her efforts at intimacy. Stubborn man!

When they passed a couple of her coworkers in the hall and no one looked her way or said a word, Roxanne smiled. *Well, I'll be damned. He really can project a mental image in others' minds that we aren't here. That's so cool!*

When she saw Susan from her accounting department approaching them, she stuck out her tongue as the woman passed. Roxanne stifled a giggle. She'd always wanted to do that to Susan. The woman had resented her from the moment she arrived. Roxanne knew it had to do with Susan wanting her job, but that didn't mean she had to like the woman's cold treatment of her.

As they passed through several cubicles to get to her office, Roxanne put her hand over Rafe's on her shoulder to warn him she was taking a detour. She couldn't help stopping by Arlene's desk. The woman was known to be quite the ball buster in the building. She'd always put on such a formal front, but Roxanne knew all she needed to do was let down her hair just once and people would warm up to her.

Standing behind her, Roxanne pulled out the pair of chopsticks she constantly wore in her hair. As the woman gasped and tried unsuccessfully to keep her hair from falling down, Roxanne backed away and giggled.

You have quite a devilish streak in you, Rocky, Rafe said, his low chuckle echoing in her head.

"Watch," she whispered as several people looked up at Arlene's frantic actions.

"Who stole my chopsticks?" she said, glaring at Tony.

Tony raised his hands in an innocent manner. "Don't look at me. I'm all the way across the room. But, you know, Arlene, you should let your hair down more often," he finished with a wink.

Arlene blushed several shades of red and for the first time since Roxanne had known her, the woman was speechless.

Roxanne set the chopsticks behind a stack of folders on Arlene's desk.

Me thinks you like this power of invisibility a little too much, Rafe said in an amused tone.

As they walked off toward her office she whispered with a chuckle, "Why not use it while I got it?"

Once they entered her office, Rafe followed her to the hiding spot as she retrieved the ledger. Tucking the book under her arm, she said, "Come on, let's go find Jake."

When they entered the hall again, Roxanne looked up and noticed Scott walking down the hall toward them. Her entire body tensed and her steps slowed until she stopped dead in her tracks.

What's wrong, chère? Rafe's concerned voice entered her mind as he laid both his hands on her shoulders and squeezed.

Roxanne closed her eyes and soaked up his heat from behind her. When she opened them again, Scott had stopped right in front of her, his expression thunderous.

* * * * *

Rafael realized the man that had Roxanne's feet frozen to the floor had to be Scott Bender. A fierce, primal need to protect welled up within him. He let go of the mental hold he had over the man standing in front of them and allowed him to see them. He wanted the prick to see who was about to rip his throat out.

Then the asshole reached out for the ledger saying, "You stupid bit—"

Rafael's hand shot out before the conscious thought entered his brain. He encircled Scott's throat and squeezed, relishing in the gulp the idiot made.

"So much as finish that statement or touch her in anyway, and I'll snap your scrawny neck in two," he said in a menacing tone.

Scott narrowed his gaze on Rafael. "Who the fuck are—"

"Don't give me an excuse to put you out of your misery," Rafael bit out, interrupting him once more. "I've got more than enough anger for what you've put Roxanne through."

Rafael spoke to her. "Go see Jake, Roxanne. I'll keep Scott here company while you explain everything to his father."

Roxanne eyed his grip on Scott's throat warily.

Yes, I could kill him with my bare hands, Rocky, but I'll let you take care of it the legal way. He did feel intense, ready to kill, but more than anything, he wanted to let Roxanne handle the situation on her own as much as possible. He sensed it was important for her to do so.

"Be good," she said to him in a stern tone before she walked off toward Jake Bender's office.

Rafael's gaze followed Roxanne's swaying hips until she turned down another hall. Then he returned his gaze to Scott's brown one as he pinned him against the wall.

"Stay put."

Clutching at his hand, Scott looked around, his voice frantic, "You can't do this. I'll have you arrested for physical assault."

"No one is going to help you. For that matter no can see us," he replied in a flat tone.

Scott's eyes bulged when Rafael gave him a humorless smile, displaying his fangs. His anger at this sorry excuse for a man only intensified his own pent-up desire for Roxanne and the knowledge he'd never act on the instincts that were running rampant through his body.

But man, did it feel good to help Roxanne, even if was in a small way. The realization that he'd fulfilled his debt to Charlotte by helping Roxanne hit him hard. But what was Charlotte's answer to his question? She never did tell him. He furrowed his brow and tightened his hold on Scott when the shit tried to escape once more. Charlotte said he'd know the answer once he fulfilled his end of the bargain, but he didn't feel peace. If anything, he felt more alone than he had in a very long time.

"Scott Nathaniel Bender!" An enraged, booming voice reverberated throughout the office.

Rafael met Scott's gaze, noted how white the man's face had become, and smirked. "I think that's your cue, my boy." He grinned and pulled Scott away from the wall by the collar of his shirt.

When he entered Jake Bender's office and released Scott, Jake Bender, his face beat red, pointed to a chair in front of his desk and barked, "Sit!"

Jake turned to him and said, "Thank you, Mister...?"

"Delacroix."

"Delacroix. For your assistance in this matter." Glaring at his son, who had flopped into the chair he'd indicated, he continued, "The police have been called —"

"Dad!"

"Not a word, Scott."

"But that man's a —"

"I said, not a word, son!"

Jake looked back at him. "I'm going to make sure my son pays for his crimes."

Roxanne gave Rafael a grateful look and then turned to Jake when he addressed her.

"Roxanne, I'm gonna need you to stay and make a statement to the police. You up for it?"

Roxanne nodded.

"That's my girl."

Mine, too, Rafael thought. His heart contracted as he realized he already thought of her in those terms.

Frustration mounting, he knew he needed to get the hell out of there. When he turned to go, Roxanne ran after him and grabbed his arm.

"Where are you going?" Her confused gaze searched his face.

Her sweet scent surrounded him, making his gut clench and his cock rock hard.

Pulling him over to the door, she stepped outside the office and shut the door behind her. "We need to talk," she said in a low voice.

Rafael stared into her green eyes, heard her heightened heartbeat and the rush of blood through her veins. His gaze dropped to her full lips...a mouth that pleased him to no end. If he were alone with her, even for five minutes, he'd have her naked and underneath him. Guaranteed. Rafael clenched his jaw at the thought. No way.

Running his finger down her throat, he stared at the column of soft flesh one last time, knowing he'd never taste her blood again. "I'm not the man for you, Roxanne."

"Is this about your need to protect me, Rafe?" she asked, her brows drawing together in frustration. "Because if it is, you've done a wonderful job of doing just that."

Anger mixed with embarrassment swept through him. "Why do you think that?"

Roxanne blew out a sigh of frustration. "Cordelia told me about your past."

He clenched his fist at the old woman's intrusion.

"Don't be mad at her, Rafe. She had your best interests at heart," Roxanne said, placing her hands on her hips.

"It's not the same thing, Rocky," he heard himself saying before he thought better of it. "Scott is human."

"Humans, vampires, werewolves...who cares. We're all creatures in the end and we *all* have weaknesses of some kind," she insisted.

Rafael pressed his lips together. Yes, they all certainly did. He knew better than anyone.

"My point exactly," he replied. Turning away, he said as he walked off, "As I said, I'm not the man for you, *chère*."

Walking away from Roxanne was one of the hardest things he'd done in his life. But for her own sake, he knew he was doing the right thing. Rocky needed someone who could give her everything and Rafe didn't have anything left to give. He would never forgive himself if anything happened to her because he couldn't adequately protect her in his supernatural world.

* * * * *

Roxanne drove up Rafael's driveway, trepidation skittering through her body. The day had been a long one with several interviews with the police, statements to sign and an office to move into. Yep, Jake had made her senior accountant and insisted she move into Scott's office immediately. Scott's two accomplices had been arrested, so she felt safe to swing by her apartment and change clothes.

The evening's warm air blew through her open window and scents of jasmine and gardenia invaded her senses as she parked in front of the house.

Roxanne was thankful for the full moon's light that lit her path as she walked to the door carrying the shoes Cordelia had lent her. With the house completely dark, she realized Cordelia had probably left for the night. Roxanne sighed in disappointment. She'd hoped to personally thank the older woman for her help and maybe talk to her a little more about Rafael. Instead she laid the borrowed shoes, along with the thank you note she'd written just in case, on the front porch near the door.

As she walked off the porch toward her car, Roxanne turned back to the house to take one last lingering look when she noticed light reflecting off the tops of the huge oaks in the back of the house. Rafe? she wondered, her heart racing as she quickly walked around the side of the huge house. When she rounded the corner, she saw the source of the light came from Rafe's studio.

Her heart sped up as she quietly made her way to the secluded house. Her sex throbbed in memory of what she and Rafe had done the night before in his art studio. The passion they had shared within those four walls made the cozy house a very special place in her heart.

Roxanne held her breath and opened the door, wondering what type of reception she would receive from Rafe. Would he be angry that she was there? She peeked around the door and released her breath in a disappointed sigh when she saw the studio was empty.

As she turned to leave, the vivid colors in the painting across the room caught her eye. Roxanne walked up to the easel and stared at the picture.

As her gaze scanned over the painting of her standing naked in the swamp, Roxanne smiled. Rafe had painted in vivid detail all the way down to the water droplets glistening on her body.

She was looking away in the painting, but from her profile she could tell a smile graced her face. Provocative and sensual, the mood of the painting struck a chord in her and a deeper yearning for Rafe began to thrum its way through her body.

The painting didn't look quite finished and Roxanne looked down at the charcoal drawing Rafe used as his guide while he painted. In the charcoal drawing, she saw the bull gator just a few feet from her. The mood the gator in the charcoal created was very different than the mood Rafael had created in the painting. He had stopped painting right when he would've had to draw the gator if he had wanted to keep in line with the charcoal drawing.

Roxanne's heart went out to Rafe and the turmoil he must be going through. She had to convince him to let go of the past. Her decision made, she knew exactly where to find her were-vamp.

Chapter Ten

As Roxanne entered the forest, she immediately noted the change darkness brought upon the surrounding area. Frogs croaked, crickets and unknown insects buzzed and chirped. Roxanne smiled at the deafening rhythmic harmony their nighttime noises brought to the bayou. She inhaled and grinned as the evening dew enhanced the bayou's natural scent, causing the damp, earthy smell to overpower the floral scents so prevalent during the day.

She turned her head at the fast flutter of an owl's wings as it dove past her, winced when she heard the pained squeak its prey made, and jumped at the bellow of a bull gator off in the distance. Their sounds reminded Roxanne that as peaceful and beautiful as the bayou appeared, danger always lurked—that someone was always on someone else's menu for the evening.

When she heard a distinct wolf's howl near the swamp, Roxanne looked up at the full moon through the foliage above her and shivered in anticipation and fear—fear she wouldn't be able to convince Rafe to forgive himself, fear he wouldn't give them a chance.

Thankful for the light that filtered through the thick foliage above her enough to lead her way, Roxanne took a deep breath to calm her nerves and headed in the direction of the swamp. She'd only taken a few steps when she saw a wolf's form emerge from the woods in front of her.

Rafe!

Roxanne smiled and walked toward him. But her steps slowed and an inner warning bell went off when she was within a few feet of the wolf. It was the way he looked at her, His eyes narrowed, his mouth closed, his stance...predatory. The sound of rustling underbrush in the woods behind the wolf drew her attention. Two more shadowy forms emerged as two gray wolves walked up behind the tan and black wolf.

Her heart jerked when the first wolf, after sniffing the air around her, bared his teeth and a low growl emanated from his throat. As the two wolves moved to stand on either side of the obviously alpha wolf, they too began to growl. Panic gripped her. Roxanne knew the wolves could sense her fear. They seemed to be feeding off of it. She took a slow step back and realized the harder her heart pounded, the deeper their growls became.

The first wolf stopped growling and let out a sharp bark. Instinctively she knew, he wanted her to run. He wanted the thrill of the chase so he could hunt down his prey. Roxanne turned and bolted deep into the woods, thankful she had worn serviceable shorts instead of a skirt this time.

Her heart pounding, her chest heaving as she took short, frantic gasps of breath, Roxanne swiped the hanging moss out of her way as she zigzagged through the woods, trying her best to lose the wolves.

When she heard the sound of their heavy paws pounding on the ground, the excited panting coming at her from three different sides, her heart sank. They would overcome her soon. Their bodies were built to hunt. She knew they were holding back, toying with her.

But the will to survive was strong, she was a good climber...and wolves—a wide grin spread up her face when the realization hit her—wolves weren't. Adrenaline kicked in, giving her the burst of speed she needed to put a little distance between them, just enough to give her a chance to scope out a tree to climb.

Up ahead, she spotted the perfect oak, its low limbs silhouetted against the light of the moon—limbs low enough for her to get a quick foot up if she could just get to it in time.

With the wolves gaining, Roxanne's chest burned as she pushed herself to get to the tree. But in her effort to keep her line of vision on her goal, she lost sight of the dangers of the forest floor and hit the ground hard as she tripped.

Her hands and knees dug into the damp forest floor as she skidded to a stop. At the sound of the wolves approaching, all Roxanne had time to do was roll over and hold her breath as she awaited the inevitable.

The tan and black wolf snarled and leapt through the air toward her. Roxanne's heart nearly stopped. She inhaled sharply and held up her arms to ward off his ferocious jaws as his body descended on her.

Roxanne looked on in shock when a huge brown and black wolf rammed into her predator's side, eliciting a yelp as he knocked the other wolf to the ground before he could connect with her.

Rafe! In her heart she knew, the wolf was Rafe.

The two wolves snarled and snapped at one another as they rolled on the forest floor. Roxanne had never heard such feral sounds coming from animals before. Rafe was amazing to watch as he finally pinned the other wolf to the ground by locking his jaw around the other's neck.

Roxanne wanted to applaud him, but his voice entered her head, strong and commanding, *Get your ass into that tree, Roxanne. Now!*

Roxanne scrambled to her feet and noticed the two gray wolves' gazes darting between her and their pinned leader. She didn't want to leave Rafael but she wouldn't disobey him either.

Her movements spurred the two wolves into action and they split up, one going after her while the other went after Rafe. Roxanne doubled her efforts to get to the tree. The rough bark bit into her hands as she grasped the lowest limb and quickly hoisted herself up on it. Just in the nick of time too, for the gray wolf chasing her literally snapped at her heels as she made it to safety.

But Roxanne felt far from safe. Her attention focused on Rafael and the wolves below, her heart rammed in her chest and fear for Rafe gripped her entire body. She shook all over when the wolf who had been chasing her turned to attack Rafe as well.

But he didn't quite make it to help his buddies out for another gray wolf emerged from the woods, his teeth bared. Scout! Roxanne recognized Scout's distinctive black markers on the tips of his ears as the wolf pounced on the other gray wolf, protecting Rafe, his alpha.

Roxanne's gaze darted to Rafe who had to release the other wolf to fight off the gray one on his back. Now all three wolves fought, the gray and tan/black wolves each took turns attacking Rafe.

Roxanne saw blood coating the wolves' fur and the need to protect her own took over. No! She couldn't loose Rafael. She started to climb down when a large wolf, his coat so black she only saw him due to the flash of his white canines, leapt on top of the gray wolf attacking Rafe. With the skill of a practiced predator, in one swift jerk of his head, the black wolf snapped the gray wolf's neck, instantly ending the animal's life.

At the same time the gray wolf hit the ground, Roxanne heard a pained yelp from Scout as he fought with the other gray wolf. A fearsome snarl came from Rafe right before he went berserk. He fought with fierce, deadly precision and the tan/black wolf suffered the same fate as his comrade.

But Rafe wasn't done. The black wolf moved out of his way as he shouldered past him to leap on the gray wolf attacking Scout. Roxanne almost felt sorry for the gray wolf. The beast didn't stand a chance against Rafe and he gave the animal no mercy. The sudden silence in the bayou after all that snapping, snarling and feral growling now seemed eerily appropriate for the occasion...almost as if the animals of the swamp lands knew to give a moment of silence to the dead.

Rafe stood panting over the gray wolf he'd just killed. He moved over to Scout who was lying on his side and nudged him with his nose. Scout whimpered. Roxanne's heart went out to Rafe as he transformed back into a human and patted his friend's side. Rafe whispered something into Scout's ear and the wolf immediately perked up, sat up on his haunches, and panted as if eagerly awaiting a treat. Her heart soared in relief.

Rafe laughed out loud, stroked the wolf's head and said, "I do believe I've been hoodwinked. Go home, 'ole boy."

Scout made a happy yipping sound and took off in the direction of Rafael's house.

Rafe walked over to the tree where she stood, clinging to the branches and held his hands up saying, "For his prize Scout gets to sleep on your bed." He grinned. "Jump down, *mon amour*. I've got you."

In an instant Roxanne was in his arms. Once she lowered her feet to the ground, she clung to his sweat-drenched, blood-soaked body and let her hands roam to make sure none of the blood was his.

Rafe hissed out in pain when she hit a gouge on his shoulder.

"Oh, I'm sorry. I just wanted to make sure you were okay. I see you suffered a few wounds yourself," she finished, her stomach clenching at the pain he must have felt from the deep teeth marks on his shoulder.

He grasped her hands, stopping her nervous movements. His intense gaze met hers as he said, "I'll be fine, Rocky. One benefit to being a werewolf. We have an amazing regenerative gene in our genetic makeup."

"Plus, he gets the added bonus of vampire blood to boot, a very beneficial combination," a man said from directly behind her.

Roxanne turned to see a tall, black-haired man staring back at Rafe. He stood a good three inches taller than Rafe and everything about him exuded confidence...even in his birthday suit! Roxanne avoided looking down when she realized the stranger, like Rafe, was completely naked.

Keep your gaze leveled upward, chère. Rafe's voice warned her mentally.

Rafe almost sounded jealous, Roxanne thought with a smile. Well, the stranger did have a gorgeous face. Pitch black, short-cropped hair framed a face with a highly defined bone structure and vivid green eyes. Roxanne decided she didn't mind complying with Rafe's request one bit.

"I see you didn't really need my help," the stranger said, indicating the dead wolves in a sweeping glance.

Rafe held out his hand to the man. "No, I didn't, but then they weren't here for me were they, Baine?"

Baine? Now where had she heard that name before? Roxanne racked her brain trying to remember. Then it hit her, the story Cordelia had told her about Rafael's past. Baine was one of the twin brothers who had saved Rafael's life when he was to be exterminated by the pack.

Baine's entire countenance turned as hard as stone. "No. They're after Ethan."

He clenched his fists and continued, "A small group has accompanied me to help protect Ethan, but Haden's men split up in their search for my brother, so we did the same."

Clasping Rafe on the shoulder he said, "I'm so glad to see you alive and well, Rand." His lips twitched in amusement as he dropped his hand and continued, "You've no idea how personally satisfying it is to see that you, the only living were-vamp I'm aware of, survived despite himself."

Rafe laughed as he pulled Roxanne into the circle of his arms and pressed her back against his chest. "My name is Rafael now and I couldn't agree more. Having a reason to go on makes all the difference."

Roxanne's heart leapt at his words. Could he have been referring to her? She didn't dare hope. Instead, for now she snuggled closer to Rafe's heat, enjoying the safe feeling of his arms around her.

Baine tilted his head to the side, an expression of interested curiosity on his face. His gaze drifted to her and then back to Rafael's. "Ethan asked you to join his pack, didn't he?"

Baine's question surprised Roxanne, but not near as much as Rafael's response.

"Yes. He came through here a couple of months ago."

Baine shook his head and grinned, his white teeth flashing in the dark. "That's my brother. Stubborn as a mule. Going off on his own. Doing his own thing."

He sobered and met Rafe's gaze with a serious one. "I take it you turned him down since you're still here."

Rafe's arms tightened around her. "Yes, I turned him down."

Why? Why would he turn down an opportunity to be a part of a pack? One that obviously wanted him and accepted his were-vamp status, Roxanne wondered.

Rafe kissed the top of her head. "I'd like you to meet Roxanne Waters."

Baine's green gaze met hers. Obviously totally at ease with his naked state, he clasped her hand. "Nice to meet you, Roxanne." Baine's smile turned positively devilish as he leaned over and kissed her hand.

When Rafe made a growling sound low in his throat, Baine straightened, a mischievous smile on his face. "Wish it could've been under different circumstances though."

Good Lord, these 'creatures of the night' were some of the sexiest men she'd ever met in her life. Roxanne wondered what Liv would say about Baine? If she thought Rafe was hot, her friend would probably fall over in a dead faint at the mere sight of Baine...especially a naked Baine, she thought with an inward chuckle.

Baine met Rafe's gaze with a challenging one. "I'll take care of these wolves, my friend. I believe you should go clean up a bit." He raised an eyebrow and glanced at the moon, a feral grin on his face. "The night is still young."

"Thanks, Baine," Rafe said as he clasped her hand and literally dragged her in the direction of the swamp.

Chapter Eleven

"Rafe!" Roxanne said in exasperation as he walked with purposeful strides, pulling her along beside him.

When he reached the edge of the swamp, Rafe released her hand and dove into the water. Roxanne's heart pounded as she watched him bathe off the blood that coated his body. When he emerged from the swamp, water sluicing off his beautifully carved form, her throat constricted at the gorgeous sight he made.

Rafe walked straight toward her, his expression aggressive and completely focused.

"Take off your shoes," he ordered.

Roxanne's stomach fluttered at this commanding side of Rafe. She did as he asked and before she could say another word, he'd swept her up in his arms and walked right back into the swamp.

Roxanne wasn't at all prepared when he let her go, dropping her in the shallow water.

She came up sputtering, too angry to worry about her fear of swimming.

"Why the hell did you do that?"

His gaze wasn't on her face. He reached out and touched her wet nipple through her shirt, sliding his finger over the tip. Man, was she ever glad she didn't wear a bra tonight.

Roxanne gasped at his intimate touch. Before she could respond, Rafe swiftly pulled her wet shirt over her head and tossed it on to the embankment.

Fire burned in his gaze as he grasped her waist and yanked her toward him, clamping his mouth on her distended nipple. Roxanne's hands landed on his shoulders to steady herself but as Rafe's teeth scraped her sensitive bud, then nipped the pink tip, her fingers speared through his wet hair, pulling him closer.

Excitement shot through her, a heady rush of adrenaline that went straight to her sex, making her ache for more.

Rafe kissed his way up her collarbone and then to her neck. "If we continue, I'm not going to stop, Rocky. Tonight is for keeps."

He pulled back and met her gaze. "You're ripe to breed and my body is primed to mate. I helped you get your life back today. I'm asking you to help me get back mine." He cupped her face, rubbing his thumbs along her jaw. "I want to make love to you, to make you my lupina mate."

Her heart sang with the knowledge Rafe had finally forgiven himself enough to accept another in his life. At the same time the realization that Rafe had just asked her for a favor…a favor she couldn't refuse if she wanted to pay her debt to Charlotte. Thank God his request was something she also wanted. But she realized giving Rafe the thrill of the chase would make his night that much more exciting.

"And if this isn't what I want?" she asked, breathless.

Rafe's eyes narrowed and his hold tightened. "Then you'd better run, *chère*, as if your life depended on it."

Her blood thrummed and her sex throbbed at his acknowledgment that he wanted her so much she'd have to run to keep him from mating with her.

Roxanne pushed away from him, saying, "I'm not sure that's what I want." Backing away toward the shore, she teased, "Maybe you need to do a little more convincing."

"Rocky," he said in a dark warning tone, a scowl on his face.

As soon as her feet touched the embankment, Roxanne made a show of wiggling out of her wet shorts and underwear. Throwing him a kiss she said, "Show me whatcha got and maybe, just maybe, I'll let you in."

Roxanne took off running when Rafe let out a long howl and shifted to his wolf's form. Her heart pounding in her chest, excitement pumping through her veins, she ran through the woods to the sound of Rafe's huge paws pounding the ground behind her.

Knowing she could never outrun him in wolf form, Roxanne decided to circle around and head back in the direction she came. The water in the swamp would hide her scent. She didn't want to make this hunt easy for Rafe. Panting, she ran as fast as she could. When she reached the swamp, Roxanne's thighs shook and her lungs burned from her exertions. *I really need to exercise more*, she thought, taking big gulps of air.

As she stood there on the embankment waiting, she realized Rafe should've emerged from the woods by now. Where was he? Trepidation filled her at the quiet that seemed to descend over the swamp.

The sound of flapping wings drew her attention as a large bird swooped past her, Roxanne turned to see the black bird shift and change to human form right before her eyes. Rafe laughed at her surprised expression. Picking her up in his arms once more, he carried her into the shallow water.

When he set her down, Rafe continued to hold her close.

"You're mine, Rocky." He kissed her temple and then her jaw before claiming her mouth with his.

Roxanne's arms went around his neck and she held him as close as she could as he deepened their kiss, taking all she had to offer and giving her just as much in return. His hard chest brushed against her sensitive breasts while his erection jutted against her belly. She couldn't get close enough to him, his heat, his seductive lure.

Rafe broke their kiss and swiftly turned her around. Pressing his chest against her back, his erection nudged her backside, letting her know just how much he wanted her.

Sliding his hands down her arms, Rafael threaded his fingers through hers and leaned his entire body against hers while he laved at her neck with his tongue.

"I'll never get enough of every treasure your body has to offer, *chère*," he whispered against her neck as he moved their clasped hands down her belly.

Cupping his hand over her sex, Rafe kept her fingers locked with his and said in a husky voice, "Show me how you like it, Rocky."

Roxanne's blood pounded in her ears at his suggestion that she show him how she pleasured herself while he played an intimate part in learning her body.

When he touched her clit she arched against him and used her hand to guide him to the right amount of pressure and rhythm she needed. When his fingers delved inside her walls, Rafe groaned against her neck and sank his fangs into her throat.

Her knees started to buckle at the erotic sensations slamming through her, but Rafe slid an arm around her waist to support her while she rocked her hips to the thrust of his fingers in and out of her body.

Roxanne's orgasm washed over her in wave after crashing, pleasurable wave. She moaned as Rafe pressed the heel of his hand against her pubic bone, giving her additional friction while he continued to slide his fingers within her.

When the tremors stopped and her heart rate slowed, Rafe withdrew his fangs from her neck. While he licked her wound closed, he continued to skim his hands over her breasts and down her waist as if cherishing every part of her body while he memorized her form with his hands. Roxanne sighed and laid her head back against his chest as he stroked her skin, his movements seductive and arousing.

"I have to taste every part of you, Rocky," he ground out as he grasped her wrist and tugged her down into the murky water. "On your hands and knees, *mon amour*."

Roxanne fell to her hands and knees, her movements stirring up the murky water underneath her. She inhaled deeply, taking in the gardenia scent all around her as Rafe slipped his hands between her legs, pushing them further apart. Roxanne moaned in anticipation and moved her knee in the water, opening her body to him.

Rafe slid his hands across her spine and pressed down slightly saying, "Arch your back, *chère*."

Roxanne did as he asked, feeling completely decadent in such an open position.

When he swiped his tongue across her clit, she whimpered at the brief touch and pressed back against him.

"I didn't think you could taste any better, Rocky but damn, your gorgeous pussy tastes even sweeter now that you're ready to mate," he groaned against her before he thrust his tongue deep in her core.

His actions caused heat to radiate throughout her body, shooting to all of her extremities. Roxanne curled her hands on the swamp bottom, the sensation of the wet dirt squeezing through her fingers only fueling her desire.

The smell of the swamp, the lush greenery surrounding them, overpowered the gardenia scent, reeling her senses with its raw, musky odor.

The bellow of a bull gator along the edge of the swamp made her heart jerk and she froze, fear gripping her. How could she have forgotten about the dangers that lurked all around them?

"Rafe," she started to whisper.

"He won't bother us," he said with confidence as he stroked her body.

The gator forgotten as her body raged for release, Roxanne begged, "Rafe," and pressed against him. She needed him inside her, his thick cock filling her completely, taking her breath away.

Rafael grasped her hips as he pressed his cock against her opening.

"I love you, Rocky," he rasped as he thrust inside her, plunging as deep as her body would accommodate.

Roxanne closed her eyes and moaned at the feeling of completeness their joining brought. She clasped her muscles around him, smiling when he groaned, withdrew and thrust back in.

Again and again he rammed into her until she screamed out in sheer ecstasy as she came, her body shuddering around him.

Roxanne opened her eyes in time to see the gator slip into the water.

Fear and desire raged within her. "The gator," she whispered while the curling sensual suspense built in her belly once more as Rafe continued to move within her, his breathing rampant. Her gaze followed the gator as the creature swam lazily toward them.

I see him, he replied mentally, his voice unconcerned. Her stomach clenched in fear while her core throbbed in desire and the dual emotions caused her heart to speed up to a rampant pace. Adrenaline surged though her veins. With each thrust of his hips against her buttocks, she noticed Rafe withdrew from her less and less until he no longer withdrew from her at all.

While he rocked his hips, penetrating her deeper and deeper, Rafe laid his chest across her back and laced his fingers with hers in the water. She felt safer with his warmth surrounding her.

His masculine scent mixed with the smell of sex and sweat and blood, permeated her senses, causing her to inhale in short rampant breaths. God, she'd never get enough of Rafe's scent. A low, feral growl came from Rafe, rumbling down her back. Suddenly, the gator turned away, moving back toward the shore.

Roxanne's fear subsided allowing her to focus on Rafe's body thrusting inside her, taking possession. With each thrust of his hips against her, Roxanne felt a change take place.

Rafe's cock suddenly felt at least five degrees warmer and it certainly seemed a hell of a lot wider, like there were two of him inside her rubbing along her walls, creating a body-consuming sensual friction. Roxanne froze when an intense cramping sensation gripped her own pelvic muscles. As if it had a mind of its own, her body clamped around the base of his cock and remained that way. Rafe groaned and thrust once, then again as his semen, warmer than it had ever felt before, spread inside her.

The constant gripping sensation of her pelvic muscles created an ache deep in her belly, as if she were on the verge of an orgasm and couldn't quite get there. "Rafe," she whispered, her heart thudding as she panicked at the strange sensation. She wanted to move and give herself release.

"No!" he barked out and held fast to her when she tried to pull away. His own breathing was so erratic, he had to finish his answer mentally, *If you move, you'll hurt both of us, Rocky. What you're feeling is the wolfen mating knot. We're locked together to assure your pregnancy. Soon your body will relax and you'll instinctually know when to move.*

The acute, constant build-up of desire that spiraled through her for several minutes almost had Roxanne in tears. Her arms and thighs shook with the supreme effort it took to remain still. Finally she felt the muscles within her core began to contract on their own in rapid fire succession as if rebounding from being held in one position for too long.

"Can I move now?" she all but sobbed.

"God, please yes." Rafe's groan sounded painful.

Roxanne began to move her hips. Rafe's large size still hadn't subsided and the added fullness was all she needed. She screamed out in sheer delight as she came, in one orgasm after another.

Rafe's groan of satisfaction followed on the heels of her own as he rammed into her in the throes of another release.

Their bodies slick with sweat, Rafe withdrew and carried her to the embankment. Laying back on the grass, he let her roll on her side, but continued to hold her close.

Kissing her forehead, he said, his voice full of deep emotion, "My lupina mate."

Roxanne smiled. "I love you too, Rafe."

When Rafe splayed his fingers over her belly, she asked, "I could really be pregnant?"

"You *are* pregnant," he responded with a confident chuckle.

Roxanne's heart pounded in excitement and she covered his hand with hers.

Lifting her head, she asked, "So when are we leaving?"

He gave her a quizzical look. "Leaving?"

"Yes, to join Ethan's pack."

Rafe sat up on his elbow and stared at her intently. "You want to leave your job and move away to live with a pack?"

She smiled. "Our child will be part wolf and I wouldn't want him to grow up and not know his heritage." She grinned. "With Jake's glowing recommendation, I should be able to get a job anywhere." A frown furrowed her brow for a brief second. "Of course, I'll probably be the only human in the pack."

Rafael gave her a sheepish grin. "Um, a little something I forgot to mention. You will soon have the same capabilities as a hybrid were-vamp."

At her shocked expression, his grin widened.

"I will?" she asked, surprise and excitement coursing through her.

Rafe ran his hand through her wet hair. "When you have the baby, his blood will mix with yours during the delivery, assuring that his mother will be a werewolf. My taking your blood will assure your vampire conversion."

"I'll get to run with the wolves, so to speak?"

Rafe laughed and kissed her forehead. "Yes, you'll hunt with me if you so choose."

She thought for another minute, absorbing and accepting the knowledge of how drastically her life was about to change. She'd sort out the whole hunting thing later, but most important was their child.

"Our baby will be part were-vamp and part human, right?"

Rafael nodded. "Yes, but I'm not sure what powers he or she will have."

He ran a finger along her cheek and said, "Being part of a pack is a very different life, Roxanne. You'll have very little privacy except within your own suite of rooms."

After growing up without a true family, the idea of an extended one really appealed to her. But Rafe sounded as if he were trying to talk her out of living in a pack. Then it hit her...he was afraid he'd lose his solitude, the privacy he'd enjoyed for decades.

"I'll make sure you get your quiet time to paint, Rafe, but I think you should do everything in your power to embrace your heritage, for yourself as well as our child." Glancing at the moon above, she laced her fingers with his and laid her head back down on his chest saying, "Let's embrace the moon together, *mon amour.*"

Rafael's chest swelled, his heart soaring at her words of acceptance. He blinked back tears of joy, then smiled, genuinely smiled, for the very first time in over four decades.

About the author:

Patrice Michelle welcomes mail from readers. You can write to her c/o Ellora's Cave Publishing at 1337 Commerce Drive, Suite 13, Stow OH 44224.

Also by Patrice Michelle:

A Taste For Passion
Bad In Boots: Harm's Hunger

MALÉDICTION

Annie Windsor

Chapter One

Hungry...hungry...hungry...

More urge than word. More drive than thought.

Wind whipped his broad wings and body as his tail shifted to steer him in a circle. Pennsylvania woodlands stretched beneath his sharp gaze, an endless panorama, reeling at mind-altering speeds. Each color caught his attention as he watched for movement, even the twitch of grass above a field mouse. What he really wanted was a rabbit, but he would settle for a squirrel. Even a snake or a frog.

Hungry. Starving!

Nothing moved below. No food. No relief.

Chank Arceneaux's head ached. He was too deep in his predator-host's mind. Deliberately, he concentrated on his physical body for a moment, shifting in his hiding place far below on the ground. The ache of his muscles and the sweat on the back of his neck anchored his soaring consciousness. He was man, not hawk. Only his mind was flying.

Fighting the wind.

Feeling the hunger.

A cry broke from his beak, ripping across the cloudless morning sky—and the woodlands gave way to fields, roads, and a school.

Wrong...wrong...wrong...

The red-shouldered hawk attempted to bank back toward the forest, but Chank gently asserted his will over the bird. The bird fought bitterly, images of its nest and life-mate twisting Chank's gut.

"Not yet," he murmured from the small stand of pines near the elementary school's back entrance. "Just a few more minutes."

The hawk panicked from the psychic contact and flapped too hard, almost tumbling down in the treacherous wind currents. Chank withdrew his consciousness a fraction, but kept his mental hold on the hungry predator.

Slowly, the bird complied with Chank's direction and circled above the elementary school. Through the hawk's eyes, Chank scanned a small hill patched with dirt, gym sets, and clumps of grass wilting in unseasonable heat. The school, a crooked crescent made of brown brick and cream-colored aluminum, spilled down the hill and curved toward an affiliated junior high complex. A battered chain-link fence separated the two facilities.

At Chank's careful urging, the hawk pumped its wings and soared around the hill, staying neatly within the confines of the elementary schoolyard, as if the chain-link were high enough to put a barrier in the sky. Chank once more surveyed the territory, and—

There. Standing beside that mower on the Middle School side of the fence.

Roosevelt James. A piece of human garbage. A child-murdering psychopath from the hottest reaches of hell who had been arrested, escaped jail prior to trial, and eluded the police for nearly fourteen years...doing God knows what to pass his time.

*Why do such monsters look so...*regular? It was all Chank could do to rein in his rage and remain calm until he understood the entire situation.

James scrubbed his sunburned cheeks with a worn red handkerchief. He was a tall, spindly man who looked like a scarecrow because his long arms and legs were too flexible. *Stuffed with straw instead of bone.* That's what the surviving child had told police all those years ago.

Some sort of genetic skeletal problem, Chank had figured. This deduction had led him to hospital birth records within the perp's age range and over forty possibilities, scattered all over the United States.

Roosevelt James was possibility number thirty-seven.

Chank Arceneaux was a patient man.

"Nose like a banana, and he hadn't shaved." The kid had been one hell of a witness.

When Chank read through the Cold Case file, he had imagined what he now saw through the hawk's abnormally keen eyes: dark fuzzy stubble on Roosevelt James's pointed chin. Matching stubble shaded the top of his head.

The hawk screamed its hunger again.

A contest of wills now, with the predator in the air and the predator on the ground.

Chank braced himself for the final test, squeezing the radio in his hand. His thumb brushed the page button. Two punches and an army of special agents would descend on the school. The doors had been locked. The students had been moved to an auditorium for an impromptu presentation on drug laws and safety.

All ready. All arranged.

Just…one…last…step.

To be sure.

Chank grimaced, staying in the bird's mind a moment longer. He knew he needed to make the leap, but his soul recoiled against it.

Roosevelt James stuffed his handkerchief back into his rear pocket and stared skyward. His face was somber, and his mouth formed a tight line at the sight of the hawk.

Chank watched through the bird's eyes. Was the bastard secretly a wildlife fanatic? Did he know the hawk's transgression on man-territory was unusual? Somehow, cagey asswipes like Roosevelt James always seemed to have just the right bit of useless knowledge to help them evade justice.

As if reading Chank's thoughts, James trained his cool blue eyes on the bird. He rubbed his pencil neck, instinctively trying to look casual, as if he were taking a well-deserved break.

Chank-in-the-hawk continued what he hoped looked like an innocent search and hunt pattern. Anxiety gripped him as it always did at this crucial juncture. An icy voice rang from the depths of his tortured past.

Well, hello there, little sparrow. Welcome to the big sky.

He would never forget that moment, the first and only time a predator-host felt and understood his presence. He had been miles from home, but sensed something amiss. He had gone sailing back toward his family's bayou mansion, using the consciousness of a small Kestral—a Sparrow Hawk. Damn, but it had been devilishly hard to keep the bird off its evening diet of grasshoppers and lizards.

When he reached the boundaries of his family's land, he had sensed a powerful dark energy, something he associated only with large predators, like wolves. Lions, tigers—those he had never felt, but he imagined them, and when he did, they felt like the dark energy at Sanctuaire.

Chank had tried to leap from the Kestral's mind into the huge predator's thoughts, and...

Well, hello there, little sparrow...

Such a backlash!

The Kestral had plummeted to swampy earth, lying half-in and half-out of the black bayou waters, dying as the screaming started.

Chank's family, being murdered.

He had been stunned and helpless in the dying Kestral's mind, his body too far away to help. He had been too slow to save even one of the people he loved.

Well, hello there...

Chank forced himself to take slow, relaxed breaths. The hawk let out a cry of rage.

Below him, James shuffled back a few steps, then stopped. "Fuckin' birds," he grumbled. "Give me the creeps, screamin' like that." He squinted up, and Chank had a sudden feeling that James sensed he was being watched.

With a flick of wings, Chank widened the hawk's circle, straying over the edge of the chain-link fence before he dared to glance back at his quarry. Roosevelt James drew his thin eyebrows together. He started to turn his back, made ready to walk away—and Chank knew he had to act.

Shoving his old pains and fears aside, he steeled his gut, clenched his teeth, and dropped from the hawk's mind into the consciousness of Roosevelt James.

The entry into the man's thoughts was seamless, which answered Chank's first question. Yes, Roosevelt James was a human predator. Chank could only enter, track, and influence the minds of true predators.

In short order, after flipping through only a few of the bastard's memories, Chank's second question was answered. Yes, this man was definitely the depraved, murdering son of a bitch they were after. Genetic testing would later prove that. For now, Chank's word would be enough for his waiting team. Even though they had no idea *how* Chank found killers so efficiently, they knew that to date, he had never been wrong.

Keeping his consciousness in the back of James's mind like a time bomb too quiet to tick, Chank struggled to control his actual hand back in the pine bower, some 300 yards away. His thumb punched the radio page button twice.

Almost as one, the FBI Cold Case Squad and approximately 30 additional special agents burst from cover, weapons drawn and aimed at James.

"Freeze! Hands up! On your knees!"

Twenty or more voices, shouting at once.

Chank heard them through James's ears. He felt the flare of James's panic. The scarecrow man reached the separating fence in two strides and started over it like a minor obstacle. He had visions of running down the south hall of the junior high school.

"Stop! Hands up and on your knees! We will shoot!"

Concentrating all his energy, all his power, Chank thought *FALL.*

James wavered in his climb.

Fall, you bastard. Mais, oui. *Fall!*

"Who are you?" the killer bleated.

And then Roosevelt James fell, right into the waiting circle of agents.

Less than an hour later, Chank watched the car drive off with the babbling child-murderer. He felt more tired than triumphant—and relieved to be in his own head again. The gut-level satisfaction of catching the monster pleased him, sure. But, damn. Being that close to sick bloodlust and madness...

"Another one bites the dust," muttered a nearby agent, filling out forms. The young man cut his eyes toward Chank. "Batman strikes again."

Suppressing a sigh, Chank moved away from the cluster of his peers and stood, arms folded, against the dividing fence.

Batman.

He had been called Batman since his first day at the Academy, when he effortlessly climbed to the roof of a training building to investigate a bit of staged evidence. His longer-than-FBI-norm black hair, deep voice, thick accent, and brooding Cajun features only strengthened the mystique—not to mention his uncanny solve rate when he worked active cases. And now, even in the Cold Case Squad, the nickname followed him.

He supposed there were worse nicknames.

Maybe.

As he tried to relax, the school doors opened. With the threat over, the building was out of lockdown, and kids headed out for phys ed and recess. The principal was answering questions at the side door, an I'm-so-sued look on his face.

He had, after all, hired a child molester and murderer with no background check.

Chank watched the bouncing kids and hoped Roosevelt James had injured none of them. He felt the usual temptation, to track and reinvade James's mind and torture him with the pain he caused his victims. Chank didn't do that, however. He also didn't find a new predator-host and cause James's escort to wreck in some bloody, final fashion.

Judgment wasn't Chank's job. Only tracking and capture. He had learned little from his family before their slaughter when he was nine years old, but he had learned that much.

You're part human, son. Here to help, so help. But don't overstep. After all, you don't know everything.

Chank's headache intensified. The mental impulses of nearby hunting animals knocked at his consciousness. A few children on the playground and more than a few of the agents had predatory tendencies. Their aggressive instincts bothered him, too. He rubbed his eyes. God, he needed to go home for awhile, back to Louisiana, to Sanctuaire. He needed some peace.

The imprint of the hawk lingered in his thoughts, and he remembered the bird's fierce, protective impulses for its life-mate.

There was no life-mate waiting for Chank Arceneaux at Sanctuaire. Only quiet. Only loneliness. Chank had vowed never to marry and pass on *le malédiction*, the curse of his *Trakyr* senses.

For a moment, Chank's focus narrowed to a group of playing children. A little girl, smiling, twisting her blonde braids. A little boy hopping on one foot, huge grin pasted in place.

The pounding in his head neared unbearable. Once more, that hateful voice from his past echoed sharp in his mind.

"Hello, little sparrow," he muttered, staring at the happy kids but seeing only his oldest and most vicious nemesis: Bordelon, last of the *Huntyrs*.

Bordelon was the vicious beast who murdered Chank's family.

There's a madness that comes from being the last of a species, he thought grimly. *A relentless sense of desperation. But it ends with him, with me.*

If Chank never loved, never married, never reproduced — and if he succeeded in capturing or killing Bordelon before he died, the *Trakyrs* and *Huntyrs* would become a footnote in forgotten volumes of paranormal lore. Hell, only the oldest of Voudon practitioners and true Wiccans even knew the two races exist.

"It's better this way," Chank told himself for the millionth time, believing it with most of his heart.

The hawk's feral love for its mate — there was no room for such emotions in Chank's life, even if there was one woman who almost made him change his mind every time he saw her.

Damn good thing she tended to ignore him. *Oui.* Damn good thing she probably hated him.

A sharp buzzing sound startled him from his reflections.

He jammed his hand into his pocket and grabbed his pager. The numeric code made him lift one eyebrow in surprise. The director wanted his help on an active case. In Philly. Now. Car en route.

The squeal of tires in the school parking lot made him look up.

"Scratch that. Car here."

Without a backward glance at the scene of his latest conquest, Chank Arceneaux strode toward his waiting ride, trying not to think about where he might be going — or the woman he would see when he got there.

Chapter Two

Too late, too late. A Ph.D. in psychology, the best training in criminology – all for nothing. For shit! Kiri Auckland's agony scalded her insides. She didn't know what was worse – the barely contained rage threatening to blow her head apart, or the horrid feelings of guilt, of regret, of such complete failure.

Clearly oblivious to the lamentations of an FBI profiler who should have delivered them from such a chore, medical examiners taped off the scene across the street from Kiri. A non-descript row house on Marlyn Road, in Overbrook, a quiet Philadelphia subdivision on the nicer outskirts of town.

"Not South Philly, where I saw it happening." Kiri cringed. The sound of her own voice doubled her headache, and the square lines of the house, eerily outlined in Pennsylvania's hot afternoon sun, seemed to form and distort, form and distort. The cloudless summer sky should have lifted her spirits a little, but nothing could soothe her today. She wondered if anything would ever soothe her again.

How could this happen? She adjusted her sunglasses and wished her head would go ahead and burst, it hurt so badly, right at the temples. *I was riding the bastard's mind. I saw him in South Philly. Damn it!*

Had her special awareness of the killer been thrown off because of her lunch date with Jon? The bastard left her hanging. Yeah, she'd been a little pissed, but she couldn't imagine that disrupting her special "radar."

Granted, Jon's sexual impulses were enough to static even extrasensory perceptions, not that he'd ever acted on any of them. Nice-looking or not, the guy was plain weird, and Kiri had figured she was well shed of him. No more older men. Never again. Four dates were more than enough, especially since the jerk didn't show for their fifth.

Maybe she should give up men completely. After all, she'd never had a truly satisfying relationship, never found a man who could keep up with her sexually, much less please her. Work was her god, her hero, her all and everything, and she didn't see that changing. Men just weren't worth her time, beyond the occasional fling. And Jon had certainly been no exception to that fact. Distant laughter, a few chaste kisses—he was as cold as they came. An evening with him left her bored, frustrated, and in the end, a little angry. Which was unusual in itself. Typically, Kiri's emotions were reserved for work and work alone.

When Jon stood her up, she had stalked out of the downtown restaurant, thinking of ten wicked messages to leave on Jon's voice mail—and *known* something was wrong.

The knowing had struck her with the force of a storm, much stronger than usual. She had felt the primal, evil stirrings of the serial murderer she had been tracking for almost four months. It had taken no effort to home in on his location—or his intentions. Making her usual calls, Kiri had mobilized the task force…and sent them to the wrong address. The wrong neighborhood, the wrong side of town.

What the hell? She scuffed her flat black shoe against the grass and dirt in the median marking midpoint between the two strips of row houses on Marlyn Road. This had never happened before. From the moment Kiri had profiled her first case at Quantico, she had connected with the killer she sought without much difficulty. All it took was studying the method, the motive. Getting into the murderer's head figuratively—and then getting into his head literally.

Like a faint smear of blood on the fabric of the universe, Kiri would begin to sense the stain of the murderer on humanity itself. And then she would sense the killer's emotions, track him, and take him down.

Well, she did the tracking. A task force actually did the muscle work. At the ripe old age of twenty-nine, Kiri Auckland had become the most successful profiler the FBI had ever trained. No completed homicides once she caught the killer's emotional "scent." A few paperwork mistakes, a couple of rookie missteps in that first month, five long years ago—but since then, clean as polished glass and twice as smooth. She had a gift, for God's sake.

And now this. Fat lot of good my gift did…

Her thoughts trailed off. She still didn't know the victim's name. She knew what was in that house, though. Pain and suffering beyond mention, and a body almost beyond recognition. There would be no signs of struggle, as if the victim had gone willingly to her horrid death. She would have been cut and burned and misused. And around that, the bastard would have drawn a *vèvè*, a Voudon symbol signifying one of the many Voudon gods, in the poor girl's blood.

Kiri had been reading all about the true religion of Voudon, as well as its cinematic perversion, Voodoo. The asshole was practicing a twisted version of the actual faith, performing rituals at certain times, in certain ways, to increase his own power. This murder, so close to the full moon—no doubt the *vèvè* would be a paen to one of the fiercer, more frightening gods.

Voodoo nonsense, some of the medical examiners would say as they photographed the nightmare, but Kiri didn't agree. She was from the deep South, from the Gulf Coast. Her own unusual gifts and her time in the swampy backlands had taught her there were more forces on Earth than mortal beings understood. Whether or not this murdering bastard tapped into those forces was anyone's guess. He had been dubbed the *Houngon*, pronounced "ooo-gon," by some smartass reporter who knew the name for male priests.

Maybe he was an *houngon*, and maybe he wasn't. After being wrong about a murderer's actions for the first time in her career, Kiri wasn't ruling out anything.

She folded her arms against another wave of bitter regret and self-blame. At least the sunglasses afforded her some protection from the glares of the ten or so nearby agents and the onlookers clotting on either side of barricades protected by Philly's finest. News vans hadn't arrived yet, but they wouldn't be far behind.

Damn the sun. I'm going to go blind and fry. She felt her sensitive skin beginning to blister. Even though her hair was long enough and black enough to shield her cheeks and forehead, she kept it pulled back, professional-style, while she was on the job. The black knee-length skirt, the long-sleeved white blouse, and the black suit jacket also served the cause of professionalism. Her full figure strained against the seams, swelling slightly in the stifling humidity. Maybe she'd get lucky, puff up like a balloon, and drift out to sea.

Luck, however, wasn't on her side. That fact was yet again confirmed by a lone figure, striding along the row house's roof. The dark-headed man seemed to be a phantom in the heat shimmering off the roof's flat surface. No doubt who he was, though it twisted Kiri's guts to acknowledge his presence.

Batman.

Chancellor Arceneaux, her counterpart in the investigative unit, the "golden child" who had wowed the Bureau with his solve rate and unbelievable instincts before she came along, had arrived. If the Bureau had already brought him in, then the magnitude of her blunder was even greater than she first imagined. She'd likely be fired, just as soon as media attention waned.

Kiri had displaced Batman in her first few weeks on active duty. Sent him packing to Cold Case, the unit assigned to older murders where the scent had chilled and the catch-rate plunged to around ten percent. Word had it that Batman was none too pleased with that turn of events, but Kiri didn't know for certain. They crossed paths nearly every week, but managed to avoid talking to each other.

He was too quiet. The way he looked at her made her sweat. And looking at him…definitely risky.

Because he's too gorgeous for human eyes. Because he'd never be interested in a woman like me — guys like that don't go for Plus size. Besides, I just swore off men five minutes ago.

But Batman wasn't a man.

He was a dark god.

Kiri groaned inwardly. Arceneaux had been on leave when she got assigned, and by the time he came back — well, too late. There was a new girl in town.

A girl who'll likely be on the first bus back to the Mississippi coast.

Kiri glared through the dark filters of her lenses as Batman lowered himself from the roof of the victim's row house. Philadelphia's "trinity" homes, three-story turn of the century structures packed 25 to a half-a-block, weren't as tall as high-rises, but still, seeing someone rappel from one of the linked, flat roofs disconcerted her. Batman was known for climbing up and down at will, examining scenes like a half-mad monkey.

"Son of a bitch." Kiri's partner Dane Hughes, special agent in charge, stalked over to her, coat flung over one shoulder. His midnight skin glistened, and he held his lanky frame rigid. Sweat stains were spreading around the neck and sides of his white shirt. "Looks like a goddamned stunt actor."

Kiri said nothing. Dane sounded too cheerful, and his moustache twitched repeatedly. Something was wrong, beyond the obvious.

"Director's flying in." Dane spoke evenly, as if reciting a movie schedule. His teeth seemed too large and too white when he smiled. "We fucked the dog, big time."

Dully, Kiri turned her attention back to the scene across the street. She catalogued Batman's impressive height and the way his muscles bulged in his black t-shirt and black jeans. Men could wear jeans to work, even at the FBI. If she did it, she'd probably be demoted in a day. Women had to "keep up appearances," and all that—and doubly so for big women. Kiri doubted she'd have ever gotten her spot in Profiling if it hadn't been for her too-strong-to-ignore instincts.

Arceneaux could get a job anywhere, though. Just by walking in the door. She watched him move around the raised porch of the row house, descend the stairs, and drop to one knee, placing his hand on the sidewalk.

Dane cleared his throat. "Vic's name was Carolyn Demeter. She was twenty-eight, getting her Master's in Nursing over at U-Penn."

Probably a nun. Or married with five kids. Kiri blinked furiously, refusing to cry. Across the road, Batman stood and spoke with three uniformed officers. Medical examiners swarmed like termites, dusting and bagging and scraping everything in sight. A dull whump-whump-whump announced the approach of a news chopper, or maybe the venerable Bureau director.

"She wasn't married," Dane finished, "but she was engaged to the governor's son."

Kiri didn't know whether to laugh or finally cry. "Is that why the director's coming? Only because she was a somebody—no, wait. Engaged to a somebody. I should have known."

This time, it was Dane who said nothing. They had argued politics and ethics enough times for him to know better. Kiri knew he thought she was foolish for focusing so fully on the job and the job alone.

Do you want to be in the field forever? What about the future, girl…

She sighed, just about the time one of the medical examiners handed Batman a small baggie, gesturing back toward the row house's open door. Arceneaux stared at the bag's contents, then shielded his eyes and glanced upward in the direction of the chopper noise. Despite his fame within the Bureau, the man was known for being camera-shy. He avoided publicity like a plague. Said it compromised his anonymity in investigations.

Be anonymous, be arrogant, be whatever you are, Kiri thought fiercely, ignoring the ins and outs of politics and the weight of the forces aligning to punish her for her failure. *Be better than me, I don't care. Just find the hateful prick who did this.*

Once more, Batman stared down at the baggie in his hand. Then he looked up—and straight at Kiri.

For some reason, her heart began a staccato march, keeping time with Batman's strides as he moved toward her across the sidewalk, the road, and the few steps of grass between them. Kiri was vaguely aware of Dane Hughes speaking gruffly to nearby agents, but she had no idea what the words meant. Her world had narrowed to Chancellor Arceneaux and the ten feet, nine feet, eight feet separating them.

Kiri's nostrils flared as she took in his strong but enticing man's scent. Something like pine, but not as sweet or overpowering. Almost cedar-like, with some salt and earth mixed in for good measure. Her profiler's mind clicked off other features, like his hair, which was thick and darker than hers, if that was possible. She realized it was pulled back into a short ponytail that hung just past his shoulders.

A crack Fibby with a ponytail. How does he get away with shit like that?

But he always did.

Must be the looks.

High cheekbones, a tan so dark he looked baked to well-done, ink-black eyes with a hawkish cant—and dear God. They just didn't make real men with bodies like his. Arceneaux was so tall he shaded her as he stopped about three feet in front of her.

He looked arrogant, yes. And intelligent, forceful, even overpowering—and yet, his features had a weary edge, as if he had been burdened too long with secrets and grief.

Even though she had tried before and failed, Kiri instinctively reached out with her extra senses. Half-staring, half-concentrating, she tried to find his emotional signature, the essence that would tell her if he was friend or foe, sane or insane, and so many subtleties in between. In her mind's eye, her thoughts grew wings and fluttered outside her head to circle around him.

And hit an invisible wall, and ricocheted back to lance through her eyes like so many flying swords.

Kiri cried out, swayed, and almost fell.

Strong hands caught her. Dane Hughes on her left and Arceneaux on her right.

The helicopter they had been hearing finally crested over the row houses of Marlyn Road. Numbers reflected off the side in garish television colors.

"R-Reporters," Kiri managed to stammer, and then the powerful hands pulled her toward Dane's standard-issue brown Ford Taurus with no whitewall tires. Kiri could sense her partner's concern and embarrassment. Curiosity, disdain, distress, and a smattering of smug satisfaction emanated from nearby agents and police officers. From the crowd came a low hum of emotional excitement, blended with horror and fear. Rabid desire floated at her from above, and Kiri knew this would be the reporters, moving in for the scoop.

From Batman on her right—nothing. Not so much as a ripple of feeling. What was he, some sort of Cyborg? She had never failed to "read" another person, but every time she tried to sense Arceneaux, he came across in a flat line. And this time, he seemed to have pushed back, shoved her away from his thoughts.

Kiri struggled with a sudden terror as Dane opened the back door to his Taurus and helped her inside. She slid across the seat, wrenched her arm out of Arceneaux's grip, and stared at him as he eased in beside her.

Batman offered her a brooding frown, slammed the door, and punched a button, locking Dane Hughes out of his own car. Dane didn't seem to mind. He was straightening his jacket and going into press-mode.

Don't leave me! Kiri's mental shout followed Dane as he walked away from the Taurus, but of course, he didn't hear her. Thank God the car was running, the air blasting, because another dose of heat on top of her fear and vicious head pain might have knocked her flat.

Turning her attention back to Arceneaux, she opened her mouth to ask him who he thought he was, *what* he was—but all she said was, "I can unlock the door on this side."

Arceneaux shook his head. "*Coo-yon.* We got no time for those media bastards."

His rich bass tones and the depth of his Cajun accent shocked Kiri so badly that her head cleared. *Coo-yon.* Spelled properly *couillon*— Cajun slang for foolish. Foolishness—he was telling her that getting out of the car would be stupid. God, it had been years since she heard the cadence of her grandmother's voice. Decades.

Chank had never talked much around her, and now she wished he had.

Before she could ask him where he was from, his liquid-black eyes bored into hers. Something like puzzlement contorted his perfect face, followed by surprise, then irritation. As if remembering at the last second, he whipped the medical examiner's baggie out of his waistband and held it up.

"What you know about this?" he asked in that spine-tingling rumble, shaking the little package. "The *Houngon* left it behind in the *vèvè*, where we couldn't miss it."

If the circumstances had been different, Kiri might have melted into a puddle at his feet just from the sound of his voice—and she was no easy mark. Damn, this man had some kind of power, but this was work, and he was dangerous. He could be feeling anything. He could be a hero, a killer, or an alien from Pluto, for all she could tell. How could she even think about such things when a poor woman lay dead across the street—because she, Kiri, had failed?

Because I couldn't read the killer. Because the bastard fooled me somehow. Her eyes narrowed. She moved her gaze from Arceneaux to the baggie, and then her head really started to spin.

Inside was a single long lock of jet-black hair with a slight curl on the end, just like hers. Tentatively, she reached out, and Arceneaux allowed her to take the little bag into her hands.

Even through the plastic, she could feel her own emotional spoor. She reached a hand up and stroked the side of her head, as if hunting for where the hair came from, all the while trying to piece together how this was possible.

Sinking deeper into the spoor, she caught a trace of someone else. A familiar, yet frustratingly pungent remnant.

Kiri's eyes widened.

Oh, my God. Heat consumed her, this time from inside instead of outside. She nearly crushed the baggie in her hand. *Son of a fucking bitch!*

Jon.

Jon Bordelon!

Chapter Three

Most of the time, Chank Arceneaux's mind and heart resided with the dead. His past, his present, and his future intertwined with lives stolen away too soon, and he himself lived wrapped in the near-suffocating cocoon of his own five senses.

It was safer that way, for him and for any woman he might otherwise pursue.

Like this one.

Kiri Auckland had been the first female to jolt him back from his self-enforced emotional exile—literally the first moment he met her five years ago. She had a force of spirit, a personality that walked in the room before she did. In a sea of dark suits and jaded attitudes, she…glittered.

He had tried to read her then, get a sense of her true heart, but he couldn't.

That only increased his desire to get to know her, so of course, he avoided her. Somehow, though, they ended up at the same lunch spots, the same meetings, the same trainings.

Now, here she was, distracting him in the middle of a crime scene investigation.

Dieu.

He gazed at her, amazed, once again captured by the mix of innocence and almost carnivorous strength. Her soft southern accent, that skin, her coal hair, even the warm depths of her dark eyes—she had to have Creole blood, maybe even more than she knew. Sometimes Creole babies came in porcelain instead of sultry brown. Throwbacks to the more European mix, before the newcomers adapted to the differing climate of this continent.

She was well-proportioned, soft to look at, rounded and full and womanly. God, but he hated the walking skeletons who threw themselves at him. He had no desire to bed cadavers or little girls. This woman, though—damn, but he could get used to looking at her more closely. All the time. She would fill his arms, feel so soft against him when he pulled her close…

Stop. Merde!

Without shame or hesitation, she seemed to sink into the baggie she held tightly in her sun-pinked hands.

Foolishness, he chastised himself in a voice surprisingly like that of *Maman* Rubie, the old *mam'bo* on Daemon Swath who once ministered to the needs of his family. *Don't look at her long. This curse you carry, you swore you'd never pass it on.*

Maman had seen to him at Sanctuaire after the tragedy, and she was the only living being who knew what he *really* was. And until Chank met Kiri, *Maman* Rubie had been the only human he couldn't "read" with his special senses.

Why? He directed the question to the absent *Maman*, as if she were sitting in the front seat. *I am* Trakyr. *Why can't I sense this woman's basic nature?*

He could read all other living essences within his range. And as always, every predator from overzealous agents and cops to a fox in a hole some miles away. At the moment, the small, mean impulses of sewer rats hammered on his defenses. Must have been thirty of them, scuttling along the tunnels below the pavement. Predators came through like screams on his radar, and all he had to do was flick his attention this way or that to absorb what they experienced. Chank Arceneaux had spent his life seeing, hearing, tasting, touching, and smelling the world through such blood-hungry beasts.

Saner minds like Kiri Auckland's — well, of those, he knew little.

Kiri shifted in her seat, clearly using some sort of enhanced perception to examine the hair he had presented to her. The color and texture left little doubt that the hair might be a match for hers. It could have been his, but he was almost certain it wasn't. His abilities didn't extend to the inanimate, but he suspected hers might.

Chank had been watching Kiri since she took his place in Profiling, but he had never approached her alone or asked her about the special senses he thought she had. All along, he'd been aware that she would be too much of a temptation. Living a celibate life was a real bitch sometimes, *oui*.

Besides, she was educated and cultured. Very…proper, from what he could discern. Swamp rats from Louisiana wouldn't be her speed.

She seemed more a Vanderbilt University and mint julep type. Probably screamed if she saw a crawfish up close.

And yet, here she was, princess in the flesh, in the back seat of an FBI Taurus. She was…right next to him, so close he could smell the gentle scent of woman's perspiration and warm vanilla. If he tried long enough, he could probably peg the brand of lotion and bath soap.

The hunger of a nearby predator, a cat, made Chank turn his head just as Kiri flinched and crumpled the evidence bag like she wanted to fling it out the window. Something had upset her deeply, and now proceeded to etch itself along every line and muscle of her sunburned face.

"What is it?" Chank shifted his focus back to her so fast he got dizzy. He hadn't felt so off-balance since he was ten years old and stealing his first kiss from Marie Beauregard over at St. Elizabeth's Parish. The sudden urge to throttle whatever or whomever had bothered this woman made him narrow his eyes. "Tell me what you see, *chère.*"

Kiri looked stricken. "I don't know what you're talking about."

"*Mais, oui,* you do." Chank did his best to ignore the cat—closer now, hungry, on the prowl. He managed a smile despite the telltale hardening of his cock and *autre.* Damn things had minds of their own, and the worst timing. "You see things, know things others don't, just like I do. We don't need these secrets, you and me."

"Don't speak to me like we're old friends, Agent Arceneaux." Kiri's eyes flashed. She scooted a little ways away, then attempted a glare and failed. They locked eyes, and for a moment, she seemed pliable, a little more open.

Chank's heart ached, watching her struggle with herself. He knew how badly it could scar a sensitive soul to see death all around, and he knew how difficult it was for women to achieve respect in the old boy's club of the FBI. Don't feel, don't cry, stop being female, deny your woman's strengths, be *male* if you want to get ahead. This insistence that femininity was somehow weak infuriated Chank.

Most FBI agents had never known a woman as powerful as *Maman* Rubie, and they wouldn't likely notice her if they did. They wouldn't sense the depth of inner strength, the well of passion and feeling in a woman like Kiri Auckland.

So much worse for them, oui.

Seconds passed. Chank smelled fresh air and meat as the hungry cat scented prey. A bird. Yes. *Bird, bird, bird...* He rubbed his eyes to shut out the feline, as usual with minimal luck. *Maman* Rubie had taught him some tricks, made him some potions, but peace was hard to come by.

The silence between Kiri and Chank grew, obscured by the crowd noise outside the Taurus. He didn't dare break it. She was skittish, this one, both professionally and personally. The next move needed to be hers, or she would never trust him.

Gradually, her harder veneer reasserted itself, and Kiri Auckland became all business again.

"Is that your hair in the bag?" Chank asked, his voice huskier than he intended.

She nodded.

"How?"

A sigh, a shrug. "I don't know."

Chank tensed. His *Trakyr* senses might be failing him, but his lawman's instincts told him she was holding something back. He cursed himself for not befriending her before this, so that she might share her secrets.

"Would you tell me if you did know?" Lame, but he couldn't think of better.

Kiri evaluated him with eyes like glittering black diamonds. Her closed expression was answer enough.

"I'm not your enemy," he offered, turning his hands palm up. "If you hadn't taken my spot in Profiling, I would have let it go, *oui*."

"Convenient." Her curtness increased as her hands strangled the evidence baggie. "Nice to know I wasn't chosen on my merit—that you were leaving anyway."

"Not every man in the FBI is a competitive, self-absorbed bastard." His upturned palms clenched into fists. "Give me a chance?"

"Are we finished here, Bat—er, Agent Arceneaux?"

Now Chank couldn't help another smile.

Batman. She almost called me Batman. From her, I wouldn't mind, non. *Where's my cape?*

"We aren't finished until you tell me what you're holding back." He intended to sound friendly, but knew his words came out surly.

She glared at him, and an insanely protective urge rose as he thought about the *Houngon* involving Kiri in his crimes. Was the bastard becoming obsessed with her? Could it somehow be Chank's fault, for liking Kiri?

No. Mais, non. *Please!* But the worry rang true, much to Chank's dismay. Yes, it made an awful sort of sense, that the *Houngon* would use such a woman to bait him—a woman Chank admired, even if from a distance.

His lack of focus cost him.

For a moment, the scene in the car shifted to pavement and grass. The top of a bush scrubbed Chank's head as he hungrily eyed a nearby Mockingbird. His stomach rumbled. He kneaded the earth with his paws, unsheathing his claws as he crouched—

Damn!

Chank blinked hard, jerking himself out of the cat's mind and forcing his attention back to Kiri.

"Tell me what you're hiding," he urged with new vigor. "You need an ally. I understand the burden of...extra senses."

Kiri answered by staring past him, out the side window of the Taurus and into the crowd beyond. From the corner of his eye, Chank could see Dane Hughes working the reporters, pandering to the audience. Dane was a born publicist, the ideal special agent in charge.

"Don't want to embarrass you or cause you trouble, *catin*." He deliberately made his voice calm, as soothing as possible, despite a powerful urge to roar with guilt and frustration. "I just want—"

"I'm not your doll, damn it. Or your honey, or your sweetheart, in English or in French." Kiri's expression turned bland. She wasn't being waspish, only firm. "I grew up on the coast. I speak enough *patois* to get along, so save your Cajun charm. My name is Kiri Auckland. Agent Auckland to you. Yes, it's my hair, and no, I don't know how it got in the *vèvè*."

She paled as she said this. Chank wondered if she was thinking about the dead woman or the woman's blood, used to paint the symbol.

"You're lying," Chank said quietly. "And we both know if you don't tell somebody the truth, the next *vèvè* might be drawn in your blood."

Kiri's upper lip curled in answer. She fixed him with a cold stare and said the last thing he expected to hear from her beautiful cultured mouth.

"*Bec mon chu.*"

With that pronouncement, she threw the baggie on the seat between them, slid sideways, punched the lock release, and left the Taurus in a swirl of black skirt, vanilla musk, and indignation.

Bec mon chu. Kiss my ass.

"Love to," Chank murmured, watching her ample, enticing hips sway as she stalked into a gaggle of milling black suits and white coats.

Too bad it could never be.

Chank knew in his gut that her involvement *was* his fault. He also knew he had to get as far from Kiri Auckland as possible, without confession of his interest. Her only chance was for him not to care—and that would be hard, indeed.

Chapter Four

Two Weeks Later

"Son of a bitch." Kiri rubbed her grimy neck. Sweat drenched her cotton blouse and black jeans, and mosquitoes treated her *Skintastic* like an aphrodisiac. She smacked at her exposed cheeks and arms as her pirogue sliced across the bayou's inky backwater.

Son of a bitch, son of a bitch...

She wasn't thinking of the stooped man poling the boat through Louisiana's largest, deepest swamp—the man with the leather skin and three-toothed smile. Pascal. Yes, that was his name. He'd charged her a small fortune to take her where she wanted to go, and mumbled lots of nonsense about poisoned ground, hexes, monsters, and the walking dead. She had cash, though, and he caved in a big hurry when she flashed the green.

Son of a bitch, son of a bitch...

She wasn't even thinking of Batman, Chank Arceneaux, though the memory of his intense eyes and scorching touch intruded at every opportunity. Arceneaux was probably miles from here, doing something important and well-publicized. Kiri could care less.

Son of a bitch, son of a bitch...

Her litany was for Jon Bordelon, the *Houngon*, and the way he had played her like a smooth hand of poker. He had *touched* her for God's sake. On the hand. On the neck. Even kissed her on the cheek a few times, which was probably when the dickhead snipped the lock of her hair he used to set her up in the Overbrook killing. And then somehow, he'd misdirected her with his mind, made her look like a fool—and murdered a girl just to show her he could.

Nothing had ever made Kiri want vengeance so badly. She could see Jon in her mind, with his salt-and-pepper black hair, cropped military-style—and that maddening little beard, covering his lips and chin, cut as close as his hair. The bastard had a scar from his left ear to his nose, sweeping under his eye like an extra cheekbone.

Had she ever really found him handsome? *Damn!* At least they had never been intimate in any way. The very thought made her want to vomit.

He was insane. All those killings, the dark rituals to increase his "power"—for what? Friggin' pathological asswipe.

Kiri had tracked Bordelon halfway to hell and back since that awful day in Philly. She'd had plenty of time to do it, considering her suspension from the Bureau while certain "irregularities" in her handling of the *Houngon* case were investigated—but the bastard's spoor seemed to pop up here and there, then vanish completely. Kiri finally decided to go to the source, to the Atchafalaya, where public records indicated one Jon Debrais Bordelon had been born, with a birth date that matched Kiri's guess about Bordelon's age—about seventeen years older than her.

Assuming she had his real name, of course.

She thought she did, because it would be his style to bait her. He'd give her a few true clues, betting on the fact she wouldn't share them with the Bureau. He'd bank on her to do exactly what she was doing: invading the Atchafalaya like an Amazon scorned, intent on vigilante justice, armed to the teeth, ready to kill—and completely alone except for the toothless wonder poling her pirogue.

Well, the hell with Jon Bordelon. He underestimated women, and especially *this* woman, because he was used to being the hunter, not the hunted. Yes, she'd come to the bayou alone. Yes, she was playing his game, but only so far. No matter what Bordelon thought, Kiri fully intended to win, whatever the cost.

She had revised her profile of the bastard minute by minute since she found out the truth. The son of a bitch had some sort of Hannibal Lecter-Agent Starling fascination going on with her, something she couldn't quite figure.

Why her? Because she was good at her job? Because of her special senses, which clearly didn't work on him?

Despite the oppressive heat, Kiri felt a slight chill. She cleared her thoughts and mentally scented the area. The place was nearly empty from a psychic standpoint. Here and there she caught a snatch of human spoor—mostly like Pascal's—busy, furtive, but not evil. Cajuns were a stand-offish bunch, often gruff and temperamental, but rarely plain bad, like Bordelon.

Bordelon, who seemed to allow her to sense him when and if he chose.

The bastard could be anywhere in the world — or right beside her, or right over there, in that clump of overgrown bushes. Maybe even coming up quietly in his own pirogue, or waiting past Cain Island on Chien Stretch, the patch of mud and rushes where she planned to land.

According to the records Kiri reviewed, Bordelon had come from the Stretch. The Bureau had a file on the little piece of land, along with Daemon Swath and Cain Island, because of an old mass murder case. Sanctuaire, a mansion on Cain Island, had been the scene of horrid brutality — a woman, two men, and seven children, slaughtered. One of the unfortunates had been a federal agent, an Alcohol, Tobacco, and Firearms man, which caught the Bureau's attention.

A ten-year-old boy had survived, found cut up and bleeding but well-tended in the care of a Voudon *mam'bo* on Daemon Swath. The old woman had cursed the two agents who tried to take the boy for treatment and questioning. She fought them so fiercely with her machete and shotgun that they'd been forced to summon the local law — who left the boy with her after all, since she had been named guardian in his family's papers.

The only irregularity Kiri had noticed was that the identities of the dead and of the lone survivor had been obscured, marked *private and classified eyes-only* for the Bureau director. Unusual, but maybe the ATF agent still had family on the job.

Kiri's chill faded, replaced once more with a drenching sweat. In the hazy, heat-filled distance, she could make out a break in the endless mass of cypress, Spanish moss, and cattails.

"Is that it?" she asked Pascal, trying hard not to whine as she slapped another dozen mosquitoes congregating on her right elbow.

The man grunted and didn't look back. After a moment, he muttered "Dat Cain Island," then crossed himself as if warding off great evil. "We still a ways off where you goin'."

Kiri suppressed a snort of frustration. She didn't believe in the sort of mythical monsters conquered by holy symbols. There were plenty of real, live humans on Earth much more frightening — and they didn't give a damn about God. "Does anyone still live there?"

At this, Pascal actually gave her a heavy-lidded glance over his shoulder. "*Oui.* Every now and then — but what on Cain Island ain' human, *chère*. Don' go wanderin' where you ain' welcome."

Once more, Kiri bit back a retort. She didn't want to piss off the man and find herself unceremoniously dumped into the brackish river.

Pascal kept poling, and the long, thin pirogue eased through lily pads, driftwood, and cypress knees, emerging from tree cover around the surprisingly green edge of Cain Island. Kiri realized with a startle that the outcropping seemed to be part of a giant lawn, carefully trimmed. In the distance, she could make out the lines of an antebellum home the likes of which she had only imagined through her grandmother's tales of the old south.

Squinting in the sunlight, she tried to make out the house's color, the exact shape — but she couldn't. And as she stared, other parts of the island seemed to grow more obscure, like some slow-working giant hand was erasing them.

The heat's getting to me, she told herself, and wished for an icepack and twenty gallons of nice, cold tea. Lemon, no sugar, lots and lots of ice. Trembling, she gripped the sides of the pirogue and forced her gaze forward.

They were heading for another curtain of Spanish moss.

"Wait," Kiri said suddenly, and Pascal obligingly slowed the boat before they fully passed the patch of green. "Let me off at Cain Island first. I think I'll start there."

Pascal stiffened. "We don' make no deal a'go dat place. We make our deal for the Stretch."

"So? Cain Island's closer." Kiri shifted in the boat, feeling the weight of the pistols in her ankle holsters, her chest holster, and her visible waist holster. Never mind the bowie knife she had taped to her back, down in the small where it wouldn't be so visible under her shirt. "I'm paying you plenty. And I can give you more for the extra time."

The little man didn't even look tempted. "*Mais, non.* Besides, you don' be gettin' far on Cain if you ain' welcome."

Kiri felt half-annoyed, half-intrigued. She glanced toward the patch of green, then once more turned her eyes on the gables of the mansion. For some reason, she couldn't see it. But that was impossible. They were lined up with where it should be, albeit off in the distance. She leaned forward as much as she dared, gazing hard across the long tree-lined lawn. Before her eyes, vines seemed to grow and wend about tree trunks, making a barrier and further obscuring her view.

Crack!

A black woman dressed in a shocking red gown and turban materialized on the shore, arms raised.

Kiri fell back, hand on the grip of her visible pistol. Pascal swore, then muttered a prayer as the woman began to chant. Her low, melodic voice bounced over the stream's obsidian surface. The dialect was so thick Kiri had no real idea what the woman was saying, but her meaning was clear enough.

Stay away!

Pascal fumbled with his pole, giving the boat a hard push.

"Stop!" Kiri ordered, regaining her balance, but the little man only pushed harder.

"*Couillon,*" he muttered. "*Oui.* Me no fool, me. That *Maman* Rubie, grand-cousin to Marie LeVeaux." He whispered the last name like a thousand ears might hear him and disapprove. "You wan' go see Queen Marie's blood when she mad, you swim."

Kiri's instinct moved into high gear. She felt a humming in her head, and caught a mental whiff of the spoor she had been looking for.

Bordelon!

Was the son of a bitch making them see the woman on the shore? No matter. He was close. Yards away. Maybe only feet.

Without allowing herself to think about what she was jumping into, Kiri vaulted out of the pirogue and into the thick, hot water. Her feet struck the marshy bottom of the bayou, and water sloshed high, almost to her neck. She walked as fast and hard as she could against the resistance of sticks, plants, and the surprising cool undercurrent, all the while ignoring the swearing from Pascal in the pirogue. Her jeans and weapons seemed to weigh two tons, and she tried not to think about the water seeping into her guns.

Kiri kept her eyes fixed on the woman in red, who could only be a *mam'bo,* the way she danced and chanted. The woman might have been sixty years old or six hundred, Kiri couldn't tell. Kiri didn't hold much stock in Voudon practices, but thanks to her upbringing and research, she was familiar with them. This *mam'bo* was casting major spells, if such mystical acts held any true power.

Please, don't let there be leeches in this muck. Or alligators.

Her feet splitched and splotched as she struggled up a small slope toward the shore, closer and closer to the *mam'bo.* The woman didn't notice her. She continued her flailing dance and incantations, looking somewhere over Kiri's head.

Kiri thought about her guns again and hoped they would bear up after getting soaked. At least the knife was impervious, not that she would need it against an old woman.

Another few feet, and she pulled clear of the black waters. Green fronds and oily patches of black clung to her clothes, and her skin now wore a fine coating of silt. Cold breezes struck her, swirled up and down her body — then seemed to blow right through her. Kiri held back a shriek, but couldn't stop herself from pitching forward and landing on her knees.

The soft dirt cushioned her. She felt no pain, only a distant dizziness and ringing in her ears. The breezes stopped abruptly, leaving her hot and cold at the same time. Muttering her annoyance, she got to her feet and walked from the dirt to the trimmed grass.

"Excuse — " she started to say to the *mam'bo*, but the words died in her throat. The red-clad woman was nowhere to be seen.

Kiri whirled around, spraying slime-water in every direction. No *mam'bo*. And no Pascal and no pirogue.

At least the vines and bushes had disappeared as mysteriously as they had appeared. She could see the island clearly again — and in the distance, the splendid mansion. It looked about the size of a two-story city block, with Grecian columns, a wrap-around porch, and balconies all along the second level. It gleamed white in the afternoon sunlight, heat shimmering off the black shingled roof. Several outbuildings, also spotless white, lay to the left, and to the right was an overgrown arbor and garden. In the distance, she could make out what looked like a dock, jutting into the bayou on the far side.

"Bordelon," Kiri reminded herself aloud, trying to focus on why she had waded ashore.

Instantly, a new round of cool prickles traveled her flesh. She turned slowly back toward the swamp. In the distance, near the curtain of Spanish moss between Cain Island and the distant Chien Stretch, an empty pirogue floated.

Kiri felt a squeezing in her chest.

Was it Pascal's boat? Had something happened to the little man?

But, no. This pirogue looked newer and cleaner. And it was a different color. Red paint gleamed beneath the black coating of muck and water.

Red...red...red...

The color rose like water, covering her head, competing to fill her senses. The day suddenly grew still and completely silent. Kiri's eyes ached from the red. Her ears hurt, too, and she realized the incessant hum of frogs, insects, and birds had just...stopped. Instinctively, she reached her mind toward the pirogue.

Damn! Bordelon's spoor was so pungent it nearly knocked her backward.

The boat moved as if something had bumped it—as if someone might be swimming it slowly toward Cain Island.

With a deep growl of rage, Kiri drew one of her waterlogged pistols and stormed back toward the water.

Steel arms grabbed her from behind, simultaneously disarming her and pinning her tight against a brick-hard and bare chest.

"Don't be a fool, *catin*," said a rumbling voice she recognized. Chank Arceneaux's breath felt hotter than flame against her ear. "He wants you like that, in the water, helpless and alone."

Chapter Five

Chank tightened his grip on his *catin*, his sweet Creole doll, expecting a fight. Her shapely body felt like heaven in his arms, swamp water and bottom silt aside—but, damn. She had guns everywhere—and a knife, too. Ready for trouble. Asking for it.

"Let me go," she said in air-conditioned tones.

He answered her by taking a slow breath, inhaling the vanilla musk clinging to her midnight hair. Through her thin blouse, her damp skin pressed against his bare chest, and he had wild thoughts of stripping her out of her wet clothes.

Of course, he'd need a shitload of handcuffs, ropes, and probably a big-ass whip to keep her from killing him while he did it. This was not a woman who would easily surrender to anyone's advances, that much he could tell.

Why in God's name had she come here? And how had she crossed the veil protecting Cain Island?

He hadn't sensed anything amiss until he'd heard the chanting. He thought *Maman* Rubie had come for a rare visit, but when he stepped out of the gardens he had been clearing, he had seen his dream—and his nightmare.

Kiri Auckland was standing on the shores of Cain Island. And just beyond her, outside the protective veil, the murderous bastard who wanted to kill her let himself be sensed.

This was a bastard Chank knew only too well, a deadly menace who would eat Kiri alive if she stepped free of Cain Island's psychic barriers. Chank had acted without thinking, rushing to save Kiri from a fate she couldn't possibly understand.

Delight battled with overwhelming guilt. He was so glad to see her—and equally horrified. Once more, he wondered how she had crossed through the protective spells. Cain Island's defenses were near to impenetrable after the tragedy of his childhood. *Maman* Rubie's magic and the spirits of his family guarded Sanctuaire with jealous ferocity. Here, Chank was spared the full brunt of his *Trakyr* senses. He could briefly escape his endless connections to the minds and emotions of predators, and for a time, be untouchable.

And yet Kiri Auckland was very much touching him. She was pounding the hell out of his arms. The wet cotton of her blouse slapped against his sunburned flesh.

"I said let me go, you arrogant prick! Just because you think you're some Cajun fucking Batman doesn't give you the right—"

Her scream of rage cleaved the island's silence as Chank hoisted her and threw her over his shoulder. She was strong, *mais, oui*—but not strong enough to escape him. He couldn't risk letting her stay outside. Inside, he could keep her still and safe long enough to explain what they were up against.

Maybe.

If she didn't kill him first.

Dieu, but it felt good to hold her so close! His hand strayed dangerously close to her ass.

Why were the gods torturing a celibate man?

Chank strode toward Sanctuaire, managing the lioness on his shoulder the best he could. Water dripped down his bare chest and back, even splattered into his face as she thrashed in his grip. By the time he got her up the steps and into the drawing room, she had called him everything but a nice boy, and he was sure her punches had cracked at least one of his ribs. He couldn't help wondering what it would be like to see her so aroused, but from passion instead of rage.

More and more he thought of making love to her, fucking Kiri hard and fast, then slow and sure. He could see their bodies slick with heat, limp from exhaustion…and his erection grew near to unbearable as he bolted the drawing room door, turned back toward the room, and dared to set Kiri Auckland on her feet.

In the moment she touched the floor, she stood briefly in his embrace, her black eyes fixed on his, fairly snapping with fury.

Chank let his hands rest on her hips until she stepped away. Her cheeks were flushed, and she was breathing fast. It might have been his imagination, but she seemed a tad unsettled in addition to being mad enough to spit.

Damn. Damn! If she shared this insane attraction, how would he ever keep from claiming her, now and for all time?

He thought she was going to slap him, but instead she reached behind her back, up her untucked shirt, and ripped her knife free from its wet tape. The good-sized Bowie Rescue glinted in the drawing room's natural light, its wickedly serrated blade and curved tip dangerously close.

She probably knew how to throw the damned thing, too. God bless the FBI.

Chank raised his hands and tried to choose his words carefully. "I apologize, *catin*. We need to talk, but in here, where it's safe. Nothing— no evil, human or otherwise—can touch us inside Sanctuaire."

Kiri kept the slotted knife pointed at his throat. She was maybe two steps away. One good lunge, and she would run him through. Again, Chank's mind filled with images of wresting the weapon away in a sweaty, heated struggle, then throwing her to the floor and fucking her until they both collapsed.

Losing my mind. Yeah, boy.

"What the hell are you doing here?" Kiri finally asked, her voice still cold and tremulous.

"I live here," Chank answered simply. The curve of her jaw distracted him, but not nearly as bad as the way her wet clothes clung to her ample breasts. He could see her nipples beading beneath her blouse.

Confusion claimed Kiri's features and she lowered her menacing knife a fraction. "You can't live here. The owners got murdered twenty years ago. I read the file. Some asshole carved them up with a machete—"

Chank winced in spite of a strong effort to hold his expression steady. She had read the file. Of course she would have, good investigator that she was. And he could see her piece the truth together.

Kiri lowered the knife completely.

Instead of relief, Chank felt his own anger kindle. She was staring at his scarred chest and biceps now, remembering the wounds described in the Bureau's report, maybe even thinking of him as a scared little boy. That pissed him off beyond reason.

"Don't stop now," he snapped. "Why don't you describe the scene in detail, eh? How *ma mère* was found in pieces in her garden. My father, not far away. My uncle, my brothers and sisters, my cousins—all in the house, different rooms, different poses. *Oui*. The file is very thorough."

"I didn't think," Kiri said quietly, gazing steadily into his eyes. "Words on the paper, how they translate to real life—well, I can be bull-stupid sometimes."

Her frank admission and lack of apology calmed Chank a fraction. If she started that so-sorry and poor-man bullshit, he might snatch her knife away and cram it three feet into the wall.

Yet, she didn't seem to be the pitying kind. The faint roar in his blood picked up, and in seconds, he thought about touching her again.

Up and down, up and down. Chank frowned. He wasn't used to rollercoaster emotions, and he hadn't had to deal with his wilder side in a long time. No woman had kept his attention for more than five minutes, much less to the extent of waking such primal possessive urges.

Kiri turned away from him and strode to a nearby couch, imprinting the sight of how her wet jeans clung to her rounded, firm ass forever in his mind. There were six sofas in the large window-ringed room, and she picked the only leather one. When she sat, he heard the gentle slap of her damp clothing. Almost as an afterthought, she placed the knife carefully on the cushion beside her.

"Did you come here after the *Houngon*?" she asked bluntly, and now Chank found himself close to smiling again. All business, this one. Would that make fighting the attraction easier? Somehow, he thought not.

"Yes and no," he admitted, feeling a tightness all across his dampened body.

I came here to get away from you, to save you by my distance...

"I came here to rest, to sharpen my senses for tracking. I also knew the bastard might turn up close by."

Kiri leaned forward, her damp cotton blouse parting to give him full view of her cleavage. "Because he's from here, over on the Chien Stretch, right?"

Chank snorted. "He's from hell."

"The file—"

"Will tell you nothing." Chank forced himself to look at the many bookshelves or one of the Persian rugs—anywhere but at Kiri's breasts.

"Not about the true nature of Jon Bordelon. If you're ready to be honest, we can share information, maybe catch the bastard, *oui*?"

For a moment, Kiri didn't speak. Her hand drifted absently to the hilt of her knife, stroking it from tip to blade, tip to blade. Chank imagined her fingers on his cock and almost fell over when she rubbed the knife again.

"Why should I trust you?" she asked at last.

Against his better judgment, he crossed the room and eased onto the same couch as Kiri, mindful of the knife between them. A steel chaperone.

Better something than nothing, he supposed.

"I have answers you won't find anywhere else." He forced himself not to reach for her hand. "Together, we might bring this son of a bitch down. Apart, we have half the chance, at best."

Another long silence ensued. Kiri stroked the knife again, and Chank couldn't stand it. He carefully placed his hand over hers and felt gratified when she didn't pull away.

Her skin felt like satin beneath his rough palm, and this time, when her black eyes fixed on his, he thought he saw a spark born of something other than anger.

Wishful thinking. She's scared and frustrated, that's all. I'm offering her a lifeline.

"If you would feel better," he murmured, "I'll begin."

Kiri nodded, still leaving her hand in his. Chank felt both the warmth of her flesh and the coolness of the Bowie Rescue's custom finger-grooved hardwood handle. He let his gaze travel from her soft-looking hands to her softer-looking cheeks. She reddened under his stare, and once more, he felt that lurch in his chest—and his cock. Halfway down his shaft, his *autre* threatened to emerge, but he suppressed it.

Dieu, he wanted her. "I have extra senses that allow me to track...predators. Do you have similar skills?"

Kiri swallowed. Her eyes lit on his bare chest again, seeming to trace his scars. "Yes," she confirmed at last. "But I think a bit different from yours. I sense...the essence of people, the emotions they're feeling and often their intentions. It's like a mental scent, a spoor. If I concentrate hard enough on the spoor, sometimes I can ride with the person for a time—be in their head."

Chank felt a mild surge of surprise. "Very useful. Do you know where it came from? Your gift, I mean."

"No." Kiri's dip of the head was both graceful and shy. "My mother died when I was born, and I never knew my father. My grandmother raised me, over in Pass Christian, Mississippi."

"It may be just an anomaly then. One of life's many miracles." He smiled at her, grateful to see her features soften some. Perhaps building trust wasn't hopeless after all. "Can you sense me?"

Kiri looked up sharply. "No. It's the first time I haven't been able to read someone. Well, the second I guess. I thought I could sense the *Houngon*, but he tricked me somehow."

"You thought you were riding with his mind, but you weren't." Chank understood now. It made perfect sense. "He fooled you in Overbrook."

The narrowing of Kiri's eyes answered him. Her hand stiffened in his, and he knew he had to say something to restore her fragile cooperation.

"It's one of his skills," he said quickly. "You can't read the *Houngon* correctly because he isn't fully human, and he used his abilities against you."

"He isn't—oh, now wait a minute." Kiri did pull her hand away then. "Don't start sounding like that boatman Pascal and all the other suspicious idiots around here. I grew up with that crap."

"Think, *catin*. You just said you have never failed to read a person." Chank gestured like a showman without meaning to. "Other than the *Houngon*, other than me—you can accurately sense all humans, *oui?*"

With a frustrated groan, Kiri stood. She stretched her legs and arms, then shook her head. "Right. Sure. So, what, this guy's a werewolf? A vampire? No, wait. An alien. Yeah, that's it."

"I am sorry you were drawn into this. It's an ancient war, older than both of us." Chank got to his feet and found himself so close to Kiri that he was nearly rubbing his chest against her breasts. Doing his best to think despite his raging hard-on, he said, "Jon Bordelon is *Huntyr*, one of an ancient race bred for one purpose: thinning the human herd. We won't be able to go after him in the usual ways. The usual rules won't apply."

Kiri still looked skeptical, but he could tell she had begun to work out the implications of the rest of what he had told her. "So, I can't sense him because he's not fully human," she said slowly, raising her chin. She moved toward him, just a bit—but enough. "And I can't sense you because..."

"Because I am *Trakyr*. A part-human, like him." Chank opened his mouth to explain further, but instead gave into his deeper urges. He took her forearms with both hands and pulled her against him, loving the wetness of her clothes and skin. Her cheeks flushed a deeper red, exciting him further. Her lips, plump perfect hearts, drew him forward until he kissed her, harder than he meant to, deeper than he intended.

She didn't fight. In fact, she pressed against him. He knew she could feel his erection, but she didn't pull back. Her lips parted, admitting his tongue, and her hands gripped his sides fiercely.

Somebody moaned.

Was it him? Her?

Couillon, Arceneaux. Couillon!

Chapter Six

Kiri's lips ached as she pulled back from Chank's kiss. She inhaled the earthy-salt scent of his sweat and wondered about her sanity again. All her training as an agent, her experience as a criminalist flew out the nearest bay window. The only thing left in Chank's powerful embrace was one hundred percent woman.

This man made her senses spin. He talked crazy and looked like a god. He smelled like all things natural and healthy, like honest work and fresh wind. Her hands traveled his damp back, appreciating the column of muscle on either side. She indeed felt like a *catin*, a doll in his massive arms. His body, granite against hers—and those eyes! So deep-black and haunted, she felt like she could slide into his hot gaze and stay forever.

He wanted her. The way he touched her, like she belonged to him—no doubt about it. His cock hardened against her belly, making her pussy throb.

"I'm filthy," she whispered, suddenly aware of her silt-covered clothes and skin.

"*Mais, oui,*" he purred against her ear, making her shake. "Me, too. Swimming in swamps can have that effect. Come with me."

When he leaned back to look at her, Kiri could breathe only in short gasps. The angular lines of his naturally dark face, his laser-like gaze, the way his lips quirked on the left when he grinned—*damn*. He let her go and stepped to the side, and she instantly ached to feel his arms again. Her mind filled with images of being naked in his embrace, his mouth on her nipples, his cock poised to thrust into her aching core.

For a long moment, she thought he might grab her and pull her against him once more, but instead, he extended his hand. She took it without comment, and he led her out of the drawing room and up the mansion's wide marble steps, toward the second level.

I kissed Batman, she thought, working hard not to stumble. She felt like she had walked into some freaky dream, or fallen down the Cajun version of a rabbit hole. Part of her didn't care how dirty she was. She wished Chank would stop, lay her down on the steps, and fuck her until neither of them could breathe.

"*Trakyrs* have opposed *Huntyrs* across the centuries, able to sense the world but blind to each other." Chank's body-tingling bass rumbled through Kiri's mind as they reached the main landing. Stained glass windows cast colored shadows on marble floors, and portraits hung in evenly spaced intervals along two opposing hallways. Kiri couldn't help but notice that the place felt older than it should. *One hundred years? Two hundred?*

Three?

"The *Huntyr* Bordelon murdered my family," Chank intoned, startling her from her musing.

His statement was so flat, so simple that at first, Kiri couldn't accept it. Her emotions jolted, then jolted again, trying to re-start and failing. Pictures from the old FBI file on Jon Bordelon streamed through her thoughts. Her blood sizzled in her temples.

The bastard killed Chank's family. Of course, it was obvious when she considered it, but still…

She wanted to reach out, stroke Chank's arm, but he looked utterly unapproachable as he continued. "When he struck I was away from home, fishing. He came for me, but I was…I am…protected by a magic he didn't expect. His Voodoo killings and the *vèvès* – he's trying to grow powerful enough to break that magic. But he can't. He never will. He doesn't have what he needs to work the last spell. My…protector saw to that, all those years ago."

The blood of his first-born, given willingly, Kiri thought, remembering the rituals she had read about in books and briefings. Jon Bordelon needed the blood of his own first-born child, and he couldn't just take it. The child had to give it up freely.

Obviously, the bastard didn't have children.

My protector saw to that.

Kiri chewed her bottom lip. *What does he mean? What did that old mam'bo do to keep Bordelon from reproducing?*

Chank glanced at her, but Kiri didn't know what to say. He sounded so logical, and he looked so serious. Truth had a sound, a rhythm, and she knew she was hearing it.

But all this fantastic nonsense about *Trakyrs* and *Huntyrs* — impossible.

Wasn't it?

"Now it seems the *Houngon's* attention has settled on you." Chank's dark gaze raked across hers, asking questions she couldn't answer.

"Why?" she whispered, battling a dry catch in her throat.

"If you don't know, then it's a mystery." Chank shrugged, his well-defined muscles rippling in the landing's multi-hued light. "He may think you're one of us, but *le malédiction*, the curse—well, my family is the last of the *Trakyr* blood. Whatever gift you have, it's a strange blessing I know nothing about."

Does he believe me, that I don't know where my abilities came from? Kiri felt a surge of frustration because she couldn't "read" Chank except by traditional means. He was standing only a foot from her, arms folded, perfect chest bulging. His tight-fitting black cotton pants seemed old-fashioned, like breeches worn in the 1600's—and sweet God, they showed off his splendid erection. Her pussy flooded again, and she wanted him more than she could remember wanting any man.

Did he have some irresistible alien sexual aura? If he was part-human as he claimed, was his equipment…normal?

Maybe he has two cocks, she thought giddily as she dared to reach out and touch his naked chest.

He took a slow breath as her fingers made contact with his steel-hard muscles. Like a hawk striking prey, he swept her up again, holding her firmly as he claimed her mouth. Her lips parted, and his rough tongue found hers. They moved together, almost dancing, at the head of the imposing staircase. Chank's hips ground into Kiri's, and she moaned into his mouth. Making love to him seemed right, like a refusal of tragedy and the insanity of the *Houngon*.

And then he stopped them again, gently but firmly. "We'll need to make a plan and call in some help from my friends." His hands massaged her shoulders as his words tickled her ear. His breath moved down to her neck, giving her thrill after thrill—but she sensed him distancing, almost at light speed. "It's the new moon tomorrow. Best time to go after a *Huntyr*, when their senses are dullest."

Kiri felt like her skin was on fire. She kissed him again, trying to persuade him to act on their mutual desire, but he prevailed and pulled away. With a wry smile, holding her arm tightly in his like a prince escorting a princess to the ball, he led her down the right hallway to a suite all her own.

"You can stay here, *catin*. Safe from me, safe from everyone. Have a bath, relax, *oui*? We'll eat later—and plan our strategy."

"I don't want to be safe from you," she asserted, stepping into the circle of his arms once more.

He groaned and rubbed against her, such a bald admission of his own desires that it took her breath away...but then he said, "I can't. *Le malédiction*—I won't risk passing it on."

"Damn, Arceneaux." Kiri reached down and caressed his swollen cock through his soft cotton breeches. Heaven. The man was beyond well-hung. "Haven't you ever heard of condoms?"

"*Oui*," he growled, moving her hand away, though his blacker-than-black eyes screamed his wish to do anything but. "They break. Go now, bathe. We'll talk afterward."

His tone brooked no argument.

Quick as a blink, he propelled Kiri through a door and closed it between them. She sighed and leaned against the carved wood, wishing she could melt back through and rip off Chank's pants. Instead, she made herself turn around, slowly and carefully remove her many concealed weapons, and take stock of her surroundings.

The room was breathtaking, and once more, she had a sense of being in an ancient, almost hallowed place—more castle than mansion. The floors, like the rest of the mansion, were polished marble. Against the right wall stood a four-poster bed complete with a gauzy golden canopy. Gilded chairs with deep green cushions filled in empty spaces between four windows taller than two grown men—and outside, Kiri could see a balcony all her very own.

The bathroom was another study in old southern elegance, replete with clawfoot tub with circular white curtain, two pedestal sinks, a toilet, and even a bidet. Kiri stripped off her clothes, feeling once more like a woman lost in a dream. There was a laundry bin, white wicker with painted golden edges, positioned between two fat white towels monogrammed with a flourishing golden *A*. Kiri half-expected a silent servant to materialize and remove her garments as she dropped them in and closed the lid, but the suite remained empty and silent except for her movements.

After doing some rudimentary cleaning and drying in hopes of saving her guns, she surrendered to the urge to wash away the day. In minutes, she stood in the clawfoot tub enjoying the warm thrum of a well-pressured shower inside the quaint circled curtain. Overbrook, death, the *Houngon*, and the FBI suddenly seemed a million miles away.

Kiri couldn't remember the last time she felt so wonderfully and totally distracted, so freed from the drives of work and the daily struggles of being a woman in a man's organization. And a big woman at that—not even one of the perfectly-shaped dolls they could ignore on the basis of beauty and sex appeal. That made her a target, even if the other agents were smart enough to keep their comments quiet.

Chank might be Batman, but she was Blunder Woman. Oh, and She-Whale and sometimes Superpudge.

Except, of course, when she was tracking a killer. Then she was Whatever-You-Say-Just-Do-It-And-Advance-Our-Careers.

Men. No, thank you.

Her hands traveled her body like an old friend as she slowly remembered what pleasure it could offer her. She was more than a mind, an agent, a large-sized joke—she was still a woman, no matter what her coworkers and her last slew of boyfriends might think.

"Bordelon not included," she said aloud, spitting his name into the water to cleanse herself of *that* mistake.

Chank didn't seem to mind her larger size. She had long ago grown comfortable with herself, but she had never found a man who truly saw past her appearance. This guy seemed above-board, though. He seemed different.

Kiri soaped up and caressed her breasts, smiling as her nipples ached under her touch. His rough hands would feel so good instead of hers! Whatever held him back—outside the obvious—she'd break through it.

Her hand delved lower, to her still-swollen lower lips, and she sighed with pleasure and need as she rubbed her clit. Warm, soapy water coursed over her fingers, spilling across her pussy. Bayou silt washed off her in waves. Kiri felt her muscles relax.

When had she been this at ease?

On a haunted island with a Cajun FBI agent who claims to be half-human tracking a murderer who could have seduced me—also half-human, let's not forget that. Never mind Pascal of the three teeth or the mam'bo *in red, or the fact that you're probably double-fired from your job now. Triple-fired. Damn, Auckland. You've gone over the fucking cliff.*

The *fucking* cliff.

Kiri stroked her clit faster, feeling the pressure build in her belly. Her nipples went super-sensitive, and she pinched one with her free hand. A bolt of pleasure fueled her excitement. Chank's teeth would cause a lightning storm, biting, holding the pebbled flesh still for his tongue to tease...

His hard cock would feel perfect against her mons, pressing into her throbbing core...

He'd enter her slowly, then let the sweetness mount with each thrust...

"Yes!" Kiri's small orgasm rattled her. Too bad the tub had no walls to fall against—but at least she took the edge off her raging need. Next step, plowing through Chank Arceneaux's penchant for stopping romantic moments and getting some *real* satisfaction.

As she got out of the tub and toweled off, Kiri wondered again if Chank's half-human status might mean his manhood was...well, different.

If he did have two cocks, I could take them both. She ran her towel hard between her legs and shivered again. *That would be interesting.*

The thought had barely formed when something tickled the back of Kiri's brain. She straightened and absently wrapped the towel around her as she left the bathroom.

A fluffy white robe in a size plenty large enough, also monogrammed with a flourishing *A*, lay across her bed.

Kiri flushed with pleasure and triumph. Chank had come back in to leave it for her. Had he stolen a glance into the bathroom?

Did he like what he saw?

The tickle in her head came again, this time strong enough to make her turn toward the French doors leading to her balcony. Sunlight slanted through glass panes at long angles as she approached.

"Sunset soon," she murmured, hearing the thought even as she spoke it. She felt oddly dizzy, as if she'd had a drink or two, but it wasn't unpleasant. Probably the heat.

Her hands moved automatically to the handles, and she threw the doors open wide. Unmindful of her barely-covered body, she stepped into the bayou swelter. Late in the afternoon, the air had a muggy weight. Haze made Kiri squint at the grounds of Sanctuaire—endless strips of green divided by overgrown reds, yellows, and oranges— flowers, out of control everywhere except where Chank had cut clear paths. Beyond the island's boundary, black waters drifted lazily by or stood in stagnant, bug-veiled pools. Cypress trees rose like dark sentinels, draped with Spanish moss and thick, gnarled vines.

Kiri's dizziness grew worse. Almost drunk, she clung to the edge of one door and stared out, out, out, just beyond her range of vision, where something waited.

A distant part of her mind told her to be afraid, or maybe angry. The rest of her brain felt besotted and drowsy, and didn't really care. She moved forward, feeling dreamy and relaxed, to a black wrought iron chair beside a glass-topped table. The chair felt wet and warm as she climbed up on the circular seat, all the while keeping her eyes trained on the strange spot in the distance.

It seemed to flicker. Swamp lights. A little pocket of bayou fire.

Now a voice called to her with no words, only urges. Images of her mounting the balcony, jumping off, and flying to meet her destiny. She moved her feet in the chair as she imagined soaring high above Sanctuaire, over the dark water. The wind would feel splendid on her damp skin, like a lover's touch.

Come to me, chère. Words now. Hypnotic. Beyond tempting. *Test your wings.*

Kiri smiled. She never knew swamps had voices. She leaned forward, tipped, and her hands closed over the balcony's railing. The sun-heated metal tingled against her hands as she lifted one leg to climb over.

"*Dieu!*" The loud exclamation from behind her nearly made her pitch forward. Strong arms snatched her back from the brink of take-off. She struggled, still dizzy and confused, but couldn't escape. Without ceremony, Chank Arceneaux hauled her back into the suite, put her down, slammed the balcony doors, and locked them. Clad in nothing but a towel about his waist, he wheeled on her, eyes spitting black fire.

"What were you doing?" he demanded.

Kiri looked past him through the doors' gauzy curtains, her brain straining to catch another hint of the swamp's voice. The thickness around her thoughts wavered, then slowly began to clear. Bit by bit, the feeling of drunken serenity passed.

She dropped her towel.

"The swamp's voice?" She covered her mouth, then dropped her hands back to her sides and clenched her fists. "Oh, my God! I was about to jump off the balcony. Chank, I thought I could fly. The swamp told me—"

She trailed off, realizing how absurd she sounded, but Chank's expression held fear and rage, not ridicule.

"*Bâtard foutu*," Chank snarled, clenching his fists. He whirled toward the balcony doors as Kiri's mind sluggishly translated the fairly proper French curse. *Fucking bastard.*

And then she knew.

Jon Bordelon had just played with her mind again.

Chapter Seven

Chank stared out Kiri's balcony windows and seethed.

It wasn't possible. The veil of protective spells around Sanctuaire was absolute, and Chank hadn't sensed a breach until it was almost too late. Somehow the *Huntyr* had laid hold of Kiri's mind. Thank the heavens she possessed an usual ability to fight his commands.

Bordelon had attacked his woman. *His* woman! In *his* home! If the bastard were within arm's reach, Chank would have torn his head from his shoulders.

It's happening again. He's coming for what's mine, and I can't stop him. Blood pounded in Chank's temples, and he ground his teeth. *No! I can bond with her, bring her under the magic's protection as my mate. If I'm careful…but would she…damn! I couldn't burden her in such a way.*

Only the light touch of fingers on his bare shoulder brought him back to the present, to himself. He stepped away from the contact, shaking with rage at the monster who stalked his very heart.

When he turned to Kiri, he fought to keep his voice even. "I'm sorry, *catin*. From now on, unless I'm with you, please leave the doors and windows closed. I didn't think he could touch you here. I would have never left you alone if I'd known. This is my fault."

At that moment, Chank took in the full measure of Kiri's nakedness, and his anger faded to nothing. Her pretty face flushed as she took hold of his biceps and gazed past him, through the panes in the doors and out into the bayou dusk. Her breasts—incredibly full with light pink nipples, beaded and damp from her shower—made his mouth water. Her rounded hips enticed him, as did the black thatch of hair between her legs. Moisture glistened on the fine hair, and Chank wanted nothing more than to lick it off, drop by drop.

She seemed to feel the touch of his eyes right about the time his cock nearly jutted out from his towel. Her skin turned a deeper, even more desirable pink.

"What do you mean, your fault?" Kiri's voice was nothing but a whisper.

"I know one reason for Bordelon's attacks." Chank forced his gaze to the side, but Kiri's naked image blazed in his mind's eye. "I believe the *Houngon* realized my...interest in you."

Her response to his admission was a wordless stare. She was clearly waiting for more explanation.

Chank squared his shoulders and faced her. "Though we haven't spent much time together, I've noticed you, Kiri. *Mais, oui*. More than noticed."

Her brows shot up, bracketing her bright black eyes. For a moment, she looked thrilled, then troubled. With a sigh, she said, "You can stop blaming yourself. I went out with the asshole three or four times. That's what I held back on you in Philly."

Kiri's words struck Chank with the force of a slap. He felt refreshed rage at Bordelon, mingled with gut-twisting jealousy—and a surge of fear. If she and Bordelon had been intimate, if she had gotten pregnant...

"What happened?" he asked, his throat as dry as summer grass.

Kiri ran a hand over her eyes. "Not even a kiss on the lips. Does that make you happy? Tickles the shit out of me, considering."

Up and down. Chank clenched his teeth as his rollercoaster emotions crested and broke again. He almost laughed at her unselfconscious humor right before her nearness overwhelmed him again.

With another masterful effort to control his mounting desire, he murmured, "Do we have any more secrets?"

"I don't know." Kiri's eyes drifted to his hard cock. "Do we?"

Chank swallowed a groan and barely kept his shaft and his *autre* in check. Definitely not time for that revelation, no matter what pleasure it might give him.

Instead, he swept her into his arms. Her embrace turned fierce, and their kiss became a deep joining, lips to lips, tongue to tongue, both of them breathing in unison. He wanted to touch her everywhere at once, needed to feel her softness, her yielding—and she gave it to him in small measures. A moan for a caress, a shiver for a kiss to her ear, her neck, her bare shoulders.

She reached for his waist and pulled off the towel, freeing his cock to strain against the softness of her belly before she gripped it and began sliding her hand up and down. Balls to tip, she explored him, as if checking to see if he had all his man's parts.

He did, of course. The tiny nub halfway down his shaft, his *autre*, caused her only the barest of hesitations. *Dieu*! He would come just from her touch if he let her continue. Briefly, he once more considered letting her see his full sex, but almost as quickly discarded the idea. That would come later, if at all.

Assuming, of course, he kept some control of himself.

"Enough," he said hoarsely, and picked her up again. This time, he cradled his *catin*, pressing his lips into her damp hair. She didn't fight him, and he carried her straight out of her suite, down the hall past the stairs, and to his dimly-lit Spartan chamber at the far end of the west hall. No more light intruded around the heavy curtains on his window, and Chank knew night had claimed the Atchafalaya.

Kiri kept her arms tight around his neck. They kissed furiously, breaking only for air, and when he finally stretched her out on his pearl-white bedspread, her lips were swollen and half-parted, waiting for his mouth again.

Wordless, keeping his gaze firmly on hers, he eased into the bed beside her, then reached inside his nightstand and withdrew a somewhat ancient foil pack. Kiri took it from him even before he could shut the drawer.

"I'll do it," she said huskily.

Chank broke a sweat at the mere thought. Sanctuaire had air conditioning, but it seemed pathetic at the moment. His internal temperature climbed to molten as he slid over her, kissing her cheeks, her nose, before collapsing on his back. Having sex as a full-human had never satisfied him before, but he knew this time, everything would be different.

Kiri straddled his thighs, giving him a vision of her full breasts and glistening mons. Her slit felt hot and wet against his legs as she ripped open the packet and tossed the foil aside. A devilish smile played on her red, red lips as she leaned down and ran her tongue over the head of his cock.

"Mmm. You taste as good as I imagined."

This time, Chank didn't bother to swallow his groan.

She didn't stop there, stroking down his shaft and the nub of his *autre* with her fingers, fondling his balls as she slid his length into the heat of her mouth.

"Damn." He clenched his jaw and gripped the bedspread, holding off an explosion as she repeated the sweet teasing, up and down, up and down, like heated silk on his skin.

And then, with a purr that almost pushed him over the edge, she stopped and raised her head. Once more, her slick mons rubbed against his thighs. This woman seemed designed to torture him.

"Not yet," she whispered, fitting the condom over the head of his cock and rolling it slowly, slowly, slowly downward—and pausing just above the tiny nub. "First, promise me that tomorrow night, we'll get Bordelon. I want the bastard out of commission permanently."

"I promise," Chank growled, feeling the heady blend of passion and rage rise then wane as the condom started moving again. When her fingers brushed the nub, it was all Chank could do not to release himself more than he should.

"Second promise: no more secrets and no more hauling me around like a laundry bag—unless I ask you to." Kiri's voice sounded like soft notes in a jazz tune, sultry and utterly feminine. And the condom stopped once more.

Chank closed his eyes, opened them, and took a deep breath. "Agreed."

The condom inched downward again. Kiri let her fingers tickle his sensitive shaft and brush across the top of his balls. At the final second, she stopped again.

"Third and last promise—but not the least. Make me happy, Chank Arceneaux. I'm tired of assholes and what did you call them? Competitive, self-absorbed bastards? Yeah." She palmed his sac, making him dig his teeth into his lip. "You don't have to promise me forever. Just—please me tonight."

Chank's only answer was another possessive, desiring growl. It was all he could manage. His body burned along with his thoughts, and he waited until she finished settling the sheath—but barely. The moment he felt it snug in place, he sat up, took her firmly by the shoulders, and laid her back on the bed beneath him. The suddenness of his action made her gasp, but she smiled as he did, looking so deeply into his eyes he could feel it in his gut.

Enough precautions, enough waiting.

He stretched himself above her, holding himself up, palms down on either side of her shoulders. Her soft, pliable body felt warm beneath his rougher skin as he lowered his head and kissed her slow and easy, letting the heat build. Her tongue met his eagerly, again and again. Her hands traveled along his sides, squeezing, tracing him appreciatively.

Shifting down, Chank nipped her neck and listened to her shivering sigh, enjoying the distant lingering of her vanilla musk. He'd have to get her more, and soon. The scent suited her perfectly, and made him crazy.

He kept up his careful descent, running his lips along the hollow of her throat and down, between her breasts. Her woman's smell was stronger there, a mingle of clean skin and new sweat, and he tasted the salt with the tip of his tongue.

Kiri shuddered beneath him. When he glanced up, her eyes were closed.

Smiling, Chank slid his lips sideways across the swell of her breast until he captured a pebble-hard nipple in his teeth.

This time, Kiri bucked beneath him. "Yes," she murmured as her hands rubbed his neck and face. She wrapped her fingers in his hair and urged him down against the soft, giving flesh.

The third promise Kiri had asked him to make, to please her—the one he had answered with only actions—*mais, oui*, that one would be pure heaven in the keeping.

Chapter Eight

Kiri wondered if it was possible to die from want.

Chank's scarred chest felt rough and sensual to her hands, and his man-smell of soap and sex made her dizzy. She could still taste the drops of his salty pre-come in her mouth, and as she raised her fingers to his face, his long hair became silk ropes around her hands. Moaning, she used her leverage to press his face into her breast. He flicked his tongue against her nipple, and her pussy throbbed in rhythm with the contact.

"Harder," she whispered, loving the fire of his mouth, the hard bite as he nibbled, then started to suck. He moved her nipple between his teeth with each forceful pull, as if drinking from her swirling desire. When she arched into his body, she felt his cock press against her leg like a hot iron rod.

God, he was going to feel wonderful inside her.

Chank switched nipples too soon and not soon enough. The minute his teeth found their second target, a small orgasm rippled through her, making her tremble. His rumble of pleasure was immediate.

"So beautiful," he said quietly, then bit her nipple again, just rough enough and soft enough to suit her. Kiri worked her hands in his hair, feeling his head go up and down each time he sucked her breast deeper and released. She closed her eyes, losing herself in the edgy almost-out-of-control sensation. Nearly pain, completely pleasure. He called her *catin*, but he was making love to her like she was a full-grown woman, not some fragile thing that would break beneath his strength.

Perfect.

She had always wanted that.

Maybe I've always wanted him. Maybe I've always been waiting not just for a man like this, but for this *man.*

"You like it a little rough." He gave her nipple another firm bite, and she moaned.

"Yes. Ah, damn!" Kiri leaned into the next bite. A few more like that as he sucked, and she'd come again—but Chank brought her right to the top and broke away, pulling free of her grip on his loosely-bound ponytail.

Before she could protest, he ran his tongue down her belly, straight into the wet hair of her pussy. She spread her legs wide, giving him access, praying he'd ease the pressure threatening to blow her insides to bits.

"Maybe you'll like this just as much," he murmured, pushing her thighs even farther apart.

Kiri felt Chank's skilled tongue plunge into her channel, taste her, move hard against the sensitive edges, then slip back out and run firmly up and across her clit. Her breath left in a sharp gasp as he did it again, and again.

"So good," she half-spoke, half-groaned, shifting her hips, moving against his mouth.

He trapped one of her thighs and held her still, spreading her lower lips with his free hand.

Kiri's clit was so swollen that his breath almost made her scream.

And then his mouth fastened on the sensitive button and sucked it just as hard as he'd sucked her nipples.

She came instantly, fire racing through her belly—but he didn't ease up. If anything, he doubled the pressure and speed of his stroking tongue. His growls of satisfaction vibrated against her labia, making her convulse against his forceful grip on her thigh.

She felt like her clit was lifting right out of her pussy, like he was swallowing her whole. It was too much. Not enough!

"Don't stop," she pleaded, unable to stand another second—or the thought of stopping.

He showed no mercy, keeping up the wonderful assault until she raced toward what would surely be a mind-expanding orgasm. As she pressed her clit into his mouth, he let go of her thigh and entered her with one finger, then two, then three. Kiri yelled and squeezed her nipples as her channel walls contracted against thrusting fingers.

"Yes. Yes!" She came with a bucking, shouting frenzy, ramming her clit into his tongue and swallowing his fingers to the knuckle. This time, he did ease back, extending the sensation until it became a creeping fire in every muscle, along every inch of her skin. She knew she was drenched in sweat. Damn. Damn! She had expected good, but—this, this was something…other.

Her thoughts were barely coherent as Chank once more moved and settled between her legs. She didn't realize he was sitting on his knees until he lifted her hips and slid her splayed legs and limp body toward him.

Drifting in a realm of complete relaxation, Kiri opened her eyes.

Chank's feral stare bored into her as he positioned his cock. She looked down at her pussy just in time to see him enter her, ramming deep as he pulled her hips forward.

They moaned together, releasing hours, days, weeks—even years—of frustration with such a complete joining.

Kiri felt his balls slap against her ass as he cupped and spread her cheeks, bringing her hard against his next thrust, and the next.

"Fuck me," she demanded, letting the forbidden words spill out, thrilling at the freedom and the wet sound of their sex as Chank did just as she instructed.

Kiri's back arched as he lifted her off the bed again and again, plunging into her aching depths at the same time he lowered her against his thrust. She ground against him each time, taking all she could, welcoming more, wanting everything.

"Deep, God, you're so deep. Your cock feels so good!" Her voice sounded alien to her, husky and hoarse, but strong and forceful.

"I've never known a woman like you." Chank kept up his slow, unimaginably deep penetration, finding a rhythm like a waltz. Kiri threw her head back and let him move her, riding every inch of his cock, loving the feel of his deliberation—and waiting for him to turn loose.

She was ready. Was she ever ready.

"More," she urged. "Hard and fast."

He chuckled, squeezing her ass hard as he buried himself balls-deep in her pussy yet again. "Patience, *catin*. You could do with more. I can teach you, *mais oui*."

The weight of the delta swelter seemed to descend on Kiri as he shifted her weight to one hand, braced her ass on his thighs, and used his thumb to massage her clit—all the while moving his cock in and out of her channel at a maddeningly unhurried pace.

Kiri felt like her entire body had been sensitized. Every motion, every touch made her tremble and shake. She thought she was going to have a heat stroke. When she looked at Chank, he glistened with sweat, as if his muscles had been rubbed with oil. His face was relaxed, yet she could see the firm line of his jaw and the determined blaze in his coal-diamond eyes.

Damn, but it was erotic to see his big, thick cock sliding in and out of her in slow motion. He toyed with her clit, then stopped, toyed, then stopped until she knew she couldn't take another instant.

"Please, Chank," she whispered, barely able to choke out the words. "I want you so much!"

The magic words.

Yes, yes, yes, yes!

He rolled forward, resting her feet on his shoulders, and drove himself into her with the force and fierceness of his earlier bites.

Kiri actually screamed and didn't even feel embarrassed.

Nothing had ever felt so filling, so satisfying. Chank's cock seemed twice as thick, twice as hot as he pounded into her pussy. The heavy smell of come and sweat and flesh intoxicated Kiri as her breasts bounced from the force of Chank's thrusts.

She could tell from his short, sharp breaths he was close.

"So sweet," he rumbled. "So beautiful."

Kiri's orgasm felt like the end of the world. Electric bolts sizzled through her clit, her nipples, up and down her spine and arms and legs. Her body shook from head to toe as she clenched on Chank's cock. He lurched and bucked inside her as he came, shouting her name, fucking her hard until the last wave of sensation pushed her into an absolute stupor.

Unbelievable. If he thinks I'm letting him go after this — ha. No way in hell.

She was vaguely aware of Chank collapsing beside her and pulling her onto her side, into his strong, safe arms.

"*Catin*," she thought she heard him whisper. "See? I always keep my promises."

And then, "I would die for you. Sleep, *mais oui*. You're safe now."

Chapter Nine

Chank drifted toward sleep cradling his prize against his chest. He felt wary, but better. Through their lovemaking, and with the depth of his feelings, there was no doubt he had bonded to Kiri even if he couldn't "read" her. Even now he could hear the beat of her heart, the rhythm of her breath, in ways mere humans could not. She would be his family always, whether or not she returned his feelings or chose to stay with him. More importantly, he would know immediately if a predator threatened her.

Maman Rubie couldn't give him back his murdered family, but she had protected him and given him the gift of being able to extend some of that protection to his family of choice.

Chank intended to convince Kiri to remain on Cain Island if she could face a childless future. He intended to make her his. After touching her, kissing her, making love to her—how could he ever let her go? As for the curse, they would simply have to be careful.

Heavy-lidded, he kissed the top of her head and let his exhaustion claim him.

Minutes later—hours?—Chank woke to Kiri's soft mouth on his cock.

Was he dreaming?

No. It was still dark out. The only light in the room came from a single candle on his night stand.

He was lying on his back, arms flopped to the sides, legs apart. Kiri knelt between his thighs, pumping his erection, sliding her pretty lips up and down his sensitive shaft.

"Damn, woman!" He groaned from the exquisite feel of her tongue running over his balls and moving up the sensitive vein and *autre* on the underside of his cock. She worked hand and mouth together, like a glove, gradually increasing the pressure.

What would it feel like to release the rest of my sex? Chank's mind reeled at just the thought, and he had to clamp his teeth to keep it from happening. Even in his youth, he had never revealed that particular secret to a woman. He hadn't even been tempted.

Kiri's kisses became deep sucking, and her grip became a well-timed squeeze-and-release. The flickering candlelight played off Kiri's flawless skin and midnight hair, making her seem that much more a vision, a dream. Chank could feel her breasts rubbing against his groin.

Dieu. This wouldn't take long! He concentrated hard, making sure his cock stayed as she expected it to be. To err now—well, that would be unthinkable.

Kiri hummed with pleasure, sending shocks along Chank's every nerve. He imagined himself fucking her in every possible position, every room in the mansion, every alcove on the island. So much exploring. So much enjoying.

She was perfect for him, and he was perfect for her. He'd show her. He'd convince her.

But in the meantime, he had to survive her.

She brought her free hand into the game, keeping a steady, sensuous massage on his balls as she took his entire length in her mouth. With her other hand, she reached up and tweaked one of his nipples, hard.

That did it.

Chank tried to croak a warning, but Kiri ignored him.

With a low groan, he spilled himself into her mouth. She kept up her efforts, stroking and sucking until he had nothing left but a smile on his face.

"Come here," he murmured, and Kiri complied, stretching out beside him and caressing his chest and belly. "You're incredible, *catin.*"

"I think this has been the weirdest and best day and night of my life," she answered before falling asleep with her head on his shoulder.

Chank held her, enjoying how she had draped herself over him. One day, he would tell her more about the growing depth of his feelings for her. And maybe, just maybe, she'd feel the same way.

The next time Chank woke, he wasn't in Sanctuaire, but walking the hard-packed dirt of Daemon Swath as he had done countless times as a boy.

Maman Rubie was there, machete at her side, dressed in red and tending the trunks of her trees. Chank frowned. The *mam'bo* only wore red in dreams and visions, never in real life.

"*Oui.*" She shifted her bulk to complete the painting of the tree base. Red, like her gown and turban. "In dreams. You been back on Cain Island near two weeks, *chér.* Why you make me meet you in dreams?"

"Bordelon's about. I didn't want to put you in more danger."

"Oh, him. You think I be worried about that *couyon?*" She used the more vulgar pronunciation of *couillon,* suggesting "little dick" or more precisely, a shriveled testicle. Chank had to smile. Some things never changed. *Maman* Rubie had never feared the evil in the Atchafalaya.

Most folks thought she *was* the evil in the swamp, after all.

No human or part-human in his or her right mind would challenge the *mam'bo* of Daemon Swath unless they had a *loa* on their side. And last time Chank checked, the Voudon gods hadn't yet deserted his foster mother. She still meticulously pleased and contained the most ill-tempered *loas* known to the religion.

As if in response to Chank's thoughts, *Maman* Rubie dropped her brush, picked it up, and began painting the tree trunk with dirt and bits of grass, something she would never ever do. Chank slowly realized she was using blood, not paint to coat the tree. All around her and the tree, a *vèvè* glistened. It was large and garish and crudely drawn— again, nothing *Maman* Rubie would tolerate.

His heart started to beat faster. Instinctively, he reached out his *Trakyr* senses, searching the island.

Hawks, rats, mice, a badger, snakes, a fox—Chank tasted blood in dozens of different mouths, on dozens of different fangs. He coughed.

Other than nature, he found no lingering dangers.

"Dangers, ha." *Maman* Rubie sniffed and dropped her paint brush again. This time she didn't pick it up. "Mademoiselle Charlotte, she put me in danger, yeah. Murderers, ghosts, wolfmen, vampyrs—been a long bunch of days. Now you, too. That woman you keepin'—she ain' what you think, *mais, non.* Come see me, boy. Come soon."

Suddenly distracted by the senses of a thousand predators, Chank barely processed her words. When he did, he asked, "Why?"

"You know why."

Chank startled. A bitter memory gripped him, of running across the Swath so fast that bushes and brambles cut him deeply enough to scar. He had only one thought—getting to his family before it was too late. *Maman* Rubie caught him, refused to let go.

I have to go home. He pounded her arms. She was holding her blood-stained machete in one hand.

No, boy. Mais, non. *You can' go. Ain' nobody to go home to.* Her voice, so heavy, so sad.

Why?

You know why.

"You know why," *Maman* Rubie repeated, gut-punching Chank with the phrase. "He done been...and gone."

He glared at her, and she lifted her face to meet his gaze. Unnatural white eyes gleamed as she stared like a dead thing animated just to horrify him.

"Some things do change," the zombie-*mam'bo* said in a voice eerily like Kiri's. "Things always change."

Chank backed away, falling, stumbling, until he plunged headlong into the bayou's unforgiving black depths.

Chapter Ten

Kiri woke slowly from a series of disturbingly violent dreams.

She never had nightmares, much less such bloody ones. She must have killed and eaten ten different kinds of animals.

Raw.

And she danced, too, talking to gods she had never heard of, calling on powers she didn't even understand.

It was all disgusting. Just at the moment she thought she would vomit and die, she woke up, draped safely across Chank like he was the best pillow in the universe.

She blinked, clearing an almost reddish haze from her vision. As her thoughts settled, she found herself in the yellow half-light of a bayou dawn. Outside Sanctuaire, frogs, crickets and endless hoards of insects kept up a steady rasping, as if mourning the passing of darkness. Released from her nightmares, Kiri didn't have the slightest mourning urge. She snuggled against Chank and wanted to dance and shout and swing from a rope like Jane, only halfheartedly trying to escape her hunky swamp god.

With a smile, she tightened her arm around Chank's midsection. "You've graduated from Batman to Tarzan. Is that okay?"

Chank, still sleeping soundly, cradled her like a favored doll, with one arm under her head and the other resting against her hip. She felt small and protected in his embrace, utterly new and unexpected sensations. Being a big woman had taken some toll on her self-esteem, though not as much as it could have. It had, however, robbed her of the simplicity of feeling a man's greater size and power on many occasions.

Obviously, that would never be an issue with Tarzan here.

Nah. Batman. He'll always be Batman.

Last night, minus the nasty dreams, well...it had been the most exciting, most fulfilling night of her life. Sex with a rougher edge—not too rough, but just rough enough.

Yes, yes, *yes*.

A man strong enough to please her.

What a miracle-find.

Her nipples and pussy ached with a sweet, desiring soreness. If he woke up horny, she'd fix that in a hurry. She wanted more of him. Maybe she wanted all of him.

As she shifted against Chank, the sheets brushed softly across her damp skin, accentuating the hot iron of his muscled body. Her toes brushed against his leg, and her head rested against his chest as it rose and fell. His heavy male musk still lingered in her nose, and she could still taste the salt of his seed on her lips.

Smiling like a naughty teenager, Kiri let go her hold on Chank's mid-section and reached for his cock. It was already halfway to erect as she slipped her fingers around the soft, firming flesh. She brushed the small nub halfway down, a mole, she figured—a beauty mark. It felt interesting and she rubbed across it again.

It seemed to swell with his shaft.

Grinning, Kiri pinched the little mound of flesh.

Chank woke with a start and grabbed Kiri fast and hard. He moved so forcefully she didn't have time to think, much less react. One moment she was on top, shifting her hand lower to cradle his balls. The next, she was on her back, arms and legs splayed, pinned by his weight and his fierce hold on her wrists.

Damn!

She struggled and didn't move him an inch. Surprise competed with irritation. Years of self-defense training...but Kiri had never used it. She stayed out of the hand-to-hand, profiling and directing the troops—never fighting!

Did she need to fight now?

Chank's ragged breathing gave her no clues. He lay with his legs between hers, cock pressed hard against her thigh, his face only inches from her nose. His black eyes blazed fiercely in the low light.

Kiri had insane thoughts of goading him, making him angrier and angrier until he took her hard, fast, relentless. Until he left her screaming for mercy, and she left him limp and spent. Once more she struggled, this time harder.

"What are you hiding?" he growled.

"Fuck you!" She pushed against him with all her strength, and with a feeling that was almost a color. A red emotion, binding her senses to its will. Red. Red. Red! Like her vision in the awful nightmares.

Above her, Chank seemed loose and wild. Dangerous, even.

Something equally wild rose within Kiri, speeding from the depths of her consciousness to engage him. Her pussy flooded so fast she could barely stand it.

I've lost my mind, her rational side insisted.

Her irrational side only bellowed silently. Against her will, her eyes narrowed. "Let me go," she demanded.

"Make me," Chank countered. His voice sounded thick, his accent too heavy. Was he even awake? Did she care?

Kiri clenched her jaw, holding back a literal scream of challenge. A powerful aggressive urge rose, crested, and nearly pushed her to reach up and bite Chank's bottom lip.

"*Maman* Rubie told me you aren't what I think." Chank lowered his face until Kiri could feel the heat of his breath bathing her face. His eyes glittered in the morning sun—but they were distant, unfocused. "What are you?"

Thoughts spinning, body burning, Kiri was too far gone to answer. She wanted to claw at Chank. She wanted to punish him and prove what she was—a woman, all woman, his woman—and at the same time, she wanted to kill him. She literally wanted to kill him!

Or screw him silly.

I have gone completely nuts. It's hopeless.

Her nipples felt like hot, aching rocks against Chank's rough chest. Her clit throbbed and burned, and more than anything, she wanted to find a way to shift his cock toward her center, raise her hips, and take him deep, straight to her core.

Chank didn't seem the least interested in continuing. In fact, he seemed like he was on another planet.

"Are you still asleep?" she managed to mutter. Realizing she was right, she kneed him in the belly as best she could. "Wake up, damn it!"

Wake up and fuck me. Wake up and die! Shit. What's wrong with my brain?

Chank grunted as she kneed him again. Gradually, his eyes cleared, and he seemed to return to himself. In a flash he let go of her wrists and sat up, straddling her thighs.

She wanted to roar at him to come back and finish what he started.

"What happened?" His expression communicated shock blended with worry. "Did I hurt you?"

Kiri opened her mouth to swear at him, but instead said, "I'm not that fragile, remember?"

At this, Chank's dark face grew a shade darker and his lips tugged into a smile. He still seemed disturbed, wary—but more connected now.

Disconnect. Disconnect! Lose it again, and this time fuck me!

Kiri was quickly aware of Chank's cock, still hard against her belly. If she could only move a few inches...

"*Mais, oui.* You're not fragile." A deeper, fresher husk in his voice made Kiri's body vibrate. "I'm very glad. Fragile women are dull women, in my opinion."

Her arousal waned just enough to let her think—but not for long. Her breath caught anew as Chank eased off her thighs and trailed his cock through her thatch as he stared at her. She had kept her arms where he let them go, straight out, as if she were tied to the bed. Her nipples were still painfully hard, begging for his mouth, his teeth, and she knew he had to see her heart beating too fast. Her pussy more than ached as she felt the nudge of his erection.

She opened her legs wider and rubbed her clit against the tip of his cock. The sensation sent shocks up and down her spine. Kiri let out a long, slow sigh, still keeping her arms pasted to the bed. She still wanted Chank to grab her again, with that fierce look. With the edge of power and anger.

Why did that excite me?

The image of Tarzan and Jane intruded into her thoughts.

"I want you," she murmured, moving her hips in a circle, tempting and teasing. "Hard and fast. Now."

Chank responded instantly. In seconds, he had reached over to the drawer, removed a condom, opened it, and positioned it perfectly over his shaft.

"Hold me down like you did before," Kiri asked, barely suppressing a note of begging.

Eyebrows raised, Chank complied.

Once more he lay above Kiri, holding her down, completely in control. Only the wildness was missing. He seemed excited, but not over the edge.

Biting her lip with frustration, Kiri managed to squeeze her thighs together and trap his cock. She saw his eyes widen, first from pleasure, then from pain.

"Don't hold back." She pinched his shaft harder, then let it go. "Don't you dare."

"You start early, *catin*," he rumbled.

"Your fault."

"Mmm." He positioned his cock, ready to plunge into her pussy — but didn't. Instead, he shifted down and bit her nipple so hard she cried out.

That was perfect!

Kiri thrashed beneath him as he sucked the same nipple, biting and flicking his tongue over the top all at once.

No wonder other men had bored her so quickly. She wanted this kind of passion, this kind of power.

She *needed* it.

Struggling against his grip, Kiri tried to shift his attention to her other nipple — but Chank refused to move. He held her firmly. She felt his muscles growing more and more tense.

With excitement for her.

He bit her nipple again, just hard enough. Her clit throbbed, and she felt the tremors of a small orgasm.

"Yes. Like that!" She wriggled, but Chank held her right where he wanted her. With a deep groan of satisfaction, he seized her other nipple, sucked it into his mouth, and swirled his tongue around the edge.

Kiri shivered.

"Harder," she pleaded, but Chank kept up his gentle licking and sucking. "Please! Don't tease."

His laughter rumbled against her flesh, giving her new shivers and trembles. "When I'm ready," he murmured, then sucked her nipple between his lips again.

Kiri thought her pussy might explode.

And then Chank bit down on her nipple, gently. Once. Twice. Three times.

"Damn you," Kiri whispered, rocking her head back and forth. She was seeing red again, thinking of murder. Shoving the thoughts aside, she concentrated on her body's needs, her heart's wants.

Chank trailed his tongue over the sensitive flesh of her nipple once more, then bit down hard enough to bring tears to her eyes—and make her come. A bigger spasm this time.

He didn't let it pass.

Almost at the moment her orgasm waned, he drove his cock into her pussy, following the sensation deeper and deeper until Kiri could do nothing but moan and raise her hips to take him even farther.

"So good," he said in his thick, aroused bass. "*Catin.* Ah, *catin.*"

"Fuck me," Kiri pleaded. "I can't stand any more playing!"

Chank definitely wasn't playing. His eyes flashed as he bored into her and drew back, then plumbed her depths again. Her channel walls gripped his pulsing cock, giving her ripple after ripple of extra pleasure.

The feel of her hands pinned against the bed, the way he slammed into her pussy knowing she wanted it hard and deep, the perfect sore ache of her nipples, the wet sound of him sliding in and out, in and out, the fresh smell of sex mingled with last night's lingering aromas—all of these wonderful sensations swirled together.

Kiri heard herself screaming, "Now! Now! Now!"

She knew she was bucking hard against his thrusts, felt like his cock was driving home to the center of her body—and then she came with a mind-burning rush of heat. Dizziness overtook her as he kept pounding, groaning with his own orgasm and drawing out each contraction, each new blast of fire from seemingly every nerve ending in Kiri's body.

Limp and still reeling, Kiri couldn't react when he pulled out and let her wrists go. His weight shifted, and Kiri felt the wet heat of his tongue against her clit, pressing hard, moving just enough to continue releasing sweet, lingering aftershocks.

Every so often, he paused to mutter French endearments, and some in bayou patois. Did this man *ever* know how to please a woman...

And from the looks they shared, Kiri felt certain he'd been pleased, too. She deliberately refused to think about her bad dreams, her violent urges, or the red vision. Just her imagination. Passion gone insane. That had to be it.

Who did *Batman marry, anyway? Ah, the hell with it. Me Jane.* She ruffled Chank's hair. *You my swamp-Tarzan-Batman now*, mais, oui.

Kiri smiled as much as her spent muscles would allow.

Chapter Eleven

Chank savored Kiri's rich, musky juices. He had never been so aroused by any woman, or so thoroughly satisfied. Now, he enjoyed the unhurried, unpressured tasting of her leftover excitement.

This was why he had avoided her.

This was why he knew he had to stay away the minute he saw her.

He could imagine spending hours between her legs, sucking her clit, using his tongue to explore her sensitive channel, sliding his fingers in and out of her wet core, her tight ass, until he learned the taste and feel of every last inch of her. He wanted to memorize each sound of pleasure, each moan of delight, and learn her guarded fantasies and fill them, one at a time.

He wanted to show her what his body could *really* do, when he thought she was ready.

Then he wanted to start over, maybe make up a few new fantasies as they went.

It no longer bothered him that he couldn't "read" Kiri. Somehow not knowing for sure what she wanted was exciting, challenging. He found that without the noise of her direct impressions, he could feel at peace and concentrate on hearing what she truly needed and wanted. His five senses brought him plenty enough information. He wished he knew every detail of her past, and all her dreams for the future. No doubt he could talk to her for weeks and months and never run out of topics. Her sharp mind, her dry humor, her heart-twisting self-doubt — all of these things added up to an incredible woman.

He could see himself on Cain Island ten years from now, making love to Kiri into the wee hours of the morning. Twenty years from now. Forever, as long as they had.

This is past dangerous, mais oui. *And I'm a fool.*

He gradually stopped running his tongue up and down Kiri's wet folds. When he lifted his head and glanced up at her face, he felt surprised by a certain hardness to her features. She was gazing at him with relaxed happiness and desire—but deep in her eyes, he caught an unnatural gleam.

And then it was gone, just like that.

I'm anxious from my dreams, that's all. My dreams…

"What's wrong?" Kiri's voice carried through his sudden rise in worry. She must have felt him stiffen, depart from the moment and their feelings to a place of more urgency.

He sighed.

"As much as I'd like to stay right here for the next week, we can't." *Week? Hell. Would you stay a year,* catin? *Fifty, maybe?* Chank made himself smile. "I think we need to go see a friend of mine."

"This *Maman* Rubie you mentioned?" Kiri shifted beneath him and propped herself on her elbows. "Is she a *mam'bo*?"

Chank sat up and stared at his new and surprising lover. "*Oui.* But, how did you know?"

"I saw her when I first came here, when I was still on the boat. She was dressed in red and dancing, casting spells I think." Kiri shrugged. "By the time I made it ashore, she vanished. I mean, she left."

A deep sense of unease claimed Chank at Kiri's words. Obviously, she had seen *Maman* Rubie in a vision, making her protections for Cain Island.

But that was impossible. Only *Trakyrs* and *Huntyrs* could do that—along with ghosts and Voudon gods, and a few true believers.

Kiri didn't seem like a ghost or a god, or even a true believer. And she couldn't be a *Trakyr* or a *Huntyr*.

So…what was she?

He worked to keep his face impassive as he studied her.

That woman you keepin'—she's not what you think, mais, non. *Come see me, boy. Come soon… Things do change… Things always change…*

Chank broke a light sweat. He eased off the bed, smiling at his mysterious *catin.* "We have a lot of planning to do if we want to go after Bordelon before he kills again. And *Maman* Rubie could help us. Will you come with me to her little patch of swamp?"

Kiri sat up and grinned. All vestige of…other, of that hard gleam, were gone. "Sure thing. Let me get my guns, if any of them aren't rusted beyond repair. And oh, God. The mosquitoes. I wish I had—"

"Don't worry." Chank winked. "That I can handle."

An hour later, his belly full of toast and eggs, Chank suffered from a painful erection as he slowly and carefully rubbed a thick copper-tinged cream along the lines of Kiri's cheeks, her ears, her neck, and lower, to her chest.

The drawing room seemed too bright, too large. He wanted her in a small, quiet space, all to himself. He didn't want to be taking her off Cain Island, but the *Houngon* had already proved he could get to her in Sanctuaire. No way was he separating from her at this critical juncture. It would be just like the murdering bastard to strike tonight, during the new moon, when Chank least expected it.

No, they had to go to Daemon Swath and see *Maman* Rubie, to find out what they could. And they had to take out Jon Bordelon once and for all. Kiri wouldn't be safe any other way. As he ran his hands over her breasts, then down to her waist and back up again, his heart clenched.

He had to make her safe. He couldn't lose her.

Kiri held up her hair and smiled at him, clearly oblivious to his dark thoughts and enjoying his sexual frustration. He couldn't even kiss her because his family-recipe bug goo would numb his teeth and tongue.

Her skin felt as soft as flower petals even if her soul was as steely as the two functioning pistols she had cleaned, and her Bowie Rescue—currently waiting with her clothes on the leather sofa.

"Having a good time, Arceneaux?" Kiri winked at him, and he realized he'd been lingering over her still-swollen nipples, stroking them gently with his thumb.

"*Oui.*" He winked back and forced his hands lower, to her belly. "Never had better. Now don't go tempting me, or I'll rub this in places it shouldn't go."

"Mmm. Would you have to get a warm rag to wash it off then?"

Chank nodded. "But by then, I fear you'd be in serious pain."

Kiri grimaced and lowered her hair as he worked the goo into her hips and shapely ass. "Best be careful. I don't like *that* kind of pain."

Her sultry teasing made his cock hurt. Hellfire and damnation, but he wanted to fuck her again, bent over his leather sofa, breasts bouncing as he rammed into her hot juices, cock and *autre* alike…

I may die before I finish this. His jaw ached from clenching as he knelt and finished his task, covering the curves of her calves, working hard on her ankles and feet.

Thank the gods he had done his own coating. If he'd left it to her, she would have killed him sure, *mais, oui.*

"There," he said hoarsely. "When it cures, we'll be ready."

"For what?" Kiri teased as she picked up the black T he loaned her and struggled into it. It fit her like a shirt-dress and made him want to pick her up and take her back upstairs to bed. Her jeans had been rinsed out, but they weren't dry. As they had the day before, they clung to her hips, making him sigh before she dropped the T down to hide at least those assets.

Only the goo saved them from his raging desires.

An hour later, as the sun crested over the swamp, Chank poled the hand-carved Arceneaux pirogue through the Atchafalaya's black, black waters. Cypress branches blocked much of the sky, and Spanish moss hung in great green sheets all around them.

Kiri sat in the pirogue's far seat, balancing Chank's weight as mosquitoes and midges hovered around them. No biting, though. The family recipe was good as ever.

"The file said your *Maman* Rubie held off FBI agents until she was declared your guardian," Kiri said in a slightly forced tone. "With a rifle and a machete."

Chank nodded. "Two days. And it was a shotgun packed with rock salt and nails. You'd rather take a bullet than that stuff, yeah."

"Ouch." Kiri rested her hands on the sides of the pirogue. "Has she always been that fierce?"

"*Oui.* If they had taken me, Bordelon would have killed me." Chank felt his insides stiffen against discussing the tragedy, but it felt right to give Kiri what knowledge he could. After all, she was his family now, even if she didn't exactly know that yet. "The FBI didn't understand enough to protect me, or Human Services. Not even the local law, *non. Maman* Rubie saved my life twice over."

"Then I'm twice-over glad to meet her." Kiri's smile lit up the shadows cast by moss and vines. "Did you…know about Bordelon before he attacked Sanctuaire?"

"I knew of the *Huntyrs*, but there had been a peace between us for a generation. My father and Old Bordelon felt the time of our people had passed. What was the point, to fight with only one heir left to each?" Chank rammed the pole into the swamp harder than he intended, feeling the impact in his shoulders. "The *Houngon* — when his father died, he had other ideas. That or he went mad after his first kill. Many *Huntyrs* do."

"Can Bordelon shapeshift, or anything?" Kiri's gaze was direct, and her question held no ridicule. "If he's part-human, I mean."

Chank felt a small wave of guilt, but told most of the truth. "Back in our history, long ago — yes, both races could shift, mostly into beasts that hunt and prowl. Now, we just have the senses and use predator-minds as hosts."

And we have an interesting genetic modification in an interesting place…

Kiri sniffed and swatted at the hoard of frustrated mosquitoes. "The curse. Experiencing the world through the senses of predators. Is that happening now?"

"*Oui.* But I block it fairly well, especially close to home." Chank shifted his gaze easily back and forth from Kiri to the brackish water, measuring his next stroke with the pole. "Other times, I tap into it, use it to my benefit. I can't sense Bordelon, but I can borrow the eyes and ears and noses of animals to find the bastard."

This seemed to be enough to satisfy Kiri for a bit. Chank couldn't think of anything else relevant to tell her. *Trakyr* vs. *Huntyr* was a simple battle, uncomplicated and easy to understand. It was kill or be killed. Triumph or be tortured and eaten.

Such dramas played out every day and night, every minute, perhaps every second in the Atchafalaya Basin. The boat sliced quietly across the swamp's surface, and Chank wondered how many dead things, human or otherwise, had fertilized the rich silt. Millions. Maybe trillions.

For a moment, the hundreds of nearby predators felt loud and overpowering, but he quickly mastered his attention and realized something was odd. None of the predators were very close. Even the snakes were keeping a distance. It was as if someone had drawn a large circle around the pirogue and marked it as off limits.

Or maybe the predators were frightened of the only thing that scared them: a bigger, more effective predator.

With practiced force of will, Chank directed his mind back to navigating between massive cypress trunks and their knee-like roots jutting out of the water.

Kiri's voice was quiet when she next spoke. "Do you think Bordelon's bloody rituals have made him stronger, or is he delusional?"

Chank tightened his hands on the pole. "I believe in the *loas*, and the ability of some to call them. Whether Bordelon is a true *houngon*—anybody's guess, *oui*. But *Maman* Rubie, she's a true *mam'bo*, that I promise."

Once more, Kiri fell silent, leaving Chank to wonder exactly where Bordelon was and what the bastard was doing. The fact that he had let them get away from Cain Island with no attack disturbed Chank for some reason—but not nearly as much as the odd distance-keeping of the normal animal predators.

Something definitely wasn't right.

Bordelon must be close.

In fact nothing at all felt right in the bayou except Kiri's presence with him and his anticipation of seeing *Maman* Rubie again.

Chank glanced at Kiri, only to see that strange, hard glint in her eyes once more. She was gazing past him in the direction of Daemon Swath. Her knuckles were white from the force of her grip on the pirogue.

I should ask her what she's thinking, Chank told himself. *But I'm not sure I want to know.*

Chapter Twelve

It's not my imagination. Louisiana sun is hotter than Pennsylvania sun. Kiri wrinkled her nose, feeling a slight burn despite the thick bug goo and the shadows of tent-like cypress branches.

As Chank poled the pirogue across the bayou's thick black water, Kiri had a good time studying his T-shirt-clad muscles. She also had a blast noting the way his ass filled out his tight black jeans. They hadn't been in the water five minutes when the man broke a full-body sweat. His ponytail quickly fell limp against the back of his neck, and Kiri enjoyed the way his white T stuck to him like a second skin.

Then, her brain started to short-circuit.

At first it was a moment of splashing water when no water was splashing anywhere she could see. And yet she experienced the sounds, the sudden fresh-dirt smell of the water, just as clearly as if it happened next to her. A few minutes later, Kiri felt herself slithering over some leaves. Just a flash, quick, there and gone, running away—but she felt it.

She had "borrowed" the consciousness of animals before, ridden with them just like she rode with perps, in the back of their minds—on purpose, never by accident. This was different. This was out of her control.

Is it Bordelon? Is the bastard playing me?

A real, tangible snake swam through the plant-filled muck far in the distance, racing away from the boat but still within Kiri's eyesight. For a moment, she could see the reptile's intricate skin patterns too well, as if it were right beside the boat. As she stared, she had passing thoughts about grabbing the snake and eating it. Raw.

"I'm losing it," she muttered.

"What?" Chank gave her a smooth gaze over his shoulder as he pushed hard with the pole. His muscles bulged.

Damn the mosquito goo. She wished she could jump him where he stood. Her emotions were a swirl of fear and desire. Rage and lust.

"Something's wrong," she admitted through clenched teeth, after dreaming up and discarding five steamy in-the-pirogue sexual fantasies—all of which ended with the little boat upside down and the two of them getting their naked asses chewed by alligators.

Kiri expected Chank to question her, but instead he said, "*Oui.* I sense it too."

"I keep seeing things I shouldn't. Stuff like what you told me about—the world through a predator's eyes, only they're all running away from something."

At this, Chank's lips tightened to a straight line. He said nothing for long, long seconds, then offered only, "Unusual. Has that happened before?"

"Yes and no." Kiri fretted with the oversized black T-shirt Chank had loaned her, tying a knot in the side so it wouldn't hang to her knees when she stood. Her jeans, still damp from rinsing out, felt absolutely wet with added sweat and humidity. "I've never ridden in a mind by accident. It's never been out of my control. Is Bordelon doing something?"

Chank shrugged, then poled harder. "Maybe. I don't know."

And then he got as quiet as the boatman on the River Styx.

Pole, glide. Pole, glide.

Kiri felt almost hypnotized by the rhythm, but at least she could block out the surges of sexual fire and anger that seemed to be coming from nowhere.

"We're almost to Daemon Swath," Chank murmured as they passed beneath thick tendrils of Spanish moss. "*Maman* Rubie, she'll help us."

After a few more minutes, Kiri felt the harsh, unforgiving grip of anxiety. Her heart thumped so hard she heard blood pumping in her ears, and her fingers kept balling into fists she had to consciously release. She became sure they shouldn't go to Daemon Swath, and almost shouted her sudden realization of that fact.

Chank, oblivious to her distress, made a smooth landing on the shore of an island more packed with dirt and trees than anything else.

Kiri started to shake.

Her eyes darted left, then right. If she had been in a movie, no doubt some deep and god-like voice would have screamed about evil and warned her to run away.

"What's that smell?" she asked suddenly, her stomach heaving. The aroma was thick and sweet. Her mouth watered crazily despite her desire to vomit.

"Fresh chicken on the spit," Chank answered evenly. He was eyeing her in a way that told her he saw she was nervous. "*Maman Rubie must be cooking for the loas*. You okay, *catin?*"

NO!

"Sort of," she muttered as she climbed out of the pirogue, relieved Chank couldn't read her. Whatever was happening in her head couldn't be real. She had reached out with her senses, and no dangers lurked nearby. Bordelon was a wildcard, but they knew he could be anywhere, at any time—so, he was a given. And if he was waiting on Daemon Swath, so much the better. It would save them the time and trouble of hunting him down.

To comfort herself, she flexed her shoulders, enjoying the feel of the Bowie Rescue taped firmly beneath her shirt, snug against the small of her back. She had a newly cleaned and oiled standard-issue sidearm in an ankle holster and another secured by a holster to her waist. The remainder of her guns waited at Sanctuaire, ruined by her swim in the swamp.

Chank was unarmed. *I rely on my wits. Guns won't kill much in this part of the Atchafalaya,* catin.

Whatever. If she got nervous, she'd shoot first and interrogate later. Until now, she'd been spared that horror in her work, but she had a feeling Bordelon would leave her with no options.

Kill. Murder. Blood. Red. RED! Her vision blurred to crimson, and she swayed. Another wave of fear wracked Kiri as she joined Chank over by a dirt path. When she shook her head and tried to think, all she could do was tremble.

Chank reached her in two steps and wrapped her in his firm embrace. He said nothing, and for that, Kiri was grateful. She took a deep breath, inhaling his man's scent of sweat, sun-browned skin, and fresh earth. His touch seemed to reach her mind, easing her tension and calming the riot of her thoughts. Bit by bit, the visions of red receded. She focused on Chank's strong arms and hard chest, and how good it felt to be—just for a few seconds—protected when she felt so afraid.

The smell of roasting chicken suddenly seemed pleasant.

She raised her head and kissed Chank on the cheek. "Better now. I think I got too hot, or something. I'm just…more nervous than I'm used to being."

Her Cajun Batman gave her his quirky smile and took her hand. "The Swath would make a priest carry Holy Water, *catin*. Come. She's not as fearsome as you think."

Kiri walked beside him, squeezing his fingers, absolutely sure he was lying at least a little bit.

It took only a few minutes to reach the center of Daemon Swath. Kiri absorbed the sights silently, from the board home to the large *oum'phor* to the bottles and bones hanging from trees—each of which had a painted base. Smoke rose in fits and puffs from behind the house, and Chank escorted Kiri around the corner. She clung to him, still a little woozy and fearful, which pissed her off.

By the time she caught sight of *Maman* Rubie, she was grinding her teeth and digging her fingers into Chank's forearm.

The old *mam'bo*, skin as black as Chank's fathomless eyes, wore a white peasant's smock and head wrap that made for a blinding contrast. Despite the dirt and smoke, the cotton fabric seemed spotless, almost luminescent. She had her back to them and she bent over, poking at coals under a hand-crank spit with a long stick. Four pullets roasted over the low flames. Small pots made a circle around the fire pit, and some of them were smoking, too.

Kiri sensed rather than saw power radiating from the woman in slow, lazy arcs. Impulses to pull her knife or a gun pounded on her instincts, but she refused to respond. This was Chank's godmother. The woman who saved him and raised him. Why was she filled with such a desire to disrespect her—or more to the point, flee her sanctuary like a hunted rabbit?

Maman Rubie stood and straightened herself. Her shoulders stiffened. Slowly, she turned, holding the stick like a fire-tipped spear.

Kiri had to hold her breath to keep from screaming.

She saw *two* women. One old and gnarled and bent, innocuous and even subservient in expression. Behind that façade, or under that skin stood a warrior of fearsome proportions—red eyes, a necklace made of teeth, crimson garb from head to toe, and the most menacing snarl Kiri had ever witnessed on a human being. Smoke lifted and swirled about the double-figure, like a cloak or a screen. The woman studied Chank, then turned her fearsome dual eyes on Kiri.

Chank had stopped walking and had placed his hand over Kiri's. Good thing, or she would have bolted then and there.

The *mam'bo* gazed at Kiri for so long even Chank fidgeted. At last, she lowered her stick and cast it down. Without speaking she turned and kicked dirt over the fire, smothering it quickly. Not so much as an ash or dust speck settled on her dress. She raised her arms and chanted something Kiri took for a prayer, then bowed and backed out of the circle of pots.

As she left the smoke, her double-persona faded slowly into the hazy sunlight. Now she became a kindly but somewhat shrewd-looking older lady, dressed in reasonably fresh cotton, arms open, smiling at Chank.

Kiri waited quietly as Chank embraced his foster mother and spoke to her gently in patois. *Maman* Rubie's teeth flashed when she smiled, and she kept the smile as she let Chank go and walked over to Kiri.

Trying her best to smile back, Kiri extended her hand. *Maman* Rubie clasped it. Kiri felt a painful shock and cried out as a cracking sound tore the silence on the Swath.

Both women jumped backward, and Kiri fell to her knees holding her hand. She just knew all the bones had been broken, but the searing, wringing sensation passed in a hurry. All that remained were her strange, unsettling emotions—rage, fear, distant lust—and the reddish gauze on her vision.

Her head throbbed. Surely her brain had to be splitting in half.

"Easy," she heard a woman's heavily-accented voice saying. Then, "Get her to the house, yeah. I'll take care of her there."

Chank knelt beside Kiri just as her mind switched off like an overloaded circuit. She barely felt him catch her as she pitched forward into darkness.

Chapter Thirteen

The inside of *Maman* Rubie's house seemed too dark and too hot.

Chank's gut burned as he watched his foster mother hover over the small, flat bed in the main room—the bed she used for special healings. Deftly, *Maman* Rubie anointed the woman he loved with an uncrossing oil mixed from patchouli, sandalwood, myrrh, cinquefoil, and ammonia no doubt distilled from swamp gasses. His eyes watered from the overpowering scent as she spoke low and forcefully, to drive away any evil clinging to Kiri.

Something unnatural had happened outside.

Chank had that "wrong" feeling again, now so strongly his *Trakyr* senses were on high alert. A thousand questions competed for asking, but he knew better than to interrupt his foster mother while she worked. He had seen her do this too many times, and he knew the score.

If someone or something tried to hurt these two women—his blood revved like hot oil in an engine. He would maim. He would kill.

He thought about taking Kiri's guns, then decided to leave them with her in case she needed them.

All he needed was his bare hands.

Maman Rubie put down the uncrossing oil and changed to a fouler smelling concoction of mandrake and petitgrain with a touch of angelica.

"Protection," Chank murmured.

His foster mother nodded. She anointed the still unconscious Kiri once more, then handed the small brown pot to Chank. Automatically, he crossed to the door and rubbed the oil on the handle. After that, he dabbed oil on all the windowsills in the house. The ritual felt as familiar to him as dressing or eating, since he had completed it every night of his childhood, until he left the Atchafalaya Basin.

When he finished, he came back to Kiri's bedside and gazed down at her pale, sleeping form.

"What is it?" He finally allowed himself to ask, heart aching from the sight of her so weak and vulnerable. "Did Bordelon attack her thoughts?"

"*Non*." *Maman* Rubie sat down in a cane-bottom rocker close to the bed, keeping watch over her patient. "Her own mind attacked her."

"Like mine does sometimes." Chank let out a breath of relief, understanding, but his foster mother shook her head.

"*Non*. Not like yours. Boy, don't you know what she is?"

Chank tore his eyes from Kiri and stared at *Maman* Rubie. "A damn good agent and fine woman—with some abilities like mine."

"Not...like...yours." *Maman* Rubie's tone was stern. "Lookin' away don' make nothin' disappear, Chank Arceneaux."

"Not, possible." Dread eased into Chank's mind, cooling his rage and worry into thick, motionless ice. "When he came to the Swath hunting me, you cut his face. You cut his manhood, *oui*. You told me he couldn't have a baby, that we'd be the last!"

"He was near to grown, boy. His dick worked before I took his balls. What if—"

"No!" Chank's shout rang through the muggy, still darkness of the house. He turned his back on his foster mother and stared at Kiri, half-blind with shock and anger.

And then, somewhere out in the swamp, someone started laughing.

Bordelon!

Chank acted before he thought, wheeling around and stalking toward the door.

"*Couillon*. Be still." *Maman* Rubie was already there, blocking his exit. He raised his arms to push her aside, but faltered at the full sight of her, bent and shaking with the fatigue of magic already worked, using the facing to support herself.

"Please, get out of my way. I don't want to hurt you."

"You want to hurt somethin', yeah. Why not me? I'm handy." *Maman* Rubie laughed, just a small chuckle.

As if in answer, Bordelon's laughter swelled like the wind, rising high above the swamp. If sounds could kill light, his cackling would surely jerk the sun from the sky.

Chank felt like a ball of rage. All he wanted to do was get out of the carefully protected house, get away from *Maman* Rubie and Kiri and anything else that might keep him from tearing Jon Bordelon into hundreds of bloody pieces.

"Quit listenin' to him. Demons can't enter you if—"

"If you don't open the door." Chank exhaled the rest of the familiar adage. His better sense returned slowly, and he realized *Maman* Rubie was right. If he stormed out of the house now, he'd break the magic she had just worked, put himself at risk, and leave both women without his protection.

Kiri stirred, and both Chank and *Maman* Rubie startled.

Chank stared over his foster mother's shoulder, filled with love and misery. For the first time since he was nine years old, he felt completely lost.

"What am I gonna do, *Maman*?" he asked. "I made her my family. I—I love her."

Maman Rubie took his arm and led him back to Kiri. She patted the side of the bed for him to sit down, and Chank sat.

"For now, boy, thas enough. Just wake her up." *Maman* Rubie winked. "We'll figure this out together."

Chapter Fourteen

Kiri woke to the sensation of an army marching back and forth between her temples. The world was spinning, and something stunk to high heaven.

"Get me out of the toilet," she pleaded, then coughed.

"Here, *catin*." Chank's voice cut through her confusion. She squinted at him in the candlelight.

Candlelight?

"What time is it?" She tried to sit up, but Chank gently pushed her back.

"Early evening," he said in that low sexy voice. Kiri would have gotten horny immediately, but she felt like she was dying. And she smelled like an explosion in an incense factory. And she was on a bed harder than granite, in a stiflingly hot board house, drenched with sweat and God only knew what else.

On top of that, a Voudon *mam'bo* was sitting beside her bed in a cane-bottom rocker, creaking back and forth, back and forth, smoking a corncob pipe.

Thoughts of wild Cajun sex faded quickly from Kiri's mind.

"What happened to me?" This time, she sat up slowly, and Chank helped her. "You touched me and—"

"I knocked you out, *oui*." *Maman* Rubie nodded. "If I'd known you were *Huntyr*, I would have been more careful."

"Excuse me?" Kiri shoved Chank away from her bed and swung her legs over the side. She faced the *mam'bo*, heart hammering, squeezing the wooden bed frame until her fingers hurt.

Then she looked at Chank, and his drawn, sad expression confirmed the woman's absurd assertion.

"Listen to her," he said quietly. "She'll explain what we know, *oui*. Then you can agree or disagree."

Damn him for always making sense.

Kiri tried to swallow, but her throat was too dry. Before she could ask for water, Chank picked up a pitcher from a tray and poured her a glass.

She drank it gratefully, feeling the cool liquid slide into her belly, dropping her body temperature from inferno to bearable. He handed her a large yellow apple then, and she didn't protest. Her stomach ached from hunger, and the fruit seemed oddly filling with each bite she took.

When she finished the apple, Chank threw away the core and came to sit beside her. He put his arm on her shoulders, and together they faced *Maman* Rubie.

"When this one was a boy, Old Bordelon died. Young Bordelon, near seventeen years old, was the only soul left on Chien Stretch—and he don't hold with the truce his daddy made. *Non.*" The *mam'bo* took a draw on her cob pipe, filling the room with sweet smoke. "He did what his daddy wouldn't allow. He killed, and like most with *Huntyr* blood, he lost his reason. Killin' became the only thing, the most important thing."

"He murdered Chank's family." Kiri leaned into Chank's hug, as much to offer him support as to comfort herself.

"*Oui.* And he came for the boy, too. Mistake was, he came here."

Maman Rubie paused for another few puffs, and Chank spoke. "He got here before I did, and he tried to kill *Maman*. She cut him bad across the face." He ran a finger from his left ear to his nose, lining out the scar Kiri knew well from her memories of Bordelon's hateful face. "And then she...cut him lower."

Kiri's eyes widened. "As in his dick?"

"*Mais, oui.*" The *mam'bo* held her pipe in her teeth and grinned. "Stupid little shit. Cut his thunder, so he don' have babies. Thing is, he was old enough to use that damn dick before I hacked his balls clean off. Never thought about that, til I met you."

"You...never knew your father, *catin*," Chank added. "You told me that. With your abilities and all that's happened, we think—"

"Stop." Kiri leaped up before he could finish, swayed with the force of her head pain, and sat back down, hard.

Chank reached for her, but she pushed his arm away. "Don't touch me! That's foul. It's stupid and disgusting, and no. Just, no! Jon Bordelon is *not* my father."

Yet even as she said it, she heard the devastating ring of truth, and she hated it. For five whole seconds, she hated Chank, too.

"My touch, it's poison for a *Huntyr*." *Maman* Rubie kept puffing, apparently unconcerned about Kiri's fomenting freak-out. "You probably 'bout busted a gut not wantin' to get off that pirogue and come up on this little piece of earth, *oui*?"

Kiri seethed in silence as her stomach clenched. She wanted to hurl curses at this know-it-all bitch, and at Chank for listening to her.

Suddenly, *Maman* Rubie leaned forward and spoke in steady, forceful tones. "I'm too old to be dealin' with bullshit, girl. When Bordelon tries to take your mind, you can push him out after a fashion. Only *Huntyr* and *Trakyr* could do that, and you ain' *Trakyr*. Tell me you've been fine since you been in the swamp, that you ain' startin' to see the world in blood-red, in terms of food and not food. Go on. Tell me that."

"I—" Kiri faltered, nearly consumed with disbelief and belief at the same time. "I've been too hot," she finished weakly, feeling more sick than ever.

No. No. No. No.

"You been too close to the source, to the first huntin' grounds." *Maman* Rubie sat back and flicked a lighter into her pipe. Kiri thought she'd gag on the smoke. "The *Huntyr* half of your blood, it's tryin' to win out."

"If you'd gone to Chien Stretch without coming here…" Chank, who had inched close to her on the bed again, trailed off, then shrugged and looked at the floor. "I might have lost you before I had you."

Kiri slowly went numb and wished she could dig herself a pit and just jump in. A month ago, her life had been normal. She'd been a crack profiler, on the rise. She'd been sane, and relatively certain about the direction of her life.

And you were dating your pops. Don't leave out that part.

Her stomach lurched.

Instinctively, she reached for Chank, and he was there on the bed beside her. Right there. Even though he'd just found out she was part of a race his people had been at war with since time began.

Chest aching, she dared to look into his eyes. She saw no revulsion or disgust, only affection.

Only naked, undisguised love.

He winked at her, then settled his arm back around her shoulders, chasing away the darkest part of her despair.

"Bordelon must have figured to use you, once he got such a dose of good luck—you crossing paths with this one here, and him wantin' you." *Maman* Rubie resumed her rocking. "If he could hook the two of you up, he'd always have a pair of eyes on Chank, until he could break my magic and take him out."

"But on the balcony, at Sanctuaire." Kiri straightened up, feeling a new flash of hope. "If all this is true, why'd he try to kill me?"

Maman Rubie's expression never changed. "Mayhap he did, mayhap he don'. Tricky bastard, *oui*. Either way, he'd win. You jump off and die, Chank goes crazy with grief, my magic fails, and he kills Chank. You don' jump, Bordelon still has his eyes on Chank and a brand new weak spot to use."

At this, Kiri recoiled and tried to pull away from Chank, but he wouldn't let her go.

"*Non, catin.* Not your fault. I don't care what the bastard thinks." He leaned down and kissed the side of her head, keeping his arm firmly in place. "Thing about him is, he sees everybody like himself, bloodthirsty and cold. That's not you. You've been resisting him."

"But once you touched me—" her voice caught, and she almost started to cry.

"*Oui.* Once I touched you, finished falling in love with you..." Chank pulled her closer and she couldn't help putting her head on his shoulder. "He thinks it's no-lose for him."

"It is, unless she never kills," said *Maman* Rubie. "And we kill Bordelon."

Kiri stopped talking, doing her best to think through everything. Her thoughts bumped against each other like cars in a demolition derby, and nothing wanted to make sense.

To their credit, Chank and his foster mother didn't intrude. They simply sat with her, affirming her with their presence, until she righted herself enough to say, "But what if killing him doesn't end it? If you're right, I'm still...half of that evil bastard. What if I lose my mind and start eating animals raw and murdering people?"

"*Non, catin.*" Chank's response was immediate and passionate. Kiri wanted to look at him again, but she couldn't. She just couldn't. "What you say, it isn't you. Your essence is good."

Kiri exploded off the bed, filling the small space between *Maman* Rubie's chair and the edge of the blankets. Her heart thumped in rabbit-like bursts, and she wanted to bite something. Everything. Anything.

"How do you know I won't go nuts?" Her voice sounded deeper than she'd ever heard it. "You can't read me, Chank. We're blind to each other."

Chank got slowly to his feet, and Kiri heard the creak of cane and wood as *Maman* Rubie quietly extracted herself from the situation. No one spoke in the long seconds it took the *mam'bo* to cross to the door to her bedroom and shut it quietly behind her.

Before she could speak any of the fears crowding her mind, Chank had her in his arms. His hot breath brushed her ear as he murmured, "I can't read you mind to mind, *mais oui*. But I can read you in all the ways that count."

More red, bleak rage frothed through Kiri's veins, but Chank's touch eased her malicious feelings. Bit by bit, she felt more like herself, and yet, less like herself than ever. She clung to him like a child rescued from a hurricane, blown by unexpected winds, drenched with her own sweat and his.

He stroked her arms. "I do love you, *catin*. It may seem odd and too soon, but since I met you five years ago…"

"I know," she said hoarsely, focusing on the rhythm of his touch. "I—you…well, damn, Batman. I love you, too."

Chank stepped back just far enough to gaze into her eyes. He cupped her cheeks in his hands, gently rubbing the outline of her ears. "The old magic *Maman* used to protect me, I gave it to you when we made love, *oui*. By caring about you so deeply, by making you my family of choice. Unless Bordelon breaks her spells, he won't find you the easy prey he thinks."

Kiri thought about chastising Chank for not telling her this sooner, but her brain had suddenly shifted gears. "If Bordelon doesn't know I'm protected, then I'm the perfect bait."

Chank's sharp eyes and anxious frown told her that he had already come to the same conclusion. She could tell he wanted to argue, insist that she take no part in the danger ahead, but they both knew better. They had been agents too long, and more than that, they were human beings with a responsibility to do something no one else could do: stop Bordelon's evil.

Using me to lure my…my **father** *out of hiding…it's our best chance.* She bit back a rush of bile at the thought. *I'd never give him my blood willingly, but I would happily lead the bastard to his death.*

Chapter Fifteen

Chank watched Kiri pole the pirogue into the darkness of the swamp, guided only by a lantern. Her course would be straight on to Chien Stretch. Her instincts would lead her just as surely as if the island had a homing beacon lodged in its bloodstained shore.

Aided by *Maman* Rubie's signs and predictions, they had decided Bordelon would be where he was the strongest and safest on this dangerous New Moon night—his own island. In the confines of his birth-home, whatever protective magic *Huntyrs* could work would be most powerful. Bordelon might expect some attempt to approach him, and he would no doubt be prepared.

Still, he was likely sleeping, restoring himself for a new round of frenzied killing, not to mention his attacks on them. Bordelon didn't know Kiri had come under the same protections that had kept him from killing Chank for so many years.

This would be their secret weapon.

Kiri's presence would jar Bordelon, gain his attention. He would come for her, to taunt and tease, maybe to hypnotize her until she gave up her blood for his dark purpose—maybe even to kill her. After all, with her blood, he believed he would be able to break the magic protecting Chank.

The *Houngon* would have to try.

But he would fail...and Kiri wouldn't let on. She would play along, fill his senses and distract him, lead him closer and closer to the island's edge, out into the water—and Jon Bordelon would meet his doom.

Kiri would not be alone as she teased Bordelon into action.

Chank would be waiting, lodged in a host Bordelon would not expect—and could not defeat.

Maman Rubie had hold of Chank's waist, joined with him body and mind as much as possible. They could share some thoughts, some perceptions like this—not all, but hopefully enough. She muttered incantations as he reached his thoughts into the endless black water and searched for the type of mind he needed. It didn't take long to find a host, and Chank didn't spend a second hesitating or remembering the past. His present and future were at stake, along with the woman he loved.

With determined yet measured force, Chank let his consciousness sink into the water and down, down, down into the muck, into the most brutal, prehistorically fierce mind he had ever shared.

The bull gator thrashed as it sensed the intrusion, and Chank flinched from the force of the beast's attempt to push back his entry. The damn beast was the size of a cow with a ten foot tail, and its jaws could open wide enough to eat an actual bull.

Maman Rubie's grip steadied him. She was still talking, a language Chank had never heard of grunts, clacks, whistles, growls…

Easy, his mind clumsily translated her words as much as possible. *Feed. Time to…feed.*

Chank felt the big beast whip its massive tail and start to swim. He could "smell", but the sense was unusual in the water—musk, mildew—he couldn't put his finger on what he was experiencing until he realized his nose was closed by skin flaps. He stared straight ahead into the dense water, eyes protected by a transparent third eyelid, but he was unable to interpret any of the shadows the gator deftly avoided or wanted to pursue. Though the beast could see in the dark, the water obscured his vision. More than anything, Chank *heard* the swamp in a completely new way, even through the water-protective flaps covering the gator's ears.

The vibrations of moving fins and tails.

Splashes both close and distant.

The sinister whisper of low-lying currents.

An out-of-place *plunk-thunk* followed by a *swiiisssh*.

This noise stood out like a hiccup in the natural flow of sounds.

Plunk-thunk…swiiisssh.

Plunk-thunk…swiiisssh.

The old alligator wanted to move away from it, but Chank carefully urged him toward it instead.

Maman Rubie had to work hard to keep the beast focused and relaxed as they headed straight for human-noise.

And then the gator surfaced near the pirogue with a quiet *pop*.

Instantly, the beast swallowed as his throat opened. Chank's hearing and vision and sense of smell cleared as if a blanket had been lifted off his head. Everything seemed sharp, crisp, even though it was beyond dark with no moon.

"Turtle, turtle, turtle…" *Maman* Rubie kept up a steady chant in Chank's ear and the gator's brain, convincing it that the boat was highly desired prey. The beast obliged their needs by powering forward, legs clawing, tail slicing back and forth.

Between the two of them, they kept it motivated to chase, but slow enough and distracted enough never to catch up.

Chank relaxed for the next half hour or so, pleased by their progress and his nearness to Kiri. Here and there, he worried about their plan, to draw Bordelon into the open and attack him with the combined force of *Maman* Rubie's magic, Chank's experience and anger, Kiri's prowess, and the strength of the gator itself.

Crude. Elementary. Simple.

And just brazen enough to work, if they caught the monster unaware.

The bull gator was more than powerful enough to take on Bordelon should he appear sooner than expected.

Mais, oui. Chank smiled to himself. *This gator could take on a pickup truck without much effort.*

"Boy, don' make me laugh." His foster mother's chastising was instant. "Keep your mind on your business."

Our boy here, he's the only predator around, Chank told her. *Haven't felt anything for the last fifteen minutes, or more.*

"*Oui*. Does that surprise you? They're scared of Bordelon. They're scared of your girl."

Kiri's pirogue kept moving, farther and farther away from Daemon Swath. At the forty-five minute mark, Chank's enhanced night vision offered him long, savory views of her strong arms wielding the pole. Sometimes he caught a glimpse, head to ankle. Her black hair was pulled back sharply, showing the elegant angle of her jaw. Her full curves made her seem all the more feminine and powerful, yet all the more vulnerable.

She saw his gator host swimming along beside her, and the lantern-light revealed her smile. Her bared teeth glinted in the yellow light, and for a moment, she looked fierce enough to kill the *Huntyr* herself—but that couldn't happen. Kiri must never kill. Ever. No matter what.

Chank's cold amphibian pulse quickened.

They were almost to Chien Stretch. Any minute now, the action would begin.

Kiri stood still in the pirogue, letting it glide toward the Stretch's dirty shore.

Dieu, but she's beautiful. If Bordelon lays a finger on her...

The gator gnashed its teeth, aroused by Chank's surge of protectiveness.

Maman Rubie pinched the sides of his physical body to recapture his attention—and the world around them exploded.

Chank's ears—his real ears—shut down from the force of the noise from behind him. His consciousness tore loose from the gator as he pitched forward, his face plunging into the bayou muck while his feet stayed on land.

Maman Rubie landed on top of him, gasping.

Chank struggled to free himself, managed to sit up, and wrapped his arms around his foster mother. He knew he had to get her to shore in a hurry, then find some way back to Kiri.

Catin! Ah, damn! If only she could hear him.

Still dizzy from his ride in the gator's mind, Chank tried to pull *Maman* Rubie to safety. His cheeks and neck took stinging blasts of hot wind and dirt. Before his mind fully settled back into his body, before he even understood what had happened, *Maman* Rubie was snatched from his grasp.

Chank blinked to clear his vision, but ash and smoke stung his eyes. The darkness had vanished, replaced by blazing yellow light. He made out a familiar figure dragging *Maman* Rubie toward towering flames.

"Bordelon!" he roared, staggering out of the water.

The *Huntyr* ignored him and hauled his prize toward the firestorm.

Chank howled as he ran forward to save his foster mother.

Every structure on Daemon Swath was burning to the ground.

Chapter Sixteen

The gator struck the pirogue so hard Kiri literally flew into the water. The sound of wood being splintered and crunched terrified her into swimming as hard as she could for the shore—for anywhere but near the big bull gator that had lost its mind.

Behind her, the beast thrashed in the water and smashed her boat between its massive jaws. Its fury rippled out in waves, half-absorbing Kiri's senses as she battled to keep her wits. She couldn't see a thing even when she desperately raised her face to breathe.

Where was Chien Stretch? How far ahead?

If I don't get to the shore…where is Chank? What on earth happened?

Her arms chopped against the thick, warm muck as the weight of her jeans and Chank's oversized cotton shirt pulled her down. Her guns were being ruined. No way they would fire now. Probably never again.

She would reach the Stretch alone, with no backup, and no firepower. Nothing but her Bowie Rescue, still taped firmly against the small of her back.

Damn. Damn!

Her heart threatened to leap into her throat. Her lungs felt like they were tearing in half from the effort of her swim. Her extra senses surged and surged, confusing her, almost leading her down into the depths to search for fish, turtles—any prey she could find.

"Leave me alone!" she shouted at her own mind, her voice muffled in the unforgiving bayou waters. She didn't dare kill, not even an animal. Not even a fly, if she could help it.

Her ears, super-alert, caught the sound of silence, followed by the sound of swishing and splashing.

The gator was coming.

And the gator was close.

Kiri's kicking feet struck bottom and she righted herself as fast as she could. Stumbling and cursing, fighting the water's deadly grip, she tore herself from the swamp and threw herself onto dry land.

Almost at once, she fell.

"Son of a bitch!" Her frustrated scream hurt her own ears—but not nearly as much as the bone-breaking roar from right behind her.

She turned on her hands and knees, slowly, slowly, and found herself facing the biggest alligator she had ever seen. His dark outline extended from a foot or so in front of her nose, back across the shore, where it seemed to become one with the inky water.

The monster's eyes glowed in the darkness like some demon straight out of hell.

Kiri thought about screaming or running, but she knew better. The bastard could run twenty miles an hour or better, at least for short distances. That, and it could see in the dark.

Though Kiri realized she wasn't doing half-bad in that respect, herself. Little by little, the gator's outline was sharpening as she stared. Her sense of smell, her hearing—all of her awareness seemed to be doubling, tripling as she sat like a dog waiting for the gator to snap off her head.

Its mouth was open. Chunks of wood were lodged between its dark, mossy teeth.

"Go ahead," Kiri growled. A red rage broiled in her belly, rising quickly to her throat, her eyes. "Do it. Do it!"

The gator swayed, as if uncertain.

Kiri barely noticed through her fog of fury. Her fists clenched. She pushed herself off the ground.

"Come on, I said!"

Her voice carried in an eerie way, sounding almost like the bellow of a female gator.

At this, the bull clamped his mouth shut and actually backed up a step. He moved his head this way and that, seeming to take in where he was, and the general absence of other animals.

"Get off my island!" Kiri screamed. She actually kicked out at the beast, catching it on the lower jaw.

Part of her mind informed her that her leg would be bitten off at any second.

Another part of her mind, much darker and more primitive, did nothing but roar and shout—which Kiri realized she was doing aloud.

The gator gazed at her with his glowing eyes, swayed for another few seconds, then turned and ran back into the swamp

Kiri watched it go with her oddly enhanced vision. The world around her seemed distinct yet dark, bathed in the red haze of madness she could no longer control. Her one urge was to follow the gator into the water, find it, tear it to bits with her bare hands, and eat it.

God, what's happening to me?

"What's going on?" Her shriek startled her in the relative silence of the Stretch. As she gulped in air, her thoughts began to calm. After a minute, she was able to release her fists.

Still panting, still with teeth clenched, she turned a circle, examining her surroundings. Bordelon could be anywhere. Beside her. Behind her.

But there was nothing but reeds and a few scrubby trees and bushes. No house to speak of. Just a broken down shack, far in the dark distance.

"Whatever," Kiri muttered, willing her heart back to a normal beat. She turned to check for the gator before heading for the shack — and came face to face with a tall, heavy-set woman wrapped in luminescent red silks.

Not *Maman* Rubie. No. This woman had skin the color of alabaster and long blonde ringlets arranged in a mound on the top of her head. Her skirts billowed out toward the bottom in the hoop-style of centuries past.

She looked…classy. European, maybe. French? English?

There's a loa *who's supposed to be white…Shit! Get a grip, Auckland! She's a friggin' vision on a haunted island!*

"Who are you?" Kiri finally managed, afraid to take her eyes off the woman lest she vanish like *Maman* Rubie did on the shores of Cain Island.

"I am called Mademoiselle Charlotte." The woman's tone was cool, but not unfriendly.

The loa's *tone*, Kiri reminded herself. She shivered despite the heat.

Mademoiselle Charlotte appraised Kiri like a prize filly up for sale. She even reached out a ghostly hand and pried open Kiri's lips to stare at her teeth. The contact felt like an ice-bolt to the mouth, but Kiri held her ground. She was starting to see red again, on the fringes of her vision.

Without comment, the woman released her lips and glanced back in the direction of Daemon Swath. It was then that Kiri noticed an odd orange glow against the otherwise velvet-black sky. Her throat went completely dry.

"Chank," she rasped. "Oh, no. No!"

"Trouble, *oui*," said the apparition in a lilting but formal French accent. She turned her piercing green eyes to Kiri. "Only a half-blood you, but you are strong. Willful. You will do. Now, *petite chou*, you must come with me before all is lost."

The old French endearment grated on Kiri's nerves. She opened her mouth to protest, but before she could speak, a swirling wind caught her around the ankles.

It felt...strange. Too strong for any normal wind.

Slowly, the moving air crept up her legs to her hips, her belly, her chest, her shoulders—she was completely encased in the chilly swirls—and then she felt herself leave the ground.

Kiri flailed for a second, almost swimming in midair as Mademoiselle Charlotte laughed.

"Easy, *chou*," said the Loa. "Let me do the work."

Not knowing whether to be terrified or furious, Kiri made herself stop fighting.

The silver funnel gently lifted them straight into the sky—just as the island below her rumbled, shook, and turned into a ball of flame.

"He blew it up!" she shouted to Mademoiselle Charlotte, her mind calculating the number of charges and the type of delay timer that would have been necessary to cause such destruction. "He blew up his own island! His own home!"

As the unnatural winds flailed her wet hair and clothes, she stared in disbelief as Chien Stretch and everything on it became an immolated orange glare. Heat covered her like a smothering blanket, blotting out her logic and strangling her heart with the knowledge of why *Maman* Rubie's island, Daemon Swath, was glowing in the distance.

Chank...

In that one second, Kiri stopped caring about catching Bordelon, her work with the FBI, and the multitude of indignities she had suffered over her size. She stopped caring about her past, her present, her future. She stopped caring about anything at all save for Chank and his foster mother. They were the only things that mattered in her world.

Her heart nearly tore in half as she covered her face against the wind and against the image of Chank and *Maman* Rubie burning to death.

They can't be dead. They can't be dead. They can't be dead.

Her thoughts whirled around and around, blending with the silvery wind. Her last coherent offering was a curse, directed at fate, fortune, all things magic and supernatural, and most especially, her murderous father.

Killing-induced madness or no, that bastard was about to die.

Chapter Seventeen

The sense of Kiri in danger followed by a distant blast made Chank stop running through the flames like a madman, desperately seeking two of the three people on earth his senses couldn't track.

He knew before he looked toward Chien Stretch what had happened — but he didn't want to believe it.

Sweat coated him from head to toe. His clothes were singed. His skin smarted and burned. His teeth ground together reflexively as his insides seemed to tear and bleed from the anguish.

Yes. There was a yellow glow in the distance.

Yes. Chien Stretch had been blown to smithereens with the same type of professional explosives the son of a bitch Bordelon had used to incinerate Daemon Swath.

"Kiri!" Chank grabbed the sides of head, shooting his senses out like arrows to find a host. Please, no. She couldn't be gone. She couldn't be dead! He had to find some sign of her. But...*Maman*...she needed him, too!

Torn between Kiri and *Maman* Rubie, Chank's heart couldn't decide, couldn't reconcile what was happening.

Nothing was nearby. No predatory minds at all.

"*Dieu!*" he shouted in frustration, his gut roiling.

"Let it go, little sparrow," came a chilling voice from behind him. "She's a memory, like your family. Like this old bitch will be if you don't come over here right now."

Chank forced himself to turn around, battling a grief that threatened to stagger him. He could barely breathe for the heat, but the flames danced around him without doing any real damage. *Maman* Rubie's magic was holding. Still holding.

Blinded by smoke and pain and despair, he stumbled through the pillars of fire, unable to see anything, searching for the taunting voice.

"A little farther, my small bird." Bordelon's tone had a maddening lilt. Chank wanted nothing more than to choke it from his throat.

Turning left, then right, he charged deeper into the island until he broke into a large circle of earth devoid of flames. The sudden break in smoke and darkness startled him, and he coughed.

Two trees, bases painted deep red, stood in the center of the circle.

The first thing Chank saw was Jon Bordelon, sallow in the light of the fire, standing within the swirls of a raggedly-etched *vèvè* and wearing fancy red robes like a priest of the Pethro rites. The silver strands of his crew cut and beard glinted in the eerie light, and his scar seemed to dance wildly from his ear to his mouth.

The next thing Chank saw was *Maman* Rubie tied to one of the trees, her head lolling against her chest. She looked ashen and weak, and so very, very old. And wet. As if she had been doused in something.

Chank's nose immediately supplied the answer: gasoline.

They were surrounded by a ring of fire, blocking out all other sights, creeping slowly inward.

There was no way to get *Maman* Rubie off the island alive.

Chank's eyes narrowed as he fought to push away the images of his childhood—his family, murdered and dismembered. The helpless feeling he had as his host sparrow hawk fell from the sky. Bordelon's horrid laugh, even now echoing through their prison of fire.

So this was how Bordelon planned to kill him. By slaying his heart and will with Kiri's death, then by murdering his protector. All those rituals had been to give the son of a bitch enough power to get close to the *mam'bo*, to break past her island's many defenses. He obviously didn't know if he could harm her directly, so he would let his bombs and the flames do his dirty work. Then, with her dead and her spells broken, he would come for Chank.

"If it's the last thing I do, I'll finish you here, tonight." Chank battled the stench of gasoline and acrid, burning wood. "You're no *Houngon*. You're just another murdering bastard, *oui*."

Eyes watering, snarling like a rabid dog, he advanced on Bordelon.

Bordelon raised *Maman* Rubie's machete to her throat and laughed. "Far enough, boy. Either way, she's dead, God rest her unholy soul."

Fighting every aggressive instinct he possessed, Chank halted. The air felt hot enough to set his lungs aflame.

Bordelon couldn't hurt *Maman* Rubie, not seriously. He hadn't been successful in beating her magic. Of that, Chank felt almost certain.

Almost.

It was possible that the bastard had broken her protections completely—but Chank wouldn't know unless he kept walking.

And if he was wrong, his foster mother would die before his eyes, just like his family had so many years ago.

Gnashing his teeth like a wild animal, Chank calculated his odds for a successful charge and take-down. They were slim to none. It might be a mercy to force the bastard to kill *Maman* now, before she burned, but he knew he couldn't do it. He had to bargain that he could find a way to spare her.

Even as he decided this, a cold fist squeezed his heart until it seemed to stop beating, until he felt absolutely nothing at all. Every muscle in his body stilled. He became granite, inside and out, glaring at his enemy.

And so Bordelon and Chank faced each other at the center of the island, in the ring of flames that once was *Maman* Rubie's grove of *reposoirs*. Bordelon had set fire to the homes of the *loas*. He had desecrated the *oum'phor* and disrespected the sanctuary of the Pethro gods. And now, he menaced their aged servant like a gleeful homicidal teenager.

When the fire got close enough to burn her, he'd simply walk forward, away from the blaze, kill Chank if he could, and keep on going.

Despite his many years with *Maman* Rubie, Chank didn't know how to invoke the Voudon powers. He called them anyway, as best he could.

Come to me. Help me. His blood boiled from the heat of the flames and his own rage. *If I'm not worthy, help her.*

Then aloud, "Please. I'll do whatever you want!"

In response, his ears popped, and sounds seemed to grow muffled. Chank imagined that the flames had slowed, that they weren't moving, as if time had stopped inside the burning grove.

A breeze cooled his heat-fatigued face, and he knew that sensation had to be a fantasy. A cool breeze couldn't exist inside a circle of fire.

Could it?

Chank's hair stirred.

Bordelon's haughty smile dimmed and he glanced toward the dark sky.

Following the bastard's gaze, Chank thought he saw a swirling silver funnel moving inexorably toward them.

He blinked.

The vision didn't vanish.

It came closer. And closer. And closer.

Chank actually felt cold in the shifting winds—and the flames weren't moving. Neither was Bordelon, or *Maman* Rubie, or anything else except the silver funnel.

It touched down gracefully between Chank and the magically frozen *Huntyr*.

Chank could make out two figures inside, one in red, the other indistinguishable. The red-clad figure proved to be a large, beautiful aristocratic looking woman. She stepped out of the wind, and Chank realized her skin was glowing.

A loa. He swallowed. *What else could this be?*

"*Je m'appelle* Charlotte," she said in perfect, lyrical French. *My name is Charlotte.*

Chank winced. *Maman* Rubie had spoken of Mademoiselle Charlotte many times, and rarely fondly—especially in the vision he had, where his *Maman* had been a zombie.

Reverting to perfectly-accented British English, the *loa* said, "You'll do whatever I want. Splendid. I'll take that bargain. Now, what would you ask of me?"

Chank cleared his throat. "I want to save *Maman* Rubie."

"Her? She's old. Nearly ready for the Reaper." Charlotte smiled, but Chank didn't return the expression. "Surely you'd rather I kill the *Huntyr* and rid you of your most despised enemy."

"No. I want to save *Maman*."

The *loa* shrugged. "As you will. I'll grant you that favor." She waved her hand, and *Maman* Rubie vanished from the tree—only to reappear seconds later, without the gasoline, right in front of Chank. He barely had time to get his arms around her to keep her from falling. She was muttering, half-conscious, and holding her machete. Chank could have sworn she looked a little younger, even.

The fist around his heart eased back some, and he felt a momentary rush of relief as he held his foster mother close.

"Put her down," Charlotte instructed.

Chank complied, lowering her reverently to the ground at his feet and using his legs to keep her in a sitting position.

When he straightened again, the *loa*'s eyes were twinkling. "I grant that she will leave here tonight, completely whole and unharmed, no matter what. And for that, you agreed to give me anything I want— one time and one time only, when I ask it of you."

With a nod, Chank sealed their bargain.

Charlotte grinned. "Very well. We will speak again later."

She turned to walk back into her silvery funnel, but paused before disappearing into the swirling wind. With a coy look over her shoulder, she said, "By the way, I agreed to just the *mam'bo*. Saving this one is up to you."

She snapped her fingers and vanished, and her funnel vanished with her.

As the dust settled and the flames came back to life, Chank realized someone lay on the ground halfway between him and the *Huntyr*, who was shaking his head as if to clear himself from Charlotte's spell.

It was...a woman.

His heart stopped all over again.

"Kiri!"

Chapter Eighteen

Kiri heard Chank's voice call her name so loudly he might have yelled in her ear. The wonderful bass sound woke her instantly.

"You're alive!" she shouted. "Oh, thank God." Her heart swelled as she sat up, looked around for him—and saw Jon Bordelon rushing at her instead.

Kiri screamed and rolled to the left. Her bastard of a father tackled the dirt where she had been.

Springing to her feet, Kiri drew one of her guns on reflex, pointed it at him, and pulled the trigger even as Chank's voice rang out behind her.

"No! Don't kill!"

Too late.

But, nothing happened. The waterlogged trigger locked before engaging.

Bordelon was on his feet in seconds.

Kiri took in his strange robes, wondering if her vision had gone red again. Then she threw the pistol at his head as he rushed her. The butt struck his temple with a decided crack, and he went down.

Kiri spun around, saw Chank and *Maman* Rubie and felt a joy like she had never known.

It wasn't a dream. They were really here. She hadn't lost them!

Opening her arms, she ran toward Chank, who carefully stepped away from *Maman* Rubie, then hurried toward her, yelling, "Behind you!"

Kiri's training kicked in. She dropped to one knee just in time to send Jon Bordelon sailing over her, straight into a surprised and off-balance Chank.

The two men crashed to the ground in a flurry of fists and shouts.

Kiri got up in a hurry.

Bordelon and Chank were wrestling so hard she couldn't tell who was who.

Smoke stung her eyes, and she started to cough.

"Chank!" she stumbled toward them, but before she took three steps, Bordelon came out on top, facing Kiri. With supernatural speed, he flipped Chank over, drew a pistol from the folds of his robes, and held it to the back of Chank's head. Chank tried to turn back over, but Bordelon had leverage.

Kiri froze mid-stride. Her breath froze too, lodging painfully in her chest. Her thoughts darted back and forth between pleading for Chank's life and wondering if Bordelon *could* kill Chank.

All the talk of spells and protections—was it real, or fancy? If she counted on it, would it get the only man she had ever loved killed?

"You want to play the odds, love?" Bordelon winked at her.

Kiri wished she could spit in his eye. "Fuck you."

"No thanks. You're too large for my tastes." Bordelon jammed the gun down hard as Chank bucked, and Chank grunted. He stopped fighting.

Once more, the grove went quiet but for the hissing and crackling of flames.

"If you want him alive, then do what I say." Bordelon's voice sounded like a snake's hiss to Kiri's ear. "First, put your other gun on the ground. Now."

Kiri nodded, highly aware of the crackle and pop of advancing flames—and what Bordelon did and didn't know about her weapons. She forced herself to take her time with his request, slowly unbuckling her ankle holster, holding it out, and dropping it on the ground as her thoughts settled. The fire hissed angrily.

Then, casually, as if complying with the bastard's game of power, Kiri pretended to clasp her hands behind her back.

Bordelon smiled, still bearing down with the pistol on Chank's head. "There's my good girl. What a love. Now, just a sip of your blood. Your wrist will do nicely—"

"Don't do it!" Chank's muffled shout distracted Bordelon, who looked down long enough to order him to be quiet.

That was all Kiri needed.

She had one chance, and she took it.

In a single fluid motion, she ripped the Bowie Rescue free from its damp tape and hurled it base over tip, straight at Bordelon.

The bastard looked up just in time to see the blade sink deep, deep into his right shoulder.

Perfect hit.

The nerves in his right arm surrendered, and the hand holding his pistol fell limp and useless. Bordelon howled as the gun hit the ground, and Chank threw him over in a heartbeat. Two swift punches from Chank's iron fists, and the son of a bitch quit moving except for the slight rise and fall of his chest.

A wild triumph flared in Kiri's belly and she had a powerful urge to open her mouth and roar with satisfaction—then grab Chank and hug him for hours. As it was, she eyed the flames, which were closer still. "We need to finish him and get the hell out of here."

"Agreed." Chank stood up in a hurry.

They both turned to where he had left *Maman* Rubie—and startled at the same time.

She was standing, machete in hand...but she seemed as tall as the tree Bordelon had tied her to only minutes earlier.

Dressed in plain, red robes, eyes wide and white, lips curving upward in a terrifying smile, the...enhanced...*mam'bo* of Daemon Swath addressed them in a voice too resonant to be only hers.

"Y'all go on now." Her words echoed as she turned her fearsome eyes on Bordelon. "Leave him to us. We'll be along when we're finished."

Kiri swallowed reflexively.

She felt absolutely no urge to argue with *Maman* Rubie in her official capacity.

Chank gave his foster mother a deferential bow, and Kiri knew he was of like mind.

She eased up beside him, brushing his arm with her fingers and feeling a flood of comfort even from such small contact. "Will she be okay without us?"

"*Mais, oui,*" was all Chank said.

Then he turned and grabbed Kiri's hand, and the two of them plunged out of the grove, clearing the flames in long, rapid strides.

Kiri felt the singe of heat, saw the glare of bright burning all around her, but she also sensed an eerie protective field moving with them as they escaped.

The magic protecting Chank. The magic he had extended to her.

Still clinging to each other's hand, they blasted through a last wall of fire and tumbled together into the bayou's warm, waiting water.

Kiri felt the welcome muck rise up to cover her. For a few blissful seconds, she rested in the silence. The thick waters of the swamp mimicked a womb, cradling her, cradling Chank, until they were forced to push upward to breathe.

Wordless, understanding each other without benefit of extra senses or conversation, they slowly swam together toward *Maman* Rubie's dock and pirogue. Water ran in and out of Kiri's ears, warping the fierce howls and snaps of the fire. Once or twice, she thought she heard harsh, unearthly laughter—and then her birth father, wailing like an infant.

The urge to roar with triumph struck her again, and this time, she didn't hold back.

Chapter Nineteen

Hours later, still tasting the delights of Chank's hastily prepared red beans and rice, Kiri stepped out of the clawfoot tub in her suite. She was completely clean and amazingly free of scratches, bruises, and burns. The fluffy white towel she used felt like pure heaven, soothing her skin and her mind as she carefully rubbed her shoulders, neck, and face.

Chank had gone to shower, too, after he saw to the needs of *Maman* Rubie, who had arrived at Sanctuaire just after they did—without her machete and riding what looked like a swirl of silver wind. The *mam'bo* had been herself again, dressed in a soot-coated white dress and turban, and clearly exhausted. When Chank offered to help her into one of the downstairs bedrooms after dinner, she had agreed immediately.

As Kiri watched Chank lead his foster mother away, she felt immense gratitude toward the woman, and even more respect. The rage that had driven her since she came to the Atchafalaya had burned clean away in the fires, then extinguished itself completely at the death of Jon Bordelon.

She would escape his curse. Her father's *malédiction*. Somehow, she would. Even if it meant no more FBI. No more law enforcement, period. Work had never seemed less important. Spending time with Chank, however long or short it might be, that was what truly mattered—at least for now. And now was more than good enough.

Kiri ran the soft towel across her back and chest, then lower, over her belly.

If I never kill, I'll never lose my sanity and become the monster he was.

"And no children," she said firmly, finally understanding all the reasons Chank had avoided her so long despite his attraction.

"Wrong!" crooned a lyrical voice from the bedroom.

Kiri spun around and dropped her towel.

Mademoiselle Charlotte was standing between the bathroom door and the bed, resplendent in her red silks. In the room's low lamplight, she seemed more imposing than she had on Chien Stretch, even without the silver swirling wind. Somehow, it seemed...*wrong* for such a creature to be indoors.

"Wha-" Kiri began, but the *loa* waved her right hand like a maestro cueing an orchestra.

What she cued up instead was a surprised, naked, wet and dripping Chank. He appeared beside the *loa*, hands on his chest, as if rinsing soap off his smooth, well-defined muscles.

The *loa* flicked her hands again.

Kiri felt a strange tug in her mind and belly, saw a flash of light—and they were downstairs in the drawing room.

She caught her breath fast.

Heavy golden curtains had been drawn to cover the floor-to-ceiling windows. No lights were on, but the room fairly danced with candlelight from hundreds of tapers placed on every shelf, every table. The room smelled of cinnamon and something Kiri couldn't place. It was sweet and pleasing, but it made her feel a little drunk each time she inhaled.

Magic, she thought, with no real fear. Chank looked more annoyed than afraid, too.

Kiri took another long breath, capturing the sweet-smelling aroma and letting it make her dizzy. Damn, but Batman looked fine. His taut skin glistened in the flickering yellow light, and his coal-black eyes sparked as he realized what had happened.

Kiri's nipples came to attention at the sight, and her pussy tingled. The *loa*'s presence should have bothered her, but after everything that had happened, Kiri couldn't have cared less. If a Voudon goddess wanted to be a voyeur, so be it.

Chank lowered his hands to his sides and bowed to Charlotte. "*Bonsoir*. Have you come to collect your payment for *Maman* Rubie's life so soon?"

"Payment?" Kiri's mind cleared enough to let her frown deeply. "What are you talking about?"

"Before I knew you had survived, I bargained for *Maman*'s life," Chank explained, looking miserable and sheepish all at once. "Mademoiselle Charlotte answered my plea."

"He said he'd do anything I wanted." Charlotte laughed and batted her eyes, then looked Chank up and down in a way that made

Kiri want to punch the *loa* in the nose. Especially when the magic hussy in red brushed her fingers across Chank's cock and said, "I definitely wouldn't mind an evening of pleasure with a *Trakyr*. Strong cocks, and *les autres*, mmm, mmm."

Autre? Kiri struggled to control her temper and remember her French. She finally came up with "other." But, "other" what?

Chank lowered his eyes, as if embarrassed. "Will you ask me to be unfaithful to my woman, Mademoiselle? *Mais, non*. You're a champion of love!"

Charlotte moved her hand from his stiffening shaft, though Kiri thought she did so grudgingly.

Good thing, Kiri fumed to herself. Another second, and she would have found a way to introduce the grabby *loa* to her Bowie Rescue. After all, it was right behind her on the bathroom counter...but, damn. She wasn't in the bedroom anymore!

"No violence will be necessary," Charlotte said as if Kiri had shouted her intent. The *loa* reverted to her more British accent as she added, "I have not come to tear asunder what fate has so wisely joined."

Kiri let out a breath, and she could tell Chank was equally relieved.

"My price is simple," Charlotte continued. "And for the two of you, quite easily accomplished." She paused, tossing her blonde ringlets, clearly for maximum drama.

Kiri decided the *loa* was either annoying, or a little nuts. Maybe both. Chank seemed the picture of patience, gazing at Charlotte without a hint of the frustration Kiri felt.

"Will you not guess?" Charlotte's smile was big and bright and more than a little chilling. She flicked her gaze to Kiri, then back to Chank.

"I couldn't possibly, *non*." He shook his head, spreading his damp hair over his deeply tanned shoulders.

Mademoiselle Charlotte clucked. "Well, well. You've disappointed me. Ah, well, I'll just tell you. In exchange for saving *Maman* Rubie's life, I require that you have children. As many as possible."

"No!" Kiri shouted at the same time Chank did. She felt like she'd just been slapped.

"We can't, no." Kiri hugged herself, protesting without thinking about the fact she was talking to a Voudon goddess. "I won't pass on the curse in my blood. Chank won't either."

She cut her eyes to Chank, who nodded grimly. "*Oui*. Please. Do not ask this terrible thing."

Charlotte regarded them both as if they were foolish kindergarteners. "But I'm not asking. I'm demanding. I don't care if you love each other forever, or marry, or don't—but you must have children, and the sooner the better. Terrible things will happen if you refuse me."

Kiri's voice deserted her. Chank kept opening his mouth and closing it again. His erection had died in the birthing, and his normally dark skin seemed to have gone pale.

"You don't understand." Charlotte sighed theatrically. "Very well. I'll make it clear. *Huntyr* and *Trakyr* must join every so often to make balance, and to keep it."

Kiri still couldn't speak. As far as she was concerned, that was as clear as an iced-over windshield. "We're the last of our races. Even if we have children, what will it matter in the long run?"

Charlotte sounded exasperated as she answered. "Your children will be neither *Huntyr* or *Trakyr*. They will be a perfect balance, and companions to the gods. With both the protective and the brutal instincts of your races, your children will have the power and strength to serve the Pethro rites."

"And when our children are dead?" Chank's quiet question affirmed Kiri's confusion.

"Then the Blood Rites will have no true shepherd," Charlotte admitted. "But I have hopes that your children will be drawn to mate with others of fierce temperament and deep strength." She twirled a blonde curl around her finger. "Perhaps that will be enough to give us strong guardians for many years to come. If not...there are other old races we could call upon...if we had to."

"The Pethro *loas* must have a guardian," Chank murmured. "Or the world will suffer untold pains. *Maman* Rubie told me that many times."

"Rubie is old." Charlotte sighed, this time with no drama. "She would have kept at her task until time's end to spare you any worry— but it has been too many generations since *Huntyr* and *Trakyr* joined. It is right to give her rest and peace. Surely you must see that."

And Kiri did see, to her great shock. She and Chank would have a baby, or babies—and one of them would become *Maman* Rubie's successor. She imagined the *mam'bo* in her mind's eye, with her timeless face and mysterious aura of power.

How old is that woman? Will some of my children live for centuries? Or maybe my grandchildren? My God. What they could learn about the world…

Lost in thought, Kiri almost didn't notice Chank looking at her. Waiting for her answer.

"I will not agree unless you do, *catin*." He folded his arms and his muscles rippled so perfectly that her body started to ache all over again. "This is our decision, together."

Kiri started to ask him if he was nuts, but ended up saying, "Of course I'll have your babies. When do we start making them?"

Chank hesitated, then gave her a bad, bad, bad boy smile. Just a quirk of the lips with a flash of white teeth, and Kiri thought she was melting. Once more, she took a deep breath, letting her mind spin with the sweet spice filling the room.

"Well, then," he said to Charlotte in a husky voice. "We're agreed. But only if you leave now, Mademoiselle."

The *loa* giggled, gave his cock a playful tap. To Kiri, she said in her original French accent, "*Oui*, I'll go. But you should make him tell you all about his *pénis*. Better yet, make him *show* you, *chére*."

And with that, the Voudon goddess vanished in a haze of silver swirls.

In moments, the sparkles faded, and Kiri found herself alone and facing a man so handsome he might have been a god himself. A man she had spent five years wanting but avoiding, adoring but denying. And then a night and a morning screwing—and a night trying to save—along with her own ass and the world in general, of course.

Now she'd promised to have his babies.

And what did Charlotte mean? *Make him tell you all about his* pénis…

Kiri's eyes traveled from his fierce eyes to his desire-sharpened smile, then lower to the steel of his chest, his firm waist, his already-erect cock…and her heart started to jump.

Was there something she didn't know about Chank's body?

Something awful or something…wonderful?

He looked mortified, yet excited in an elemental, stirring way. Underneath his self-conscious expression, Kiri read hope and want and need, and her own excitement doubled.

"So," she whispered, taking another lung-full of the enchanting spice. "Show me, Arceneaux."

"*Oui, catin.*" Chank came toward her and rubbed his rough, damp palms on her shoulders. "But, first, did you mean what you said? Will you bear my children? As my wife of course, if that would please you."

Yes! Kiri's brain and body screamed, but her practical mind quickly asserted itself. She choked back her welling emotion enough to give him a sharp and Charlotte-like glare. "I'll do it on one condition."

Chank's eyebrows shot up. "And that would be?"

"That you show me what an *autre* is, and show me right now, with no more sweet talk."

"Anything for you, *ma belle catin.*" His voice rumbled as he stepped back and looked down at his stiff cock. "Give me your hand."

Kiri extended her right hand without hesitation, keeping her eyes fixed on his erection.

He took her fingers and placed them halfway down the swollen shaft on the underside, right on the nub of flesh she had toyed with the first time they made love.

"Rub it," he said hoarsely, more a command than a request.

Feeling new shivers of excitement, Kiri stroked the nub, carefully, teasing, like she might have done the head of his cock—and the lump started to grow, down at first, then up, toward her.

Meanwhile, Chank's cock was getting thicker and longer, as if to support the new weight.

Staring, Kiri massaged the *autre* as it came into full proportions—a second, smaller penis, not as long or thick as the main attraction—and much more flexible despite its rigid state. It reminded Kiri of a magic wand, only much more tempting.

"You do have two cocks," she said in absolute amazement. She grabbed his first shaft and stroked it along with the *autre*. "You could...fuck me double..."

Chank made a noise of surprise, then growled his pleasure. When Kiri looked up to meet his gaze, his expression communicated nothing but unbound desire. He grabbed her by the shoulders and kissed her fiercely, trapping her hands on his cocks even as he thrust his tongue in and out of her mouth.

*Fuck me double…*Kiri's own words echoed in her mind as he pulled her hands free, picked her up, and carried her toward the large leather couch on the far side of the room. Her heart raced as all the possibilities ran through her mind.

Thicker penetration.

Sucking off two cocks at once.

God, he could fuck her ass and pussy at the same time. The smaller cock would fit just perfectly. No pain. Only perfect stimulation.

These erotic images, the spices in the air, and the feel of his wet, muscled chest and arms blotted out her reason as he took her around the couch, to the back side, and set her on her feet.

From behind her, he hugged her, grabbing her nipples roughly in both hands and pinching at the same moment he bit her neck.

Kiri moaned, getting wetter by the second. "Yes. Damn." She leaned into him, clit throbbing as he rolled the hardened flesh of her buds between his fingers.

"*Catin*," he whispered. The word came out ragged, ripped by his passion, and that only excited Kiri more. She rubbed her ass against his cock and *autre* and thrust her nipples more fully into his palms.

"Harder. I can take more. I can take all you give me." She lifted her arms and reached back to touch his head as he bit her neck again. The pressure on her nipples increased until pain joined pleasure in just the right blend.

Kiri grabbed fistfuls of Chank's wet black hair, shuddering as he pinched and tugged, pinched and tugged. His teeth felt like fire on the skin of her nape. His cocks, sizzling steel against her back and ass.

God, she was wet.

"*Je t'aime, catin.*" He nibbled her neck again. "I love you."

Heat flushed every inch of Kiri's body. She was covered with pleasure-chills, shaking, wanting him inside her pussy so badly she couldn't stand it.

"I love you, too—now, please. No more waiting!"

Chank's bass rumble of pleasure nearly made her come as he let go of her breasts and pushed her forward, bending her over the leather couch. Her breasts scrubbed against the soft leather, giving her more chills, and she braced her hands against the couch cushions, eyes closed.

This would be good.

This would be better than good.

Her breathing came in short, labored bursts.

Behind her, Chank parted her ass cheeks. "So sweet. So pink."

She felt his finger on her clit then, and came with a surprised shout.

Almost instantly, he drove his larger cock deep into her pussy.

Kiri screamed, spreading her legs wider as his *autre* rammed against her clit, stroking it just as surely as Chank's finger had.

No, it was more than that. Infinitely more.

"Oh, my God."

She trembled uncontrollably, barely able to stand the level of stimulation.

His cock was filling her core, and his *autre* extended from there, resting inside the contour of her wet pussy, joining with her clit like a hot, sucking sponge. Chank's extra cock had somehow mated with her swollen button just as surely as his main cock joined with her throbbing channel.

And then he started to pump, in and out, up and down. Dual action.

Fuck me double.

The first of many meanings to that phrase, Kiri had no doubt.

She closed her eyes and fisted the hard leather couch cushions, her mind expanding with her vagina as Chank took her more completely than she could have imagined. His shaft felt so good in her core, sliding deeper and deeper, and his *autre* claimed her clit like a possessive, suctioning finger. He held her hips with both hands, steadying her for ever harder, ever deeper thrusts.

"Beautiful *calin*," he murmured, and the sound of his masterful voice nearly pushed her over the edge. With force of will, Kiri held back. She wanted this to last another minute. An hour. Maybe a year or two.

"Chank," she gasped as each movement nearly lifted her feet from the floor.

Her breasts bounced against the leather couch.

She felt wanton, released, fulfilled in ways she couldn't have dreamed of a month ago.

"Come, *catin*," he demanded, driving into her again and again, making her flesh slap against the couch. "I want to hear you scream."

Kiri's orgasm felt like a wave of fire, starting at her pussy and spreading out in wide circles, to her belly, to her huge nipples scrubbing on the leather cushions, to her curled fingers and toes. She did scream, all the while keeping herself as open to his powerful strokes as she could.

But he didn't stop.

He simply pulled back a little, detaching the *autre* but leaving his cock in place as he lifted her, turned her over, settled her ass on the back of the couch, and kept a firm grip around her waist.

Kiri wrapped her arms around his neck.

She felt like a limp doll in his grasp as he stared at her with those hot, deep black eyes. Her mouth was open, fighting for air. Her skin blazed with pure passion and endless sensation. The smell of their sex laced through the intoxicating spices, taking her to yet another level of saturation.

Her legs were still splayed wide, and she loved how his expanded cock felt in her pussy.

The *autre*, wet from her juices, slid against her ass, seeming to seek a new target all on its own.

"Relax," Chank instructed, his voice so deep it rattled Kiri's spine.

"If I were more relaxed, I'd faint," she murmured.

Chank gave her a sexy grin, then pulled her hips forward. His *autre* entered her ass slowly and carefully, pushing her close to yet another orgasm just from the exquisite penetration.

He kissed her tenderly then, pausing, letting her feel the totality of their joining.

Kiri forced her leg muscles to work, closing her thighs around his waist. She felt cherished. Possessed. Adored. And totally ready.

Chank began slowly, pushing his cock in and out of her soaked pussy, making her walls contract. She shivered from the fullness in her ass, clenching around his *autre*, too. Every inch and ounce of her absorbed the electric jolts.

"You're...incredible...Batman..." she said between deep, shuddering breaths as he fucked her double again.

Picking up his tempo, he kissed her, mimicking the movement of his cocks with his tongue. His arms felt so strong around her that Kiri let hers fall away from his neck. She leaned backward until she braced herself on the couch, exposing her hard-as-stone nipples to his hungry mouth.

Chank sucked first one and then the other, and Kiri's groans became small shouts of ecstasy.

So good. So total.

Each movement brought almost-climaxes, pushing her up and up as he rammed into her pussy and ass harder and deeper each time.

One of his hands eased upward on her back, lifting her toward him as his thrusts grew frenzied.

Kiri thought she would die from the pleasure.

She thought she would explode.

And then Chank did explode, growling. Biting hard on her nipple. Spilling hot seed from both cocks. Catapulting Kiri into an orgasm so spectacular it literally shut down her brain.

Unable to control her muscles, Kiri collapsed in a haze of heat and satisfaction.

After a few long, sweet moments, her Cajun Batman picked her up and carried her slowly up Sanctuaire's wide main stairs.

To his room.

To their room.

"Do it again," Kiri murmured as he lowered her onto the soft pillows. But she fell asleep before he could answer.

In her endless horny dreams, she thought she heard Chank whispering about hawks and life-mates, and how glad he was to have her in his nest.

Chapter Twenty

One year later

Chank hung up the telephone and walked out to the balcony, smiling as he saw his wife in her element.

Dressed in light robes, her dark hair pulled back in a matching scarf, Kiri had her feet propped on the railing while she read yet another book about the history of Voudon. Her cheeks were flushed from the heat, and sweat beaded on her neck and chest.

Chank's cocks came alive as he thought about licking off the sweet salt, and about the many rooms and positions in which he had done just that. They had been married eleven months now, and it felt like only a week. He couldn't get enough of his bride. The newest *mam'bo* in the Atchafalaya. The queen of Sanctuaire, and of his heart.

My nest. My life-mate. His heart swelled, remembering the hawk, and flying, and winning the right to the perfect peace he had known across the last months.

Below them, in the full gardens of Cain Island, *Maman* Rubie walked their two-month old twins, Nicole and Solomon. She carried one on her chest and one on her back, native-style, in soft slings made of goatskin and lined with the softest cotton. Her lilting murmur drifted like petals on the breeze as she named each herb, flower, and tree, starting them early on the path of understanding nature.

"I love you," Kiri murmured without looking up from her book. "Was it the FBI again?"

"Yeah. The new director. He wants to talk to us. I told him we'd think about it."

Kiri put her finger on her place and glanced up. Her dark eyes, once flinty and cold, now seemed infinitely warm. "What is it this time?"

Chank studied his babies and *Maman* Rubie as they paused to sniff Kiri's colorful climbing roses. Nicole had her mother's porcelain skin, while Solomon had his swarthy hide. Both babies had their parents black-as-black hair. He would take on the world for them. The universe.

And he wanted more—a mansion full of dark-headed babies from Kiri, laughing and learning the flora and fauna under *Maman*'s careful tutoring.

"Some asshole killing kids in Maine, up near the Canadian border," he said finally, not wanting to surrender the perfection of the moment.

"I could probably find a good hex for that kind of bastard, if you give me a day or two."

Chank laughed. "Yeah, well, I think they'll want a little more than our magic, *catin*."

"I'm ready if you are." Kiri closed her book and stood up, stretching, giving him a wonderful view of her sexy curves and angles. "We can go together, in-and-out. Have the son of a bitch behind bars in no time. And don't give me that protective male bullshit about putting myself in danger, Batman."

"Wouldn't dream of it, Wonder Woman." He winked at her, gratified by her sensual, teasing grin. "I think we'd better talk to *Maman*, though. Get her opinion."

Kiri moved to him like a vision, wrapped her arms around his neck, and kissed him. Her lips tasted like apples and cinnamon, her favorite breakfast. Her body felt like soft, welcoming heaven.

"We'll talk to her in a minute," Chank amended, pulling his wife closer, running his lips over her ear. "Maybe...an hour, or two."

His sweet doll rubbed her breasts against his chest, bringing her knee up to stroke his dual erections.

"*Mais, oui*," she agreed. "*Mais, oui*."

About the author:

Annie Windsor is 37 years old and lives in Tennessee with her two children and nine pets (as of today's count).

Annie's a southern girl, though like most magnolias, she has steel around that soft heart. Does she have a drawl? Of course, though she'll deny it, y'all. She dreams of being a full-time writer, and looks forward to the day she can spend more time on her mountain farm. She loves animals, sunshine, and good fantasy novels.

On a perfect day, she writes, reads, spends time with her family, chats with friends, and discovers nothing torn, eaten, or trampled by her beloved puppies or crafty kitties.

Annie Windsor welcomes mail from readers. You can write to her c/o Ellora's Cave Publishing at 1337 Commerce Drive, Suite 13, Stow OH 44224.

Also by Annie Windsor:

Why an electronic book?

We live in the Information Age—an exciting time in the history of human civilization in which technology rules supreme and continues to progress in leaps and bounds every minute of every hour of every day. For a multitude of reasons, more and more avid literary fans are opting to purchase e-books instead of paperbacks. The question to those not yet initiated to the world of electronic reading is simply: *why?*

1. *Price.* An electronic title at Ellora's Cave Publishing runs anywhere from 40-75% less than the cover price of the <u>exact same title</u> in paperback format. Why? Cold mathematics. It is less expensive to publish an e-book than it is to publish a paperback, so the savings are passed along to the consumer.

2. *Space.* Running out of room to house your paperback books? That is one worry you will never have with electronic novels. For a low one-time cost, you can purchase a handheld computer designed specifically for e-reading purposes. Many e-readers are larger than the average handheld, giving you plenty of screen room. Better yet, hundreds of titles can be stored within your new library—a single microchip. (Please note that Ellora's Cave does not endorse any specific brands. You can check our website at www.ellorascave.com for customer

recommendations we make available to new consumers.)

3. *Mobility.* Because your new library now consists of only a microchip, your entire cache of books can be taken with you wherever you go.

4. *Personal preferences are accounted for.* Are the words you are currently reading too small? Too large? Too...**ANNOYING**? Paperback books cannot be modified according to personal preferences, but e-books can.

5. *Innovation.* The way you read a book is not the only advancement the Information Age has gifted the literary community with. There is also the factor of what you can read. Ellora's Cave Publishing will be introducing a new line of interactive titles that are available in e-book format only.

6. *Instant gratification.* Is it the middle of the night and all the bookstores are closed? Are you tired of waiting days—sometimes weeks—for online and offline bookstores to ship the novels you bought? Ellora's Cave Publishing sells instantaneous downloads 24 hours a day, 7 days a week, 365 days a year. Our e-book delivery system is 100% automated, meaning your order is filled as soon as you pay for it.

Those are a few of the top reasons why electronic novels are displacing paperbacks for many an avid reader. As always, Ellora's Cave Publishing welcomes your questions and comments. We invite you to email us at service@ellorascave.com or write to us directly at: 1337 Commerce Drive, Suite 13, Stow OH 44224.

Printed in the United States
24182LVS00001B/172-321